TO
DIE
FOR

∽ ALSO BY CHRISTOPHER PIKE ∾

Thirst

Thirst No. 2

Remember Me

The Secret of Ka

TO
DIE
FOR

2 NOVELS:
SLUMBER PARTY
AND
WEEKEND

CHRISTOPHER PIKE

Point

Northern Plains Public Library
Ault Colorado

If you purchased this book without a cover, you should be aware that this book is stolen property. It was reported as "unsold and destroyed" to the publisher, and neither the author nor the publisher has received any payment for this "stripped book."

No part of this publication may be reproduced, stored in a retrieval system, or transmitted in any form or by any means, electronic, mechanical, photocopying, recording, or otherwise, without written permission of the publisher. For information regarding permission, write to Scholastic Inc., Attention: Permissions Department, 557 Broadway, New York, NY 10012.

Slumber Party, ISBN 978-0-590-43014-2
Text copyright © 1985 by Christopher Pike

Weekend, ISBN 978-0-590-44256-5
Text copyright © 1986 by Christopher Pike

Slumber Party was originally published in paperback by Point in 1985.
Weekend was originally published in paperback by Point in 1986.

ISBN 978-0-545-26434-1

All rights reserved. Published by Point, an imprint of Scholastic Inc.
SCHOLASTIC, POINT, and associated logos are trademarks
and/or registered trademarks of Scholastic Inc.

12 11 10 9 8 7 6 5 4 3 2 1   10 11 12 13 14 15/0
Printed in the U.S.A.   40

First compilation printing, September 2010

Book design by Tim Hall

❧ Contents ❧

SLUMBER PARTY

❧ Chapter 1 ❧

Dana Miller's downshifting, as they rounded the tight mountain turn, was like a kick in the seat of the pants. The plowed snow looming above their VW gave the illusion of being in a bobsled run. The dazzling white landscape was more than unshielded eyes could bear, but here in the shade, Lara Johnson stared out the window in delightful awe. This weekend ski trip would be one of the high points of her life.

"How am I doing?" Dana asked, referring to her driving.

"Well . . ." Lara began, not wishing to offend her oldest and best friend. "We are still alive."

Dana chuckled. "Does that mean you want me to slow down?"

The back wheels zigzagged as they whipped out of another turn. "A bit," Lara breathed, putting a hand on the dashboard.

"I wouldn't mind being late," Celeste Winston agreed from the backseat, reopening her eyes slowly.

Dana sighed, putting on the brake. "Doesn't look like we have much choice. The road's blocked off."

A hundred yards in front, a chain was suspended across the asphalt, behind which rose a miniature mountain of snow. Three cars were jammed into a makeshift parking lot. A ranger waved them to the side. Dana buried the front end of the car before she could kill their momentum on the ice-slick surface. Lara rolled down her window.

"We're heading to Cedar Stream," she said. "Is there another way around?"

The man tugged on his white whiskers, a Colonel Sanders clone. "You must be with them other young ladies," he said, in a country-boy voice.

Dana nudged her side, pointing at a parked BMW. "There's Rachael's car," she said.

Lara nodded. "We are. Do you know how long ago they got here?"

"Must be—ohh—near two hours ago."

"That Rachael drives like a fiend," Dana said.

"She's not alone," Lara muttered.

"This is as close as you're going to get," the ranger said, answering her initial question. "But Cedar Stream's only three miles away. You got cross-country skis, I see. Should have no trouble hiking in."

Lara felt a pang of concern for Celeste.

At school she wasn't allowed to take PE because of a bad back. Indeed, since this was primarily a skiing trip, Celeste should not have come. But upon hearing of their plans, their younger friend had pleaded to be included, if only to enjoy the scenery.

"I'll be okay," Celeste said, meeting her eyes.

"You have no skis," Lara said.

"I'll walk. I walk pretty good."

"If the snow's powdery," Dana said, "you'll swim."

Lara put on sunglasses and climbed out of the car. Drifts had cut many of the pines to pint size. The miles they would have to master did not appear an easy proposition.

"There is a packed path yonder this ridge," the ranger uttered, reading her mind. He frowned as Dana dug open the hood and began to unload their supplies. He said, "Like I told your friends, you best be well stocked with food. By night, a granddaddy of a storm is going to hit. And be careful, because there's no cell reception in this area."

"I told you," Dana said, tossing Celeste a duffel bag, who caught it and promptly disappeared giggling into a wall of snow.

"Careful, careful," Lara said. "I know, Dana. I read the papers, too. I told Nell we should wait until next weekend, but she insisted that it had to be this weekend. So did Rachael, for that matter."

"Rachael's just hoping that you break a leg so you'll end up in the hospital and be out of the running for homecoming queen," Dana said, not joking. "I still think she was the one responsible for me getting kicked off the Associated Student Body Council."

"If they put a cast over my face, maybe she would stand a chance," Lara said, not taking herself seriously. Rachael would win hands down: tall, blond, tan—she looked like a cover girl. What could a short, dark-haired nobody with girlish bangs and a nose that was at least—despite what her friends said—a size too large do against a Barbie Doll? Of course, personality wise, Rachael was not everyone's dream queen. "What do we do with our car?" Lara asked the man, who was following their exchange with a wry grin.

"Leave the keys. A partner of mine and I will move them down to the lodge."

"That's awfully nice of you," Lara said, surprised. Didn't rangers have more important things to do? "What name should we mention when we pick it up?" She couldn't find a badge.

"The colonel," the man smiled, smoothing his whiskers again.

THE EFFORT REQUIRED TO BALANCE A DUFFEL BAG ON her back, while simultaneously trying to recall seldom-used cross-country ski techniques, caused muscles to ache that Lara hadn't even known she had. Yet as she paused to catch her breath and wipe off the beads of perspiration dripping into her eyes, she realized that she hadn't felt this exhilarated in ages. The air was so crisp and sweet that it was like biting into a dessert. In every direction, the scenery could have been framed and pasted on a postcard. The flawless blue sky made it difficult to take seriously the warning of an approaching storm.

"If I died and couldn't get into heaven," Dana said, "I wouldn't mind spending the rest of eternity here." Her back was bent with a weight similar to what Lara was carrying. Only Celeste, who moved gingerly between them on a ski track, stood erect. She had valiantly tried to help, but they had ended up digging her out of the snow.

"Quite a change from West Star High," Lara agreed, which was where the three of them went to school, in the heart of congested Oakland.

"Maybe we'll meet some guys," Dana said hopefully. With a great deal of fondness, Lara had to admit that Dana's face was one best loved by a mother. Yet Dana had no shortage of boyfriends, only a lack of ones that—as Dana put it—appreciated her from the neck up.

"Six single girls," Lara said. "We'll have to meet a whole herd of them." Though she would settle for one. She hadn't gone out on a date in six weeks. At first she had thought that she was being too picky, but then again, she hadn't said no to anybody.

"What we need is a party," Dana said. "The storm can strand whoever comes."

Lara noticed ever-silent Celeste blushing, and asked, "Do you date much?"

Celeste was startled by the question. "Oh, I've never gone out with a boy."

"You should," Dana said. "They need us. Believe me."

"I . . . can't," Celeste replied hesitantly.

"Won't your aunt let you?" Lara asked.

"She . . . I don't think she would mind."

"You're too shy, is that it?" Lara asked gently.

Celeste looked at the ground. It seemed as if an envelope of sorrow had enfolded her. "Yeah, that's why," she said finally.

Lara thought that there was more to the matter. The doubt forced her to evaluate just how scant their knowledge of Celeste was.

ON WHAT HAD BEEN ONLY THE SECOND DAY OF SCHOOL, Lara had been browsing in the library for something to read. Working at the local mall's theaters during the week was an exercise in killing time. She had picked up a Stephen King horror novel and was reading the critics' raves on the inside flap, when she noticed a slight, pale, auburn-haired girl, staring at either her or the book. What struck Lara from the first instant was the innocence of her expression.

Lara smiled at her and waved the book. "Have you read this?"

The girl approached slowly. Although the weather was warm, she was bundled up. Later Lara learned that Celeste always dressed this way.

"I've read all his books," she said in a small girl's voice.

"Do you get nightmares?"

The girl did not appear to connect the question with the reference to the horror books. "I used to have many dreams about—" She frowned. "Oh, I see. No, books never scare me."

"What's your name?"

"Celeste."

"I'm Lara. You're new here."

"I am, yes."

"What grade are you in?"

"I'm a sophomore."

"A shame. I'm a senior. We can't be seen together." Celeste looked as though she had been slapped. Lara squeezed her arm. "I was only joking, for goodness' sake! Hey, I was just going to lunch. Have you eaten?"

"No."

"Are you hungry?"

"Yes."

"Good. I'm taking you to lunch."

Afterward Lara was not sure why she had felt such immediate warmth for Celeste. Perhaps it was the girl's obvious frailness that had awakened a desire to protect.

Over lunch Lara had asked why she had been staring at her. Celeste had replied, "You looked nice."

Her tone had been filled with amazement.

Since then Celeste had revealed few personal facts. Her parents were dead. She lived alone with her aunt. She had a bad back from a car accident. She liked books.

"There it is!" Dana exclaimed, as they crested a frozen bluff. The trilevel frame house was set in the side of a natural granite wall, spacious windows opening on a breathtaking view of the valley. A thin trail of smoke drifted from a towering brick chimney. Home sweet home. They plopped down their burdens.

"Can you imagine the bucks Nell's parents must have to buy a place like that?" Dana asked with a mixture of disdain and envy.

"Money isn't everything," Celeste said.

Dana stared at her. "Were you just hatched from an egg?"

"We never told you about Nell," Lara said to Celeste. "She was one of the gang when we were all small. She moved away when we were in fourth grade. Her family's in oil. They live in Sacramento now. Over the years, she's kept in contact. She's a good friend."

"When you meet her," Dana said, "don't mind her

seriousness. That's just the way she is." She added quietly, "Nell hasn't had the easiest life."

"Why?" Celeste asked.

Lara and Dana exchanged looks. Fourth grade — long enough ago for everyone's memory to fade, except for Nell's. The facial scars she saw in every mirror made that impossible. She hadn't moved away. She had been driven away.

Except for the addition of Celeste, and the absence of Nell's younger sister, Nicole, this weekend's cast would be the same as *that* slumber party.

"When we were nine years old," Lara began, "Nell had an accident."

"It was nobody's fault," Dana interjected.

"She got burned," Lara continued. "Her face and hands. She had to have extensive plastic surgery, which was very painful. She looks okay now, but it's always there between us. You see, the accident that burned her — each of us contributed to it." Lara tried to smile to relieve her tension. "I guess you would call it our deep dark secret."

"Was anyone else hurt?" Celeste asked, stooping down to make a snowball. Obviously she did not notice how badly the topic disturbed them.

"No," Dana said quickly, before Lara could speak. "No one else was hurt." Dana pressed Lara with her eyes, shaking her head. The thought was mutual.

Do not talk about it. Do not remember.

"No one else," Lara echoed weakly, not exactly a lie. Nicole hadn't really been hurt. Nicole had died.

"I'll be especially nice to her," Celeste promised.

"Hey you penguins!!" came a shout from the house. "What took you so long?"

Mindy Casey, tripping over her scarf and enthusiasm, floundered toward them. In appearance she was a pale shadow of her idol—Rachael. Her character took after her bubble-gum chewing obsession: initially sweet, often swelled with hot air, periodically exploding. Lara couldn't imagine life without her.

"Give me that snowball," Dana said, taking Celeste's embryonic snowman and unleashing a pitch that grazed Mindy's forehead.

"I just did my makeup!" Mindy cried, wiping her face. A brief but furious snowball fight ensued. Outnumbered two to one—Celeste did not participate—Mindy soon surrendered. As part of their terms, she helped them with their bags to the house.

"Was there much work getting this place livable?" Lara asked.

"Nell's been slaving away, though she did have us clean out the basement, but Rachael and I spent most of our time on a snowman," Mindy said. "He's on the other side of the house, wearing that scarf your mother knitted Rachael when she was a kid, and my cowboy hat and sunglasses. He looks cool."

Rachael Grayson appeared on the porch.

"Hi, girls," she said in her slightly cynical tone that made the uninitiated feel that they weren't quite as important as they thought they were. Seeing Rachael, poster perfect in her skintight, blue ski outfit and dazzling shower of blond hair, Lara thought again how ludicrous it was that they were in competition.

"Look at you," Dana said in disgust. "No way I'm going to go hustle guys with you."

Rachael smiled faintly, acknowledging her physical superiority. "How are you, *Princess Lara?*" she asked.

"Just perfect, *Princess Rachael,*" Lara mimicked. Both of them had already been elected to the homecoming court. "Where is our loyal subject, Nell?"

"Preparing our royal chambers, poor wench," Rachael said, causing them all to laugh. Rachael came down the steps and hugged them.

"You must drive like a fiend," Dana said.

"We left before dawn. Had to pick up Nell. You should see her house. It should have a moat."

"How is she?" Lara asked quietly.

Rachael wobbled her palm. "So-so. She has a slight fever. I think it's caused by having us all here at once. I think it . . . you know what I mean."

"What did you think of the storm Colonel Sanders is worried about?" Dana asked.

Rachael laughed. "What's a few more snowflakes in this icebox?"

"Those few more snowflakes could bury us here for days," Dana said. "We told you to wait till next weekend."

A cold light hardened Rachael's eyes. Since childhood, Lara had sensed, but never witnessed, a part of Rachael capable of genuine violence. "It was important that we come this weekend," Rachael said flatly.

"Hello," Nell Kutroff said, causing everyone to jump slightly. She was standing in the doorway, bracing herself against the railing. Wrinkles of fatigue pinched her eyes. The scars about her nose and mouth were more noticeable than usual. This was the first time since the accident that Lara had seen Nell without heavy makeup.

"How are you?" Dana asked tentatively, not moving from her spot.

"Fine. It's good to see you again, Dana. Real good."

Lara felt herself drawn involuntarily forward. She hugged Nell tightly. Nell hesitated before returning the gesture. Unshed tears burned Lara's eyes. Why this sudden depth of emotion? Was it a flood of relief or guilt? They separated, studying each other. "You look good," Lara said finally, lying. It was guilt.

Nell smiled. "You look better."

Lara put her hand on Nell's forehead. "But you've got a fever." Actually she didn't feel hot at all.

Nell shrugged. "I'll be all right after a nap. I prepared your rooms. You each have your own, and they're all on the top floor."

"Thanks," Lara said.

"I wanted to congratulate you on being one of the top five beauties at school," Nell said formally.

"I campaigned vigorously," Lara said. The compliment was but another reminder. Nell would have, should have, been beautiful.

Celeste was hiding behind Rachael and Mindy. Lara beckoned for her. "This is the wonderful new friend that I told you all about on the phone. Nell, meet Celeste."

For the longest moment neither made a move nor spoke. Finally Nell offered her hand. "That's a beautiful name, Celeste," she said, with a trace of nervousness. "What does it mean?"

"Nothing," Celeste said.

"Heavenly," Lara corrected. Surely Celeste must have known that!

"I'm glad you could come," Nell said.

"I appreciate you having me," Celeste said.

There was a strained undercurrent on both sides. Lara wondered if Celeste's coming was an imposition on Nell. She said: "Celeste has back trouble so she won't be skiing with us. She can guard the fort."

"Speaking of which," Rachael said. "No offense meant, but I didn't come here just to shoot the bull with you ladies. Let's hit the slopes!"

"How far are the lifts?" Mindy asked.

"About four miles," Nell said. "But there's an excellent hard-packed path the entire way. Leads right to the door of the lodge. I'll show you on a map."

"Aren't you coming with us?" Lara asked.

Nell wiped her forehead. "I think I'll rest a bit first. I can join you later. Now come, let me show you your rooms."

They were taken on a tour of how the other half lived. Each bedroom was ridiculously large. The central fireplace — there were three altogether — could have roasted a prize steer. The constant smell of pine and cedar was a pleasure. They didn't go into the basement, but Nell told them of a recently installed propane tank that could supply them with enough power to endure the fiercest winter siege.

Lara was concerned that Nell did not feel well enough to accompany them, but she was pleased that Celeste would not have to be left alone. Hopefully they would hit it off.

Before leaving, Rachael and Mindy insisted that the rest of them see their snowman. They exited through a side door, where the snow was shaded by the house.

But there was no snowman.

The scarf, sunglasses, and cowboy hat rested on the ground. "Mindy," Rachael said, annoyed.

"I didn't knock it down!"

"Well, I'm sure Nell didn't," Rachael said.

"I haven't been out of the house since we arrived," Nell said, puzzled.

"Is this some kind of adolescent prank?" Dana accused Mindy.

"No! I swear. Somebody else must have knocked it down."

"A psychotic snowman murderer with an ax, right." Rachael said.

"The only tracks are ones that lead from the house," Nell said.

"It must have melted," Mindy said.

"Impossible," Nell said. "It was in the shade. And besides, it's too cold."

Lara stooped to gather up the late snowman's clothes. The scarf and hat came loose only with a sharp yank. They had been frozen in place. A concave circle of ice about six feet in diameter had taken the place of the snowman.

"He *must* have melted," Lara said, "and taken some of the surrounding snow with him. And then froze again. See how smooth it is here?"

Rachael frowned. "Weird."

Lara asked Nell, "Is there a pipe or a vent under this spot?"

"Definitely not."

"There must be," Rachael insisted. "The pipe could be underground."

Nell shook her head. "I've been coming here since I was a child. I would know."

"How the hell did he melt, then?" Rachael demanded.

"Probably saw a nude female snowman and got too hot," Dana suggested.

That broke them up. They began back toward the house. Except for Lara. She remained studying the impression of ice. It was as though the snowman had suddenly caught fire.

"I'M HUNGRY," DANA GROWLED.

"You're always hungry," Lara said.

"I wish anorexia was contagious and I knew someone who could infect me."

"Wonder what's taking them so long?"

They were sitting in the lounge next to a heating vent, their recently rented downhill skis standing sentinels on either side. Rachael and Mindy were still being fitted. Nell had provided them with lift passes. The trip down from the house had been uneventful. However, dark clouds could now be seen to the northeast.

"Rachael's probably having her skis shined to where she can see her face whenever she looks down," Dana said.

"I heard that," Rachael snapped, striding into the room, Mindy on her tail, both empty-handed.

"Where are they?" Lara asked.

"We're picking up the skis in a bit," Rachael said. "Mindy and I have some things we want to do first."

"What are these *things*?" Lara asked.

"We're meeting some friends," Mindy said, popping a bubblegum balloon.

"You can meet friends in Oakland," Dana said, sounding vaguely jealous. "Let's ski first."

"But you're hungry, Dana," Rachael said with profound concern. "You need your nourishment or you'll starve that cute double chin of yours." Dana stuck out her tongue. Rachael added, "Seriously, Lara, why don't you two eat? We shouldn't be too long."

Rachael and Mindy began to walk away as if the matter were settled, which annoyed Lara. "Is this why this weekend was so important?" she called.

They just giggled, and were gone.

"Do I really have a double chin?" Dana asked.

"Of course not."

"You liar. Let's go stuff our faces."

The coffee shop was jammed. Ski parkas from every color of the rainbow, and ski chatter from overactive imaginations filled the room. They had to wait to be seated.

Dana decided on the entire menu before finally ordering a chicken cashew sandwich and a large piece — as she made clear to the waitress with her hands — of chocolate cake. Lara had a bowl of vegetable soup. She was dieting. She was always dieting. Damn that Rachael, she didn't deserve to be homecoming queen.

"I read in a magazine that skiing burns seven hundred and fifty calories a minute," Dana said in between mouthfuls of food. "You sure you don't want some cake?"

"An hour."

"Huh?"

"Seven hundred and fifty calories an hour. I read the same magazine."

"Does that mean you don't want a piece of cake?"

Lara put a hand on her stomach. "I am still hungry. Maybe an apple will kill the urge."

At the fruit bowl, all the apples were green, so she decided on an orange instead. She had picked up and squeezed half a dozen when a soft male voice spoke behind her.

"Are you looking for a hard one, or a soft one?"

The question made her jump and drop her orange. He picked it up and placed it aside on the table. "I guess you don't want this one," he smiled.

Lara managed to shake her head. He was a few years older, and half a foot taller, than herself. His olive skin wasn't from overexposure to the mountain sun. He was of either Greek or Slavic descent, yet he had light green eyes, which contrasted sharply with a shock of unmanaged black hair. He was vaguely frightening, definitely handsome.

"The reason I ask," he continued, "is because I often see people squeezing oranges and I never know what they're looking for."

If this was a come-on, it was rather clever. "I was looking for one that was neither too hard nor too soft," Lara said.

"Up for the day?"

"The weekend."

"Supposed to snow heavily tonight."

"I know."

"Where are you staying?"

Lara nodded and smiled. "That-a way, at a friend's house. I'm with some girls from school."

Her hint that she wasn't with a guy removed a subtle barrier. He smiled again. He had nice teeth. "I'm Percy Chand."

She shook his hand. "Lara Johnson, pleased to meet you. Where are you from . . . Percy?"

"Currently, San Francisco. But I'm never in one place long."

"I'm from Oakland."

"I was there a couple of weeks ago. Do you go to school there, or what?"

The question was really, are you still in high school? "For another few months," Lara said vaguely.

Percy reached randomly into the fruit bowl. "This couple looks good. Can I join you?"

"Well . . . I am with a friend. I would have to ask her."

"My buddy should be along in a minute. We're already bored with each other."

"I . . . I guess it would be okay."

She led Percy to the table. Dana's eyes sparkled when she saw him. She stretched her neck to flatten any undue bulges. "Dana, this is Percy. He's from San Francisco." She tossed in, "He's here with a friend."

"Hi!" Dana said, a shade too loud.

"Hello."

With introductions complete, they sat down. The conversation flowed easily. Lara and Dana did most of the talking. Percy possessed the rare virtue of being a good listener. His interest in both of them seemed genuine. When asked a question, even a frivolous one, he thought for a moment before answering, taking them seriously. His personality was soft. He was originally from Canada, an orphan who hadn't gotten past ninth grade. Since leaving his foster home, he had spent most of his days drifting through the Western states, working enough to get by, then moving on. Currently he drove a truck for a furniture warehouse in San Francisco. Nevertheless, he assured them that he had a great ambition. He just hadn't figured out what it was yet. He was twenty-two.

Lara liked him. She could feel the symptoms of that magic haze, where the world was suddenly much brighter and more interesting. But afraid of the hurt of disappointment, she tried not to indulge her fantasies. After all, he was just a guy. . . .

"You sound like you've had an interesting life," Lara said. "Have you found it a handicap not having finished school?"

"Haven't picked a rotten orange yet," he smiled.

"Tell me about your friend," Dana said.

Percy hesitated. "Cal? He's more of a partner than a friend. I haven't known him long. I needed a place to stay and he had an available room. He's a character. Speak of the devil. There he is in the lobby. Be back in a sec."

With Percy gone, Lara asked, "What do you think?"

"That you're a lucky SOB. Hope his friend's got a fraction of his charm."

"How do you know it isn't you he likes?"

"I noticed no obvious symptoms of brain damage. Hey, remember what I said about a party? Let's invite these two up to the house. What with Rachael's and Mindy's fellows, we could have a blast."

"What about Nell and Celeste? This is supposed to be a slumber party, not an orgy."

"We won't let them stay. We have the whole night to slumber."

"I don't know," Lara said, drumming the table with her nails. She was more than tempted. Her hormones were being very persuasive. "If we suggest it, they might get the wrong idea. I'd have to ask Nell."

"Call her!"

"You haven't even met the guy!"

Dana laughed. "Has that ever stopped me?"

"I'll think about it." Cal was a huge redhead with a massive mouth, the antithesis of Percy. He straddled a chair and waved his tongue nonstop for fifteen minutes about what fantastic skiers the two of them were. Dana appeared to like him well enough. She probably didn't notice him eyeing her breasts. Suddenly he stood.

"Got to go, got to unload the van." He asked Dana, "Want to come?"

"Sure."

"Catch you in a few minutes," Percy said as they left. When they were out of hearing range he looked at Lara and sighed. "Just an acquaintance, you understand."

"How old is Cal?"

Percy shrugged. "I'm not sure. He spent four years in the service so he's got to be at least twenty-two. Told me once—I think he was joking—that he got a discharge for *playing* with napalm."

"Is she safe with him?"

"He won't do any permanent damage," Percy muttered absently. He touched her arm. "I'm sorry, that was crude. She should be fine."

"Maybe I should be more worried for Cal."

"Can I see you again?" Percy asked abruptly.

"I would like that," Lara said slowly, racing inside.

"When?"

"We could go skiing together."

Percy shook his head. "Cal may have exaggerated, but we do ski off the top."

"But they call that Kamikaze Run. It starts like this." Lara held her hand at a ninety-degree angle. "What happens if you fall?"

"You roll to the bottom of the mountain. Don't look so worried. I've skied here before."

Lara took a deep breath. "My girlfriends will probably be having some guys over this evening. If you and Cal would like to come, I'm sure it would be okay. But I'll have to check with Nell—she's the one who owns the house—first."

"Great. We can bring drinks."

Worried that maybe she was getting in over her head, Lara excused herself to use the phone. Nell had written down the number for her before they had left.

"Hello, Nell? How are you feeling?"

"Fine."

"That's good. How are you and Celeste getting along?"

"We—we had a long talk."

"I'm glad. The reason I called, and don't hesitate to say no if you want to, is that the four of us met some guys and we were wondering if we could invite them up for the evening? Just for a little while?"

Nell did not answer immediately. Lara was on the verge of telling her to forget it, when Nell said, "I wouldn't mind. Let me ask, ahhh . . . let me ask. . . ."

"Celeste."

"Yeah, let me ask Celeste." Nell was gone an eternity. Finally: "Celeste says that it's fine with her but not to bother finding her a boy."

Lara chuckled. "How about you?"

"Bring whatever's available."

"Coming skiing with us?"

"Maybe."

Lara knew that she would never come. "Good-bye, Nell."

"Have fun, Lara."

Such melancholy in her voice, it tugged at Lara's heart. "We'll try to get back early," she promised.

Percy was happy with the news. She gave him detailed directions to the house and tactfully mentioned that they all wanted to get to bed early.

They had scarcely begun to chat again when Rachael and Mindy slid onto the scene.

"Percy!" Rachael exclaimed. "So there you are! Where's Cal?"

Oh no, Lara thought. She braced herself for a scene.

Percy stood awkwardly. "Hi, Rachael, Mindy. What are you—Cal's with Dana."

Mindy's bubble gum slipped out of her mouth and fell on the floor. "With *Dana*?"

Rachael took a seat. "Have you met my friend, Lara?"

"We've met," Lara muttered. Percy nodded, sinking back into his chair.

"Great," Rachael said brightly, casting her a microsecond glance that communicated a reservoir of hate. "I'm glad you could come, Percy."

"I didn't know you were coming," he said, smiling. "Definitely, I mean." He had regained his poise. He could see the humor in the situation.

"How did you two run into each other?" Rachael asked Lara.

"Well—" Lara began, not getting far.

"We met at the fruit bowl," Percy said matter-of-factly.

"You met at the fruit bowl." Rachael's pronunciation was very distinct.

"Is Cal coming back?" Mindy asked.

Percy laughed, standing. "I think that I had better go get him. Time we hit the snow." He nodded at Lara. "See you tonight. Good-bye, Rachael, Mindy."

"Take care," Lara whispered.

"Tonight?" Rachael asked. "What's tonight?"

"There's a party at your house," Percy smiled. "Everyone break a leg." He went to the cashier and paid for the oranges. He left without looking back. Considering the altitude, the air at the table was very thick.

"Nice guy," Lara said finally, shredding orange peels with her fingernails.

"Where's Dana?" Mindy whined.

"Oh, shut up, you!" Rachael said. "Dana's with Cal. Cal's with Dana. They're together in the same spot. Isn't that right, Lara?"

Lara bit her lip, and waved her hand impotently. "This is crazy. I just ran into him by accident."

"At the fruit bowl," Rachael spat.

"I didn't know he was with you," Lara said, raising her voice.

"And I suppose while the two of you were talking, my name was never mentioned!?"

"Right! Why should we talk about you?"

"Because it was me he was supposed to meet!"

"So he got lucky!"

"Why you little tramp!"

"Why you bigger one!"

"How long has Dana been with Cal?" Mindy asked.

Lara began to laugh hysterically. "Long enough, Mindy. Long enough."

There was a pause. Rachael asked with a slow razor: "Why did you invite him up to the house?"

Lara stopped laughing and stared Rachael right in the eye. "Because Nell said that it was okay."

"Because Nell said that it was okay?"

Lara scratched her head. "Are we getting an echo in here?"

"Shut up, Lara." Rachael smoldered, blood burning her face. "Goddamn that Percy."

"I'm sorry," Lara said gently, not altogether sincerely. "When did you meet them?"

"At the mall, a couple of weeks ago," Mindy said miscrably.

"This is just like a soap opera," Lara said. "Always hated those shows."

Yet the best was still to come.

"What a creep!" Dana swore, dropping in on their merry group. Her hair and makeup were a mess. "I'm five minutes in that guy's room, helping him unpack, you understand, when he sneaks up behind me and begins to maul me like a—like an octopus. What does he think I am!? I should call a cop, or a ranger, or something. For your sake, Lara, I'm glad that Percy said that Cal wasn't really a friend. Rachael, Mindy, you would had to have seen this guy."

"They have," Lara told the ceiling. "They have."

"Did you sleep with Cal?!" Mindy screamed, bursting into tears. (Mindy suffered from the classically feministdeficient upbringing. It was never the guy's fault.) They were suddenly the coffee shop's center of attraction.

Dana was mystified. "Huh?"

"Rach, she—" Mindy began.

"Don't say it," Rachael interrupted calmly. She took Mindy's hand and stood. Her last words were devoid of emotion. "Looks like it will be an interesting slumber party, Lara."

"Never a dull moment," she agreed.

"See you on the mountain," Rachael said. Practically carrying Mindy, she left.

Dana watched them go in wonder. "I must have missed something."

"You'd be amazed," Lara said.

～ CHAPTER 2 ～

THIS HIGH POINT OF LARA'S LIFE WAS PRETTY LOW. The skiing was no different than running laps in PE. She slid down the mountain, rode back up the mountain, slid down again. She was more conscious of her aching legs than of the fun she was supposed to be having. The wind had begun to blow and her hands were freezing. It was all Rachael's fault.

Staring at her dangling skis and the crisscrossed snow thirty yards below her lift chair, Lara figured that if Dana and she did not come to terms with Rachael and Mindy soon, the whole weekend would be shot. Neither side had spoken to the other since lunch, timing their lift rides to maintain a respectable, hostile distance. It was three o'clock. The sun would be setting early. Soon they would have to return to the house and prepare for the party.

Lara wondered if she should find Percy, tell him to forget the whole thing. Dana had said she wasn't looking forward to a second wrestling session with Cal. Yet such a prospect left Lara feeling flatter than she did already. Daydreaming had spun in her head a book-length "soon-to-be" affair with Percy. He would call her when she returned home, ask her out, pick her up in a Porsche, take her to an expensive restaurant and order lobster, then to the theater, kissing her passionately in his leather upholstered seats afterward, promising that he would see her the following day, and the day after that. She was still working on the castle-in-the-sky and the happily-ever-after chapters. It was incredible the material an innocent half-hour conversation could generate. A shame to kiss it all good-bye, without having even gotten to kiss Percy, merely to appease Rachael.

Of course, the party, with Rachael's full armament of charm on display, would probably be a more painful death to her dreams.

Lara hopped from the ski lift. Her thoughts else-where, she immediately fell hard on her rear end, jarring her spine and not doing a damn thing for the pressure she already had inside her skull. Standing up took four frustrating tries. Finally, dusting snow off her jeans, she searched for and found Dana approaching, ten seats down on the lift. Dana trod down the run as if she had an orthopedic surgeon perched on her shoulder whisper-ing paranoid warnings. Lara had gotten fed up waiting for her.

"That was a cute fall you took," Dana said, waddling

to her side, sporting wide sunglasses designed to hide her big nose.

"Too bad you didn't have your camera," Lara said, none too pleasantly.

"Serves you right for not waiting for me. Hell, I've fallen on my butt a dozen times already. You don't see me crying."

"Yeah, but you've got built-in shock absorbers."

"Now Lara, that was low. Say you're sorry and I will forgive you. If the two of us start fighting, then we're really in trouble. Everyone else hates us."

Lara pulled off her wool cap and foggy sunglasses, brushing hair out of her eyes. Immediately the wind began to sting her ears. The once distant clouds on the horizon had gathered gray overhead, putting the landscape through a black and white filter. "Sorry," she said quietly.

"I forgive you. Come on, Lara, what is it? Or need I ask?"

"Do you think we should swallow our pride and put up the white flag?"

Dana shielded her eyes, peering in the direction of the lodge. "They're getting on the lift. If we wait here, they will come to us."

"We will wait."

"What are you going to say? You won't get to first base unless you call off the party."

Lara shook her head. "You've got it wrong. Even from a distance, I can feel Rachael's confidence. She's looking forward to the party. She thinks that when Percy sees the two of us together, he'll have no trouble with his selection." Lara fitted her cap back on, sighing. "And she's probably right."

Dana touched her arm. "You really like him? I mean, *really*?"

Lara's shoulders slumped. "I think I've talked myself into it."

"You need to see the *Rocky* films again. You're giving up without a fight. Surely Percy has enough sense to pick a sweetheart over a 'swelled-head.'"

"Assuming that I'm not the swelled-head, when have you ever seen a guy want my sweetness over her body?"

Dana paused. "Never. Still, there's no problem. Find Percy, tell him that Nell's changed her mind about the party, and give him your phone number. Don't give Rachael another shot at him."

"No good. First I'd have to find him, which would be next to impossible. Still, even if I could find him, and he did ask me for my number, Rachael would know what I'd done, that I was afraid to compete with her."

"This sounds like an athletic contest. If you want, I'll be the one to call it off. They know I despise Cal."

"Do you really? You don't say that with much conviction."

"You think I enjoyed being mauled?"

"Did you?"

"Lara!"

"Did you?"

"None of your business. Just let me call it off. Forget your having to compete on even terms with Rachael. She's got a ten-point edge going in."

"No."

"You're being dumb."

"I know. But I want to see him. I miss him already."

Dana was sympathetic. "You've fallen, sister. I hope he wants to catch you. It doesn't matter what we decide anyway. They'll be here in a sec. Let's just feel our way."

Rachael and Mindy knew that they were waiting for them, despite their phony self-absorbed conversation that was designed to deny their existence. Only when Rachael had stepped off the lift, stretched, brushed her hair, and yawned, did she grace them with a passing glance. Mindy was not so subtle, showing them her back. Lara knew she would have to take the initiative.

"Hello," she said, "oldest and best friends."

Rachael's expression was calculating. "Are you being sarcastic, Lara?"

"Not at all. Been having fun?"

Mindy turned slowly. Rachael appeared to drop her guard a notch. She said, "This snow's divine. We've been having a great time."

"A super time," Mindy put in.

"We'd like to offer a truce," Lara said.

Rachael was back in command. "Really, Lara, don't be so dramatic. So we like the same guy. So what? This isn't a war. Me, I'm kind of looking forward to tonight. Like you said, never a dull moment. We'll have a great time."

"I think we should call it off," Dana muttered, looking at her.

Rachael understood and smiled. "No way," she said.

"Fine with me," Lara shrugged, her heart sinking. Rachael would flash her ultra-bright smile when he looked at her, run her sharp nails through her golden hair and accidentally brush his leg when she sat beside him, laugh deep and sexy in her throat and lean into his side with her firm breasts when he told a joke, let her crystal blue eyes slip from his spellbound stare to his crotch, letting him know that with her possibilities were endless. Percy would come a-running. Lara felt profoundly sad. Just this once, she had hoped. . . . At least she would get to see him again.

The four of them began to cut their way down the mountain. Dana and Mindy teamed up—both being mediocre skiers—and fell behind, seemingly on speaking terms again.

The last words Lara heard of their conversation were Dana reassuring Mindy that she had absolutely no interest in Cal. Rachael was sharp on her feet, frequently spraying Lara with flakes as she banked to kill the speed she would quickly gather. Lara felt inadequate in every way beside her. Rachael's spirits were buoyant. "What do you think we should wear tonight, Lara? Should we"—with a nasty grin—"wear anything?" As they boarded the lifts, she rattled off a string of dirty jokes. Trying to catch her breath and only half listening, Lara didn't get most of them. Two more runs and their separation from Mindy and Dana was complete. Finally, barely able to stand at the top of the hill, Lara suggested that they call it a day.

"Okay," Rachael said. "But let's go through the trees this time. I'm tired of this easy slide. Think you can handle it?"

"Sure," Lara said, dreading the prospect. The trees would have taxed the limits of her skill if she was fresh. And now, exhausted, she would be risking her neck; nevertheless, it was better than admitting to Rachael that she was afraid.

Rachael surprised her by shadowing her cautious pace. Maybe she was exhausted, too, Lara thought, for she had also fallen strangely silent. They maneuvered like a linked pair, giving each pine a wide berth, until they entered the most obstructed part of the course. Here Rachael began to press her right. Lara muttered for her to back off. Rachael was quick to oblige.

Lara was eyeing a cluster of approaching trees, plotting

a strategy of turns, when Rachael suddenly accelerated, cutting directly across her path. She tried to brake, but the abruptness of the effort caused her to lose balance. It was as though a meaty football tackle had slammed the back of her knees. The desolate sky, the coated trees, the powdery snow, all blurred in a spinning collage. She was a snowball, and she wasn't slowing down. Way back in her head she remembered Percy's line about rolling to the bottom of the mountain. She wasn't anywhere near that lucky.

Lara heard rather than felt the impact, a thousand splintering wooden matches. Then there was silence. Her thoughts were a dreamy jumble. In retrospect, she realized that she had been only partially conscious, but her thoughts still held the common thread of absolute disgust for Rachael. That it had been an accident did not even cross her mind, for where was she? Lara opened her eyes, which took their time focusing. The clouds were calling her name, using Percy's voice. That must mean that she had damaged her brain, she thought. Poor girl will never be the same. Then the clouds squeezed her hand, and she knew that was impossible, even for crossed neurons.

"Lara," Percy was saying. "You're okay. Don't move."

He was contradicting himself, she thought. But she was so glad that he had come to her rescue, she ignored his advice and sat up. The landscape did a quick dance before settling down and letting her know she was entangled in a sharp-branched bush. Another foot and her skull would have smacked an ungiving thick trunk. Percy was kneeling by her side, concern darkening his handsome face.

She smiled. "Fancy meeting you here."

"Remain perfectly still. You may have a bone broken."

"I feel fine, really. Not a scratch." She wiped at a funny itch in her hair. When she drew her hand away, it was stained with blood. "Well, maybe a scratch," she muttered, flexing her arms and legs slowly. The damage appeared superficial. Ignoring Percy's protests, she tried to stand. Her left knee groaned, but that was the worst of it. "See, all in one piece," she said, untangling her pants with Percy's help.

He shook his head. "You were lucky. When I saw you lose your balance in front of these trees, I braced myself for the worst."

That he'd had such concern for her eased the pain she was beginning to feel from her cut. But the joy at seeing him was somewhat spoiled by the thought of Rachael's deed. "I didn't lose my balance. Rachael cut me off."

He was puzzled by her tone. "That happens, you hit ice and suddenly gain speed. I'm sure she didn't force you into these bushes on purpose."

Lara shut a *You don't know her the way I know her* in her mouth, and said instead, "Where is she?"

Percy's change of expression indicated that he was considering her accusation. "That wasn't very nice, leaving you here."

"Were you just passing by?" she asked, thinking, *Were you following me, thinking of me all day, mad to see me?*

He laughed. "No, I was following you."

"Really?" she beamed, then remembered that she had to be cool.

"I saw you get off the lift with Rachael. I was trying to catch up. I called several times but you mustn't have heard." He pulled back her hair near her cut. "That's still bleeding. Looks like it could use a few stitches."

"No way. Those doctors would want to cut my hair in the process." She added quietly, "Why were you following us?"

He spoke seriously. "To tell you we won't be coming tonight. I talked to Cal—that bastard—and he told me about his run-in with Dana. His was no doubt a distorted version, but I can guess the truth. I'd been having second thoughts anyway. Rachael didn't look too excited about having us over. Life's complicated enough. Why don't we just forget it?"

"No," Lara said firmly. *Fool*, she told herself, *just give him your number*. But that would be too easy. And suddenly she was confident she could win Percy's affection, and she wanted Rachael there to rub her nose in it. God, Dana was right, this was a contest. "I've spoken with

Dana," she exaggerated. "I think she likes Cal more than she—more than she gave him the impression she did. Just think, six girls trapped in a house together. We'll be so bored! Come, and don't worry about it. Please?"

Percy was unconvinced. "I don't know. You're the one who said she ran you into these trees. Maybe the party was the reason."

She shook off her skis as they started slowly toward the lodge. "If she did do it on purpose," she said boldly, "then I'll need you there to protect me."

LARA RESISTED ALL OF PERCY'S ATTEMPTS TO HAVE HER see a doctor. By the time they had reached the ski lodge, her cut had dried and she felt all she needed was a good shampoo. However, her knee was throbbing. Only with difficulty had she disguised her limp from Percy. Boys liked tough girls, so she had heard.

On the same couch where she had waited with Dana for Rachael and Mindy, they sat and chatted about snow and skiing. The colored parkas had thinned, most people calling it a day—which reminded Lara, where were the girls? Already the sun had gone behind the mountain. Probably they had started back without her. She was debating whether to call Nell when Percy mentioned that he'd like to get in more skiing.

"Isn't it too late?" Her euphoria was suddenly compromised. He wanted to ski when he could talk to her. He didn't love her. "I thought maybe we could have a bite to eat at the coffee shop."

He stood, already on his way, enough time wasted on her. "I never exercise on a full stomach," he said with his usual degree of charm. "Now, are you sure you're well enough to walk back to the house? It's a long way. I could tell you were limping and trying to hide it."

She didn't want to use that to keep him. "I feel a hundred percent better." She got up, trying not to wince with pain.

"You sure?"

"Positive."

He was in a hurry. "Catch you later, then. Between seven and eight is good?"

"Positive. I mean, perfect. Have a good time!"

An awkward hesitation followed, where they both stared at each other and fidgeted. She was hoping for a kiss. But he only patted her shoulder, told her to take care, and was gone. Feeling what she recognized as unfounded loneliness, she sat back down. The long hike on her stiff knee weighed on her mind.

At that moment, the ranger who had taken the keys to Dana's car was walking across the lobby toward the bar. "Sir?" she called. "Sir, did you bring our car down?"

He walked over to her with seeming reluctance. He was not wearing a uniform. He glanced at her bloody hair, smoothed his moustache nervously, and said, "Scratched your head, I see. Were you attacked by a bear?"

"A tree. I was wondering about our car."

He rummaged through his pockets, coining up empty-handed. He smiled, showing he needed dental work. "Must have left them in the office."

"Could we get them now?"

"I suppose so," he said, without a shred of enthusiasm. "Off duty now. You girls are staying till Sunday evening, ain't ya?"

"Yes."

"I'll have those keys waiting for you when you leave."

"I'd like to pick them up now."

"But the colonel was just going to enjoy watching a football game in the bar here. Look, they'll be here and sparkling and waitin' when you're ready to leave." He grinned again, more out of habit, it seemed, than out of warmth. He slapped her side roughly. "Watch out for them bears, you hear? They'll eat ya alive."

Before she could protest, he walked away. Suspicion dominated her thoughts. He had gone to the trouble of moving their cars and now couldn't be bothered return-ing their keys. Initially he'd worn no badge and now he was out of uniform. He seemed old for a ranger. Maybe he wasn't one, but a car thief instead. She would have to check that guy out.

Lara limped to the phone and searched her pockets for the number to Nell's house. It was gone; must have fallen out when she crashed. No matter, her memory was excellent, and she dialed what she was almost positive were the correct digits. But the phone on the other end rang and rang. That was odd, for even if Nell had gone for a walk, Celeste would not have been able to.

Her meager lunch in combination with the hours of strenuous exercise made her stomach grumble for attention. Ignoring her solemn vows to diet seven pounds away, she took a seat at the counter of the coffee shop and ordered a turkey sandwich, french fries, milk, and a huge slice of the chocolate cake Dana had eaten earlier. Nothing like a stuffed belly to uplift one's mood. She was asking for the bill when a rough voice intruded beside her.

"I hope you're more friendly than your partner."

It was Cal, crushing the adjacent stool, stinking of sweat, blowing hot breath in her face. "I hear the two of you didn't hit it off," she said carefully.

He leaned on the counter with his elbow, shoving a plate aside. "What did she tell you?" he demanded.

Lara shrugged. "Don't remember exactly. Coming to the party tonight?"

"Huh?"

Later, she would have to ask Dana's forgiveness for the liberties she was going to take with her name. "We're having a party at my friend's house tonight. Percy might have told you it was off but I talked him back into it. You're welcome to come. Give Dana another chance. She didn't sound that mad at you. To tell you the truth, she likes aggressive men."

Cal was perplexed, more so than her information could justify. His eyes lost their focus, as though he were thinking intently. "Percy told me about no party," he said finally.

"Doesn't matter. I'm telling you."

"Where is that guy, anyway? He told me he was coming to talk to you."

"He left about thirty minutes ago. He wanted to ski some more."

Cal nodded to himself, swinging his feet onto the floor. "What did he tell you about me?" he asked warily.

"Percy? Not much. That you work together, live in the same place." Lara forced a chuckle. "Is there something I should know?"

"No."

She stuttered. "I was merely joking."

He smiled, patting her back with a heavy hand. "You girls fix us up a nice party. If you by chance see Dana, tell her I'm coming."

"Of course, I'll see her. I'm heading back now."

"Sure, yeah," he told the floor.

"Have *you* seen her?"

"Noo. Hey, I've gotta split."

"Do you want directions in case you don't see Percy?"

"I know where the place is. Catch you later."

"Good-bye." Lara watched him leave. How did he know where Nell's house was if he'd never been there?

CHAPTER 3

THE CLOUDS HAD DECIDED TO GIVE UP THEIR CARGO. Stretching her head back and opening her mouth wide, Lara tried to catch snowflakes on her thirsty tongue. Despite a significant drop in temperature and a strengthening wind, she was hot and sweaty. Ages had elapsed since she had left the lodge and she was still nowhere near halfway home. Her knee no longer hurt so much as it refused to cooperate. The joint was mushy. Also, the grooves they had cut in the path on their way down were filling in. Whenever she skipped out of them, her cross-country skis sank an additional foot. All this work for a trifle of sensation; it was hardly worth the bother. If not for Percy, Lara decided, she would have given the day a failing grade.

Lara was leaning against a tree, taking a brief time-out, when she saw a figure approaching swiftly on skis from up the path. It was Mindy, obviously out of control and about to . . . thank God, she had sat down and stopped herself. Lara limped to her side and offered her hand.

"You don't belong in the fast lane," she said.

"Oh, it's you, Lara." Mindy retrieved her bubble gum from the snow and popped it back in her mouth. One of these days Mindy was going to bite her tongue off. Lara helped her up.

"You're going the wrong way. Where are the others?"

"I don't know where Rachael is. I haven't seen her since you two took off together. Dana's farther up the path. We were returning to the house when I decided I had better find you. What happened to your head?"

"The ranger said it was a bear. Now that you've found me, let's get home. This storm's getting nastier every minute."

Mindy looked unhappy. "I think I should try to find Rachael."

"How do you know she isn't ahead of you two?"

"Well, I don't. How do you know she is?"

"You were returning to the lodge to find Cal, right?"

"Nooo."

"Get off it, Mindy."

She was suddenly defensive. "What's so wrong with wanting to talk to him? I don't care what Dana says, I think he's a gentleman."

"I spoke to him just before I left. He's coming tonight to the party. You don't have to go to the lodge."

"I still want to."

"You're not. You should never have left Dana. She's a

bigger clod than you. What if she trips and sprains her ankle and has no one to help her? Come, we're going home."

"Why should I?" But there was no authority in her voice.

"Because I am telling you."

"But I'd like to see him."

Lara softened. "You will, tonight. Besides, I've hurt my knee and I'm not feeling very strong. What do you say, pal?"

"Okay." Mindy squinted. "You really ran into a bear?"

Lara laughed. "One you know all too well."

They were three quarters of an hour farther along—it took a lot longer going up than going down—when they came across a most mysterious find. *One* of Dana's skis lay half covered in the tracks. Scattered footsteps led away from it approximately ten yards up the path, disappearing in a concave impression that looked uncannily familiar. Beyond the impression, there were no footsteps.

"What the hell," Mindy muttered, sliding forward to investigate. Lara stopped her.

"Stay here."

"What's wrong?"

"Don't disturb the evidence."

Mindy was suddenly frightened. "You think we're in danger?"

Lara shook her head. "I don't know what to think." She

crept forward cautiously, squatting by the ski. If it were broken, that might have given Dana reason to leave it. She tested the spring-pressured clasps that fastened onto the boots. One had lost its elasticity, but then, hadn't Dana mentioned that earlier, that it had always been that way? These Olin skis cost a bundle, to simply discard. And then there was the impression in the snow. Of course, she had seen the same phenomenon where the vanishing snowman had been. Lara moved up the path and knelt, poking a finger through the inch of fresh snow that was filling the crater. It was hard, ice. She brushed clear a patch. The frozen sheet was flaked with dirty gray.

"Lara?" Mindy called, her panic rising. "What is it?"

As though the snowman had suddenly caught fire.

Without two skis, Dana would have littered the path with footsteps. There were no footsteps. It was as though Dana had reached this spot and gone neither forward nor backward. She had simply stopped and vanished. What had stopped her? Where could she have gone? The Bermuda Triangle didn't reach this far west.

Lara broke two branches from a nearby bush and, using the string that tightened her jacket hood, fastened an awkward cross to an adjacent tree. If necessary, she would be able to find this exact spot. Returning to a trembling Mindy, she asked, "Where were the two of you on the path when you split up?"

"I don't know. We were near here. Oh, God, do you think something's happened to her?"

"How far would you say we are from the house?"

Mindy pointed vaguely. "We just have to wrap around these trees. Fifteen minutes, maybe twenty. Why would Dana leave her ski in the snow?"

"It won't have been the first weird thing that Dana's done," Lara said. This reassured Mindy. Obviously she did not notice all the inconsistencies in the situation. Lara picked up the ski. It was cold, naturally. Yet the chill that caused her to shiver was from foreboding. "Let's get out of this place," she said suddenly.

Shortly afterward, they rounded a bend and saw the house with a warming scent and trail of smoke rising from the chimney. Nell was sitting on the porch steps, her head resting in her clasped hands on propped-up elbows. She did not notice them. Only when Mindy called, did she look up.

"Have a good time?" she asked, glancing at the extra ski Lara carried.

"Okay," Lara said. "Rach here?"

"Haven't seen her."

Lara dropped Dana's ski. "Seen Dana?"

"Yeah."

Her flood of relief made her realize how worried she'd been. "How long ago did she get back?"

"Didn't you see her on the way up? I mean, she's not here. I saw her way down on the path about an hour ago before she went behind the trees. In fact, I was beginning to worry about her. I figured that she had stopped and was taking a rest, but then she was taking so long to reappear. I was about to ski down, when I saw you two coming up. Dana should know better than to ski off the path."

"She didn't," Lara said, the lump reforming in her stomach. "This is her ski. We found it on the path, just this one."

Nell heard her concern. "She couldn't have just disappeared."

"The snowman did," Lara whispered, more to herself. Quickly she gave Nell the details of the abandoned ski and the impression in the snow. She concluded by asking, "Is there another path down to the lodge that intersects this one?"

"Not really," Nell said. "Though, if enough people ski through a place it can be just as good as a path. That's probably what happened. She probably took off on some tangent."

"Why would she do that?" Mindy asked.

"Maybe she wanted to circle back to the lodge," Nell said, checking out the darkening clouds. It was difficult to be sure, but the sun had probably set. "A little late for that."

"I don't think so," Lara muttered.

Mindy came to life, in a foul mood. "That's it! That's what she did! She knew I was going back to see Cal and she wanted to get there first. She snuck off the path trying to find a shortcut."

"And left one of her skis?" Lara asked, irritated. "Don't be ridiculous. Besides, there were no tracks except the ski grooves."

"You're right," Nell said, thoughtful. "The only logical explanation is that Dana left the path well before you found this ski, and that this ski is not really hers. Olin—it's a common brand."

"I could swear it's hers," Lara said, now not altogether certain. There still remained the question of how someone else left it without making tracks. "Yet, you must be right."

"She's stealing him away from me!" Mindy complained. "Why can't she find her own guys! Cal was supposed to be mine!"

Nell chuckled. "Who's this Cal? Is he one of the guys coming to the party?"

Lara decided to let matters rest for the time being. Nell's explanation had not erased the mystery, but surely there was a harmless, logical explanation. Plus Nell's own change in mood was supportive. Her initial gloom seemed to have dissolved. Yet Lara knew only too well how quickly that could change. "Yes, he is," she said. "Boy, have I got a story for you."

"That conniving bitch," Mindy grumbled.

"Have you got a guy for me?" Nell asked.

"I'm afraid those are in short supply for this party," Lara said. "So far, only two are coming. I forgot to ask, how are you feeling?"

"Fine, I just needed a rest."

"How's Celeste?" Lara asked.

Nell paused. An unreadable emotion flicked across her face. "She's in the shower."

Not that that answered the question. "You two have a lot to talk about?"

Nell was hardly listening. "She seems like a nice girl."

Lara left them on the porch. The house had so many rooms, she had to search for the bathroom where Celeste was taking her shower. Behind one door, the light was on. Knocking lightly, she went inside.

"Celeste?"

Through the hot steam, as if she had suddenly been cornered by Jack the Ripper, Celeste jumped behind the opaque shower curtain and wrapped it about her naked body. The water was off; she had been drying. Lara chuckled at her modesty, saying, "I didn't mean to startle you."

Well hidden, Celeste breathed, "That's okay. How was the skiing?"

"Great. Met this guy. Have to tell you all about him when you're done. What have you and Nell been up to?"

"What do you mean?"

"Nothing specific. What have you done since I saw you last?"

"Nothing. We talked."

"About what?"

"Things."

The reaction was similar to Nell's. If anything, Celeste sounded vaguely angry. She had never seen Celeste angry before. She wouldn't have thought it possible. "Do you like her?"

Celeste had wrapped herself in a towel, still behind the curtain, obviously waiting for her to leave to continue drying. "Who?" she asked.

"Why, Nell."

"She seems like a nice girl."

Like an echo. "You heard about the party," Lara said, beginning to leave. "When you're dressed, come to the kitchen. Maybe our two heads together can whip up something eatable."

Celeste's voice was enthusiastic. "I'm really glad we're having a party."

"Is Nell using the adjacent bedroom?" Lara asked idly. On the sink counter was a jar of prescription skin cream for an *N. Kutroff.* Probably Nell still had to treat the areas that had been grafted.

"I don't know."

"She must be. Me, I would have taken the master bedroom. Anyway, start drumming up your best recipes."

"I love cooking."

"Great. Hey, Nell hasn't left the house at any time, has she?"

"No."

"That's good."

The crackling fire in the living room was seductive. Lara took a minute to sit on the surrounding bricks, letting the warmth ease her tired muscles. Nell had piled high the logs. One would have thought she would have been wary of fires.

"What happened to you?" Rachael's voice rang.

Lara cautioned herself to be cool. "I ran into a tree."

"You ran into a tree," Rachael repeated, not taking her answer seriously. "What happened to your head?"

Lara had forgotten the dried blood. She would have to take a shower immediately. Curious how Nell hadn't commented on it. "Actually, it was a bush I ran into. Didn't you know?"

Rachael was either a master liar or else she was innocent. "You're saying that when you suddenly dropped behind, you had run into a tree?"

"A bush. A sharp one. Ruined my jacket."

"You poor dear. I didn't know. I looked and suddenly you were gone. Are you hurt?"

"No."

"Better wash that blood out of your hair. It looks totally gross."

Lara toyed with the idea of harping on how Percy had come to her rescue. Better to have Percy bring it up, she decided. "Have you seen Dana?"

Rachael snickered. "Nell and Mindy asked me about her. No, I haven't. Bet she's back at the lodge. Nothing she likes better than a good feel and Cal's perfect for that, though that's probably all he's good for."

"Where have you been all this time?"

"Skiing."

"This entire time?"

"Hey, what is this? If I was making out with Percy, I don't gotta tell you."

"You couldn't have been doing that."

"Sure about that, Princess Lara?"

Lara smiled sweetly. "Couldn't have been kissing two girls at the same time, could he, Princess Rachael?" Before she could respond, Lara left the room. But not before she saw Rachael's flawless jaw drop heavily. She'd won that round. Still, the final score was all that mattered.

In the kitchen, before taking an inventory of Nell's stock, Lara called the lodge. The number was on a typed sheet posted next to the phone.

"Park Administration. Can I help you?"

"Yes, my name is Lara Johnson. I'm up from Oakland with friends for the weekend. We're staying at the Kutroff residence in the Cedar Stream area. The problem is — actually, I'm not sure if it is a problem — is that my friend has sort of disappeared. Her name is Dana Miller."

He was brisk. "How has she 'sort of disappeared'?"

"We don't know where she is."

"When and where was the last time you saw her?"

"Another friend of mine was with her an hour and a half, maybe two hours ago. They split up on the path that leads from the lodge to Cedar Stream. We assumed she was walking home alone ahead of us. We found one of her skis — at least, I think it's hers — on the trail. You know where I mean?"

"Yes." He seemed to be taking notes. "You're not sure it was her ski?"

"Not positive." Lara realized how nebulous she was being. "Look, perhaps she'll show up soon. It's still early. I guess what I really want to know is if she has returned to the lodge, can she leave a message with you that would get to me?"

"Certainly. What is your number?" Lara gave it to him off the phone, identical to the number she had called earlier and gotten no answer to. "Got it."

"Good. Is the storm still on for tonight?" If Percy wasn't able to come, she might not have a chance to give him her number. She might not see him again.

"Definitely. Should be a beaut. Miss, if that's all —"

"One other thing. Do you have a ranger on staff who looks like Colonel Sanders?"

"Pardon me?"

"The chicken guy. A ranger who looks like and calls himself the colonel said he was going to move our cars for us. I was wondering if he was legit."

"I know of no one on our staff who fits that description. But then again, I am new here. Did he take your keys?"

"Yes he did."

"Then you might have a problem. I'll check into it at this end. And I'll page Dana Miller periodically until she shows up. Contact me if she returns home."

"Who should I ask for?"

"Roger McCormick. I'll be at the desk all night."

"Thank you, Roger." Putting down the phone, Lara was more worried about Dana's car than Dana herself. And the colonel had moved Rachael's BMW also. Well, there was nothing she could do about it now.

Food for the party would have to be the priority. She was pleased to discover that Nell had stocked a diverse supply of sandwich ingredients: rye and wheat bread, cold cuts, french rolls, cheese, lettuce, butter, tomatoes, plus bags of chips and cartons of dips, and an entire case of Coke. That would take care of dinner, but dessert would have to have a personal touch. She was flipping through a ten-pound cookbook, thinking that she would never be able to bake anything that even remotely resembled the luscious color photos, when Celeste came to her rescue.

Celeste was not merely a good cook, she was a certified

chef. "Cold cuts," she asked in amazement, "and you like this boy?" She installed Lara in the corner out of the way, grating carrots for a carrot cake, while she prepared two chickens, clothing them in a concoction of herbs that Lara had always assumed people had in their kitchens for looks. That was but the beginning. Soon Celeste had the entire contents of the cupboards arranged on the table and countertop, moving each ingredient toward an invisible feast.

Casually she inquired about Percy. Lara needed little encouragement to pour out her heart. "Oh, he's the cutest, I mean absolutely the best-looking guy that I've ever . . ." The other girls were working to give the house a festive atmosphere, wandering in and out of the kitchen only to stuff food in their mouths. Rachael strolled in while Lara was describing Percy's voice. More harsh nonverbal exchanges. Lara was getting used to them. But she was afraid that Nell would be upset at the control Celeste had taken of her kitchen. Yet Nell seemed to take it all in stride.

With her cake tucked in the oven, Lara left Celeste to take a shower and wash the blood out of her hair. The cut reopened and the red drops trailing down her naked body made her feel slightly dizzy. There was no way she could bandage it. The hot water also made her drowsy and a nap sounded just perfect. But before she lay down on her bed, she gave the house a white-glove inspection. Was she expecting to find Dana tucked away in a secret hideout in

Cal's arms? Not really, but she had a nagging compulsion that bid her search till she could find *something*.

The house was massive, and there were many empty rooms in which if she stood perfectly still she could hear the sighing of the timbers as they buffeted the rising wind. The end of the search found her in the basement, beside a snowmobile and the huge, recently installed propane tank that Nell had mentioned, cold to her hesitant touch. It was scary. The image of a shattered house rising on a mushroom cloud formed and lingered in her mind. Why these constant thoughts about fire? Unseen flames seemed ready to spark out of the air.

She was drawn outside a side door to study again the impression marking the snowman's disappearance. But drifts created by the storm had erased the concave dish of ice. Nevertheless, she went down on her hands and knees, feeling for the spot, numbing her exposed fingers, freezing her damp hair, eventually giving up and staggering out of the dark back into the house to her bedroom.

Thawing out beneath layers of blankets, *colorless* fire sparkled inside her closed eyes. There was a face inside the flames, a face that should have slipped into the past, but that continued to shadow her, haunt her — a melting face in horrifying pain. . . .

∽ CHAPTER 4 ∽

"Why do I always have to baby-sit her?" Nell complained to her mother.

"Because she's your little sister," Mrs. Kutroff said, pulling the long Cadillac into Dana's driveway. "You should be happy you have one."

"I'd rather have a little brother who played with trucks all by himself," Nell said.

"Hush, now. We're here." Mrs. Kutroff turned to the backseat. "Have all your things?"

"Yes, Mrs. Kutroff," Lara said politely, hugging her pillow and blanket to her chest.

"Mommy, I forgot my toothbrush!" Nicole exclaimed, terribly worried.

"Moron," Nell muttered.

"You can share your sister's," Mrs. Kutroff said.

"No way!" Nell shouted, shaking her head. "Uh-uh!"

"Nell!" Mrs. Kutroff said.

"You can use mine, Nicole," Lara said, happy Nicole was

to be part of their slumber party. Nicole was fun. Actually, she was more fun than Nell. Nicole smiled and thanked her.

Rachael and Mindy were already inside. Mindy had accidently squished a piece of used bubble gum on the couch, and Dana was trying to get it off before her parents—who were watching TV upstairs—found out. Rachael was eating cake and ice cream, and drinking a can of Coke. She ate like a pig and never got fat. Lara knew that Rachael would be beautiful when she grew up. So would Nicole.

It was already getting dark so they stayed inside and watched a rented movie on a fancy projector. Nell's parents had brought over the projector earlier. They were rich; there was nothing that Nell and Nicole didn't get. The show was Doctor Zhivago, and all of them agreed that Omar Sharif had the most beautiful eyes in the whole world. Though Rachael said he wasn't such a hot guy. When he visited Julie Christie in town, she said that he was actually having sex with her. Rachael was sure of this although Lara did not think he would do such a thing. But she didn't argue with Rachael. From listening to her talk before, it seemed Rachael really did know a lot about sex and who was doing it.

After the movie, they broke into two teams and played charades. Nicole was on Dana's and her side because Nell was still mad at her sister for having come. Too bad for their team. Nicole was better at charades than all of them put together. She seemed able to place the mystery word directly in their minds. Nell even accused her of cheating, she was so good.

Dana's father came in and said that he was going to bed. He didn't want them making a lot of noise or staying up late. After he left, Rachael said wickedly, "Now we can have some real fun."

"Do you have a boy coming over?" Dana asked, excited. Already she liked boys. Lara didn't know what she liked about them.

"No, silly." Rachael went to the bar and picked up a crystal decanter filled with dark red liquid. Lara thought it looked like dirty blood. Rachael took a gulp.

"Don't!" Dana screamed. "My dad will know. He'll kill me!"

"Shh!" Rachael said sternly. "We can put some water in the bottles. He'll never know. Trust me, my brother taught me this trick."

"I don't like alcohol," Lara said.

"That's because you've never been drunk," Rachael said, uncapping a second bottle and sniffing the contents.

"What's drunk?" Nicole asked, joining Rachael and smelling the bottles, too.

"Don't you know anything?" Nell said. "Drunk is when you have a hangover and you can't drive and your head hurts."

"My head has never hurt," Rachael disagreed, dropping ice

cubes into a row of glasses. "Drunk is when you feel good and laugh a lot. We're all going to get drunk right now."

Lara hated the taste of the brandy that Rachael gave her—it was like swallowing gasoline—but she drank it all quickly and asked for more, not wanting to seem like a sissy. They stole from a variety of colored bottles. Rachael was right about one thing: They did start to laugh a lot. Nicole threw up once but said she felt fine afterward.

Lara began to get bored and rather dizzy. She suggested that they play another game. Trouble was, nobody could think of one.

"In this movie I saw they jumped over candles," Dana said.

"And?" Rachael asked.

"I dunno the rest," she muttered, finishing her drink and belching. "I don't feel much like jumping, anyway."

"Let's play Monopoly," Lara said.

"Rex chewed up Marvin Gardens," Dana said. "Can't."

"Candles, candles," Rachael whispered to herself. Suddenly her eyes flashed in her unusually red face. "I've got it! Let's have a séance! Dana, I remember seeing a Ouija board in your bedroom. You get it, and we'll turn off the lights and light some candles and incense and talk to the spirits."

"What spirits would want to talk to six drunk girls?" Lara said, slurring her words.

"Get the board, Dana," Rachael said, ignoring her.

Their gypsy parlor took only a few minutes to prepare. Mindy and Nell cleaned off the coffee table and draped it with a sheet. Dana fetched Parker Brothers' standard brown rectangular divining board and wiped clear the dust. Rachael jammed long white candles in silver candleholders—courtesy of the china cabinet—and arranged them in a precarious circle around the board. Nell told Nicole that she was too young to help move the planchette. Lara muttered that she didn't want to move the planchette. Rachael gave her a pen and paper, and told her to take notes. Because of the poor light, Lara took a seat at the bar where there was a fold-down red pocket light. Looking rejected, Nicole sat on the floor at her feet.

"What should we ask?" Mindy said, as the four of them placed their fingers on the plastic indicator.

"I'll do the questioning," Rachael said. "Nell, lighten your touch."

"Sure."

"Who's there?" Rachael asked.

The spirits could have been asleep. Lara chuckled. Rachael told her to shut up, give it time. Minutes dragged by. Finally the indicator began to move, in small ellipses that slowly grew to where the planchette was swinging between YES and NO.

"Who's there?" Rachael repeated. "Here it goes! U . . . getting this, Lara? U . . . S . . . us."

"I could have told you that," Lara muttered.

"Hey, you moving this thing, Rach?" Dana asked.

"No."

"Then you're moving it, Mindy," Dana said. "Somebody's moving it."

"I ain't," Mindy said. "You aren't, are you, Nell?"

"We all are," Rachael said. "Our subconscious is." She spoke to the board. "Isn't that right?"

The planchette swung to YES.

"See," Rachael said.

"I'm going to ask something," Mindy said. "Will I get a B in math?"

The indicator went to F. Everyone, except Mindy, laughed.

"You moved it to that!" Mindy accused Dana.

"I did not!"

"Well I'm getting at least a C in math. I don't care what it says."

"Then why did you ask?" Rachael asked, annoyed. "I told you, I'll do the questioning." She cleared her throat. "Am I going to be a rich and famous actress when I grow up?" YES, was the answer. "See, it's working," Rachael told Mindy.

Rachael inquired after all of their futures. Dana was going to have six children and be plump all her life. Mindy was going to visit a foreign country and work in a factory until she retired. Lara was going to be an international journalist who married four times. Nell was going to write the greatest mystery novel of all time. Only for Nicole did it give no hint of the future. This depressed the young girl. Lara patted her head and told her not to worry.

"We should get serious," Rachael said finally. "Let's try to find out how this thing really works." She put on her official voice. "Are there any spirits in this room?"

YES

"How many?"

SIX

"Six of us, six spirits," Lara said.

"Are we the six spirits?" Rachael asked.

It swung between YES and NO, finally settling on NO.

"Ask if Captain Howdy's here," Mindy said, afraid.

"Who?"

"The demon in The Exorcist who made the little girl barf up her guts," Mindy said.

"Is Captain Howdy here?" Rachael asked.

NO

"Are there any evil spirits in the room?" Nell asked.

YES

"Really?" Rachael asked, frowning.

YES

"Are we in danger?"

YES . . . NO . . . YES . . . NO . . .

"Who is the evil spirit?" Rachael asked. Something seemed to be distracting her. As she spelled out the letters, her voice was strained. "N—I—C—O—L—E. Nicole," Rachael whispered, all eyes focusing on the young girl, whose lips quivered and hands trembled.

"This is dumb," Dana said, backing away from the board.

"Let's quit," Lara said, rubbing Nicole's shoulders.

"Did it really spell out my name?" Nicole asked, crawling toward the Ouija board on her knees, tears in her voice.

"Yes, but —" Rachael began, considering.

"But what?" Nell asked.

Rachael scratched her head, and spoke to Nicole. "Look, it's just a toy. It doesn't mean anything."

"Ask again, please," Nicole said, wiping damp cheeks.

Rachael looked to Nell, who shrugged. Mindy nodded, placing her fingers back on the planchette. Dana shook her head and stepped away from the table. "Couldn't hurt," Rachael said.

"Sure could," Lara whispered.

"Who's the evil spirit in the room?" Rachael asked.

The planchette did not spell. It revolved until the sharp end was pointing at Nicole. Again Rachael frowned, seemingly on the verge of complaining. Mindy whistled. Nell chuckled. Nicole burst into tears.

"Nicole —" Lara began.

"I hate this!" Nicole cried, leaping to her feet, swatting the indicator away. Unfortunately, in doing so, her hand accidently hooked onto the base of a double candleholder and dragged it toward her, off the table and onto the carpet. Maybe because they were all slightly drunk, no one reacted immediately. Nicole's eyes widened with terrific surprise, and perhaps for an instant one could have thought she looked evil. Orange light played on her face. Smoke rose through her hair, a noise crackled at her feet, the stink of something burning filled the air.

"The carpet!" Dana said. "My parents will kill—"

"Why you little snot!" Nell cursed, preparing to slap Nicole.

"For God's sake, put it out!" Rachael said, searching for something to smother the fire with.

What happened next did not appear to take place in normal time. There were frantic rushes where all of them sought to help and only made matters worse, laced with horrific pauses where they froze and begged inside for things to pass.

Nell struck Nicole in the face, forcing her back. Dana and Mindy grabbed folded magazines and banged at the burning carpet. Rachael yanked a cushion from the sofa in the event the magazines failed. Lara pulled the top from the decanter of brandy, poised to drown the fire.

Nicole began to scream. Her robe was on fire.

Nicole stood with her back to Lara, the flames climbing up her front. Still, Lara could see the quivering glow as it fanned from Nicole's sides like a deadly aura. Nell squatted at her sister's feet, her mouth transfixed with amazement and fear. Dana and Mindy buried their faces in their hands.

"Roll on the floor!" Rachael shouted, dropping the cushion

and ripping at the sheet that covered the coffee table. Ouija board and candles went flying. Simultaneously, Nell sprang and grabbed Nicole by the pink wool sweater the young girl was wearing over her polyester yellow robe, throwing her to the floor. Giving no thought to the flames that began to burn her, Nell tried to suffocate the fire. The fire was losing, and surely would have been extinguished by Rachael's sheet, when Lara forgot that she was holding hard liquor and not wine. Because it was wet, she poured the entire decanter over Nicole's lower body. And it was strange how the sudden drenching seemed to work. For an instant the fire disappeared. Nell even stopped rolling Nicole and pulled back her hands. Rachael dropped her sheet. Dana and Mindy breathed sighs of relief. Lara smiled and smelled the empty bottle.

Then Nicole exploded like a Molotov cocktail.

Fearless, Nell reached forward to pull her sister from the blaze. At once her hair disintegrated, her face lost in a closing hand of black smoke. She did not seem to feel pain or think of the consequences. Mindy fainted like a crumpling paper doll. Dana rammed both her fists into her eyes and began to gag. Nicole's screams cut off like a power failure, sending a permanent darkness into Lara's heart. Nicole lay still, no longer writhing. Lara stared at the empty bottle in her hand and thought of her terrible mistake.

"Out of the way!" Rachael ordered. Picking up the sheet, she seized Nell by the nape of the neck and dragged her aside.

Spreading the white blanket between her two outstretched hands, she brought it down swiftly over Nicole. The fire went out. Immediately, before it could stick, Rachael removed the ruined linen. A putrid cloud of smoke choked the room. Lara's misty eyes were drawn downward. *No, that couldn't be Nicole.* She shook herself. *Away, bad dream, let me wake up. But she couldn't wake up, because this was real.*

Wearing only his underwear, Dana's father appeared. He knelt by Nicole, feeling for a pulse at the side of the neck, one of the few areas not scorched. Lying facedown, Nicole did not flinch.

"Is she alive?" Rachael asked.

Mr. Miller shook his head. "I don't think so," he said, very pale.

"No," Lara whispered. "Not true, it can't be —"

"She's dead."

Lara did not know who said that. Her knees lost their strength, bringing her down to Nicole's side. She touched Nicole's left hand, amazingly cool and uninjured. A part of her desperately wanted to go into the girl to compensate for what she had done to her. "Nicole, Nicole," she chanted softly. "Please hear me."

And Nicole did stir, and did turn and look at her, with a single, bloodshot hazel eye. She had not heard the pronouncement clearly, but she had heard enough.

"I am going to die," Nicole said.

Lara squeezed her hand. "I will not let you die." It was a

promise she swore she would keep. Even when Nicole's eye fell shut and did not open again.

Mrs. Miller called an ambulance. Ice packs were made up and Rachael held one to Nell's burns. Nell was catatonic, her features a blur of soft wax. Starch-white paramedics arrived. Normal time returned.

Nicole lived an entire week, until she was transferred from the local hospital to the UCLA Medical Center Burn Clinic. There she caught an infection and all the parents, including Mr. and Mrs. Kutroff, thought that it was probably for the best. She was buried in a large funeral in Oakland, and the mayor of the city came and said a few words. Thankfully, they left the coffin closed.

Nell was operated on immediately, given a series of skin grafts. The plastic surgeons felt that her face could be restored to a "reasonable degree." None of the girls visited her while she was in the hospital, or called her on the phone. Nell had told her mom and dad to tell them that she never wanted to see them again. Yet her parents blamed no one, and no lawsuits were filed. A month after the accident, the Kutroff family moved away.

Lara carried the blame alone, although accusing words were never spoken in her presence. She tried to talk to Dana, but Dana would just start to cry. Rachael took the philosophical point of view. There was no sense dwelling upon it. Fairly sophisticated for a ten-year-old, but of no comfort to Lara. Miraculously, Mindy had blanked the entire incident out of her mind. Occasionally she would even ask where Nicole was. *Dead, Mindy. Oh, yeah.* Lara's parents tried to help, but, not having been there, they couldn't understand and alleviate the pain the way the girls could have. Six months after the accident, she wasn't eating, and was fading into a wraith, unable to do schoolwork, unable to sleep without nightmares. Her parents took her to a child psychologist. He asked many questions. She gave few answers. The medicine he prescribed let her sleep but never made her forget. Actually, matters had cleared in her own mind. Lara wanted to die because she had lied to Nicole by allowing her to die.

It was at this time that Nell called. She wanted Lara to visit her for the weekend.

Lara was a pale sack of bones; nevertheless she was shocked at Nell's appearance. The initial skin grafts had focused more on replacing the skin than on what the skin looked like. Lara didn't even recognize her. However, Nell's spirits were excellent and more effective than a thousand hours of professional therapy. They talked late into the night. The incident was not dwelled upon, nor was it glossed over. Once Lara tried to apologize, but Nell made it clear that—in her own mind—it had been absolutely no one's fault. She added, "Now we can all be friends again."

Only once did they cry, reflecting on how beautiful Nicole would have been when she grew up.

CHAPTER 5

"Lara? Can you hear me? Wake up, Lara."

"Dirty blood!" she cried, bolting upright. Hands were on her shoulders.

"Lara!"

"Oh, God," she gasped. "Ashes in the coffin."

"Stop it!"

"Nicole, Nicole," she chanted. But the face in the fire began to fade, replaced by an anxious Celeste, sitting beside her on the bed. The room was dark and warm, her T-shirt cooked with sweat, her heart thumping her rib cage. She had only been remembering. It was not happening again. "I was dreaming," she muttered in apology.

"About what?" Celeste asked, releasing her, easing back.

Lara wiped at her eyes, thankful for the poor light. She had been crying. "Nothing," she said quickly. "What time is it?"

"Close to seven. I thought I'd better wake you. Are you okay?"

"Perfect. Has Dana returned?"

"No."

Lara took a deep breath, trying to remain calm. She was far from perfect. "Has Park Administration called?"

"No one has."

They must have Dana's motives reversed. Probably she had returned to the lodge to avoid Cal. But why hadn't she called? "I guess the guys aren't here."

"No. The food is almost ready, though."

"You dear, I bet you've been working on it since I conked out." Feeling a sudden rush of love for Celeste, she leaned forward and hugged her. "I'm glad you're here," she said.

"Yeah?" Celeste said softly, slightly embarrassed, uncertain.

Lara sat back against the pillows. "Yeah, definitely." She smiled. "I hope we stay friends forever."

Celeste looked away. "I don't know."

"Sure we will. Even if I go away to school, we will write and talk on the phone."

"Where are you going?"

"I told you, Humboldt. Don't you remember? Of course, I still have to be accepted."

"What if you're accepted and you don't go?"

"Why wouldn't I go? Hey, what's wrong?"

Celeste was fidgeting, keeping her eyes averted. "I want to tell you something," she said slowly, with difficulty.

"What?"

"Oh, I don't know. It's nothing."

Lara moved closer. "Tell me."

"I don't like it here," she said suddenly.

"Why? Is it Nell?"

"No."

"What is it then?"

Celeste was searching for words. "I like the snow and trees. We saw a white rabbit disappear into a hole. But, I'm . . . I'm afraid."

"Of what?"

Celeste just shook her head.

"Maybe you're homesick. Why don't you call your aunt? Nell wouldn't mind."

"That wouldn't change. . . . I did."

"You called?"

"Yes." Celeste reached for her hand, changed her mind. "I really do like Nell."

"Good," Lara said, confident that she'd hit the nail on the head when she'd mentioned being homesick. Celeste had obviously led a sheltered life. This trip away from home was probably a first. Lara tugged at her damp T-shirt. "I better get dressed. Can't compete with Rachael in my underwear. Or maybe that's what it will take. Just kidding!"

Celeste stood reluctantly. "You're really looking forward to going away to school, aren't you?"

"Don't worry. It's only a five-hour drive. And I love to drive."

Celeste nodded. "I will check on the chickens."

"Be down in a sec to help you. And Celeste, if you want to go home a day earlier, just let me know."

Celeste left the room. Lara climbed out of bed and put on her unused pair of burgundy cords—cursing the fact that she hadn't brought a dress—and a flimsy pink shirt that needed both pockets not to be indecent. She was brushing her hair when she decided to call the lodge again about Dana. Rather than go downstairs, she trekked up the hall looking for a phone in one of the other bedrooms. She wished the house wasn't so isolated from the modern world so she could use her cell phone. The door to one of the rooms was closed, muffled voices coming through the wood. Sounded like Rachael and Mindy. Lara was on the verge of knocking when she thought she heard her name mentioned. Naturally she put her ear to the door.

"We could get in serious trouble," Mindy was saying.

"Damn your whining, you coward. Who will there be to squeal?" Rachael snapped. She continued in a softer voice, obviously into a phone: "Don't worry, I'm behind you a hundred percent. Who cares about Dana? She's out of the way. Lara's the only one that matters. She's smart, but she'll never know, not until it's too late." Rachael chuckled. "Who could imagine such power! I can hardly believe it. Fate must have brought us together. . . . Hmm, let me think about it. . . . Get me what I want first and then we'll see. . . . No problem with the car. . . . To hell with her; she's just another fly to swat. . . ."

The blood roaring in Lara's ears made it difficult to hear. She had to know who Rachael was talking to, what they were talking about. The master bedroom would have another extension. Lara tiptoed away from the door and hopped up a short flight of stairs. The light to the room was out so she was surprised to find Nell kneeling on the floor, fighting with something stuck in the closet.

"Oh, sorry," Lara said, taking her hand off the thrown switch.

Nell sprang to her feet, her eyes wide, sliding the mirrored closet door shut at her back. "Christ, you startled me! Why are you here? . . . What can I do for you, Lara?"

"I d like to use your phone."

"There are four phones downstairs," Nell said sharply.

She wanted Nell's phone because the ones downstairs could not be unplugged. If she simply picked up the receiver, no matter how carefully, Rachael would know. "I'm in a hurry," she said.

Anger, never too far from the surface of Nell's personality, flashed in her eyes. It remained even when she smiled thinly and said, "Suit yourself. I suppose you want privacy?"

Lara nodded.

"Sorry I snapped at you," Nell said, stepping by her.

"Thanks, Nell." Lara shut the door behind her. She unplugged the phone, picked up the receiver, then carefully fitted the metal prong back in the wall. Rachael was gabbing: "I never read the book, but I enjoyed the movie. It was wicked when she wasted everyone at the prom. Oh, so that's where you got this idea! Wait a sec. Don't say anything! I think there's someone else on the line. Hey, who's there?"

Lara thought fast. Hanging up would lead Rachael to suspect that her entire conversation had been overheard, probably stopping her from doing what she had planned. And Lara wanted to know what that plan was. Best to act as if she had just picked up the phone to make a call. She began to press the numbers like she was dialing. The high beeps would irritate —

"Stop that!!!" Rachael screamed.

"Are you using the phone?" Lara asked with brilliant innocence.

"No, I'm dusting the furniture and just happen to have it taped to my ear. Would you please get off the line and let me finish?"

"Will you be long?" She wanted to prolong the conversation. Just one word from the other party could tell her a great deal.

"No."

"How long?"

"Six-point-twenty-three minutes. How should I know, Lara? Get off the line!"

"Nell asked that we make no long-distance calls," she lied.

"This is not a long-distance call."

"Who do you know around here?"

"It's none of your business!"

Lara faked a sexy tone. "Hi there, are you someone I know?"

"Lara," Rachael said very quietly. "I already counted to ten. I am not counting to twenty. Put the goddamn phone down. Now!"

"You don't have to get angry," Lara said, finally complying. Rachael was up to no good and she had a male accomplice. But who was he, and how serious were their intentions? With Mindy involved it seemed impossible that it was anything *really* bad. But that line about Dana being out of the way, and Dana's disappearance, did not sit well. Lara was tempted to confront Rachael with what she'd heard, but the accusations sounded so ridiculous in her own mind that she decided to hold off.

Leaving the room, she found Nell standing immediately outside the door. Embarrassed, Nell said quickly, "I wanted to get my sweater."

"I see."

"Make your call?"

"No, Rachael's on the line."

"The phones downstairs are separate."

"Are they? That number you gave me — 453-6672 — is that upstairs or downstairs?"

"Downstairs. Why?"

"Is that the right number? I called it from the lodge and no one answered."

"Yes, I spoke with you. Don't you remember?"

"No, I called a second time. I didn't have the slip of paper that you gave me, but I'm pretty sure that I dialed correctly. Did you and Celeste go out?"

"Only on the porch. Seems we would have heard one of the phones. You probably dialed wrong."

"What if you'd been in the basement?"

"I never go down there."

"I was down there."

"You were! Why?"

"Browsing around. What's the big deal? Is it dangerous?"

"My father doesn't want us fooling around down there because of the new propane tank."

Nell had had Rachael and Mindy cleaning the basement out. Couldn't be too dangerous. "I'll consider it off limits."

"I wish the stupid thing was buried outside somewhere."

"So you're sleeping in the master bedroom after all? I thought you were using the room adjacent to Celeste's."

"What made you think that?"

"I don't remember," she said honestly.

LARA SPENT THE NEXT HOUR MAKING AND APPLYING FOUR
different colors of icing to the carrot cake that Celeste
had baked. She drew a miserable carrot with two blurred
nibbling bunnies. The passing minutes were fretful. Dana
hadn't shown up, and the line to the lodge was busy. An
arctic blizzard was a more appropriate name for the storm.
With guilt, she had to admit that she was more concerned
about Percy not appearing than Dana.

"They're here!" Mindy shouted, bouncing into the
kitchen, ecstatic.

"Dana with them?" Lara asked, her throat dry. She'd
forgotten to put on makeup!

Mindy scowled. "Of course not."

Lara took off her apron, having to make a conscious
effort to keep her hands from trembling. Celeste gave her
a thumbs-up.

"I'll finish up here and join you in a minute," she said.
"Good luck."

"Take that gum out of your mouth," Lara said, following Mindy to the living room. "Makes you sound like a
cow."

"How gross," Mindy said, swallowing it.

Cal was standing with his fingers hooked — macho
style — in his pockets, talking to Nell. Percy was sitting
on the bricks next to the fire, his gray sweatshirt rolled up,
revealing dark muscular arms. Rachael, dazzling in tight

white pants and a black turtleneck sweater minus the bra, sat by his side, laughing gratefully at whatever he was saying, letting her fingers do all the things Lara had feared. Well, not *everything*. One thing you had to grant Rachael, she didn't waste any time.

"Hello," Lara said softly. There was a pause, eyes turning, Rachael's toward a window. Percy stood smoothly — every move he made had class — and squeezed the tops of her arms. Not an embrace, but it would do.

"Hi, Lara, so we made it after all," he said, smiling warmly, with a trace of amusement.

"Did you have trouble with the storm?"

"Not enough to keep us from coming."

Not enough to keep me away from you, Lara thought. This was not a crush. It was an obsession.

"Probably have to stay the night, though," Cal laughed, too loud.

"That wouldn't be a good idea," Nell said flatly.

"I smell food," Percy said, smoothing over the awkward moment. "Good food. Glad we didn't have the bite in the coffee shop."

Rachael rolled her tongue inside her mouth, not missing the reference to their having met a second time. Lara was pleased. "Celeste," she said, "she's our other friend, has been cooking us a feast. Oh, here she is now."

Like a timid deer, Celeste slipped into the room. Percy and Cal said hello. Celeste only nodded and smiled, remaining silent. Lara did not like the way Cal's eyes looked her over. There were really no two ways about it; he was a jerk.

"Looks like we're outnumbered," Cal told Percy with a snort.

"Where's Dana?" Percy asked.

"We're not sure," Lara said. "You haven't seen her?"

"No," Percy said. Cal shook his head.

"She'll show up," Rachael said, shifting the burning logs with the poker. "Nell, can we eat in here? So much more cozy than the dining room. I like fires."

"I don't care where we eat," Nell answered curtly, perhaps annoyed by the reference to fire.

Celeste and Nell took the job of servers. Back and forth they traveled to the kitchen, yet Lara received the distinct impression that they were timing their trips so as to avoid each other.

Dinner was a masterpiece. Chickens basted in rosemary, baked potatoes sliced through the middle and tucked with sour cream and butter, two casseroles of assorted vegetables coated with an inch of melted Swiss cheese, wild rice with minced green peppers and hot spices, two bottles of expensive red wine, and, of course, the artful carrot cake. They ate in a circle, Lara on Percy's right, and Rachael—ridiculously close—on his left. Nervous, Lara had no appetite, but nevertheless filled her plate. She had read in *Cosmopolitan* that men found women with huge appetites sexy.

Shamelessly, Mindy drooled over Cal, who fairly well ignored her, focusing his attention on Celeste, who couldn't have had a thing in common with him. Percy divided his attention between Rachael and Lara and, like in the coffee shop, mainly played the role of a good listener. Still, he sensed Nell's withdrawal and went out of the way to bring her into the flow of the conversation—successfully, too, with Nell relating for the first time how the house had originally belonged to a Vegas mafioso who had used it to store huge quantities of cocaine and heroin, up until his mysterious disappearance. In a subsequent probe, the FBI had found faint traces of human bones—this is what made the story interesting—in this very fireplace. Perhaps because of the wine, Nell went into greater detail than Lara cared for. Nell still hadn't bothered covering her scars with makeup.

"Reminds me of when I was in Germany," Cal said, emptying the second wine bottle into his glass. He had drunk more than all of them put together. Lara worried about the bottle of Bacardi 151 rum that he'd brought. That stuff was like kerosene.

"You were in Germany!" Mindy said, with such enthusiasm that it made even Celeste wince.

Cal broke off a corner of the half-eaten cake and stuffed it into his mouth. "Was there two years," he chewed. "Love that German beer, those German women; man, they made a boy feel at home." He belched. "Anyway, what you said about that guy getting fried reminds me of this time we accidently napalmed these four Kraut soldiers. Hell, those Krauts thought Hitler was still on the throne, I swear. Couldn't stand those bastards."

"You burned four men to death?" Lara asked, her dinner moving in her stomach, her question angering Cal.

"*Accidently*, dear. We were on a copter hop, not far from the wall, when we lost our back blade. Started spinning like a damn top. Dumped the napalm we were carrying 'cause we thought we were going down. Man, we were in the middle of nowhere! No way I did it on purpose! I told that son of a bitch colonel that it had been an accident. He wouldn't listen to me." Cal chuckled. "Took them a month to identify those Krauts. You should have seen those flames. Better than Fourth of July." He finished his wine. "Made me feel proud to be an American."

Percy was following Cal closely. Apparently he had not heard the story before. Lara understood now why Cal had been discharged. She doubted that it had been an honorable one. Whoever heard of dumping napalm? Cal felt her disgust and looked at the floor, not happy with what he'd revealed. "I thought this was supposed to be a party," he said. "Where's the music?"

"We should play some games," Rachael said.

"I'm game," Percy said.

"Are you?" Rachael asked slyly, poking his side. "Know strip poker?"

Shyness was not one of Rachael's faults. And Percy was doing nothing to discourage her attention. "We could play charades," Celeste said, coming to life.

"Now, just what is that, young lady?" Cal asked.

"Where you tell someone a word or a phrase without saying it," Celeste said. "You use your hands, gestures."

"Can you write it down?" Cal asked, trying to concentrate.

"If you know how to write," Percy said. "Charades sounds good with me."

"Could you start without me?" Lara said, getting up. "I have to make a call."

"There's seven of us," Rachael said. "We can't have even teams."

"I want to be on Lara's side," Percy said.

The thrill of joy that pulsed through her veins almost forced her to sit down. "So do I," Celeste said.

"My, aren't we popular," Rachael said.

"I'll be on your team," Nell said to Rachael. "And we'll take Mindy and Cal."

Déjà vu interrupted Lara's bliss — maybe even a memory. *Why now?* She had played charades many times since *then*. "Be back in a sec," she said, going upstairs to the master bedroom, feeling as if she was running away. The number to the lodge was still fresh in her mind.

"Park Administration."

"Is this Roger McCormick?"

"Yes."

"This is Lara Johnson. I called earlier regarding Dana Miller?"

"I remember the voice. I'm sorry, Lara, she hasn't checked in here. You haven't heard from her?"

"No."

"I don't wish to sound like we are not concerned about the welfare of your friend, but to implement a full-scale search for her in this weather would be a major undertaking. Is there any reason whatsoever that she may be avoiding returning to your place?"

"Sort of. We're having a party and there's a guy here that she had a run-in with earlier."

"And she knew this young man was coming to your party?"

"Yes. But I still think she would have at least called. Maybe she's checked into the lodge?"

"Not under Dana Miller. I went over the names of all the visitors. You probably know that we have buses leaving here every hour before eight. Maybe she just went home. Where are you girls from?"

"Oakland."

"Have you called her family?"

"I hadn't thought of that. I'll do so."

"If you get a negative response, then it's up to you. You know your friend and the circumstances better than us. If you say so, then we'll start a search."

"Not yet," Lara said. Probably Dana had hated being mauled by Cal. And she'd had plenty of money to stay elsewhere or take a bus home. "Could I call you back in an hour or two?"

"I will be here all night."

"Thanks. Oh, did you check on the colonel?"

"I haven't had an opportunity to ask the boss about him. There is definitely no one on the roster by that name."

"I'm sure it's a nickname."

"I realize that. I don't have a definite answer for you."

Lara did not want to give her head too much to worry about. "Look, I'll call you later, Roger."

"Fine."

Dana's parents didn't answer. After twenty rings, Lara remembered that they, too, had been going away for the weekend.

She had only hung up the phone, and was preparing to join the others downstairs, when it rang. *Must be for Nell,* she thought, calling on this line. To her surprise, it was Celeste's aunt.

"Lara, dear, how is your trip so far?"

"Fine." No sense bringing up Dana until she knew something more definite. "Would you like me to get Celeste? She's downstairs."

"Don't bother the girl. She'd probably be embarrassed to know that I've called. But I was sitting here alone and . . . the house seems so empty without her. How is she doing?"

"Real good. Didn't you talk to her earlier?"

"No."

"Are you sure?"

"I haven't spoken to her today, dear."

Why had Celeste lied? Lara thought back to their conversation: *"That wouldn't change. . . . I did."*

Celeste had wanted to say something else. Maybe she wasn't simply homesick.

"We're all having a good time," Lara continued. "Celeste made us an incredible meal. We were just about to play some games. You should see this house! I don't think any of us realized just how rich Nell's parents are."

"How is Nell?"

"Nell's okay. Do you know her, Mrs. Winston?"

"No—I mean, in a way, from listening to you girls talk about her. Listen, I'm going to let you get back to your friends. Don't even tell Celeste that I called. She had asked me not to."

"I understand," Lara said, not altogether sure that she did. Celeste's aunt was in an awful hurry to get off the phone. They exchanged take-cares and good-byes. Rachael was standing in the doorway.

"Who was that?" she asked.

"Celeste's aunt."

"What did she want?"

"To see that we were alive and well. She didn't want Celeste to know that she'd called."

Rachael plopped herself down in the corner in a chair. A gust of snow-laden wind shook the bedroom window. Outside was a black void. "Sometimes I wonder about that Celeste."

"What do you *wonder*?"

"Don't get hostile. Just something about her spooks me."

"She's twice the person either of us is."

"She's a sweet girl. But you've known her since the second day of school, and you don't know a damn thing about her."

"I've known you since I was four and I still haven't figured you out," Lara said deliberately, searching for a clue.

Rachael took the remark as a compliment. "Percy likes you," she said, baiting her own trap. Yet sitting face-to-face with Rachael, as she had done so many times through the years, Lara found it hard to believe that her motives were dangerously dark. She almost asked, who had been the guy on the other end of the line, what they had been talking about. Almost.

"What are we going to do?" Lara asked, taking an indirect stab at openness. "We have the whole night in front of us."

Rachael was cool. "The later it gets, the better I get. So

he wants you on his team. I'm not putting up the white flag, Lara."

"You're the one who said it wasn't a war."

"I've changed my mind."

Lara stared her straight in the eye. "This one you're going to lose."

Rachael didn't flinch. "This battle maybe. But never the war, Lara."

Lara looked away, sighing. "At least we know where we stand. Before we return to the battlefield, there are a couple of things we must discuss. First, Dana. And don't tell me she'll show up soon."

Rachael was quiet for a moment. "All right, let's take a negative point of view. What *could* have happened to her?"

"She could have left the path to take a shortcut back to the lodge and broken a leg."

"But you didn't see any tracks leading off the path. I didn't."

"Except where we found that ski, I wasn't looking for them."

"Still, you would have noticed. And Nell's right about that ski; it could have belonged to anybody. Probably someone just tossed it."

"Then what about their tracks? On one ski, they would have stood out like a sore thumb."

"Maybe they — whoever they are — broke a leg, and had a partner, and this partner carried them back to the lodge on their back, and managed to stay inside our grooves. I'm not Mrs. Holmes, but I suspect that Dana never left the path, but continued on, past the house, and wrapped around back to the lodge."

"Nell would have seen her."

"Not necessarily."

"But Nell was on the porch."

"Was Nell on the porch the whole time?"

"Did she say she wasn't?"

"Not exactly."

The answer disturbed Lara. Rachael was trying to be logical—always the approach of the villain—and that logic wasn't right. Perhaps reading her mind, Rachael added, "We have the perfect motive for her disappearing in her wanting to avoid Cal. You're making a mountain out of a . . . out of a snowball."

Lara was going to mention the two similar circular impressions in the ice but knew that it would lead to—from her side—a supernatural hypothesis, which Rachael would have no tolerance for.

"We might have another problem," Lara said instead. "That character who took our car keys—the colonel—he's probably not a ranger." Briefly, she reviewed her conversations with Roger McCormick. And once again, Rachael tried to play down the situation.

"If he was a car thief, there's no way he would have hung around the lodge where he could be spotted. So Mr.

McCormick didn't know him by the 'colonel'? You said yourself that probably isn't his real name."

"Aren't you worried about your car at all?"

"That's why my daddy pays for insurance, so I don't have to worry."

"No problem with the car," Lara remembered. *"To hell with her; she's just another fly to swat."*

"I see," Lara said softly. "And I suppose you're not worried about the melted snowman, either?"

"Huh?"

"Never mind."

"Oh, that! I haven't given it a second thought. What's gotten into you? You'd think you were on a paranoid acid trip. Let's get back to the boys. What are we going to do after charades? You should be worrying about that."

"Play with a Ouija board," Lara muttered, her nightmare nudging back in.

"With Nell here? Really, Lara, that would be gross."

"Sorry. You never think about it, do you?"

"What's the point?"

"Rach, I *want* you to think about it. Remember back to when you asked who the evil spirit was. You frowned, like something was wrong. Why did you frown?"

"Because it spelled Nicole's name!"

"No, it was something else. You had another reason."

"Isn't this a little off the wall?"

"Please, try to remember."

Rachael went to snap a quick retort, when suddenly she stopped, her eyes slipping far away. "There was a reason," she whispered.

"What?"

"The planchette, it . . . I can't remember. It was nothing important."

"Try harder."

"We were kids! I can't remember. To hell with it; it's past. Let's go play charades."

CELESTE AND PERCY HAD ALREADY PRINTED WORDS ON cards to use against the others: ecclesiastical, Lyndon Baines Johnson, rhubarb, Zimbabwe. Lara figured they had the game in the bag until she accidentally overheard one of the words Rachael was suggesting: the Rosicrucian Fellowship Ephermis 1950–1959. An uproar followed. All finally agreed to stick with current phrases.

Mindy went first. Lara gave her *Return of the Jedi* to communicate. Nell held the stopwatch, and Mindy was onstage only forty seconds—it was too easy even for bubble-gum brain. Celeste went next and drew *Romeo and Juliet.* ("Is that current, Rach?" Lara had asked.) A master of body language, Percy was able to pick up Celeste's meaning inside twenty seconds. Lara was given *milk,* and suspected that Rachael was trying to embarrass her by subtly prodding her to squeeze her breasts, which she refused to do. Still, they all had fun, except for perhaps

Cal, who was working on his Bacardi 151 and smelling totally wasted. Before his turn was up, Nell had to rewind the watch.

After an hour of play, Lara's team was destroying Nell's. Rachael demanded a shake-up. She wanted Celeste. So Rachael—Lara had to doubt her motives, because the move was totally illogical—and Celeste switched sides. Then something remarkable began to occur. No matter what word they gave Nell, Celeste guessed it almost immediately, and vice versa. Lara swore to herself that one of them must have telepathy. Cal continued to ruin their score, however. He also continued to eye Celeste, trying to charm her, actually touching her arm, her leg. She put him off politely. It was apparent that he made her nervous. Somehow Mindy had convinced herself that she didn't notice. Lara was searching for a tactful way to tell Cal to bug off, when he pinched Celeste's side. She gave out a cry of genuine pain.

Nell leaped to her feet, exploding. "You fat slob! Who the hell do you think you are?! Get out of my house!"

"Nell," Celeste began weakly.

"Huh?" Cal slurred, not yet caught up with the present.

"Just get the hell out of my sight!" Nell swore.

"Lay off him!" Mindy, shouted, standing. "You're always bossing people around!"

"What?!" Nell said, stupefied. "What!?"

"He didn't do anything wrong!" Mindy yelled.

Nell sucked in a breath, like a dragon. "Here this jerk's supposed to be with you and he's hustling Celeste and *you're* defending him!?"

"You just hate everyone!" Mindy said stupidly. *Poor Mindy*, Lara thought. Nell was probably doing her a favor, though Nell was much angrier than made sense.

"Why don't we just —" Lara tried.

"No one calls me a jerk," Cal said angrily, stumbling to his feet.

"Oh, really, jerk?!" Nell snickered.

"Shut up!" Mindy shouted.

"Tight-face bitch," Cal said.

Percy finally decided to step in. He was too late. Even as he moved to prevent blows from falling, Nell kicked Cal's left shin with her hard-tipped leather boots. Cal's howl as he doubled up in pain promised a cruel vengeance. Still, even in his agony, he did not drop his glass of rum. Nell plucked it deftly from his hand to — so Lara assumed — throw it in his face. But the fumes of the drink reaching her nose — better than three-quarters alcohol — seemed to give her a new idea. Only cursing Cal separated her from raging Mindy, who stood with her back to the fire. Deliberately, with the beginning of a laugh, Nell threw the rum at her, the fiery liquid drenching Mindy's left arm.

"Nooo!!" Celeste cried in terror.

"My new blouse!" Mindy whined.

"For Christ's sake, it's my blouse," Rachael said, sounding incredibly bored.

Cal snorted at Nell like a charging bull. "You're going to pay for that, lady."

"Enough!" Percy said, positioning himself in front of Nell. Cal heaved forward anyway, his coordination a disaster. Percy grabbed him easily by the chest. When Cal struggled and spat in his face, Percy's eyes darkened and he drew back his fist and went for his roommate's jaw. Cal fell back like a dropped sack of potatoes. Mindy, of course, tried to catch him. Cal had to weigh a good two hundred pounds. Mindy fell backward also, close to the fire.

Too close to the fire.

Lara did not immediately realize that anything was seriously wrong. Her first thought was cynical: *That's one way to ruin a party.* Then she noticed Mindy's drenched arm draped over the bricks; Mindy staring at her arm, puzzled at something going on there. Above her, the air quivered like a desert mirage. Lara remembered in chemistry class how a dish of alcohol had burned with an invisible flame. And here and now, there wasn't Nicole's polyester robe and woolen sweater to fire it. Not unless the fire spread.

"Roll on the floor!" Rachael shouted, the words echoing from the past.

Mindy began to scream. Celeste flew from the room. Percy whipped off his sweatshirt and tried to smother Mindy's arm. But Mindy launched into a dancing frenzy and he couldn't catch her. Spontaneously Lara reached for the bottle—*because it was wet*—of liquor next to the sprawled Cal. Her eyes met Nell's, who was following her rather than Mindy. Nell shook her head faintly. Lara dropped the bottle.

"Hold her, damn it!" Rachael said. From God knows where she had a fire extinguisher in her hands. Percy dove, tackling Mindy at the knees. Rachael let loose a well-aimed jet of fog. A white coat blanketed the burning arm and one side of Percy's face. The fire was gone, with Mindy's breath coming in hysterical gasps. Lifting her up, Percy laid her gently on the couch. After a quick survey of the injury, he ripped back the blackened sleeve. Lara closed her eyes, imagining ashen bone, oozing dirty blood.

"Shhh," Percy said. "It's not bad. Mindy! Listen to me! Your arm's fine. Little worse than a bad sunburn. Shh . . . You're going to be okay. That's it. You're going to be just fine."

Mindy's spastic breathing subsided. She began to cry quietly. Lara dared a look. Percy was rubbing her forehead, speaking reassuring words. Lara knew that shock was the first danger to confront, and he was handling her perfectly. Lara wondered if she wasn't in shock herself. Already blisters were swelling on Mindy's red arm. There would follow incredible pain, probably scarring, yet compared to Nicole, this had been but a—

Warning, Lara.

What was that? Lara thought that Celeste had whispered in her ear. But when she looked, Celeste was gone. Cal was going, too. Nell had picked the poker from the fire—glowing cherry red at the end—and was pointing it at him.

"Do I make myself clear?" she said coldly.

Cal sobered quickly. "Wasn't my fault."

Nell shoved the rod two inches from his nose. Perspiration stood out on his forehead. "Get the hell out of here!" Nell said.

Cal searched for support, finding none. "Should have been you, bitch," he muttered, backing off and leaving. They heard the coat closet opening, the front door slamming. Lara sat on the couch beside Percy, taking Mindy's good hand.

"Do that dance at the prom," Lara said, "and you'll win the Best Moves award."

"Rachael's a better dancer," Mindy said, not getting the joke. Her back ached. "Ohhh! It hurts!"

"That's a good sign," Percy said, wiping the white powder from his face. "Shows that the burn didn't go so deep to where the nerves were destroyed. Everyone will think you just fell asleep under the sun lamp. I know you girls will do anything for a tan, even light yourselves on fire." This made Mindy smile. "Hey, Rachael, why don't you sit here for a minute with your wounded friend."

"Sure." Rachael did not appear the least flustered. Percy ushered Lara into the kitchen. "I feel responsible for this," he said. "I only wish I'd taken that drunk's head off when I hit him. But I must have been out of my mind to hit him with Mindy at his back and the fire right there."

He was more upset than he had allowed in the living room. "If it hadn't been for you —" Lara started to say.

"Cal wouldn't have banged into Mindy," he interrupted. "And Mindy's arm wouldn't have gone into the fire."

"But her arm didn't go into the fire."

"It went close enough." He sighed. "Call the lodge. See if we can get a doctor up here."

Roger McCormick was still at work. "Has Dana Miller showed up?" he asked. Lara explained their more pressing emergency. He told her to hold the line, and was gone ten minutes. When he returned, he said that he was putting on a Dr. Kaminski.

"Can I help you?" a gentleman with a Brooklyn accent asked.

"Our friend has burned her arm," Lara said. "Can you come up? We're at Cedar Springs, the Kutroff residence."

"How bad is it?"

"She's in a lot of pain."

Doctor Kaminski exchanged muffled words with Roger McCormick, learning the distance that he would have to travel and how miserable the storm was. Lara thought that she heard him groan. "Tell me in detail how it happened," he said finally, "what the injury looks like now, her mental state." Lara described the "accidental" drenching with the rum, the mass of sprouting blisters across the entire inside of Mindy's arm. Mindy's mental state was more difficult to convey—usually she didn't seem to have one—but Lara thought she got the situation across. "Sounds like only second degree," the doctor muttered. "I take it you've removed the clothing over the wound?"

"Yes. Was that the right thing to do?" Lara asked. Nell entered the kitchen.

"How is she?" Percy asked.

"Sore," Nell said.

"Elevate her legs slightly," Dr. Kaminski said. "Also the injured arm. Do you have a first-aid kit, sterile gauze?"

Lara asked Nell, who nodded. "Yes, we do," Lara said. "But isn't there any way that you could come?"

"Everything I can do at this point, you can do also. Wrap her arm snugly in gauze. Keep her warm. At fifteen-minute intervals, give her a solution of half a teaspoonful of salt and half a teaspoonful of sodium bicarbonate to drink."

"What's that?"

"Baking soda. Your main job is to make sure she doesn't go into shock. From what you've described, that does not appear to be a danger. Nevertheless, keep her warm and keep an eye on her. Have her drink fruit juice if it doesn't make her nauseous."

"I have codeine," Nell said, handing Lara a prescription container. "Ask about these."

"Can we give her these pills for pain?" Lara asked. She read every letter and numeral on the label.

"If after an hour," Dr. Kaminski said, "she is still alert and shows no signs of metabolic depression, you may give her two, followed with plenty of liquids. But not for an hour. Call me immediately if there is a change in her condition. Call tomorrow in either case."

After thanking him, Lara hung up the phone and relayed the instructions.

"Leave her to me," Nell said. "I've had lots of experience with bandages."

Lara was sure she had. "How is Celeste?" she asked.

"She's in her room," Nell said. "I would leave her alone for the time being."

"Sure upset her," Percy said.

"It would upset anybody," Nell said bitterly, leaving.

Lara's own reaction had taken longer, but now it hit with a force that humiliated her, forcing her to sit down, bringing a gush of tears. Percy sat beside her and did the very best thing, which was simply wait. Lara fought for control, finally managing an apology and explained, "It's just that it was so much like last time, like when Nicole died. How can it be a coincidence?"

"Who was Nicole?" Percy asked gently.

Even Lara did not realize the key to that question could be to Pandora's box. The story poured out, starting when she poured the liquor on Nicole, reversing in time to explain the circumstances, occasionally jumping to the present: the fried snowman, Rachael's sinister telephone conversation, the mysterious colonel, Cal's suspicious past, the inexplicable single ski, and Dana's disappearance.

She must have been making an incoherent conspiracy out of everyone and everything, for Percy finally interrupted, saying, "The only *real* question is, Where's Dana? The rest almost certainly has nothing to do with that question."

Lara was momentarily crushed. She had been hoping for support. "What about the things Rachael said?"

Percy glanced to the kitchen entrance, careful not to be overheard. Snowflakes bombarded the blocked window above the table like mute machine-gun fire. Cold radiated through the wall at her back. Percy spoke in a low voice. "How often in the course of conversation have you said—innocently, without thinking—'I wish I could kill her,' or, 'If only we could get rid of him'? Rachael strikes me as a very attractive, shrewd young lady. But not as someone capable of murder."

Why did he have to mention how attractive she was? "You don't know her like I do." Just sour grapes.

"A conspiracy between Cal and Rachael is out of the question. They scarcely spoke to each other when we all met at the mall."

"You mainly talked to her, right?"

"Right."

"Was Cal on the phone around seven?" she asked defensively.

"I was taking a nap. I'm not sure."

"So he could have been?"

"Lara."

"I know, I know," she muttered in apology, pressing her hands against her eyes. "You see, I'm not saying what I really mean." Because she did not know. How could one explain a feeling, a haunting intuition, even to one's own self?

"I understand. You're upset over Mindy, worried about Dana."

"I'm worried about the snowman, too!" she burst out. His eyes were sympathetic, and *that* was no way to start a relationship. "All right, all right, so *all* these events are not connected. There is a pattern in *some* of them."

"What?"

"Fire!"

"Lara."

"Listen to me!" God, she sounded like her mother. "That snowman was in the shade. How could he melt by himself? And when we found Dana's ski, it was like the area had suddenly been blasted by heat, and left to freeze over. And when Mindy got burned just now, her arm didn't go in the fire."

"It didn't have to. The fumes —"

"And when Nicole exploded," Lara went on, not listening, "I could have sworn to the Pope that I'd poured wine on her and not brandy. Wine couldn't have done that to her."

"What does a nine-year-old know about different types of alcohol? Nothing! You yourself mentioned the guilt you suffered after the accident. Well, it is simply surfacing again."

"No!" Lara pounded the table, disturbing the salt and pepper shakers. "There is *something* behind this!"

"What?"

"I told you. Fire! It's coming from somewhere." She quieted. "Or from *someone*. Percy, have you ever read about pyro-kinetics, SHC?"

"Spontaneous human combustion? In the *National Enquirer*, alongside articles on people who've been taken aboard alien spacecraft from the Andromeda galaxy and had their tonsils removed."

"You don't believe in things like that?"

"I'm skeptical, very skeptical. Are you saying that Dana suddenly decided to cook herself?"

"No. I'm suggesting that maybe—just as a possibility—someone burned her. With their mind."

"Like in that movie *Carrie*?"

"Sort of."

"That was a movie, Lara. Mindy had an arm drenched in alcohol next to a blazing fire before she lit up."

Lara took a couple of deep breaths. "I know what you're saying is the logical point of view. I spoke to Nell and Rachael, and they were logical, too. But I can't get rid of this feeling. It keeps coming back."

"What are we going to do about it?"

"Stop sitting around and waiting for Dana to show up, for one thing. Where I found her ski on the path, I made a cross out of branches and fastened it to a tree. I can find that place again. Can I—would you mind if I walked part of the way back with you?"

Percy smiled, the same gesture that seemed somehow different each time, richer and warmer as she came to know him better. She was still roller-coasting in the infatuation stage, but she had crested at a peak and could see a glimmer of light in the distance that said that maybe there was something real here. At least through her eyes. He was reading her mind. "I was hoping, Lara, that you were going to ask me to stay."

"Yeah? No. I mean—I would like you to stay. But, I . . . I don't know. I don't know anything at this point." She bowed her head, trying to untangle her thoughts. What the hell, bare her heart for everyone to see. "I like you," she whispered.

"I like you."

She glanced up. "Really? No you don't. Do you?"

"Of course."

"I don't believe you."

"You better. I've already made plans for how I'm going to visit you in Oakland."

Lara felt giddy all of a sudden, yet still worried. "But you must know lots of girls. You probably like lots of them, like Rachael. I know how pretty she is."

"Rachael's very pretty."

"Oh, I know." Hard to walk this razor's edge, when she was sweating like this.

"But she's not you. I like you. What does Rachael have to do with that?"

Lara, to her total humiliation, began to cry again. "I'm sorry." She shook her head, wiping her face, looking anywhere but at him. "I'm usually not like this. I never cry. Never!"

"You've just had a rotten day." He took her hand.

She blushed. "Not all rotten. I met you."

"Still want to go to the spot?"

She nodded. "I won't sleep tonight unless I do."

"All right. But let's stay that hour with Mindy the doctor recommended before starting down."

Nell and Rachael should have been RNs. Mindy was professionally bandaged, resting on the couch with her bad arm and two legs elevated with pillows, trying unsuccessfully to convince Rachael that there was no way she was going to go into shock and why the hell didn't they give her at least one of the codeine pills?

Lara excused herself after a few minutes — under Nell's

watchful eye—and went to find Celeste. The door to her room was open, the light out. Celeste was lying facedown on the bed.

"Celeste? It's Lara. Mindy's okay. Can I come in?"

"Is the doctor coming?" she asked sadly, not stirring.

Lara sat on the bed beside her. "No. Mindy's not that hurt."

"But she was on fire."

"Rachael put it out as quick as it started. Go talk to her yourself, and you'll see."

"I don't want to. I don't want to hurt her."

"Nonsense. You'll cheer her up."

"I don't want to hurt any of you."

"Look at me, Celeste. You're beginning to sound as crazy as me. Come, let's go downstairs."

"No."

"Why not?"

"It was my fault."

"You didn't have anything to do with —" Lara stopped. *Someone burned her. With their mind.*

Celeste sensed her sudden fear, rolled over, and stared at her. Celeste had extraordinary eyes, a cat's hypnotic emerald gaze, glittering with faint light from the hall. "Don't you know?" she asked from a place far away. "I think you know."

Lara stood, backing off. "Know what?"

"Why Mindy got burned." Celeste closed her long-lashed eyes—a mild tremor shaking her body—opened them again slowly, the gesture curiously reptilian. "I think you remember."

Lara was having difficulty breathing. The air was *hot*. "Remember what? Nell splashed her with alcohol and Mindy fell next to the fireplace. . . . *Why was it your fault?*"

Celeste put a pillow over her face. "Everything I've told you is a lie," she said, her voice thick. "I won't lie to you anymore. Just get out of this place while you still can."

"I don't understand."

Celeste did not answer. Her breathing said that she had gone to sleep. Lara would have shaken her and questioned her further, but she didn't want to. She was afraid to touch her.

Downstairs, Nell asked how Celeste was. "Asleep," Lara answered.

At the end of the hour, Percy gave Mindy two pills with a glass of orange juice and carried her upstairs to her bedroom. She was asleep before they could tuck in the sheets. Awfully strong medicine. Nell left the pills atop her nightstand and the light on in case "she awoke in the night in pain."

Rachael suggested coffee, and Percy thought that sounded good. With the four of them sitting at the kitchen table, Rachael said, "You're staying, aren't you, Percy?"

"I don't think so."

Rachael smiled and refilled his cup. "Sure you are. With the two of us already out of action, you should be able to protect yourself."

"My parents wouldn't want any boys staying overnight," Nell said.

"Your parents aren't here," Rachael said.

Nell ignored her, and spoke to Percy. "Myself, I'd like you to stay. But I'm sure you understand."

"No problem."

Rachael simmered, threatening to boil. If Nell and Rachael had an all-out clash, the house would melt. It was ironic, too, since in so many ways they were similar. "Why should he have to ski four miles through this kind of weather?" Rachael asked.

The grandfather clock in the living room struck an ominous midnight. *Time to take off our masks,* Lara thought, *and show who was behind Rachael's sensual lips, Celeste's haunting eyes, Nell's plastic features.* Lara stared at her own face, which reflected like a lifeless shadow in the icy, black window. That's how she would look when she was dead.

"I don't make the rules," Nell said firmly.

"You just love enforcing them," Rachael muttered sarcastically. Lara knew her plan. Wait till they were all asleep and then tiptoe stark naked to where Percy was sleeping and ask him to scratch an itch that she couldn't quite reach. Lara trusted Percy's loyalty. Nevertheless, she also wanted him out of the house. No reason to test him. None at all.

"Shut up, Rachael," Nell said dryly.

Blood burned Rachael's cheeks. "I will pretend that I did not hear that."

Nell sipped her coffee. "Then I will have to say it again."

"You two stop it!" Lara said. "Don't you know we have a guest?"

"Sorry, Percy," Nell said.

"I'm sorry, too," Rachael grumbled.

Percy finished his cup with a single gulp and got to his feet. "Nothing worse than a guest who has overstayed his welcome. I'm the one who should be apologizing. When I see Cal, I'll be sure to hit him again. I'm going to get my skis, Lara."

She nodded. "We better get started."

"*We? We?*" Rachael said, wrinkling her forehead.

"Lara wants to recheck the spot where she found Dana's ski," Percy said. "She's going to follow me partway back."

"I was going to recommend that," Nell said. "It's a good idea."

"And walk back alone in this storm?" Rachael said. "It's a stupid idea."

"I'll be just fine," Lara said.

"You know," Percy said, thinking, "maybe someone

should be there to walk back with you." Lara shook her head minutely.

"I'll come," Rachael said.

"Don't," Lara said.

"Why not?" Rachael asked.

All tact had gone out the window earlier in the evening. "Because I don't want you to," Lara said.

"Hurry back," Nell said, chuckling.

Rachael held her wrath in check. "Hope I see you again soon, Percy," she said, getting out of her chair and giving him a blatant hug and kiss, nuzzling his chest briefly with her body, leaving the guy with something to think about. Percy, to Lara's immense satisfaction, did not return the kiss.

"I'm sure we will," he said.

"Can I help you with your skis?" Rachael asked.

"No," he said. "Why don't you two just stay here and relax and finish this pot of coffee."

Rachael took the hint and remained in the kitchen with Nell. Lara knew that they would do anything but relax together. In the short hallway at the main entrance to the house, she had finished lacing up her boots, when she remembered her scarf in the living room. "I've got to get something," she told Percy.

Resting neatly folded on the bricks by the fireplace, inches from where Mindy had caught fire, she found Rachael's scarf, the one the snowman had been wearing.

Since her own mother had knitted the scarf, Lara decided to wear it instead.

She heard angry voices coming from the kitchen.

"Cal, my foot!" Rachael was saying. "You're the one who threw the alcohol on Mindy!"

"No, I was trying to hit him!"

"You missed by a solid six feet!"

"Are you saying that I did it on purpose!?"

Lara hurried away before she had to hear anymore. She knew they were just warming up.

✑ CHAPTER 6 ✑

THE OUTSIDE THERMOMETER READ MINUS-TEN DEGREES. Fortunately the wind had abated considerably, although Percy maintained that the storm was merely catching its breath. Both of them wore nifty flashlights that hung around their necks, clearly illuminating the width of the path and the unrelenting falling snowflakes. Beyond their circle of light, the frozen landscape was a *Twilight Zone* background prop. The silence was pervasive, unnerving.

Lara spoke mainly to hear the sound of her voice. "Did Cal have a light?"

"Yes," Percy called over his shoulder, picking up speed. "You're wearing it."

"Why didn't he take it?"

"He was drunk. And Nell was about to brand him."

"How could he find his way back in the dark?"

"Good question. Don't worry about him."

She had to stop talking in order to match his pace, and to keep from running into him. Braking her momentum was more exhausting than maintaining it. She concentrated on his twin skis, imitating his moves. As a result, she almost missed the mysterious spot. Percy had crept thirty yards in front. His sudden descent and rise out of a dip clued her.

"Stop!" she called, sitting down, snow piling between her legs. Percy initiated an effortless one-eighty and helped her up. A cross hung on an adjacent tree.

"This it?" he asked.

"Pretty sure."

"What are we looking for, anyway?"

"Evidence." She went down on her knees, brushing snow away in armfuls. Her left knee, the one she had injured when Rachael had tried to kill her, began to lock up. It would be a weary road up the mountain.

"Look at this ice." She waved Percy to her side. "See how it curves down. If we brushed all this snow away, we would find a concave dish, like I did earlier. See how dirty the ice is?"

"Looks like dirt, plain dirt. Are you saying that it's ash?"

If she was, she was saying that they were standing on Dana's grave. "How many feet of snow was there prior to today's storm?"

"As much as seven or eight feet."

"Let's imagine a weird scenario. Try to be open-minded. We will assume that SHC and pyro-kinetics exist. If Dana had been skiing along this path, and had suddenly caught fire, the best thing she could have done was roll in the snow. But from experience, I know people don't do the best thing. They try to run away from the fire. She would have jumped out of her skis, maybe out of only one of them, and run up the path. Now let's say our mysterious force really began to burn her. The articles I read said that some people were reduced to only a handful of ashes. Given that, she would have melt literally a ton of snow. A pool of water would have frozen. Naturally it would be lower than the surrounding snow. There would be left only scattered tracks leading nowhere. No body. The perfect crime. What do you think?"

"I think that you have a vivid imagination, but I don't suppose that's what you want to hear. Even from an occult point of view, you're standing on — forgive the pun — thin ice. You're conveniently mixing pyro-kinetics and sponta-neous human combustion. They're separated phenomena."

"In my book, they're close enough."

"And you're talking about a power level that is way beyond anything that has even been dubiously demonstrated."

"If you accept the possibility, why does there have to be a limit to it?"

"You're beginning to sound like a parapsychologist. Okay, I'll grant you every possibility. Who's the source?"

And wasn't that the question of the hour. "I suspect everyone."

"Even me?"

She had to smile. "Except you."

Percy scared the hell out of her by suddenly catching fire! But no—God, her heart was going to burst—he had merely lit a flare.

"Don't ever do that!" she cried.

"Sorry." He saw how upset she was. "I thought all this speculating was getting us nowhere. I was going to melt some ice and study it. I should have warned you, I've always been one for theatrics."

She nodded, trying to calm herself. "I'm sorry I snapped at you. I never do that—God, I said that about crying. You must think I'm a real case."

"You're right. But you're a cute case."

"Really? No."

"Yes."

They were debating life and death, forces beyond the physical universe, and she forgot it all when he told her she was cute. "You're cute, too," she said.

He laughed. "Don't you think I know that?"

She moved closer, careful not to light herself on fire, feeling suddenly brave. "No laughs, I'm serious."

For all his class, his confidence, he seemed touched. He tossed the flare aside. "I'm going to kiss you." He put his hands on her shoulders and leaned forward. Lara closed her eyes, tilted her head back, and waited. And waited, feeling like Scarlett O'Hara. She ventured a look. Percy was worried.

"I'm not going to stop you," she said.

Poor boy, his conscience was getting in the way. "You're still in high school," he said nervously.

"Do I look like I'm in high school?"

"Not really."

"Then forget that I am. I'm eighteen!" Actually she was seventeen. "The law won't come after you."

"That's not what I was thinking! I just want you to know that I'm not the type of guy who tries to take advantage of the situation."

"Percy, it is ten degrees below zero. You're not going to take off my clothes, and I very much doubt that you want me to undress you. You *can't* take advantage of *this* situation."

He laughed. "This is a side of you that I haven't seen before."

Lara laughed, too. "I haven't seen it before either."

He kissed her. His nose was cold, his lips warm. She felt good in his arms, as if she wanted to stay there a long, long time. Hadn't a poet said that talk of death was the most potent aphrodisiac? She had never *done it* before, had always thought girls who did it on the spur of the moment without protection were fools. Yet she suddenly found herself wishing that it was a warm summer night with thick beds of grass behind the trees. He slipped his arms inside her coat at the back, picking her up slightly. His mouth tasted like carrot cake. She loved carrot cake. She leaned into him at the waist. He slipped and landed on his back. She went along for the ride, bursting into giggles.

"What happened?"

"The flare melted some snow," he said, slightly dazed. Men were such pushovers. "I slipped in the water."

"Are you okay?" She brushed snow off his ears. "I'm just glad you didn't bite my tongue off."

"Could have done worse," she smiled, amazed at her own nastiness. Good old honorable Percy didn't get the joke. He rolled over onto his knees, killing the intimacy of the moment.

"Let's check your ice. The flare has melted a good chunk of it."

"That is what I came for," Lara muttered, disappointed.

Their diagnosis was uncertain. The snow had a dark substance in it, could have been ash, probably wasn't. Lara wanted to dig deeper. Percy was reluctant, mentioning the time, how far he still had to hike. "Now if I was staying at your place," he said, "we could dig up the entire path."

"I'd love to smuggle you in." She hugged him from behind. In the morning she would not believe the things she had said and done. "But Nell would freak. Not to mention Rach."

"We'll be quiet."

"Ohh, I'm very loud," she said, on the threshold of hearing.

"What?"

"Nothing! And you were the one who was afraid to kiss me!"

He was indignant. "I wasn't afraid. I was just —"

"Being a gentleman. I know."

He drew from his coat pocket what looked like a swollen pistol. "Take this, it's a flare gun. It's loaded, and there's a refill. You just snap the flare in. You should always have one of these if you're hiking at night. Hold it out and away from your body, pointed at the sky, if you have to fire it."

"Looks dangerous," Lara said, stuffing it in her pants pocket.

"Just don't shoot anyone with it."

"Maybe Rachael."

"Hey, she's okay."

"Okay, huh?"

Percy hugged her tightly. "Don't worry, you're more than okay."

"Hey, I didn't give you my phone number."

"I'll probably see you before the weekend's up."

"You might not."

"Sure I will."

She broke free of his hold. Her stomach began to ache. "Don't you want my phone number?"

"What for?"

"What? . . ." She was stumped. He laughed.

"I have it already."

"Who?"

"Oakland Information. I even got them to give me your address on Park View Lane."

She slugged him in the stomach. "Don't do that to me!"

"You look cute when your face falls."

"When did you call them?"

"I'm not going to tell you."

"Probably *immediately* after you met me in the coffee shop."

"Now listen to her!"

"Where does Rachael live?"

"I'm not going to tell you." She went to hit him again. "Okay. Okay. I don't know."

"You said the right thing, partner." She fixed his wool cap on his ears. A gust of wind had knocked it askew. The eye of the hurricane was passing. And so, it seemed, was the gaiety of the moment. Perhaps the cold was finally beginning to penetrate. Percy felt it, too.

"You're still limping. I'm going to ski back with you. Then I'll leave."

"You wouldn't leave. I wouldn't let you." Intuitively she knew Percy must not return to the house. Not because of Rachael, but because she really did care for him, and—*Just get out of this place, while you still can*—she wanted him to be safe.

Celeste had some explaining to do. All of them did.

"Go now, before I change my mind," she said, kissing

him briefly on the lips. "Call me Monday if we miss each other."

"At six in the morning."

"I'll be up and waiting. Good-bye, Percy. Don't . . . forget me."

He turned and waved once as he skied away. Before she could respond, he rounded a bend and was gone. It would be a dark road for him. Maybe darker for her.

Haven't forgotten you, Dana. Laughter had disappeared with her best friend. Arguing and suspicion had dominated the night. Lara stepped to the center of the impression and dug the snow aside, using a sharp-tipped granite rock at the side of the path to crack into the speckled ice. The flare had gone out. She spent twenty minutes getting a foot deep, the gray thickening. A large chip, particularly dark, broke free. It would have to do. Her knee had gone passed tightening to cramping. Lara put the lump of ice in her pocket.

If the wind hadn't been at her back, she wouldn't have made it. By the time she sighted the house, her lungs were on fire and her leg was saying not another step. Except for a dull orange glow spilling through the living room windows, the house was dark.

She rested on the floor of the entrance hall for a spell before her hands thawed to where she could unlace her boots. No one came to welcome her home.

Nell was lying alone in the living room on the couch by

the fire. Lara thought she was asleep, until she spoke, not opening her eyes.

"Did you find what you wanted, Lara?"

"I didn't find Dana." Lara sat across from her. The fire should have felt good, but it didn't. "Did the lodge call?"

"The phones are dead."

Lara's pulse quickened. "How?"

Nell didn't care. "The storm."

"Do you have a walkie-talkie?"

"Somewhere."

"Where's Rach?"

"Asleep."

"Celeste?"

"Asleep, I suppose. Her door is locked."

"Why did she lock her door?"

"I guess she doesn't want to be disturbed."

"You and Rachael were really going at it when I left."

"We resolved our differences."

"That's good." Sparks burst from the logs. Lara's nerves were shot, and she jumped a foot out of the chair. Nell opened her eyes.

"Did you find anything?"

"No."

"Nothing?"

"Snow. Dirty ice."

"You've had a bad day, haven't you?"

"I met Percy. But otherwise, yeah, it's been rotten. I've been worrying all day, that's for sure."

"I had a lot of bad days," Nell said, shifting from laziness to anger.

"You mean, after the accident?"

"My whole life's been 'after the accident.' I don't remember anything before then. Do you?"

Lara took a chance. "I remember Nicole."

"Do you really? I don't think so. In fact, I know so."

Lara had no good response. "I'm sorry," she whispered.

"I knew you would recheck where you had found the ski," Nell said, as if that were related. She sat up, stabbed the fire with the poker. A flare illuminated her face, the shifting shadows emphasizing her scars. "You're looking at my scars," Nell said.

"You didn't wear makeup this weekend. Why?"

"What have I got to hide from any of you?" Nell chuckled. "Did Percy tell you how cute you were?"

"You still hate me, don't you?"

Nell dropped the poker, closed her eyes, held her breath for the longest time. "If it wasn't for —" she began, cutting herself off quickly. A single tear formed slowly, rolled down her cheek, divorced from the rest of her features, which remained as impassive as a mask. "The strangest thing is," she whispered, "I don't. I should, but I don't. Now I feel—I feel nothing." She shook herself, picked up the poker again, prodding the flames. "Go to sleep, Lara. It's late."

"You, too. You need to rest." Lara circled behind the couch, squeezed Nell's shoulders.

"In a bit I will rest."

"Are you worried about Dana?"

"I worry about all of you."

"A moment ago, you were going to say, 'If it wasn't for Nicole,' weren't you?"

"No, I wasn't. Not exactly. Good night, Lara."

Lara dragged her feet slowly up the stairs. An exhaustion that penetrated her bones began to overwhelm her. In one day she'd walked more miles, suffered more nervous traumas than she ordinarily went through in a year. To close her eyes and forget everything, if only for a little while, was the answer to her most fervent prayer. But to reach her room she had to pass the others' rooms. Tired as she was, would she be able to sleep without questioning them?

Mindy's light was on. Not knocking, Lara tiptoed in. Mindy's loud snores didn't miss a beat. The top of the codeine pills was off. She reread the label. The container was supposed to hold forty tablets. There was no way that many pills that size would have fit. Lara hoped Mindy hadn't swallowed any more. Yet shock victims didn't snore and she left reassured after retucking Mindy s blankets.

Rachael's door was shut, the light out. Lara knocked, called softly. There was no answer. Rachael mustn't want to speak to her. Lara knew that she was an extremely light sleeper. She contemplated forcing the issue, but decided against it. She didn't have the strength left for a major confrontation.

At Celeste's door, she went through the same motions. No answer. She tried the handle. Locked.

"It's Lara, Celeste. Open up."

Fatigue prevented her from persevering. She pulled herself into her room, leaning on the door to shut it. The chunk of ice in her coat pocket banged her leg, calling for attention. But it was still frozen. She put it on the desk beneath the heating vent. In the morning the water would have evaporated and she could study at leisure what was left. In the dresser mirror she saw how red her eyes were. She pulled her pants half down, fell back onto the bed, her coat still on. In a minute she would go the bathroom and change into her pajamas and brush her teeth and turn off the light and get into bed properly. In just a second . . .

Yet already she was sinking, gliding gently down a dark well with the promise of a wet bottom where all images of fire and ash would be washed clean. Rachael wouldn't kill her. Nell didn't hate her. Cal was far away. The colonel was a good guy. Dana was safe. Celeste wasn't a second Carrie. The snowman had gone peacefully. All was well.

LARA AWOKE WITH A JOLT, AN ALARM SCREAMING INSIDE her skull. Before she could even figure her location, she fell off the bed and smashed nose first into the floor. It was a fire alarm, and this was it, they were all going to burn.

In reality her alarm clock was merely shouting that it was three A.M., twenty-four hours to the minute since she had gotten up to come on her wonderful weekend in the mountains. She had been unconscious exactly an hour. She flattened the ringing with her palm. A bottle of double-extra-strength aspirin wouldn't have dented her headache. Her mouth was as dry as the desktop! The ice had dematerialized, giving up its secrets. Lara scampered to her knees.

Ten seconds later found her vomiting in the toilet. There had been flakes of ash surrounding a single black piece that could only have been charred bone. All along, it had only been in her head. She could tell others of her worries and they could reason with her and then she would feel better. Dana was at the lodge. Dana was on the bus. Dana was at home. Sure, guys.

Dana was dead.

If I couldn't get into heaven, I wouldn't mind spending the rest of eternity here.

Part of Dana was on the desk. Which part?

Lara choked on dry heaves. She wanted desperately to pass out but she knew if she did she would never wake up. She had to get out of the house! Too many horror flicks had made it clear that if she stayed she would end up as dog meat. And — God forgive her — she had to leave alone. Mindy was drugged. Rachael had no scruples about swatting another fly. Nell couldn't forget. Celeste had no past. None of them could be trusted.

Lara stood slowly, pulling up her pants, ordering herself not to make a false move. Don't flush the toilet. Don't let anyone know you're awake. Zip up your jacket. Get your gloves. Put on your shoes. Turn out the light. So far, so good. She stepped quietly toward the door. Her knee buckled. Pain, Lara, as if it was actually on fire. She stifled a cry of despair. She would never get down the mountain on this leg. The walkie-talkie? Even if there was one, she would have to ransack the house to find it. A pyro murderer wouldn't go for that. Had Cal really left? They'd all heard the door slam, but the house was big enough to hide him and his supply of napalm. The snowmobile in the basement! The keys were in the ignition! And Nell had said it was as easy as driving a car!

Lara crept into the black hall, wondering if the pyro murderer had burned out the lights. Of course, they probably had a multitude of wicked weapons. She took a step forward. Maybe a cold steel knife in her spine, a stainless razor across the soft flesh of her throat. She steadied herself against the invisible wall. She knew she'd feel the blood spurting, warm and sticky; no one died immediately. She passed Celeste's room, Rachael's, Mindy's, all dark. Her parents would have to identify her body. The red glow coming from the living room reminded her of a descent into hell as she started down the stairs. There wouldn't be much left. Cut to pieces, then poured with gasoline. Or else fried by the hyperactive frontal lobes of a witch. The living room was filled with moving shadows, otherwise empty. No way she was going into the basement without a weapon. But the shotguns on the walnut mantle were unloaded. Is that all that's left of our daughter? her parents would wail. She approached the fireplace, the poker. There would be an article in the local paper, beneath her happy senior picture: was on the homecoming court, such a nice girl. Had her whole life in front of her. She weighed the poker in her hands. Swung hard it would split open someone's skull. Survived by Clara and James Johnson. Whoever she saw first was going to get it.

The door to the basement was ajar, casting a silver sliver of light onto the thick carpet Lara peeked in, opening the door a millimeter at a time. A row of steps, three quick hops, and she could be behind the wheel with her hand on the key. Never mind the garage door, she would rev into first and waste whatever was in her way, all in only fifteen seconds.

But Lara took an eternity to open the door to where she could squeeze past. Even standing on the platform at the top of the steps, she did not have a clear view of the basement; hanging fiberglass insulation got in her way. She waited, trying not to breathe or think, listening. Had she been breathing normally, she probably would have noticed the smell of kerosene immediately. When she did notice, she would have vomited again had she anything left in her knotted stomach.

Who are you, evil spirit in the basement?

An unseen plastic container contacted the basement's cement floor. A gurgle of kerosene followed; another container bounced. Lara did not remember dropping the poker, but she definitely heard when it hit the hot water tank. The noise must have echoed through the entire house. The pouring kerosene halted. She did not wait for the Who's there? She leaped back, slamming the basement door shut. Pursuing feet rushed up the steps. She threw the bolt. Fists pounded from the other side. She ran out the front door without her skis, down the powdery path in her thin canvas sneakers that sank two feet with each stride, on a knee made of foam rubber, not once glancing over her shoulder.

Her chances were lousy. The storm had regrouped into a thousand vicious tornadoes. The flakes stinging her eyes were more painful than blasted sand. Nothing in her experience had prepared her to even imagine a blizzard of this intensity. With no light, no strength, no Percy. She was almost doomed to die. But she would not go back. Death was not always the same. Freezing was infinitely preferable to burning.

She was stumbling blindly when her hands encountered a wall of ice. There must have been an avalanche of sorts;

it had not been there a couple of hours ago. She tried to circle around, almost trapping herself in sharp bushes that lined the path. Swimming straight through was the only course. She was well on her way to the other side of the snow heap when her feet lost all support. *Down, Lara, you'll smother if you won't burn.* Quicksand, the wind-torn sky vanishing as snow covered her head. She screamed. Ice stuffed her throat. Sinking. Sinking. Only seventeen years old. It wasn't fair!

When she came to a standstill, she realized that if she stopped all her shouting, she could breathe quite easily. But what was the use? The lodge could just as well have been on the far side of the moon for all the hope she had of reaching it. And she was *so* tired. She closed her eyes, thinking to rest for a moment. Cold seeped through her coat. Not an uncomfortable cold that made her wish to be warm again. But a cold that whispered that if she just remained still a while longer, then she would never have to be cold again. There was no reason to fight the inevitable. A delicious warmth spread through her chest. How fine, not to even have to breathe anymore. *That's right, Lara. Rest and relax. Everything is all right. Soon you will be with Dana.*

"No!" she cried in horror, recognizing her folly. "No! Damn you, whoever you are, I will not die!"

Lara clawed at the ice in front of her. Terror was no longer her sole inspiration. Revenge gave her strength. Dana's

～ 131 ～

murderer, even if it was the Devil himself, was going to pay. Snow shoved through her jacket collar. A razor edge of ice sliced her cheek. Blood spurted and froze. Suddenly the wall of ice tumbled, and she fell forward, the biting wind returning. She was through.

Yet anger brought her less than a mile farther. Her legs would no longer work, no matter how she bullied them. On hands and knees she gained at best an additional two hundred yards. Then she could no longer feel her hands and knees, or her arms, or her face, or even her blood pumping in her heart, only a pain inside that cried at all she would miss. Percy would call early Monday morning, and no one would be awake to answer. At graduation there would be a diploma with honors with her name on it, and she wouldn't be there to accept it. Her birthday would come, and her mother would have no reason to bake a cake. Her mother had always hated to bake, anyway.

"I will not die," she croaked, huddling into a ball. To revive her fingers to wipe the freezing tears out of her eyes, she pulled off her gloves with her teeth and shoved her hands into her crotch. She met an obstruction pressing through from her pocket.

The flare gun! She pulled it out and reached for the trigger, but it promptly slipped from her numb grasp and sank in the snow. Practically ripping her cheeks, she shoved her right hand in her mouth and licked her fingers frantically, getting a painful tingle. Next she banged her hands together so hard that she was sure she must be breaking bones. Still she could not master the delicate trigger. Inspiration gave her a third method of defrostation. She squeezed her hands back in her pants and—what the hell, she was going to die anyway—peed on them. That worked.

Like a firework from Mexico, the flare popped into the sky, a bulb of yellow light that detonated in a red brilliance that was nevertheless almost entirely swallowed by the low flying clouds. A ranger a mile away wouldn't even have seen it. Nice try, Percy. She reloaded the gun, but didn't even bother to fire the flare, shoving it in her belt under her coat. The brief crimson dawn faltered and died. The returning darkness was devastating.

I will not die, she thought, knowing that she would. Already her body was no longer attached to what was left of her mind. At least she didn't feel it. She hardly felt anything. Funny how she could still see. Her eyes must have frozen open. They would find her that way, staring forever down the path for help that never came. And this person surrounded by a bright light coming up the path to her rescue was surely a hallucination. Or perhaps it was tomorrow and she was already dead and simply hanging around to see herself found. Or maybe he was even an angel. The light was so bright, she wanted to blink, but couldn't. He moved closer. He was tall. He was overweight and had an unshaven face and baggy trousers and wasn't even that handsome. Some angel; you would think because she had been such a good girl and had gotten good grades and hadn't even had sex once that they would have sent a beautiful seraph.

"Lara," he said, staring down at her from an Olympian height of six feet. He was no angel. And she was not dead, though she suddenly wished that she were.

It was Cal.

She remembered nothing else.

⁓ CHAPTER 7 ⁓

THERE WERE VOICES, WARM LIGHT, THICK AIR THAT smelled funny. The voices—they were rather annoying— were trying to wake her up. Lara wished they wouldn't bother. She'd had enough excitement for one day.

"Wake up, Lara."

"Leave me, Dana, I'm dead," she muttered.

"Wake up, you jerk."

That was Rachael, and how dare she call her a jerk. Lara opened her eyes. She was on the floor of the basement. "What's the deal?" she asked the sagging insulation and the hot water tank.

"I think she's awake," Dana said.

"Maybe it would have been better to leave her unconscious," Rachael said.

Lara went to sit up and couldn't. She was no longer numb but bound. She rolled on her side. Dana smiled at her.

"Dana! What a relief! I thought you were dead."

"I wouldn't start celebrating just yet," Dana said. "You

will note the fact that we are tied up in a basement filled with kerosene."

Dana lay to her left, wearing the same clothes as when Lara had last seen her, plus yards of clothesline string and spools of duct tape—as were they all—around her feet and hands. Rachael was flat on her back on the other side, her once shiny blond hair streaked with blood, her face ashen. At the far end of the basement, under the massive white propane tank, was a pond of kerosene and rows of unopened plastic containers of the same.

"That Cal!" Lara cursed. "I should have known."

"From what we have been able to gather from our limited point of view," Dana said, "Cal had merely been coming back after sobering up to apologize for what happened to Mindy. He found you in the snow and carried you back here to the nursing hand of Nell Kutroff. Rach and I tried to shout to him; we could hear them talking upstairs, but Nell had our mouths professionally taped. Cal actually saved your life. For the time being. While you were blissfully defrosting, after Cal left, Nell tied you up and dragged you down here."

"I don't understand," Lara said. "Where have you been?"

"Oh, I've been in the house all along. After I got back from the lodge, Nell offered me a delicious, steaming cup of cocoa, and I woke up in her closet next to one of my skis, tied and taped like you wouldn't . . . like you are now.

Plus my mouth. I heard you calling the lodge, and arguing with Rachael concerning my whereabouts. I appreciated your concern. Man, have I got to pee!" She sniffed. "I see you couldn't wait. You know, Lara, I bought you those pants last Christmas, and you've ruined them."

"How can you joke at a time like this!" Lara cried.

Tears swelled out of Dana's eyes, and Lara could see that she'd been crying already. "What else is there to do?"

Lara turned the other way. "How's your head, Rach?"

"It's felt better. Am I still bleeding?"

"Yes. A lot. What happened?"

"After you left with Percy, Nell and I adjourned our fight to the living room. I thought I was getting the better of it until I turned my back for a sec and felt the poker cracking my skull. I came to down here, and Nell brought Dana down a few minutes later to keep me company."

Lara could not keep up with the revelations. Especially when they left so much unexplained. "I'm so sorry, Rach."

"Don't hassle it. If I had a choice between drinking coffee with Nell or going for a late night stroll with Percy, there wouldn't have been a choice. Did you kiss him? I bet he's a good kisser."

"Just once."

"Who made the first move?"

"He did, of course."

"You liar, Lara, you're hornier than me. But you don't have to apologize; I understand."

"No, I'm sorry because I suspected you as the murderer."

"Me?" Rachael said softly, a sadness in her voice Lara had never heard before. "Not me, Lara. How could you think that of me?"

"I overheard you on the phone."

"Ohh, I see. I was just talking to Ted McDannel. You know, that creep with the mold on his teeth? He did a brake job and a tune-up on my car for free, and to compensate him I invited him over to watch a movie on TV and let him have a small feel, nothing big. Anyway, the movie we watched was *Carrie*. From that he got the idea of a way to fix the balloting for homecoming queen. Ain't I a jerk? I never told you, Lara, I know I'm prettier than you, but in every other way, I've always felt way behind. I didn't think I could win honestly. Since Dana was no longer on the Associated Student Body Council, and Ted was Sergeant at Arms, we figured we could pull it off."

"How exactly were you going to fix the balloting?" Lara asked, knowing it was an absurd question, given the situation.

"You don't want to know."

Lara fought with the tape and string, not getting a quarter of an inch of play. "Rachael, you nut, you would have won hands down. Even I was going to vote for you."

Rachael sighed. "We'll never know now, will we?"

"Where's Nell now?" Lara asked.

"Upstairs," Dana said.

"Celeste! She'll kill Celeste!"

"Lara, she's going to kill all of us," Dana said.

A lightbulb exploded in Lara' s mind. The glare of the obvious had covered the truth. Celeste had been right.

Don't you know? I think you know. I think you remember.

"Maybe," Lara said.

"What special exempt status does Celeste have?" Rachael asked. "Because she wasn't at the slumber party?"

Lara did not answer, but asked instead: "Rach, I asked you before and I'm going to ask you again. Why did you frown at the Ouija board when it spelled Nicole's name?"

"Lara, I realize that we're all about to be killed, but could you please stick to more pertinent topics."

"That's a weird question," Dana agreed.

"Someone was moving the planchette, wasn't she?"

"We all were," Rachael said.

"But wasn't one person moving it *consciously*?"

Rachael took a moment. "I thought at the time . . . yeah, maybe."

"So what?" Dana asked.

"Probably nothing," Lara said, "possibly everything."

"Someone's coming," Rachael said tightly. "No begging. Don't give her any satisfaction."

There were feet on the steps, moving carefully for they lacked flexibility from being too long in the hospital. Dana and Rachael gasped. Lara didn't. From the moment they had met in the library, a part of her had known.

"Celeste!" Dana cried.

"Untie us!" Rachael said. "Quick!"

Celeste ignored them, having eyes for only Lara. Such beautiful green eyes, like a child's, a child who was never supposed to have grown up.

"Hello, Nicole," Lara said.

Nicole—Celeste—acknowledged her insight with a slight nod. "I tried to tell you."

The truth had been crying for her to notice. The awkwardness when Nell and Celeste "first" met, overcompensating for the fact that they had spent their entire lives together. The prescription cream in the shower, really for Nicole Kutroff. Nell and Celeste's unspoken rapport in charades, not unusual for two who had always been together. Nell's overreaction when Cal had pinched Celeste. A dozen other hints.

"And you didn't want to hurt any of us," Lara said.

Nicole's face changed horribly, innocence fleeing from the memory of years of torment. "I could not hurt you enough," she said bitterly.

Rachael and Dana were shocked speechless. Lara wanted to plead that it had been an accident when Nicole reached down and pulled off her thick sweater. She was naked underneath. Dana began to choke. Rachael closed her eyes. "Oh God," Lara breathed.

Scars of a decade of constant surgery were there; swollen and convoluted red flesh stitched together with only thought for a chance for life—not for what that life may have to be like. Grotesque lumps were her breasts; a tight band of knotted tissue was her abdomen. No nipples, no bellybutton. A touch would bring pain. *I've never gone out with a boy.* The sight brought revulsion.

"I could take off my pants," Nicole said with a feigned laugh. "It gets better, more interesting." Lara shook her head.

"You can't be," Rachael stuttered. "You're dead!"

"Wouldn't that have been better for all of us?" Nicole sneered. "Oh, I wanted to die. And I did, again and again and again, every time the pain shots wore off. My parents told you I was gone because they didn't want anyone to know they had such a *thing* for a daughter. Of course, that's not what they told me. They said that they were trying to give me a chance for a new beginning, a normal life. Hah! Even on the hottest days, even in the backyard, I always had to be totally dressed. They were just ashamed. But it's funny, you know, there were unique compensations. I got to see pictures of my own funeral!"

"You don't want to do this," Lara said with a conviction that came from knowing she spoke the truth. The hate Nicole was trying to project wavered.

"But I do!" Nicole smiled nervously. "I've been waiting for this all my life. I've dreamed about it."

"Not you," Lara said. "I remember —"

"You remember a happy little girl!" Nicole interrupted, turning away, putting a hand on the propane tank, the equivalent of a warhead if there was the tiniest spark.

"Maybe. But what about Celeste? I knew her pretty good."

"Yeah, right, sure," Nicole said sarcastically. "Didn't even know she was a monster, did you?"

"You're not a monster."

"Dana almost threw up! Rachael couldn't even look at me!"

"You were such a good friend. I can't believe —"

"It was all an act, Lara! I was never your friend. Never!"

"No one's that good an actor," Lara said. "Do your parents know about this plan? They don't, do they? It was Nell's idea."

"It was my idea!"

"I don't believe you. Why did you come to live with your aunt if you simply wanted to kill us?"

As though she could no longer support herself, Nicole leaned on the tank, her head turned down. "I wanted to know what I was going to destroy."

"No," Lara said, taking an awful gamble, with nothing to lose. "You came because you didn't trust Nell. You wanted to see if we were as rotten as you had been told."

"And you are! All so happy! Going to your football

games, and your movies, and out on your dates! Never once thinking about what you had done! I even asked you! Was anyone else hurt? And you said no! You'd forgotten! How could you have forgotten me?"

"It was too painful to talk about," Dana said.

Nicole fought to calm herself, standing away from the tank, staring at all three of them. "I came to live with my aunt to find out why. That's all. Why. I was only a little girl."

"There is no *why*," Rachael said. "It was an accident."

"Lara poured gasoline on me!" Nicole shouted.

"Brandy, she was trying to put you out," Rachael said. "And I did put you out. And I burned my hands doing so."

Nicole shook her head. "That's not how it happened. Nell put me out. Nell saved me."

"Nell tried to," Lara said. "We all tried."

"No! You didn't even want me there. You all hated me!"

Lara decided that the moment had come. "You're wrong, Nicole. Nell was the only one who didn't want you there. She was the one who spelled your name on the Ouija board as the demon. She was the one who pointed the planchette at you. *Nell caused the accident!*"

"Oh really, Lara," Nell said quietly, coming down the steps, dressed for the cold, handing Nicole a down jacket. Lara was struck by how at ease she was, how calm. "You want to go now, Nicole? Mindy's not going to wake up."

"Wait," Nicole said, the opposite of her sister, torn with anxiety. "I want to know exactly what happened."

"I told you," Nell said, moving to the propane tank, checking the pressure gauge, kerosene thick at her feet.

"Liar," Rachael swore.

Nell smiled. "You weren't much fun, Rach. You have no imagination. Lara was the only one who was worth the trouble. She was perfect, obsessed with the missing snowman, Dana's ski, the ash in the ice. That last *omen* was almost too much. It almost frightened her away. You look surprised, Lara. This is the juicy part, you're all pissing in your pants. But I wanted revenge to last, where I could savor it. I wanted to haunt you. With a hand torch, while Rachael and Dana were cleaning out this basement, I melted the snowman. Took two minutes. And it was I who knocked out Dana, and slid down the path on your previous tracks, and planted the ski, and melted the snow, and threw in a bag of ash and bones from an old barbeque."

"How gross," Dana said.

"I was safe," Nell went on without a pause. "I could see you and Mindy still miles away. Everything worked my way. Foolish Cal and his napalm, an accidental plus that helped set the mood. And I even got to light Mindy up! And best of all, my plan worked! I overheard you talking to Percy, Lara. Spontaneous human combustion! Pyrokinetics! *Carrie*! Your head was in the palm of my hand.

You were afraid you'd catch fire any second." Nell pulled a lighter from her pocket. "And you see, you won't be disappointed. This place is going to blow. Nicole and I can hover around the flames, keep warm, until help arrives. And no one will go to jail, for there will be no evidence."

"Wait," Nicole said again, eyeing her sister. "That night, on the Ouija board, did you spell out my name?"

"Of course not."

"Lara said you did."

"At this point, Lara would say pretty much anything," Nell muttered, hardly listening, opening a box containing four more bottles of kerosene. "Give me a hand with this, will you?"

Nicole did not move. "If I hadn't suffered so much —"

"Maybe you would let us go," Lara said.

"She's my sister." Nicole bit her lip, talking to herself. "She took care of me."

"She lied to you," Rachael said.

A flash of anger distorted Nicole's face, but it didn't last. Nell unscrewed a cap and savored the smell as though it were a fine wine. "You poured brandy, not gasoline?" Nicole asked.

"Why would we have gasoline in our living room?" Dana said.

"But brandy's full of alcohol," Nicole moaned.

"I panicked," Lara said. "I used it because it was wet. I just wanted to put you out."

"I suffered so much. . . ." Nicole whispered, squeezing her eyes shut, trembling.

"But you've been happy these last couple of months," Lara pleaded. "Remember when we went to the show, and ate all that chocolate ice cream afterward, and got sick? Remember when the five of us all went —"

"I remember burning!" Nicole wept. "That's all I remember!" She turned on Nell. "Stop that!"

Nell put down her bottle of kerosene and glanced over, unruffled. "Yes, Nicole?"

"I want you to stop."

"We can't go back."

"We are going to stop."

"But—"

"You lied to me! You said that it was gasoline! You said that she poured me with gasoline! On purpose!"

Straining her head as far off the floor as possible in order to follow the exchange, Lara noticed a bulge in her pants beneath her coat. The flare gun! Nell had failed to remove it. Now if she could just get her hands on it, and aim at Nell while she stood in the kerosene.

"You see my face, sister?" Nell said quietly. "It's not very pretty, is it? In fact, it looks like the rest of you. Now look at them. They all look fine. So, who's lying to you?"

"No one has to be lying," Nicole said, obviously fighting a tremendous internal battle. "Before I moved in with Aunt Martha, I told you —"

"That was a mistake, anyway," Nell interrupted. "If these ladies hadn't been such dimwits, they could have traced the Kutroff name through her."

"I'm glad I did! I'm glad I got to see and hear both sides of the story! Nell, we don't have to —"

"Stop!" Nell said, raising her voice for the first time. Nicole cowered. "We will not argue about this again. Go out on the porch. Wait for me. It's already done."

So close, yet with a draining heart Lara saw that it was not to be. Blood was stronger than truth. Nicole bowed to her sister's command, pulling on her sweater, her jacket, limping toward the stairs, not looking at them.

"Good-bye, Celeste," Lara said sadly.

Nicole turned. "Why did you call me that?"

Nell had returned to her kerosene bottles. "Because Celeste was my friend," Lara said. "And because you're not. We were right all along. You've shown us nothing new. Nicole is *dead*."

Nicole's frail shoulders sagged with the burden, and Lara thought she would fall to the floor. Yet suddenly she smiled, as tears watered from her eyes. "Celeste means 'heavenly,'" she murmured, in a faraway space and time. "I picked that name to fool you. Celeste. My mommy has a picture of me in a long, golden dress when I was seven years old. No, I had to have been six. Couldn't wear dresses when I was seven. It's my favorite picture of myself. I have it in my bag if you want to see. . . . But that picture, it's like looking at another person, someone I don't know, someone I'd like to be. That's the real reason I moved to Aunt Martha's, to be that person, to be happy. I was standing by our pool in my dress, laughing happily. My mother took it just before I fell in the pool and ruined the dress. Got all wet, got all burned. Is that why you said, 'Good-bye, Celeste'?" Nicole's expression focused, hardened. "But I didn't actually fall in the pool." She stared at her preoccupied sister. "Nell pushed me in. She ruined my dress. She was always doing things like that. Always."

Nicole came to a decision. Moving swifter and more silently than Lara had ever seen before, she came down the steps. With a finger to her lips, and her eyes glued on Nell, who knelt with her back to them, she removed an unattached hacksaw blade from the pegboard above their heads. In moments she had cut through the tape on Lara's hands. The string was more stubborn. Nicole was working on it when Nell sent her flying with a kick to the ribs. Nicole dropped to the floor like a shot animal, the wind knocked from her lungs.

Nell spat, knocking the hacksaw blade to the corner. "You're no different than them! Get out of here! I should have left you in the fire! You're always getting in the way!"

Nicole was beaten, wheezing, sobbing, nursing her side; she staggered to her feet. Relying upon the railing of the stairs, she tried to pull herself out of the basement.

Disgusted, Nell returned to the corner and grabbed a

kerosene container, saying, "For that, ladies, you're going to drink some of this first."

Lara began to rock. Four swings and she had the momentum to sit upright. Her hands were still tied, and it would take time that she didn't have to free them completely; but because of Nicole, they were loose enough to where she could remove the flare gun from her belt. Simultaneously Nell unscrewed the cap of her bottle, and said, "Hot stuff, girls." She moved toward them.

"Damn you to the deepest hell!" Rachael cursed.

"I second that," Dana said, keeping her composure, neither wanting to give Nell the satisfaction.

"Going somewhere, Lara?" Nell asked.

Lara raised the gun, putting four pounds on a five-pound trigger. Nell halted, lifted a penciled eyebrow. She had put on makeup after all. "You're full of tricks, aren't you, Lara? Why don't you shoot?"

"This is a flare gun," Lara said slowly. "Makes a lot of sparks, and you're standing in a puddle of kerosene."

"Fry her!" Rachael said.

"Do it!" Dana urged.

"No!" Nicole cried from the steps, coming back down.

"No one move!" Lara ordered, climbing to her knees. Nicole paused. Nell smiled.

"Shoot," Nell said. "We can all burn."

"You would go first," Lara said, "and the tank would take time. We could get away."

"Maybe, but you're afraid to chance it," Nell said. "To me, this is nothing new. I am not afraid." She took a step forward.

"Stop!" Nicole screamed. Nell hesitated. "I am afraid!"

"No one has to die," Lara said. "Let me untie the others. We can forget the whole thing."

Nell laughed deeply. "Forget? I'll never forget." She whipped out her lighter.

"It would be worse this time," Lara promised. Another move, and she would pull the trigger. She swore that she would.

"Please, Nell," Nicole begged, actually falling to her knees. "Would you kill me, too?"

Puzzlement flickered across Nell's face. "But this was all for you."

"Don't you see, I don't want it." Nicole wept.

"It would be as though none of this ever happened," Lara said.

For the first time, Nell allowed her madness to surface. "Then I would have nothing to look forward to," she said, eyes dilated, voice dreamy, shuffling slowly toward them. "Nothing to plan, nothing to think about, except how ugly I am." She paused before a dirty round mirror attached to the hot water tank, and smiled at herself, brushing her hair back. Then she wiped at the dust, receiving a clearer reflection, and her face crumpled. "You see this cheek? It's plastic. It's not me."

"Nell, listen to me," Lara said. "We can help you."

Nell picked up the mirror, scrutinizing her features as though for the first time, appalled at what she found. "How would you help me? You're not a doctor."

"By being your friend," Lara said.

"I have no friends." Nell dropped the mirror, a shattered silver array circling her feet. Still she stared at herself in the kerosene-soaked pieces, perhaps trying to arrange them together in a way that made her beautiful. She sighed. "I'll never have a boyfriend."

"Sure you will," Lara said.

"No." Nell shook her head, splintering the glass with her foot. "Never." She struck the flame on her lighter, saying calmly, "And neither will you." And with every trace of lethargy suddenly absent, she pounced. Lara fired at her feet.

The flare shot through Nell's legs, ricocheting off the back wall, landing like a squirming snake in front of Nell on her right, where it detonated. The kerosene lit immediately, swallowing flames engulfing her like a hungry maw. Yet she stood her ground silently, not moving. A glimpse through the incandescence revealed an expression of acceptance. Lara thought she had never seen Nell so peaceful. Up until her childhood friend's face began to melt.

"Nell!!!!" Nicole screamed, running clumsily, uselessly to her sister's aid. Lara tried to trip her to stop her, but she was too slow. On the borders of the spreading bonfire,

Nicole wavered before plunging her hands, two of the only parts of her body that had not been burned before, foolishly into the flames. Finally dropping to her knees, Nell made a shoving gesture, as if to say get back. Then she fell forward and was lost.

"Nell!!!" Nicole wailed, her heart breaking in the cry.

"Get the hacksaw blade," Rachael said.

"Quickly," Dana added.

Frantically Lara rolled to the corner, banging and bloodying her nose in the process. The binds to her feet took a lot of sweat. Smoke stung her eyes. Finally, she was able to rush to Dana's side. While hacking at the string, Rachael commented. "I knew you wouldn't do me first."

"I won't leave without you," Lara said.

"I might," Dana said. "Hurry!"

Rachael twisted her head toward the propane tank, licked on all sides by the fire. "You owe me one, Nicole," she demanded.

Moving like a zombie, Nicole stood and removed an ordinary saw from the wall above their heads. It was more effective than the loose hacksaw blade. Rachael was freed the same moment Dana was.

"Let's quit this joint!" Rachael shouted, moving Dana in front of her, up the stairs.

Lara was on their heels when she realized that Nicole was not following.

"What are you waiting for!?" she yelled, coughing.

"I'm staying," Nicole said, her eyes fixed on the blackened heap that had been her sister.

Lara grabbed Nicole by the ear and yanked her onto the steps. "I'm not in the mood to argue with you!"

Nicole gave no reply. Nevertheless, she cooperated. They had exited the basement and were in the hall heading for the living room and the front door beyond, when a shock wave—had to have been from exploding kerosene bottles, couldn't have been the propane tank—took their feet out from under them. Rachael and Dana backtracked and helped Lara and Nicole up. Lara's leg was on fire. Nicole blotted it out, her hands a terrible sight.

For once, the cold swirling snow was welcome. Rachael stumbled away from the porch and fell down behind a tree, the back of her head still bleeding. Dana ran down the path. Lara helped Nicole to Rachael's side and collapsed herself, pressing a handful of snow on her burned leg.

Rachael bolted upright. "Mindy!"

"I knew we'd forgotten something!" Dana called from somewhere.

"Stay here," Lara said, hugging a tree, pulling herself upright. "I'll get her."

"You'll die," Rachael said, trying to follow, unable to stand.

Lara wobbled toward the porch and the rectangular orange lantern that was the open door. Nicole tried to stop her.

"This was my doing," she said. "I'll get her."

Lara nodded. "We'll get her together."

The fire was spreading from the north wind, which was to their advantage, allowing them to cut through the kitchen and take the back stairs to the top floor. The power was out. Currents of black smoke and dancing red light pursued them. Lara slammed each door shut at her back. It would be a literal hell getting back out — if the propane tank didn't solve that problem for them.

Lara kicked open Mindy's door, shouting into the dark room, "Get up! The house is on fire!"

There came a deep breath, a contented sigh, the resumption of snores. Lara closed the door. Nicole led her to the bed. She felt for Mindy's head, took the glass of water from the nightstand, threw it in her face. "Wake up, Mindy!"

"Not thirsty now," Mindy muttered from a dream.

"Mindy!" Lara touched her eyes. They were closed. The house trembled as support beams crashed below. "What were those pills!?"

"I don't know!" Nicole shouted over the noise. "They weren't codeine. They were for after operations, real strong. We'll never wake her up. I know."

"We'll carry her." Lara threw off the blankets. "Take her feet. I'll get her head."

"Okay." They stumbled about. Nicole screamed. "Ohhh!!!!"

"What's wrong!?"

"My hands! The skin's coming off!"

"Oh, Nicole. . . . Get back. I'll get her." Lara sat on the bed, and yanked Mindy's listless arms around her neck. But when she tried to stand, her knees turned to mush and she hit the floor in pain that went beyond reason. Who was she fooling? Her leg couldn't even support her own weight.

"Where are you?" Nicole cried.

"Here." Lara rolled over and slapped Mindy across the face. "Wake up, damn you!"

"Sleepytime," Mindy mumbled, hugging her as though she were a pillow.

"Get out of here," Lara ordered Nicole.

"You first."

In a rush of smoke and fiery light, the door burst open. Dana and Rachael stood there, hacking their lungs out. "What are you doing here?" Lara asked.

"One for all, and all for one, and all that crap," Dana said, grabbing Mindy by the hair.

"I figure that being a hero has got to help me in the homecoming voting," Rachael panted, lifting one of Mindy's feet.

With Dana taking the bulk of the weight, and Nicole leading the way, they carried Mindy in the direction of the living room. Flames whipping up the stairs forced them to reconsider. Even as Lara fought not to panic, she could feel her skin reddening from the heat. Billows of bloody fog engulfed them.

"Any ideas!?" Dana coughed.

"I can't breathe," Nicole gasped, doubling up. Rachael shook her. "You know this house! Can't we go out a window!? Nicole!"

Nicole nodded weakly. "Lara's room," she croaked.

Fortunately Lara had left her door closed. Once inside, they were able to catch their breath. But in the dark and confusion, the window refused to open.

"Nell locked them all with keys!" Nicole said.

"Out of my way!" Rachael ordered, picking up the desk chair. The crash of glass and the blast of freezing air gave Lara her first real hope that the five of them would see tomorrow. Dana led the way, dragging Mindy by her arms, followed by Rachael and Nicole. The door began to burn. Lara noticed the scarf the snowman had been wearing, lying on her bed. Realizing she was wasting precious seconds, she limped to the bed and, as the floor sagged ten degrees, secured the knitted wool around her neck. Her leap through the jagged window was so hurried that when she hit the icy wooden shingles she immediately fell on her rear end and slid right off the side of the house, burying her self deep in the snow. Moments later Nicole fell out of the sky and landed beside her. Rachael and Dana were dragging Mindy to safety like a side of beef.

"It's going to blow," Nicole said, struggling.

"I feel it, too," Lara said, helping her up.

They were fifty yards from the house, stumbling down a steep incline, when the world erupted in a deafening light. A giant's slap catapulted them head over heels toward suddenly brilliant trees. Lara felt as if she was flying rather than falling, and again briefly wondered if she were dead. Like a flying arrow, she pierced the crest of a drift. When she finally came to a stop and opened her eyes, she saw a spewing volcano top in place of the house. *Right, Nell, no evidence.*

"Hello!" she called.

"Over here!" Dana yelled, off to her right. Lara swam toward them, beginning to think that she must be invincible. The landscape was bathed in an enchanting, shifting blend of yellow, orange, and red, the temperature swiftly climbing. Mindy sat propped up between Dana and Rachael, a mist over half-opened eyes. "Why are you in my room, Lara?" she mumbled.

Rachael asked quietly, "Did Nicole get out?"

"She was right behind me," Lara said, searching. Would this night ever end? If the shock wave had thrown Nicole into a tree . . .

"I see her!" Rachael exclaimed. "Over there!" She began to reel, putting a hand to her head, sitting down. "You go, Lara. I don't think I want to see."

Lara understood. Near where Nicole lay unmoving, the snow was splattered with blood. The walk to her old friend seemed to take an eternity. Yet as she knelt by the young girl's head, she heard faint moaning. "It's me, Nicole. You're going to be okay."

"I am going to die," she whispered.

Lara squeezed her arms and said, as she had said years before, "I will not let you die."

Nicole smiled. "You told me that before."

Lara nodded. "And I was right, though I never knew it until now."

They were huddled around the unconscious Nicole when the old man with the sunburned face and white moustache walked down from the fires of the ruined house and asked if they would like a ride back to the lodge.

"The colonel," Lara beamed, surfacing from the depths of an exhausted trance. "You've come to rescue us."

He pulled off his gloves and checked Nicole's pulse at the neck, examining her. "This is bad," he muttered, removing his jacket and covering Nicole. "I have a radio in the tractor. I'm calling for a copter. Be back in a moment."

When he returned, Rachael asked him, "How did you get here so quick? The house only blew twenty minutes before you found us."

The colonel began to massage Nicole's legs. "Watching the football game in the bar, I got so drunk by the fourth quarter that I passed out. Can't hold my liquor like I used to. The bartender, Old Ed, he and I go way back. He just let me sleep. So when I woke up it was here in the middle of the night. I was heading back to my place when I stopped by the ranger on duty at the desk to chew the fat for a while. I'm actually retired five years now but I still like to keep my hand in to help pass the days. Anyway, this here fellow—McCormick was his name—was a new guy. I introduced myself, and we got to talking a spell—in fact, he asked if I had moved cars for you gals and I told him that I had—when this tall fellow, a shy overweight with a swollen jaw, comes in and says that he thought maybe there was some kind of trouble up at your place. He told us how he'd found one of you ladies half dead in the snow and how he'd returned you home but had a funny feeling about it. We gave a call up there but got no answer. Naturally I began to worry and thought I'd better take a ride up in the tractor. That guy—Cal, he called himself—wanted to come also but I wanted to keep room in case I was going to be giving any of you rides back down. Nice fellow, that Cal. Real conscience."

"Sure is," Lara said, thinking that he had probably saved her life twice.

Coming to at the mention of Cal, Mindy said, "I'm his girlfriend."

"Oh, God," Dana muttered.

"Which one of you was the one out in the snow?" the colonel asked.

"It was me," Lara said.

"What in heaven's name for?"

"Just for a breather," Lara said, searching the others, shaking her head slightly. "I got lost, wandered too far from the house, then couldn't find my way back."

The colonel nodded in understanding. "That can happen in these storms. But it looks like this one is weakening." A faint glow could be distinguished in the east. He glanced up, a mechanical roar tearing the night, fanning the flames, as a helicopter approached. "A pity, it was a fine old house. Any of you know what happened?"

Rachael went to speak. Lara stopped her with a slashing hand gesture that the colonel didn't see. "We all woke up with the smoke," Lara said. "There was fire everywhere. We don't know where it came from."

"You were all lucky to get out," the colonel said. Suddenly his jaw dropped as his face paled. "My Lord, weren't there six of you?"

"Yes." Lara bowed her head, touching Nicole. "Nell was our other friend. We did everything we could to save her. But it wasn't enough."

� Epilogue ⟿

Lara leaned against the hospital window on her tender nose, feeling the warmth of the barren sandy landscape beyond. The sky was a hard blue, allowing a clear view of the distant snowcapped peaks. The storm had passed.

"I'm back," Nicole said weakly from the bed.

Lara turned, silencing a pang of sympathy. Suspended on wires from the ceiling, both of Nicole's arms were heavily bandaged. Lara swung on crutches toward the bed. Her own knee needed cartilage surgery. Blood blisters from frostbite tipped her ten fingers. Her burned leg throbbed. Every breath reminded her of her cracked ribs.

"I was hoping that you would wake up before I left," Lara said, sitting on the edge of the bed.

"When is it?"

"Monday afternoon. You're at St. Vincent's, in the valley. You were flown here in an ambulance helicopter. Rachael,

Mindy, and I just got discharged today. My mother should be here in minutes to pick us up. How do you feel?"

"I'm alive," she said, shutting her bloodshot eyes. "Did it really happen?"

"Yes."

"Nell's—?"

"She's dead, yes."

Tears, and there would be more in the days to come. "You must hate her, Lara. You must think that she was insane. But to me, to me she was a good sister. She took care of me when I was sick. When I had pain, she would stay up all night and read to me. She wasn't what you think."

"I don't hate her. I was afraid that you would hate me for firing the flare."

Nicole shook her head, grimacing. "I'm going to miss her."

Lara took a tissue and wiped Nicole's cheeks. "So will I."

"Really?"

"I still think of her as a friend," Lara said honestly. Paradoxically, the feeling made the loss easier to bear.

"What did you tell them?" Nicole asked, hesitantly.

"The police know nothing. Officially it was an accident. There was no evidence to say otherwise."

"Thank you. Are my parents here?"

"Yes. They were waiting with me up until a few minutes ago. They went down to the cafeteria for a bite."

"Then they know that you know about me?"

"True. But about Nell, they know the same as the police."

Nicole was worried. "Will it always stay this secret?"

"The four of us have taken a solemn vow, and none of them would dare say a word with the skeletons I could drag out of their closets." Lara hugged her carefully. "In my house, if you like, you can still be Celeste." She kissed her forehead. "I have to go now, but I will come visit in a couple of days."

"Can I call you tonight?"

"Whenever you want." She ran her fingers through Nicole's curly auburn hair, silky like a child's. "How blind I was, only you're this beautiful. I love you, Nicole. I love both of you."

LIMPING OUT OF THE ELEVATOR INTO A HOSPITAL LOBBY, Lara saw Rachael and her mother talking to a handsome young gentleman. Rachael, a white bandage wrapped around the top of her head, had her hand on his shoulder and was laughing.

"Percy!" Lara called.

"Lara!"

She momentarily lost her crutches with his enthusiastic hello. His hug murdered her broken ribs, but it was worth it. "You look a mess," he laughed, gently touching the bandage on her face.

"Thanks a lot!"

"Seriously, are you okay?"

"I had the best brain surgeon on the West Coast. How did you get here?"

"I was so mad at Cal, I didn't talk to him until today. At six this morning, I called your home as we'd planned. Your dad answered. Sounded like I'd woken him up. I almost hung up! That was the first I'd heard of the *accident*." He hung on the last word, waiting, his face an unspoken question.

"It was a terrible accident," Lara said deliberately.

He understood, probably everything. "Always hard to lose a friend." She couldn't think of anything to say. "Anyway, your mother told me she was picking you up today. I sort of invited myself along."

"I'm glad you did."

That helped. She saw her mother approaching. "Hi, Mom!" she called.

Lara's mother was a nervous wreck. She shook as they touched, and began to cry when Nell's name was mentioned. So unfair for tragedy to strike their family twice. Lara prayed that Mr. and Mrs. Kutroff didn't appear. Mindy and Dana joined them in the midst of comforting each other. Mindy's arm was in a sling. The doctors promised a minimum of scarring. Dana hadn't even required hospitalization. Though she, too, had ended up ruining one fine pair of pants.

"We'd better hit the road," Dana said, after they had inquired after one another's health. "I have to have the van back by six."

"Mom and you didn't come together?" Lara asked.

"When I heard that she already had company," Dana said, poking Percy, "I thought that I'd better get Rachael myself."

"That was very thoughtful of you," Rachael said, with sugarcoated spikes in her voice.

"You don't have room for me?" Mindy asked.

"Not really," Dana said quickly.

"In a van?" Rachael said.

"We have room for another person," Lara's mother said. "Either of you girls could come back with us."

Lara's eyes rolled at the word *either*.

"Perfect," Dana said. "Mindy, you don't mind riding with them, do you?"

"Noo . . ."

Rachael frowned. "Why Mindy?"

"Why not Mindy?" Lara asked.

"Why not Percy?" Rachael mimicked. All eyes went to him.

"Hey, leave me out of this," he chuckled.

"Did Cal come with you?" Mindy asked Percy suspiciously.

"Here she goes again," Lara moaned.

"Not with us," Percy said innocently. Dana had

developed a sudden fascination with the lighting fixtures on the ceiling.

"Is Cal out in your car?" Mindy demanded of Dana.

"I didn't bring my car," Dana muttered.

"Is he out in your van?"

"Don't be ridiculous, Mindy," Lara said.

Mindy lost her wad of gum, accidently stomped her foot on it. "Is he!?"

Dana was fixing her blouse. "Well . . ." she began.

The coffee shop all over again.

With the exception of her mother, they all rode home in the back of Dana's van. Never a dull moment.

WEEKEND

❧ CHAPTER 1 ❧

THE ROAD WAS PAINFUL. LAST SUMMER'S HURRICANES had dug strategically placed potholes across the narrow asphalt highway. Every time their dusty Camry hit one — every sixty seconds — Shani Tucker's head kissed the car's ceiling. She wanted an aspirin, but they upset her stomach, and it was already worse off than her head. Long drives were not her forte. She wished that there was room in the front seat with Kerry and Angie, where at least it wouldn't have been quite as bumpy. But Angie was driving, and Kerry's hand was glued to the radio, searching vainly through static bands. Though the road was doing its best to slow them down, they were, nevertheless, too far south into Mexico to catch San Diego's stations. Glancing out the window at the brittle tumbleweed; the baked orange hills; and dry, cracked ravines, Shani felt as if she had crossed into another world, rather than merely into another country.

"Can't get anything on this damn thing," Kerry Ladd said, fretting as usual.

"Turn it off," Shani said. "I have a headache as it is."

"I've got to have music," Kerry said, sliding in a CD. A thumping beat filled the car. Kerry wasn't the most considerate of friends. But Shani didn't complain. The loud music was the lesser of two evils. Constant external distraction was necessary to keep strung-out Kerry from exploding.

"I've got to turn off the air conditioning, again," Angie Houston warned, wiping a long straight strand of blonde hair from her hazel eyes as she flipped a switch next to the radio. "We're beginning to overheat."

"I don't want to sweat," Kerry complained. With the cool air turned off, the rise in temperature was almost immediate.

"Do you want to walk?" Angie asked, turning down the song's volume. "Shani, how far do you think we have left to go?"

Shani studied the map her father had insisted she take. The trip from Santa Barbara to San Diego yesterday after school had been a breeze. They had checked into a Motel 6 and had gotten away early for what they had anticipated as a six-hour jaunt to Robin and Lena's vacation house located on the beach near Point Eugenia. Today was only Friday—unofficially, Senior Ditch Day—and they'd felt that they'd managed a good jump on the weekend's fun. But they were now over eight hours on the road, and making miserable time.

Odd, how they hadn't seen anyone else from their class

on the road. Supposedly, Robin and Lena had invited the whole gang.

"Well," Shani said, "we passed Point Blanco over three hours ago, and going by map inches, that's only a hundred miles from where we're supposed to turn off, so we should be getting close."

"Could we have passed it?" Angie asked.

"I haven't seen anything *to* pass," Shani said. "But no, Lena said that we'd see a Margarita Ville Canteen—that's the name she gave me—about half an hour before the dirt road that leads to her house. She said the canteen was impossible to miss."

There was no cell phone reception down here, so they had to rely on Lena's directions.

"What does Lena know?" Kerry grumbled. She hated Lena, and Lena hated her. If either one of them died this weekend from mysterious causes, Shani would not be terribly surprised. Only the promised presence of Sol Celaya—Kerry's ex, stolen away by Lena—had given Kerry the incentive to approach her archrival's house. At least, Sol was the reason why Shani figured Kerry had come. Despite having known her since first grade, Shani didn't altogether trust her. Kerry was too temperamental, too impulsive. But then again, she didn't trust Lena, either. God probably didn't trust Lena; she could be one shrewd terror.

"Don't start that again," Angie said.

"She had just better not hassle me," Kerry said.

"And you had just better not fight with her in front of her sister," Angie said.

"It sure was nice of Robin to organize this weekend," Shani said, wishing to change the subject.

"Yeah . . . it wa—was," Kerry agreed, stuttering, as she often did at odd moments. "How . . . how is . . . Robin?"

They—everyone at school—always asked her this question: How is Robin? Have you seen Robin? Is Robin better? Shani did not resent the concern, nor even the painful memories the questions always brought. After all, Robin was her best friend. It was only natural others should come to her for updates. What she did dislike was the false optimism she felt she had to project, to give them what they wanted to hear, and to salvage her own guilty conscience. But one sad day she would have to speak the truth, for then it would be too late: *Robin is dead. We killed her.*

"I talked to her on the phone Tuesday night," Shani said. "She sounded in good spirits, into getting everything organized. She was spending a fortune on food."

"Hope she isn't buying local," Angie chuckled. "But that's great she's feeling better."

"Yeah," Shani muttered. Didn't they understand that when your kidneys were gone, you didn't *get* better?

"Has she been singing much?" Kerry asked.

"I don't know. Probably," Shani lied. Lena had said

Robin's voice was all but gone. Prior to the accident, Robin could have rivaled professional singers.

"I wonder what her nurse is going to think of having all us wired teenagers sleeping on the beach outside their house," Angie said.

"The nurse won't be there," Shani said. "Lena can do the dialysis." Lena was Robin's sister. They were the same age, both of them having been adopted at infancy by Carlton Records emperor Charles Carlton. Mr. and Mrs. Carlton had no other children. They were getting to the stage in life where one had to shout at them to be heard. However, despite his wrinkles, Mr. Carlton, like so many other self-made millionaires, was intimidating. Whenever Shani talked to him, she always felt like a fool if she didn't agree with all his opinions — he had that kind of influence over people. Neither he nor his wife would be there this weekend. With their unlimited capital, they had bought Robin two dialysis machines, one for their mansion in Santa Barbara, the other for the beach house that was taking forever to get to.

When Mr. and Mrs. Carlton died, Lena and Robin would inherit a mint. At least Lena would.

"I wouldn't trust Lena to cut my nails," Kerry said.

"Ouch!" Shani said. They had hit another hole and her head had received another slap. "I understand that she's quite competent, has been trained by the doctors and all. The procedure is supposed to be simple."

"Hey!" Angie burst out suddenly. "Shani, I forgot to tell you! I called Park from the motel last night and guess who's riding down with him and Sol and Bert?"

"Who?"

"Guess!"

"Bono. I guessed, now tell me!"

"Flynn."

"Flynn!" Flynn Powers was the new boy in town, from England. He'd only arrived in February, at the semester break. He was a dream: curly brown hair; dark green eyes; a walk as smooth as liquefied charisma; and a hypnotic, accented voice that could literally put her in a trance. He had the largest hands, beautifully formed and eloquent; they could have been stolen from a Michelangelo. Everyone said it—even the guys. Flynn had something about him, an indefinable aura of depth that spontaneously commanded respect. He was neither tall nor well-built, but he was a babe. All the girls wanted him, and Shani was trying to get in front of the pack. Trouble was, he probably didn't even know she walked the earth. He didn't seem much interested in the girls at their school. Lena—she was an exception to everything—thought he was gay.

"Do you have a plan of approach?" Kerry asked. She was neutral as far as Flynn was concerned, as she was still trying to get Sol back.

"Jump on him, I don't know," Shani said, the concentration of acid in her stomach abruptly doubling. Thinking about doing anything made her nervous. Sometimes she swore she was getting an ulcer. She chewed Rolaids instead of gum. "What can I do?"

"What you suggested might work," Angie said.

"If I thought there was a chance, I would do it," Shani said, not taking herself seriously. She had to be the most sexually inexperienced girl in her senior class. She hadn't even "gone all the way" through a *Playgirl* magazine. Getting dates had been no problem, but the guys would only kiss her cheek at the end of the night, or else shake her hand; she had that kind of reputation. Perhaps she should talk to Lena, have a filthy rumor started in connection with her name. Not that she was obsessed — she was merely very, very interested in sex. What she really wanted was what all of them wanted: a relationship. Unfortunately, she had taken physics, and had received a good grade, and had won a scholarship to the University of California at Santa Barbara, and had listed "psychiatrist" as her ambition in the yearbook and had read too many of the classics, and had the repulsive habit of sounding intelligent, all of which was enough to make any adolescent male ego insecure. But in reality she had hated physics, and had gotten an A only because she had studied hard. She was not that smart, not that secure. Often, she felt lonely. Often, she watched Flynn from the other side of the campus, and wondered if he couldn't change all this.

"Accidentally lose your bikini top while swimming beside him in the waves," Angie said. "Better yet, lose your bottoms. It'll take a lot to catch that guy's cool eye."

To her own amazement, Shani realized she was actually considering the idea. She was afraid to say hello, but accidentally stripping seemed within her reach. "Is that how you got Park?" she asked. She had known Park Jacomini since they'd been two. He pretended to be intellectual—and *he was* smart, their class valedictorian—but there had never been born a more natural peeping tom. He was one of the closest people to her in the world.

Angie laughed. "That's personal. But I will tell you, to keep them, you've got to come up with pretty exotic —"

"Could we please change the subject?" Kerry interrupted, extremely agitated. Angie was quick to apologize.

"I'm sorry, Kerry. I'd forgotten. That was thoughtless of me."

"You said it to . . . upset me . . . on purpose."

"I'm the one who brought it up," Shani said. "Sorry."

Kerry turned off the music, leaned her head back, and closed her eyes, taking a deep breath. "I don't know what's wrong with me, I'm so jittery. I'm the one who should be apologizing. I guess it still bothers me."

"That's okay. We understand," Shani said.

From that point on, the conversation sort of died. The potholes thickened. Sentinel cacti and sleeping lizards bumped by while the Camry interior warmed and they sweated. To pass the time, Shani reached for her yearbook, browsing through the pages, reading notes from her friends and from those she had not spoken to during her entire four years at Hoover High. They had only received the book Tuesday, and there were still many she wanted to have sign it. This weekend would fill it up. She chuckled when she came to the place where Park had placed his note, across a full-page color picture of the varsity football team.

Dearest Shani,

Of all the girls I've known these four blissful years, you have been — with only a handful of exceptions — the closest one to my soul and body. If not for you, and two or three others, I would not be where I am, king of the class, the one voted least likely to end up on welfare. I owe all my magnificent accomplishments to you, and another girl or two.

I hope that when you become a psychiatrist that you don't discover that you're nuts. You see, I understand you — your dark lusty longings — and that would mean that I'm nuts, too, along with perhaps my close female friends. However, if in the middle of analysis you uncover deep Freudian inhibitions, feel free to come to me for relief, for the sexual freedom I have given to other girls of your like predicament, a few here and there.

All my love, all that Suzy and Bunny and Clairice have not drained, I give to you. And once again, if in the lonely years to come you should ever need — or simply desire — an intimate pal, be sure to think of Pretty Park (and friends) and make an appointment to visit us.

Love you (amongst others),
Park

Park had quite a wit, but, in his own way, street-tough Sol outdid him. Shani flipped to the picture of their pudgy, smiling school principal, whom Sol had practically obliterated with a thick, black permanent marker.

Hi!
I hardly know you and I don't think you're that interesting a chick, but you've got something I want and you know I've got something you need. If I let you see me, we don't go nowhere fancy and I expect my money's worth right from the start. I don't want to hear about your feelings and your goals cause I have no feelings and I can tell already you ain't going nowhere. If we get together, it will be for one thing only. My number's in the book. Look it up.

Wait a sec, this isn't Debbie's book? Hell! Pay no attention to what you just read, Shani dear. It sure has been grand knowing you and I just know deep in my heart that you will go far and better the world for all of mankind. I really feel that you are an "extra special person." I have found our friendship profoundly satisfying, and I will treasure your memory in the many days to come. God bless you!

Hey, by the way, Shani, how's about you calling me this summer and us getting together and going to a drive-in. I'll buy you popcorn, with butter. We can rock my van's shocks.

Love your legs,

Sol

She had better be careful not to let Kerry see his note. Thankfully, he hadn't written it on *that* page. Sol could be crude, but—once again, in his own way—he was also sensitive. Though he was now seeing Lena, he was extra careful to treat Kerry kindly. However, his politeness was a mixed blessing. Kerry took it as a sign that he was still interested in her. Neither Angie nor she wanted to drive home the harsh truth, that Kerry didn't stand an outside chance, hadn't from the moment Lena had curled her little finger and let Sol know she was available, hadn't from the day of that disastrous pep rally.

It wasn't that Kerry was ugly. Though on the short side and a few pounds overweight, she had a pleasant face and a fine figure, plus a genuinely striking smile, which she—sadly—flashed all too seldom. Lost somewhere between blonde and brunette, her short shag hair needed styling. But with a good cut and the right clothes—which neither she nor her parents could afford—she *could* have competed with almost any girl at school.

Except for Lena. Except for a perversely timed rip.

It happened in November, during the week preceding the homecoming game when they were to play their crosstown rivals and crown their new queen. Yet it had happened many times before, in cheap teenage exploitation films, the thoughtless kind without a shred of realism or warmth. Perhaps that was what had made the trick seem so especially base. However, though the fundamental idea had been boringly simple, its implementation had never been so wickedly crafty.

In those days, Sol was going with Kerry. When he was not cutting classes, they could be seen laughing hand-in-hand, one of the few happy couples on campus. Now Lena already disliked Kerry from eons past, and she began to take a fancy to Sol, and spread hints to the effect, thinking that would be sufficient. It probably would have been, but Lena wasn't used to waiting. When Sol didn't immediately come running into her arms, she *apparently* decided to hasten his breakup with Kerry. To this day, Lena's guilt had not been definitely established. However, few believed her expressed innocence. Simply no one at school had the mind to hatch an elaborate, evil plot—other than Lena—and the facts pointed a mighty guilty finger her way.

Along with Angie and Robin, Kerry was a cheerleader. In honor of the homecoming festivities, they had developed a new routine to perform at the pep rally to be held at lunchtime in the gym, the day before the big game. It involved the usual bouncing through the air and spread-eagled stretching. Lena was well aware of the specifics of the routine. Though not a member of any cheering squad—she had passed such adolescent displays, so she said—she contributed, through her sister, extra twists. One of Lena's exotic suggestions was the straw that broke the camel's back, the twist that tore the panties.

Because the cheerleaders' uniforms were warm and Santa Barbara was sunk in a rare heat wave, the girls wore regular clothes to the morning classes, leaving their uniforms in their gym lockers. While on her way to the locker room at the start of lunch, Kerry was stopped by Lena, who wanted to chat. Under normal circumstances, Kerry would not have had the slightest inclination to "chat" with Lena, and now that she was in a hurry to change, she was less anxious. Nevertheless, Lena succeeded in delaying her to the point where Kerry was cutting it close. To top it off, as they parted company, Lena *accidentally* spilt her Coke on Kerry's shorts, the soft drink soaking through to her underwear. No big problem, though Kerry was mad. She was going to change into her uniform in a minute, anyway. The only difference now was that she *probably* wouldn't be able to wear her underwear. When Kerry reached the locker room, she rushed into her uniform, not having a chance to take note of any irregularities.

The pep rally started like so many other boring pep rallies. The punchy football coach strutted to the microphone and mumbled a couple of slow lines about how smart — football-wise — their team was this year, and introduced a few key players that everyone already knew. Shani was sitting in the front row of the audience with Park. They cheered loudly for good-natured "Big Bert" — an unusual member of their unusual gang — but otherwise they were hardly listening. It was only when the cheerleaders came on that she sat up and took notice. Of course, three of her friends were in the group, but perhaps she also had a premonition of danger, for her stomach had begun to ache like it did when she was worrying deeply. Park also stirred to life. His girlfriend, Robin — whom he supposedly loved very much — was the leader of the group. He had his camera primed and was clicking away the second they launched into their routine. Even then, Shani had felt that he had taken an unusually high number of pictures of Angie.

In the middle of the skit, Kerry flew spread-eagled over Robin's shoulders and Shani thought she heard a rip. But at first she decided that she must have been mistaken, for no one else appeared to have heard anything. Then a low murmur began to spread through the audience, a sound that quickly built to loud whistles and hoots. This was an example of how fast gossip could spread, for, although she was sitting in the front, and although the cheerleaders' dresses were short, Shani could see nothing unusual as far at Kerry was concerned. Neither could Park — Shani asked him twice what was going on. But a few people, probably only a handful in the entire crowd, had *thought* they had caught a flash of Kerry's bare bottom. Afterwards, of course, there were *dozens* of guys who *swore* they were one of the chosen few. The fact that they were *all* liars made no difference. Ironically, Kerry was probably the last one in the gym to know there was a problem. The song they performed to continued on, though it was practically drowned out in the commotion, and Kerry continued to swirl and twist and bend, not noticing any draft. Shani finally got the word through the grapevine of what was *supposedly* happening, and then it seemed ages to her before Kerry found out. In reality, from the moment of the rip to the instant of her bewildered halting, possibly twenty seconds had elapsed. It was Angie who finally stopped her and whispered something in her ear, probably just a line to get Kerry to leave the gym as quickly as possible. Angie even escorted her to the door. As they crossed the basketball court floor, the audience granted them a brief respite. But the second they were out of view, they flew back into ecstasy.

Shani left her place in the stands and hurried to the girls' showers. There she found Kerry slumped on the bench that ran in front of the lockers, Angie standing nearby. The place was otherwise deserted. Kerry was more confused than upset. She did not understand what the big deal was. Her dance pants had ripped and she had flashed her underwear. So what? Shani agreed with her that there was nothing to worry about. She was lying. She didn't tell Kerry that those flesh-colored panties she'd been wearing could be mistaken for bare flesh, at a distance. That they *had* been mistaken for Kerry's backside, by more than one person.

As Kerry began to change into her street clothes, muttering about how she hoped the confusion would get cleared up quickly, the three of them made an interesting discovery. Someone had replaced Kerry's nylon dance pants with blue cotton *paper* pants of the same size. No wonder they had ripped. Normally, Kerry would have immediately spotted the switch. But she had been in a hurry before the pep rally, and hadn't detected the difference in the fabrics.

When Kerry remembered how Lena had soaked her underwear, forcing her to be late, Shani immediately put two and two together. The connection was obvious. Lena must have figured Kerry would discard the wet panties. Lena must have also been the *someone* who had switched the dance pants. She had undoubtedly been hoping that Kerry would be caught flashing her bottom. This fortunately hadn't happened, but it easily could have. Lena later denied the accusations, but she did so with a sly smile, and her deepest admiration for whoever had thought up the plan.

In the following days, Angie and Shani told anyone who would listen that Kerry *had* been wearing underwear beneath her dance pants. Few believed the truth; they apparently preferred not to. Kerry had to endure ceaseless catcalls. She also lost Sol to Lena. Shani had been disgusted with him for deserting Kerry in her hour of need, but he swore that the pep rally incident had absolutely nothing to do with their breakup. He explained that Lena had simply made him an offer that he couldn't refuse.

SHANI CHECKED ON KERRY IN THE FRONT SEAT BEFORE opening the yearbook to page fifty-eight. As a further example of how unreal Kerry's "flash" had been, there had been at least a dozen people taking pictures at that pep rally and not one of them had caught anything even remotely X-rated. Nevertheless, tucked in one corner there was a small black-and-white picture that had captured all but the "highlight" of the afternoon. It had been taken from the rear of the audience, and showed the crowd on its feet laughing and pointing at an innocent smiling Kerry, whose life was about to come to an end. There was nothing for the guys to gloat over, but it clearly brought back the day. Park had been on the yearbook staff. Shani would have to speak to him about who had allowed the picture in the yearbook.

Was it a coincidence, Shani often asked herself, that Robin's accident had happened less than a month after Kerry's humiliation?

"Hey girls," Angie said. "Looks like we're no longer alone. Sol's van is just up ahead."

Shani tossed the yearbook aside and peered between Angie and Kerry. The glare of the blazing sun made seeing difficult, but it was clearly Sol's faded black Dodge. Farther down the road, perhaps a half mile, was a solitary brown clay building, probably the Margarita Ville Canteen. That meant they were almost there. But who cared? Huddling near the rear of the van, beside Sol and Park, was a guy with the smoothest walk this side of England.

"Flynn!" Shani cried.

"God, Shani, not in my ear," Angie said.

Shani grabbed her Rolaids and downed the whole roll as if it were candy. The furnace in her stomach roared on unchecked. She had been dying to see Flynn again, yet, all of a sudden, she wished that she was invisible.

CHAPTER 2

"THIS TIRE ISN'T GETTING LESS FLAT WITH US LOOKING at it," Park said.

"Why didn't you go to the cantina down the road with Bert and Flynn?" Sol asked.

"I still can. Why don't you come with me?"

"I have to guard my van. No way I trust the Cholos down here."

"You're a Cholo."

"Used to be," Sol muttered, lighting a cigarette. Sol chain-smoked.

Park was tempted to split. The inside of their lame van was incredibly stuffy, and out here on the broken asphalt it was like standing on a frying pan. They had a much brighter sun down here than they did in the States. His nose would peel this weekend. It would probably rot and fall off. He sure could use a cold beer. Unfortunately, the strap on his sandals—his only available footwear—had snapped and it was a good ten-minute walk to the canteen. He should have taken Big Bert up on his offer to carry him. He knew Sol was intentionally mocking him, standing barefoot on the blistering pavement. Sol had feet like a caveman.

"Why don't we check on your spare?" Park asked for the third time.

Sol chuckled, the sound oddly frightening coming from him. But Shani knew Sol just acted tough on the outside. The truth was, he had a heart of gold. Park could attest to the fact that he had a heart, but it was made of a far less precious metal. Sol was tough to the core. Brought up in L.A.'s barrios, he'd once admitted to stabbing his *first* person—a member of a rival gang—at the age of twelve. He had never said it outright, but Park had the clear impression that not everyone who had gotten in his way was still alive. He'd been arrested twice in his fifteenth year; once for stealing a car, the other time for carrying a gun—a sawed-off shotgun. He hadn't told him these stories to impress him. Sol didn't give a damn what anyone thought. Park knew the horrors he'd related had only been the tip of the iceberg.

Once, old friends—the meanest, most wired Cholos he'd ever seen—had visited Sol while they were playing a rough game of one-on-one at the school yard on a Saturday afternoon. Both wore wads of jewelry and picked at their oily nails with shiny switchblades, talking in guttural Spanish with Sol about Satan only knew what. In the midst of the conversation, they said something that bothered Sol and he snapped at them. They paled noticeably and apologized frantically, like their lives depended on it, which may well have been the case. Afterwards, Sol explained that they had made an obscene reference to Park. The loyalty hadn't comforted Park.

Park wasn't sure how Sol's father had managed to get his two children — Sol had a ten-year-old sister of which he was maniacally protective, the cutest little thing — out of the barrios; probably hard work. Mr. Celaya currently had a flourishing gardening business in Ventura. But apparently, he hadn't felt that Ventura was far enough north of his son's friends. He rented a house on the outskirts of Santa Barbara, and Sol ended up in laid-back Hoover High like a wolf among sheep.

Park still remembered the first day they ran into each other — literally. Sol had knocked him out of his way in the hall. Initially, no one could understand his Spanglish, and it was probably just as well, for in the first few days, he seemed one angry young man. But first impressions are not always complete. The passage of a couple of weeks presented a different profile. Sol had his mean streak, and it cut pretty deep, but he could also be kind, and no one could doubt his intelligence. A month after arriving at Hoover High, after a couple of expulsion threats from the principal, he apparently made a firm personal decision to develop his positive qualities, and to only behave like an animal when he could get away with it. The most immediate demonstration of this decision was the change in the way he spoke. He would never be mistaken for an upper-middle-class white boy, but he developed a knack for using English concisely. And damn if he didn't take to spending hours in the library. He wasn't easy to fit in a category. Of course, he seldom returned a book.

At the end of his junior year, he went out for track and smashed the shot-put record. His bulging muscles and blinding reflexes made him a natural at the event. Park was also on the team—he ran a mediocre mile—but what really brought them together was Sol's sudden discovery of surfing. Before moving to Santa Barbara, he once confessed, he hadn't even seen the ocean and he'd despised, because of his upbringing, anything associated with the word *surfing*. Yet the sea proved an asylum to him that seemed to wash away the weight of past cares. Park had already won two minor surfing championships. Hearing of Sol's interest in the waves, he boldly loaned him a board and taught him a few tricks of the trade. Soon they were surfing together regularly. Park still wasn't sure what Sol liked about him outside of his skill on the waves. He had asked once, and Sol had said that hanging around with the school brain was good for his "tough-but-heart-of-gold-guy image." On the other hand, Park didn't fully understand what he liked about Sol. Certainly, there wasn't anyone else quite like him.

Shani didn't know anything about Sol's background.

She didn't know that five days ago he'd been kicked out of his father's house and was now sleeping in the park in his van. She didn't know that he was low on money and was looking to his old ways to get some. Without explanation, while driving through Tijuana, Sol had dropped Park, Flynn, and Bert off for an hour. Afterwards, he had only allowed ever-agreeable Bert to sit in the back, with strict orders that he not touch or smell anything. Why didn't Sol want him to check on the spare? Probably because he'd dumped the tire and jammed the space with illicit substances. Sol was reading his mind.

"What's the matter, Preppy Park?" he asked. "Don't you trust me?"

Sol had taken to putting "Preppy" before Park's name, since Harvard had written saying that one Park Christopher Jacomini looked like Ivy League material to them. Park did not resent the title. It reminded him of that old movie, *Love Story*. He strongly identified with the main character. He also had an annoying rich dad, and also was going to go to Harvard, and also wanted to be a lawyer and marry a girl with a hot body. He even fancied that he resembled the main character, somewhat. Angie said that he did. Of course, she was always quick to flatter. Robin hadn't done that . . . hadn't needed to.

Before she'd been hurt, Robin had had a hot body. And he'd always figured that he would have married her. She had been — still was — the one with the heart of gold. He glanced south down the road, in the direction where she waited to see him again. He didn't want to think about it. People his age got busted for smoking dope, they got depressed and made fools of themselves over meaningless crushes, they got lousy grades and hated their parents. But they didn't die, not in his world. They couldn't die slowly and take a piece of him with them. God, how he hated himself for having left her for Angie! But what could he do? He simply couldn't handle it. Was this the real reason he identified with the main character in *Love Story*? What can you say about an eighteen-year-old girl who died. . . .

Park kicked the flat tire. "What the hell. I don't care if we ever get there."

Sol went right on reading his mind. Blowing smoke in his face, he said, "You're such a wimp."

"Just because I won't go back across the border with you and your stash?"

"Who said I picked up anything? But don't change the subject. A real man would stand by his babe when she's in a tight spot. Robin's a great chick. She gets in trouble and you dump her." Sol spat.

"You should talk," Park snapped, throwing all caution aside. "What about Kerry and tight spots?"

"That was not the same. Kerry got humiliated, and we all felt bad for her, but it was only a joke. Dying is . . . it's no joke." He added quietly, "I know."

Park wondered at the change in his tone. Probably a memory of a friend stuck with a bloody knife had surfaced. Park pulled off his shirt, and wiped the sweat from his face. "I'll have a talk with her," he said.

"If that's the best you can do, then do it."

Park wanted to change the subject. Peering in the direction of the canteen, he remarked: "What are those guys doing? They've been gone awhile."

"Probably getting drunk."

"I don't think Flynn drinks."

"Bert will down enough beer to make up for him."

"Hey, Sol, what do you think of that Flynn?"

"I don't think he's a wimp."

"Give me a break, would ya?"

Sol patted his cheek lightly. Up close, Sol's features were thick and fearsome; however Park had to admit he was probably handsome. Strangely enough, he looked part Slavic—his mouth especially, which was large and sensual. Also, his dark hair had a hint of red, and fine curls that girls loved to run their fingers through. But his sharp black eyes; his calculating expressions; and swollen, tattooed biceps were clearly from the wrong side of the tracks.

"Okay, Preppy," he said. "I don't know nothing about him. He hardly talks. And besides, who cares?"

"I sometimes wonder about him. He looks—it's weird—he looks familiar."

"Yeah, now that you mention it," Sol said thoughtfully, then shrugging. "But who cares?"

"I can see that you don't. I wonder why he came to Santa Barbara."

"Probably for the climate."

"You're a hopeless degenerate. I don't know why I associate with you."

"Because hanging around me makes you look more interesting to the chicks than you really are."

Park thought that was pretty funny, if not true. "How's Lena been treating you?"

Sol groaned, but before he could elaborate, his eyes narrowed. "Someone's coming."

Park turned. Approaching from the weed-choked desolation of a nearby eastern hill was a tall Indian, clothed in a tan tunic tied at the waist with an orange sash. His long stringy hair was the same color as his robe, bordering a deep red beardless face that disallowed an accurate age guess. He seemed to have come out of nowhere. The uneven ground and dry shrubs at his dusty, sandaled feet did little to slow his floating gait. A hundred feet directly over his head, a blackbird circled. A minute, and he would reach them.

"Who is he?" Park whispered.

"He's Indian, maybe. . . . He has that look. Maybe he's a holy man."

"A what?"

"Not like at church. A sorcerer. Treat him with respect. I'll do the talking."

"Good. I don't speak Spanish."

Sol threw away his cigarette. The man was fifty yards away and the next moment he was standing before them. The blackbird had vanished. Their visitor's eyes seemed to focus through them, or rather, they appeared turned inward, as though he saw them from an Unusual perspective. Park felt as though he was being subjected to a thorough scrutiny. However, it was not an uncomfortable feeling.

"Puedo ayudarle, senor?" Sol said.

"Has traido ayuda y odio contigo," the man answered. Park had expected a dry rasp but the voice was smooth and melodious. A closer inspection of his face revealed lines from long years, yet his skin retained a surprisingly soft sheen. A flawlessly straight, but at ease, posture contributed to his youthful bearing.

"What's going on?" Park muttered.

"I asked if we could help him," Sol replied. He seemed unable to break away from the man's eyes. They *were* strangely fascinating.

"And?"

"He said something like, we've brought help and hate with us."

"Great. If only we had an anthropologist with us to figure that one out." But though he spoke in jest, the man's words had sent a cold shiver through his spine; quite a feat in this heat.

"Shut up," Sol said. He spoke to the man: *"Hay problema?"*

The man gestured south with his covered left hand, which perhaps held something, hidden beneath the folds of his gown. *"Paloma petirrojo. Culebra. Culebra. Veneno. Veneno."*

Park noted Sol's right hand sliding slowly toward the pocket where he carried his switchblade. Sol had a sensitive antenna for danger. Nice voice or not, Park took a step back. Sol said, *"No comprendemos. Explique usted!"*

In answer, the man jerked free a blackbird, letting it fly in their faces. Sol had his knife in hand and open in an instant, but the bird did not attack them. It screeched loudly as it wheeled into the sky, vanishing south into the glare of the sun. Trying to settle his pounding heart, Park noticed Flynn coming up the road from the direction the bird had disappeared. For a moment he imagined Flynn had grown wings and a beak. The sun must be short-circuiting his brain. Rubbing his eyes, he snapped at Sol. "What the hell was that for?"

"Cuervo. Águila. Culebra veneno. Petirrojo," the man said, undisturbed by the blade pointed his way. Sol lowered it in measured steps, frowning.

"I asked him if something was wrong. And he rattles

on about a dove, an eagle, a robin, and a snake. You saw what happened when I asked him to explain."

"Don't put your knife away," Park advised, the man smiling faintly at his remark. Despite his fear, he did not feel a danger from the man per se. But that damn bird could have pecked their eyes out. He asked, "What was that last thing he said?"

"More of the same: raven, eagle, snake, robin."

"Wait a second. Does he mean robin the bird, or Robin the person?"

"Robin the bird. I don't think there is a Robin name in Spanish."

"Ask him anyway."

Sol pressed a button. His blade vanished. But he kept the knife handy. *"Tú conoces a Robin Carlton?"*

"Hermana," he said, holding up one hand. *"Hermano,"* he added, pointing to where the bird had disappeared.

"Sister . . . brother," Sol muttered. "He doesn't know her."

"Ask him if she's going to be all right."

"I said, he doesn't know her."

"Ask him if he knows where we can get our flat fixed."

But the old man was already speaking, shaking his head sadly. *"Veneno. Culebra. Veneno. Culebra."*

"I don't suppose those were directions to a Shell Station."

Sol was wary, puzzled. "He's going on about poison and snakes."

"I wonder why."

He probably shouldn't have asked. An unmistakable rattle started in the dry bush ten feet at his back. Park looked—and looked again—and found a snake slithering right for his foot. He knew he couldn't outrun a grizzly, but he'd never read about rattlesnakes. It didn't matter, anyway. His trusty, well-educated reflexes had him frozen on the spot. It took a hard shove from Sol to get him out of the fang's crosshairs. The snake swam in between them, divide and bite, its pointed head and tongue snapping at both of them. The old man was forgotten.

"What should we do?" Park cried.

"Don't panic."

"I'm already panicked!"

"Don't let it bite you."

Park backed up several paces, moving to his left to place the van between him and the serpent. Unfortunately, the snake seemed to like the smell of him better. It slid beneath the rim of the flat tire with its mouth open and hungry. Park knew intellectually that he should turn and run, but his upper-class, manicured body would not cooperate. *It* thought that the moment *it* turned *its* back, *it* would get a huge chunk out of the back of *its* calf. And maybe *it* was right. The snake seemed to keep its distance—six feet—as long as he didn't move.

"Are you trying to stare it down?" Sol asked, picking up a hefty rock and creeping closer. The snake, bent on Caucasian meat, was leaving its flank unprotected, or so it seemed.

"Where's your knife?"

"You can't kill a snake like this with a knife." With both hands, Sol raised the rock over his head. Still, their assailant paid him no heed.

"Why aren't you carrying a gun when we need one?"

Sol whipped down his stone with a force sufficient to crack the miserable road. But the snake had only been baiting him. This was Mexico; it wanted a Mexican. It was not in the rock's path, but rather, incredibly, was closing its teeth on the hem of Sol's faded blue jeans. Sol made the best possible move, which was to trounce its midsection with his free leg. This caused the snake to lose its grip, and Sol scampered back, but he did so hastily and stumbled on an ill-placed rock. He ended up flat on his back. Rearing up its slimy head and hissing with glee, the snake charged. Sol's heavily calloused feet wouldn't be armor enough. Park felt sick. Too late his friend was reaching for his knife when the snake made an unstoppable lunge at his exposed right ankle.

"Sol!" Park cried.

A gun exploded.

The snake tore into bloody halves.

Resetting the safety, Flynn slipped a small black

pistol back in his belt, covering it with the tail of his white silk shirt. Lying on the road, with his head twisted around, Sol asked, "Where did you learn to shoot like that?"

Flynn smiled the charming smile that made the girls sigh, and Park nauseous with jealousy. But he couldn't begrudge him this time. "I usually can't hit a Coke can at five feet," Flynn said.

Park regained the use of his legs and came over and helped Sol up. "That was close. Did he catch any flesh?"

Sol brushed off his T-shirt, and shook his head, his tough, external cool somewhat ruffled. Only Flynn seemed unshaken. Park couldn't believe the guy. Sol slapped Flynn's shoulder. "Thanks, man, I owe you one."

Flynn looked at his kill with a mixture of curiosity and disgust. Already, flies buzzed about the remains. "That's okay; I just won't chip in for gas on the way home."

"Fair enough."

"And I owe you one," Park told Sol.

"Yeah. Say you fix me up with Angie for a couple of nights and we'll call it even."

Park laughed, realizing he was still shaking. "Only if I get Lena."

"You don't know what you're asking," Sol said. "Lena's worse than a snake. She's got nails along with teeth."

"Do you always carry a gun?" he asked Flynn. They knew little about him: He was from England, had his own apartment, no family, drove an old VW, played tennis, spoke seldom.

"Whenever I'm in a foreign country."

California was a foreign country to Flynn. Sol snapped, "It's none of your business."

"It's no problem," Flynn said smoothly. "I'd tell you more, but there's nothing to tell."

Park didn't believe him. His marksmanship hadn't been blind luck. He was a practiced shot. Park wondered what Flynn had practiced for.

This was weird. Here he is on a fun-and-games weekend outing, and two of his buddies are carrying deadly weapons. "I didn't mean to pry," Park said.

"No problem," Flynn repeated.

"Well, I guess the old man must have seen the snake coming and was trying—" Park paused, looked around. "Hey, where is that guy?"

"Over there." Sol pointed in the direction from which the man had come. He had already reached the bluff of the neighboring hill, and was disappearing over the other side. He must have run. "Man, that cat can move," Sol said.

"Did you talk to him?" Flynn asked casually.

"Sol did. He only spoke Spanish."

"What did he say?" Flynn asked.

Sol shrugged. "A bunch of crap."

"I'm curious. Tell me," Flynn insisted.

But at that moment, they saw Angie's blue Camry,

weaving a path that failed miserably to miss the many potholes. Kerry and Shani were with her. Park felt dismayed at his lukewarm reaction to their rescue. Of course, having an alternative ride was no major relief. Sol had had them on the road at five in the morning, but they all knew it was only a matter of time before others from their class stumbled by. Sure he was happy to see Angie, but meeting her here so close to Robin made him feel guilty. What would the weekend be like? He also had to worry what Shani thought, though she had never so much as hinted that she thought he had stabbed Robin in the back by dumping her so soon after the accident. In fact, he was actually happier to see Shani approaching, than Angie. Often he wished that it was she he was attracted to, and vice versa.

With the possible exception of Lena, Shani was the prettiest girl in the school. She was too thin, and her breasts were nothing to grab—Sol had tried once—but her hair was as black as the old man's raven, toppling in a curling cascade to her butt, and Mother Nature had granted her facial structure every break. Park had often admired her innocent, pondering profile. Junk food had no part in her diet. Consequently, the glowing skin he'd appreciated even in grade school had passed, unmarred, into young womanhood. But her claim on the hearts of Hoover High's male population was due to her eyes. They were a shade of dawn's darkest, clearest blue, like large, round mountain lakes an hour before sunrise. Yet with all this, Shani saw herself as nothing more than a bag of bones with a boring personality. True, she did bore him on occasion, but then, he had known her a long, long time. Kissing her was like kissing his sister, and he didn't even have a sister. He supposed that leading her home early by the hand in kindergarten, with her pants soiled—his free hand blatantly clasping his nose—had ruined the romance at the beginning. Whenever he reminded her of the incident, every other week, she would get terribly embarrassed. Despite all this, he had once tried to seduce her. Afterwards, she hadn't even realized that he had made the effort. She was a good girl.

Angie was attractive also, but in a more traditional, less exotic fashion. A bleached blonde, she had a tan in midwinter and brown legs longer than his own. He didn't know what color her eyes were, but they were nice. Yet they never had that much to talk about. Only when she had her clothes off was she really interesting. Not that she was dumb—she had a B average and planned on going to college—but there was nothing in her personality that stood out. She was like a collage of her friends: a bit of Shani's charm, an ounce of Kerry's nervousness, a glimmer of Robin's sweetness, a slice of Lena's craftiness, all lumped together with no definitive result. He doubted she loved him—though she had murmured the three words—so he did not feel absolutely terrible about not loving her. He liked and respected her; that was enough. Love, he had decided, was something he was incapable of.

Laughing, the three girls drove right by them. Only when Sol jumped into the center of the road and shouted something obscene in Spanish did they return in high-speed reverse. Park put his shirt back on, his pulse still not settled from the wrestling match with the snake. Angie was the first out of the car. She smiled and waved and hugged and kissed him. He reminded himself to tell her later not to do such things in front of Robin. He hugged her in return, briefly.

"We've got to quit meeting this way," he said.

"But it's so romantic," Shani laughed, coming up. "Mind if I butt in?" she asked Angie before planting a quick kiss on his lips. She tasted like Rolaids.

Angie shook her head, took his hand, not looking altogether pleased. "I don't mind."

Sol got Shani next, hugging her like he might eat her, while Kerry remained aloof. But then he grinned slyly at Kerry, and said, "Hey, babe, why don't you just slide on over here and give me a big . . . give me a little taste?"

It was an absurd line, but Kerry smiled with happiness, and Park was glad. Kerry didn't have Shani's brightness or Robin's warmth, and she was too quick to gossip, but he felt she was essentially a good kid who'd had to beat a pretty tough rap this year. He had always wished that it had been Lena's butt they had seen. Besides probably having a far more stimulating rear, she would have *enjoyed* having an excuse to flash her goods.

Without batting an eye, Sol tried to give Kerry a quick feel right there in front of them. "Animal!" she squealed in delight, making a halfhearted attempt to slap him.

"You know it," Sol said.

"Some things never change," Park muttered.

"Some things do," Shani whispered, standing close by. He glanced at her, surprised. For a moment she seemed sad. But then she turned away, toward Flynn, and he could feel her tremble. He knew she was wild about Flynn, but had sworn a vow not to leak the news, which he had no intention of breaking. Flynn had watched their reunion from a detached distance. Now he stepped forward, nodding slightly like an English officer. He always appeared in perfect control.

"Hi, Shani," he said.

"Hi! I didn't know you knew me — I mean — knew my name." She blushed. "How are you, Flynn?"

"Fine."

"I'm happy to . . . ahh . . . that you're fine."

"I'm happy to see you," he said, the perfect gentleman.

Shani bowed her head, embarrassed. "Oh."

"You should have been here a few minutes ago," Park said. "Flynn saved Sol's life. He killed that rattlesnake over there just when it was about to bite Sol's ugly feet."

"Really!!?" the three girls cried.

"I wouldn't say that," Flynn said, winking at Sol.

"Nah, that snake was dead when we got here," Sol said.

"What?" Park said.

"I touched it with the tip of my shoe," Flynn said, feigning confusion, "but that was all."

"What are you talking about, Park?" Sol asked. "I don't have ugly feet."

"We can tell that Flynn's brave by looking at him," Angie said. "We don't need your wild tales."

"What?"

"It sure is gross-looking," Shani observed. "It looks like it was shot in two."

"Must have been someone handy with a gun," Flynn said.

"A marksman," Sol agreed.

"Looks like it's been dead awhile," Kerry said.

"What?"

"Would you stop that?" Angie said, getting annoyed. She gestured to Sol's van. "Did you get a flat?"

"No, a snake bit the tire," Park grumbled. Sol must have wanted to abide by Flynn's obvious wish not to have to talk about his gun. Or else Sol wanted to make a fool of him. Or both.

"Do you have a spare?" Shani asked.

"Not with me," Sol said, laughing at Park.

"Before we left," Kerry said, "my father gave us one of

those cans that can inflate a tube and seal any small holes. Would that help?"

"With all these dangerous snakes around here," Sol said, pulling out a cigarette, "it might end up being a lifesaver."

Everyone laughed except Park. He was not amused, but he was sure it was bad karma. He was always playing practical jokes on others. Maybe it was his turn.

Angie fetched the can from the Camry's glove compartment. Kneeling by the flat tire, Sol read the instructions softly to himself in Spanish. White foam squirted briefly over the tube's nipple as he secured the can's tip into place. Thirty seconds later, the tire had regained a semblance of its former roundness.

"Will it hold?" Angie asked.

"We should be able to get to the house," Sol said, kneading his thumb into the tire.

"Where's Bert?" Kerry asked. Bert liked Kerry. He liked everyone. Kerry *used* Bert. So did everyone. Bert liked being used.

"Consuming mass quantities," Park said.

"No, here he comes," Flynn said.

There were those who said that Big Bert Billings was not a genius. Those were the same people who said the Leaning Tower of Pisa was not straight and that the earth was round—typical unimaginative fools. Italy was crooked, the tower was fine, and everybody of consequence knew the astronauts' photos of Earth had been touched up. Bert was obviously a genius. Who could lead the basketball league in rebounds and not be able to jump more than three inches straight up, never mind his two hundred and fifty pounds and six-foot-five height? Who could get to only a minute left in the SAT, be only half done, and guess at the remainder of the questions and end up with a high score, never mind the black market test complete with answers in his lap? Bert was simply humble. He hid his intelligence, so well in fact that he couldn't remember exactly where he had put it. Everybody loved Bert. He was awfully big.

Bert was walking reasonably straight up the swaying road, managing to keep his half-inch-long blond hair out of his wild blue eyes. Usually, he was rather fair, but this afternoon gallons of alcohol-saturated blood were pumping through his cheeks. Usually when Bert saw you again, he slapped you heartily on the back. One could end up in the hospital after saying hello to Bert. He waved excitedly to them. They would have to have been heartless not to wave back.

"Boy, am I glad to see you!" he shouted, coming up. His volume dial was broken at ten. "I thought you guys might have left without me!" He went to slap Sol's back. Sol hadn't moved so fast for the snake. Sol was strong, but he wasn't built like the Statue of Liberty.

"Why would we have left you?" Sol breathed from a safe distance.

Bert noticed they had company. "Hi ya, girls!"

"Hi ya, Bert!" the three replied in unison.

Bert rubbed his massive hands together eagerly. He positively stunk of beer. "Boy, have I got a story for you folks! I'd just gotten out of the canteen, and was walking back here, when this snake came out of the weeds and tried to bite me!"

"Really?" Park asked, incredibly pleased. "What did you do?"

"I stomped on it, and kicked it," Bert beamed. "Tore it right in two."

"Oh, no," Park groaned, as the others broke up in laughter.

⌇ CHAPTER 3 ⌇

SOL'S VAN WAS STILL IN THE REARVIEW MIRROR, SO THE tire must be holding up. Shani hadn't realized that they still had so far to go from where they had joined the guys. They had left Margarita Ville twenty miles behind and there was still no sign of the road Lena had mentioned. Lena's thirty minutes past the canteen was probably in an expensive, high-powered Porsche in fifth gear when the road was in one piece.

Their caravan had undergone personnel rearrangements. Kerry had wanted to ride in the van with Sol, and Angie had wanted Park to ride in the Camry with them. No one had objected. To give Angie a chance to devote all her attention to Park—who needed a lot of attention lest he get lonely—Shani had taken over the role of chauffeur. Every time she hit a pothole, Park's head would smack the ceiling. She would have laughed each time it happened, but Flynn was sitting three feet to her right, and she was having enough trouble breathing.

She was trying to start a conversation, but he was terribly quiet.

"I bet the weather down here is a lot different than it is in England," she said, thinking that was probably the dumbest thing she had ever said.

"England's much cooler," Flynn said pleasantly, his accent far less noticeable than when he had first arrived at school.

"Where are you from, exactly?"

"Southern England."

"What city?"

He hesitated. Perhaps she was being nosey. "Plymouth."

"Do your parents live there?"

"My mother does."

She would *not* ask if they were divorced. "I've never been to England, or anywhere outside of California." *That* was the dumbest thing she had ever said. "I mean, except to Mexico . . . this place . . . today, that is." She took a deep breath. "Why did you come to Santa Barbara? Am I asking too many questions?"

Flynn smiled. "Not at all, Shani. I love to hear your voice."

Did he really say that? She would have to write it down later in her diary. Slightly flustered, she weaved into a pothole. Park's head got another millimeter flatter. "Watch it," he growled.

"Thank you," she said. "I mean, I'm sorry."

"Tell me about yourself," Flynn said.

"About me? There isn't much to say about me." She couldn't think of anything offhand.

"Why do you want to be a psychiatrist?"

"Oh, how did you know that?"

"I read the caption under your picture in that book — the yearbook. It said: Ambition — Psychiatrist; Favorite Subject — Psychology; Happiest Memory — Coming out of the womb; Hoover High Bulletin Editor; Homecoming Court."

"You must have an incredible memory," Shani said, awed.

"I only read a few of the captions."

"Did you read mine?" Park asked. For some mysterious reason, his senior picture — in everyone's yearbook — had been faded to a ghost outline. Indeed, nowhere else in the book was his lost little boy face to be found. Though he had an ongoing fantasy that he looked like a certain tall, tan movie star, Park could not have chosen a more inaccurate model. Sturdy and wiry from hours of surfing, he was nevertheless short and pale. And with lips rosy to the point of appearing touched up, and a mop of hair as black as his coal eyes, he was closer to a member of the Vienna Boys' Choir than a movie star. He was not handsome, but a lot of girls — Shani included — thought he was a doll.

The absence of his picture in the yearbook was no real mystery. He had been the yearbook editor in chief. The thought of some jerk scribbling on his face, he had confided, had been unbearable.

"You read it to me, Park," Flynn answered. "Your happiest memory was going into the womb."

"I was speaking for my father, there," Park grinned.

"Who else's did you read?" Shani asked. She was flattered—she was in seventh heaven—that he'd taken special note of her, but already she was worrying about the competition.

Again he hesitated. "Robin Carlton's."

They had handed in the information for the captions before Robin's accident. Robin's ambition had been to become a doctor and join the Peace Corps and help poor people. The conversation went out the window right there. Shani decided she would tell Flynn why she wanted to be a psychiatrist when he told her why he had come to Santa Barbara.

Her reasons weren't complicated, just confusing. In school, there was no specific subject that fascinated her. She did well in all of her classes, largely because her mother was strict, but biology or history or literature just couldn't compete with real, live people. She loved to study her friends, try to understand their motivations, their hopes and fears. Lunch in the crowded, talkative quad was her favorite period. This is why she wanted to study the mind. Perhaps she was trying to figure out herself through others. Maybe she relied too much upon others. Sometimes, it seemed, she had no internal anchor, nothing that couldn't be blown away by the cruelties of the world. She needed those around her, though she saw faults in all of them. Except for, perhaps, Robin, who wouldn't always be there. . . .

Ten bumpy minutes later, they came to Lena's road, which was nothing but a dirt path scarcely wide enough for Sol's van. However, it was flat. Making a right onto the road, heading west in the direction of the hidden ocean with the potholes behind her, Shani accelerated sharply.

"Don't lose sight of Sol," Park warned. "Those cans don't put out enough pressure to keep a tire up for long."

"If he doesn't show up ten minutes after we get there," Shani said, "I can always go back for him. I want some breathing space there so I can talk to Lena, ask her to lay off Kerry."

"You'd have more of a chance of success if you prayed for rain," Park said, noting the trail of dust they were stirring up. He added absently: "If it did rain here, the Carlton Castle would be an island. No one would be able to get in and out with the mud."

They sighted the house twenty minutes later. Mr. Carlton was not one for pinching pennies, and he had spared nothing on his resort home. Shani had forgotten the number of rooms Lena had said it contained, but she remembered having laughed at the size of the number. Largely paneled on the outside with redwood, the mansion itself was a haphazard three stories of spaciously windowed boxes bolted precariously to one another, as if the architect had been fretting over a drawer full of incomplete Rubik's cubes while designing it—very modern. In this heat, the practicality of twin chimneys at opposite ends was hard to imagine. Tall, prickly cacti guarded the long white driveway, and shady trees that couldn't have done all their growing since the house had been built cooled the front porch and roof. Off to the left, separated from the house proper by fifty yards, was a carport and garage housing a boat and two foreign cars. However, it was the ocean beyond that was the real visual treat, six-foot green glassy waves sliding onto a white carpet of sand that would be their class mattress for the next couple of nights. Park and his surfboard must be in bliss. The waves were sufficient to rip off any bikini bottom, but Shani was having doubts.

They parked in the carport, Angie's Camry a sorry sight next to the Ferrari and Porsche. Lena was standing next to a cactus near the front porch, holding clippers. She waved to them as they walked up.

"Did the border authorities arrest Sol?" she asked.

Lena was a bombshell, her hair a frightening red, bushy

and wild and always in her face, through which peered brown cat eyes and a heart-shaped mouth that made the guys think of nothing but sex when it smiled slyly. Kerry swore Lena'd had implants, and if size was any testimony of guilt . . . But no, that was just sour grapes. However, Lena had fabricated her walk; it hadn't been there last year. Her butt winked with every step. The bikini she now wore flaunted her endowments to indecent advantage. There wasn't a clue of tan lines. That meant she had been sunbathing nude. Despite Angie's presence, Park was drooling. If Lena went swimming in the waves in that tissue paper when everyone arrived, Sol would have his hands full stemming the riot.

Lena was ferocious. When she wanted something, she got it—Lena's First Law. She could be subtle or overwhelming. If sweet suggestion didn't work, she would just as soon shoot a cannon off in your face. Shani had never heard her apologize or admit a mistake. A legion of female followers paid obeisance to her at school. If they had a problem, she had the solution. She would do anything for a friend, as long as she was loyal—Lena's Second Law. If you crossed Lena, your astrological chart suddenly got a black hole in it. But she was not petty. The opposite of Kerry, she never spoke ill behind your back. If you were a jerk, you weren't worth her attention. But if verbal abuse was necessary, she would blast you in your face in front of everyone. Even Sol was afraid of her.

"They dragged him out of his van and shot him," Park said.

"How many did he take with him?" Lena asked. With her clippers, she was trimming the cactus' stickers. She couldn't have been more poorly dressed for the task.

"Twenty-six," Park said. "His van's about ten minutes behind us. Hey, that's one fine bathing suit you've got there."

Angie poked him, irritated. Lena curled a corner of her lips. "I just put it on. You should have been here a few minutes ago. . . . " She let the vision hang. Park would start panting next.

"Aren't you going to ask how our trip was?" Angie asked.

"Nope."

"Lena, you know Flynn, don't you?" Shani said. "Flynn, this is Lena, Robin's sister."

"Of course I know him," Lena said. "I've only been going to class with him since the beginning of the semester. He's been to our house a few times in Santa Barbara, haven't you, Flynn?"

"Yes," Flynn said.

"Really?" Shani said, putting down a stab of jealousy. Neither Robin nor Lena had told her this before. But, then, why should they have? Funny how with a couple of compliments she was already thinking of him as hers. She was getting as bad as Kerry.

"You know how I like to break in all the new boys," Lena said. "Don't blush, Shani, you know I'm only joking. Flynn spent all his time talking to Robin."

"How is Robin?" Park asked.

"She's not well. She's just maintaining," Lena said, as straightforward as ever. Many would have considered her cold, but Lena did not baby Robin. Kerry was always quick to say it was because she didn't care. But no one really knew how Lena felt. From the beginning, when Robin had been fighting for her life, Lena had not publicly shown the slightest trace of sorrow. Lena added, "She's inside, resting. She's been looking forward to seeing you all."

Shani had not seen her in a month, since Robin had moved down here on what seemed to be a permanent basis. Was Robin withdrawing? What was here except the ocean and sand? Yet Lena had said it had been Robin's idea to have the party.

"I'd like you to do a favor for me," Shani began. "Kerry's riding in the van with Sol and—"

"And you want me to be nice to her," Lena interrupted. "Funny you should say that. And I was just collecting these needles to stuff her pillow with."

"Please, you don't want fighting at your own party."

Lena's eyes sparkled. "Oh, I don't know, it might liven things up. Look, I'll make a bargain with you, and you can pass this on to Kerry. If she leaves me alone, I'll leave her alone. Otherwise, she'll wish she had never come."

"Now that sounds like a fair deal to me," Park quipped. Shani felt far from relieved.

They were on the verge of entering the house when Robin's nurse, Ellen Porter, came out the front door carrying a small suitcase. Ms. Porter looked like a nurse even without the white uniform. Well into her sixties, she had helped take care of Robin and Lena when they had been infants, and had been with the Carlton family—off and on—ever since. She was a stern lady who believed firmly in discipline and suffering for the sake of character. Shani had once seen her slap Lena in the face for cussing. The fact that Ms. Porter was still alive indicated that she was as lucky as she was strict. When Robin had taken ill, Mr. Carlton had sent her through special training for the care of critically ill kidney patients. Much of this knowledge she had passed on to Lena. Her salary was equivalent to that of most M.D.'s. She had never married.

"Hi, girls. Hi, Park," she said, setting down her suitcase on the steps of the porch. "How was the drive down?"

"Dusty," Angie said.

"And bumpy," Shani added. "How are you, Ms. Porter?"

"As well as can be expected in this heat." She turned to Lena. "I thought you were going to get dressed, young lady. Running around like that . . . what will the boys think?"

Lena was bored. "It's too late to worry about that."

Nurse Porter frowned and checked her watch. "Well, I must be off if I'm to catch my plane. Are you sure you don't want me to stay?"

Lena shook her head. "I've done the dialysis over three dozen times with you here. It will be no different with you away. Trust me."

"We should have done Robin already today, before her friends started to arrive."

"You're right," Lena said. "But she was too busy getting things ready."

It was obvious that Nurse Porter would have been more comfortable staying. "One thing, Lena, don't touch anything inside the kidney machine. I've replaced the cellophane membrane, and the dialyzing solution is fresh. All you have to do is put the needles in her shunts and throw the switch. Call if you have a problem." She hugged Lena. "I hope the two of you have fun."

"I'll take care of her," Lena promised.

"I know you will, dear."

"Can I help you with your bag?" Park asked.

"There's a gentleman for you. Yes, Park, thank you. I'll be taking the Porsche in the garage." She came down the steps, searching for the keys in her purse. Park hopped onto the porch and grabbed her bag, following on her heels.

Only as she passed him did Ms. Porter seem to become aware of Flynn. As was his habit, he had been standing back from the rest of them. Her initial reaction was, Shani was sure, one of pure amazement. But it was only a flicker, and then she was peering at him with undisguised curiosity.

"And who do we have here?" she mused.

Shani took a step toward Flynn. "This is a good friend of ours, Ms. Porter—Flynn from England. He only started at Hoover last semester break. Flynn, this is Robin's nurse. You never met her while visiting Robin?"

"I didn't have the pleasure," Flynn bowed slightly. "Nice to meet you, Ms. Porter."

"Nice to meet you. Are you a . . . friend of Robin's?"

"We've only spoken a few times."

"I see." Ms. Porter seemed to be thinking. "Flynn—that's a nice name. Sounds adventurous. What is your last name?"

"Powers."

"I have family in England," Ms. Porter went on. Shani had thought that she was in a hurry. "Maybe you lived near them. Are you from London, by chance?"

"No."

"Plymouth," Shani said. Flynn cast her a quick look.

"Plymouth," Ms. Porter whispered. The word seemed to go deep inside her, like a piercing needle. Yet again, the unusual reaction lasted only a second. Then she smiled. "Does your family live there?"

"Yes."

"Your mother?"

Flynn paused, and it was his turn to scrutinize Ms. Porter. "Both my parents live there," he said.

Shani was confused. Why hadn't he said the same to her? She also wondered why the nurse was so interested in Flynn. Ms. Porter continued, "I used to travel a lot. I've been to England several times. I love that country, the green you see everywhere. And their passports always made American ones look so dull. When you crossed into Tijuana, did they ask for yours?"

"No."

"They'll ask for it on the way back. You did bring it, didn't you?"

"No."

"How are you going to get back into California?"

"I can fake the accent."

Ms. Porter forced a laugh. "American or Mexican?"

"Whatever it takes."

It was a subtle hint to quit prying, and Ms. Porter must have caught it. She rechecked her watch. "Well, I've chatted long enough. But it's been worth it to hear such a marvelous voice. We must talk again in the future."

Flynn smiled. "If you'd like."

Toting the bag, Park accompanied her to the car. She waved as she drove away. In the distance, coming the opposite way, Sol's van could be seen, doing at best ten miles an hour; the tire must be giving out.

"That was weird," Lena said. "Nursey was really digging into you."

"She seemed like a nice lady." He scratched his side thoughtfully, near a bulge in his belt. Then he asked a peculiar question. "When we drove up, Lena, I noticed a couple of big tanks at the side of the house. They looked like they had just been installed. Are they part of Robin's dialysis machine?"

"No, you would never put any of the kidney machine outside. Those are water filtration tanks. For cosmetic reasons, we're going to have them enclosed. If you don't filter the water you drink down here, you know what hits the fan. One of the tanks is new. Before, we used to only filter the water that led into the kitchen tap. Now you can take a shower without getting amoebas and protozoas all over you."

"How gross," Angie said.

"I was just wondering," Flynn said.

Shani was surprised Flynn would ask such a silly question. Who heard of putting parts of a refined medical instrument outdoors?

Flynn offered to unpack the Camry. Park suggested that Angie give him a hand. Judging from her expression, Angie did not appreciate the suggestion. However, she must have understood that he wanted to see Robin without a new girlfriend by his side, for she accompanied Flynn back to the carport without complaint. Park was nervous. Shani patted his hand.

"She'll be glad to see you," she said.

Park nodded. "I know." Lena held her tongue.

The entrance hallway was brief, spilling into a sunken living room with a towering open-beam ceiling and giant windows that practically invited the ocean in. The blend of furniture, drapes, wallpaper, and paintings was refreshingly old-fashioned, conveying warmth and taste. White carnations and red roses bloomed in china vases atop four separate corner tables. It seemed a sin to tramp on the divinely soft vanilla-colored carpet beneath their dusty feet.

Robin was sitting on a burgundy sofa reading a book. As they entered, she smiled and rose to greet them. "My friends," she beamed, spreading her arms.

Robin was jaundiced—even the centers of her once emerald eyes were stained a sad yellow. The sheen and curls had fallen from her brown hair. Perhaps in concession to the spreading gray, she had it cut very short. There wasn't a spare ounce on her emaciated frame. Her pretty blue blouse and smart white skirt hung on her like old sheets. As she approached, it was as though she were treading through a thick liquid, with effort being required for every few steps. Shani told herself that this could not be her dear friend. She had deteriorated rapidly in these last four weeks.

Robin was the best of them. Since they had both been adopted, it should have been no surprise that Lena and Robin bore no similar personality traits. Nevertheless, it was hard to believe they had grown up together in the same house. Robin never asked for anything, never complained. Not that she worked at being a saint. An inborn lack of egotism had her naturally more interested in others' cares. However, she was not perfect. A follower, prey to everyone's idle influence, she seldom asserted her personality. Fortunately, Lena—a leader at heart—never tried to dominate her. But Robin's greatest fault was her laziness. Though no moron, her grades at school had never risen above a C. What Robin could do today, she put off till next year. Yet maybe that bad habit was passing. From what Lena said, she appeared to be trying to get the most out of her time off the dialysis machine. Maybe because she might not have a next year.

Of all the people in the world, Shani loved Robin the most.

Shani hugged her, feeling Robin's ribs. "I missed you," she said, fighting to keep her voice easy.

"I missed you more."

Shani took a short step back, still holding her shoulders. "But you're so skinny. Aren't you eating?"

"I'm dieting," she joked, fingering a tiny gold eagle

pendant that hung from a tiny silver chain around her neck.

"Hello, Robin," Park said at Shani's back.

Robin's lower lip quivered before she could hide it with a smile. "You look well, Park."

"I feel okay. How are you?"

"Good, great."

"Give her a kiss, you bastard," Lena said.

Robin laughed, spreading her arms. "And a hug, too. I'm not contagious."

Park took her in his arms, and only because she knew him so well was Shani able to see that he, too, wanted to weep. "It's good, real good, to see you again," he said.

"Really?" Robin sighed doubtfully. But she quickly chuckled to lighten the mood, undoing his embrace. "But I'm forgetting my duties as a hostess. You must all be thirsty. Was that Angie's voice I heard? How many have arrived?"

"Sol's coming up the road," Shani said. "Bert and Kerry're with him. Other than that . . . Oh, Flynn's here."

Robin brightened. "Flynn! I'm glad; he's such a sweetheart. I'll get plenty of drinks, then. Don't any of you go anywhere. I'll be right back."

"I'll help you," Shani said.

"No," Lena said firmly. "She can handle it herself."

When Robin had left, Park leaned against the wall as though suddenly weary. "She looks terrible," he said.

"She has looked better," Lena agreed.

"Why has she suddenly lost so much weight?" Shani asked.

"She's been depressed, hasn't been eating," Lena said. "Ten days ago we got a letter from Stanford Medical Center. It was nicely phrased, but essentially it said that they had her at the bottom of their transplant-candidate list."

"But why?" Shani cried, taking the bad news hard. A transplant was Robin's only hope for a normal life. "Robin only has one kidney now, and it's ninety percent failed. Who could be more needy?"

"*More* than ninety percent failed," Lena corrected. "But you would be amazed at the number of people in her predicament. Stanford figures she had one transplant, and rejected the organ, and is therefore not a prime candidate. In other words, they feel that they gave her a chance, and now they have to give someone else a chance. Plus, she has another strike against her. You might have seen in the news, there's been a big backlash against rich people being able to buy organs and get transplants sooner than poor minorities. All those human rights fanatics are watching the Carlton name closely to make sure Robin doesn't get any special favors. Stanford's gotten paranoid, and Daddy's offer of a big donation hasn't eased that paranoia. It's all a bunch of BS. Robin will probably be the last one to be given a second chance. I swear, sometimes it doesn't pay to be rich."

"Stanford isn't the only medical center that does transplants," Park said.

"The situation would be the same elsewhere," Lena said.

"Is there no hope?" Shani asked. In a moment, she would have the nerve to make her offer, she hoped.

"If Robin had a blood sister or brother with a matching tissue type," Lena said, "who was willing to donate one of his or her kidneys, Stanford would have to take her. But since she doesn't, I would have to say there's no hope of her getting off the dialysis machine in the next couple of years."

Shani swallowed thickly. It was a thoroughly premeditated offer. "I had myself typed last week. I'm the same type as Robin. I would be willing to . . . I want to give her one of my kidneys."

Lena stared at her a long time before responding. "You are not blood-related. Stanford would say no."

"But I'm her age. I —"

"It was a noble gesture," Lena interrupted. "If there was a chance they would go for it, I would be on the phone now. Thank you, Shani."

"It was just an idea," she sighed.

Park squeezed her arm. "I'm proud of you."

"One thing," Lena added. "Don't tell Robin of your offer. It might give her hope, and then Stanford would just slam the door in her face again. Two no's in two weeks and she might stop eating altogether."

"I understand," Shani said.

"Knock, knock," Kerry said at the front door.

"The door's open," Lena said. "Hello, Kerry."

"Hi," Kerry mumbled, munching on a wad of gum, trying to look bored. "Where's Robin?"

"In the kitchen getting drinks," Lena said. "Where's my boy?"

Shani cringed at the word. Kerry played the fool. "Who?"

"Sol," Lena said.

"He's in the garage."

"What's he doing there?"

"How should I know? He's not my *boy*," Kerry said. "And I don't think he'd appreciate being called that."

"I call him that all the time," Lena said.

"So do I," Park said. "But never to his face."

Kerry scowled at Lena's bikini. *That* was a mistake. "Don't you think you should put on some clothes?"

"What's it to you?" Lena asked, sharpening her tone.

"You're practically naked."

"If it's Sol you're worried about, he's already seen me naked, many times."

"Him and a couple dozen other guys," Kerry muttered, looking out the window at the rolling ocean swells. *That* was a bigger mistake. Lena smiled her special smile, a red-lipped warning, to those who knew her, that she was going to stick in the blade.

"In this area, I have to bow to your vastly superior numbers," she said pleasantly. "A couple dozen? I should be embarrassed. That must be a pittance to someone like you."

Kerry did not say anything. She gave no reaction whatsoever except to turn and leave through the same door she had entered.

"Lena," Shani moaned.

Lena shrugged, still smiling. "She started it."

"Do you think she'll leave?" Park asked.

"I'm sure she already wishes that she had never come," Shani sighed. It was going to be a long weekend.

‏ CHAPTER 4 ‏

NIGHT HAD COME BUT NONE OF THE OTHER KIDS HAD.
Lena confessed that the printer had accidentally put June
twelfth on the written invitations, which was tomorrow.
Because they talked to Lena on a regular basis, neither
Shani nor Park had received such an invitation. Yet, Shani
was still confused. She had spoken to many of her friends
about how she had planned to get to the resort house
by Friday afternoon. Why had not a single one of them
commented on the fact that they were not coming till
Saturday?

They had a late dinner, waiting for Robin to finish with
her dialysis and join them. Though monitoring her sister's
blood cleansing, Lena had somehow managed to oversee
the preparation of a turkey, a ham, a basketful of baked
potatoes, and two huge pots of steamed vegetables. There
had also been a ton of assorted junk food: ice cream, potato
chips, cola, and pastries. Shani had indulged in none of the
junk, but she had discovered that even good food could
make you sick if you ate too much of it.

After dinner they gathered in the living room, sprawling on couches, chairs, and the floor. The light breeze through the open windows was warm and salty. When they paused in their talk, they could hear the crash of the waves and the stir of the tide. Big Bert had one quarter of the room to himself. He was working on a bottle of wine Lena had dug up from the cellar—a bottle that probably cost more than he made pumping gas thirty hours a week at an all-night Shell Station. Bert, Park, and Sol had been next to impossible to get out of the water at dinnertime, pleading, "Just one more wave!" Already, Park was a solid shade of red. At the moment, Angie was massaging aloe vera into his bare back. Robin had given her the oil. She did not seem to mind Angie touching her ex intimately in her presence, although Park appeared ill at ease, telling Angie to hurry and be done. The late-day dialysis had done nothing to improve Robin's color. She looked exhausted. She was nervously fingering the miniature golden eagle around her neck, as if for strength. Flynn sat beside her on the love seat, his eyes following her every gesture. Shani did not know what to think, but she knew she was jealous.

"Ahh," Sol moaned with pleasure. Park was not the only one getting a rubdown. Lena had Sol facedown on the floor clad in only his swimming trunks. She was sitting on his butt. Naturally, Kerry was pretending that none of this was happening, sitting in a dim corner furthest from the center of their group.

"We should play some games," Robin suggested. A sudden gust in the ocean breeze caused her to shiver.

"Should I close a window?" Shani asked.

"I like the wind," Robin said.

"Can I get you a blanket?" Flynn asked.

She appreciated his concern. "Thank you, I'm fine. I just need to be more active. What can we play?"

"Let's have an orgy," Sol muttered into the floor. Lena smacked him on the back of the head. "Let's play chess," he said, reconsidering.

"Let's play charades," Shani said.

"Sure," Bert said.

"I hate charades," Park said.

"We always play that," Angie complained.

"I'm terrible at charades," Robin said.

"It's a terrible game," Sol said.

"Let's play Monopoly," Shani tried again.

"Great," Bert said.

"I hate Monopoly," Park said, putting on his shirt.

"We played that last time," Angie said.

"I've never once won at Monopoly," Robin said.

"It's a terrible game," Sol said, rolling over, capsizing Lena.

"Oh, brother," Shani said.

"Let's play that game where we make up names for each other," Bert said, finishing his bottle of wine, belching. "I love that game."

"Huh?" Park said.

"The one where you make up a famous personality and tape the name to someone's forehead and they try to figure out who they are by asking yes and no questions," Shani said. "Is that the one you mean, Bert?"

"I think so."

Sprawled on the floor in white micro shorts, it was Lena's turn to reconsider. "I'd rather have an orgy."

Bert's suggestion prevailed. Through quick maneuvering, Shani got to choose Flynn's pretend name. As she taped it on his forehead, his curly brown hair got in the way. He helped her out, his large beautiful hands brushing against her clumsy fingers.

"I hope you made me someone nice," he said.

She had chosen *Luke Skywalker*, for Flynn—if anyone—seemed to have The Force with him, some kind of power. "I did," she smiled. "Is that hint enough for you?" He pulled out her pretend name, and, brushing back her hair, pressed it firmly in place.

"I bet I'm an old meany," she said.

"No, you're young and romantic."

She, or her character? Blushing, she retreated to her chair. Sol made Park *Tweety Bird*. But Park—unconsciously—returned the favor, making Sol *Mr. Rogers*. Seeing Flynn's name, Angie gave Robin *Princess Leia*. Robin, in turn, gave Angie *Dino the Dinosaur*. Bert was a group effort. He ended up as *Paul Bunyan*. As fate would have it, Lena and Kerry were left to choose each other's names. To no one's surprise, Lena became *Satan*. And Lena gave Kerry's character a real twist. She made Kerry *Kerry*.

And so they went in circles, asking questions of the group, getting another turn when the answer was yes. Flynn took only three turns to guess who he was, and everyone booed Shani for being too easy. Sol was a close second. Apparently *Mr. Rogers* was one of his baby sister's favorite shows, and the character was fresh in his mind. Lena followed shortly afterward, pleased at Kerry's selection. They had gone about a dozen cycles when Park figured out his name, having already made several unsuccessful stabs with the premier cowards of history. From then on, the rest of them were stuck, and the winners, getting bored, started to drop more and more flagrant hints.

"Am I important?" Angie asked, exasperated.

"Sure," everyone said.

"And I'm a cartoon character," Angie muttered to herself, having picked that up earlier. "I don't know any important cartoon people."

"You're not a person," Lena said.

"You're a pet," Sol said.

"You're a pet dinosaur," Park muttered.

"You didn't have to tell me!" Angie said, mad. "I would have got it."

"Sorry," Park said.

"So, who are you?" Lena insisted.

"I'm . . . I'm . . . Dino?"

"Perfect," Park said. "Okay, Bert, it's your turn. You've got to start narrowing down your name by asking good questions."

Bert had been guessing names randomly, three times choosing the same name. He had drunk too much wine. All he knew for sure—hopefully—was that he was not Mr. T. The weird thing was, Shani would not have been surprised if Bert did pluck the name out of the air. Luck followed him like a shadow. Pounding his head with his fist, he said, "I got it right here. I just can't say it."

"But you don't even know if you're male or female," Park said.

"I'm one of those, I know," Bert said, trying to concentrate.

"Somebody get him a mirror," Park muttered. "While he's divining the answer, why don't you go, Shani? You're—"

"Don't tell me! Don't tell me! I'll get it." She performed a quick mental review. She was: young, pretty, in love, European, a fictional character, female, dead. . . . Inspiration struck. "Did I kill myself over my love?"

"Yes!" everyone shouted.

"Am I a Shakespearean character?"

"Yes."

"Did I stab myself with a knife?"

"Yes!"

"Did my boyfriend drink poison?"

"Yes!" Park adding, "Come on, Shani!"

But she was enjoying herself. "Do I have a pet dinosaur?"

"Huh?"

"I'm Romeo!" She clapped her hands together. "I mean, Juliet. Thanks, Flynn, that's one of my favorite stories." Was he trying to tell her something?

"All right, Kerry," Park said. "Last chance."

Kerry had been keeping a low profile. "I know I must be someone rotten."

"Don't say that; it's not true," Shani said.

"I know Lena wouldn't have made me someone nice," Kerry said. Lena chuckled. Kerry went on: "I'm not Hitler, Mussolini, Nero, Charles Manson, Genghis Khan, or Pontius Pilate. Am I a female terror?"

"You're a girl," Sol said.

"Am I pretty?"

"Ehh," Lena said.

"Yes," Robin said.

"Am I alive?"

"Ehh," Lena said.

"At times," Angie said. "Yes."

"Am I well-known?"

"Amongst a small circle of friends," Shani said.

"And amongst a larger circle of football fans," Lena said.

"Lena!" Shani said.

Kerry ripped off her name, crumbling the tape and throwing it away without a look. "Your turn, Robin," she said tonelessly.

"That was rotten," Shani said.

Lena laughed. "I can't help who she is."

"Shut up, Lena, it's my turn," Robin said pleasantly, probably averting a fight. Robin was not the marshmallow of before. She fingered her pendant, the gold eagle catching the lamplight, flickering like a star. "Could I have a minute? I'm thirsty; I want to get a drink." She started to stand. Flynn stopped her.

"I'll get you one," he said. During dinner, he had done the same, waiting on her hand and foot. Robin had eaten like a bird.

"My very own butler. Thank you," she smiled. "I just want a glass of water."

Flynn was back in a minute, but he had brought apple juice instead. "You can't trust the water down here," he explained.

"Oh, but it's filtered," Robin said.

"That's right, I'd forgotten," he said, sitting back down beside her. "Apple juice is better for you anyway."

A sharp cold, like cracking ice, pumped through Shani's heart as Robin lifted the drink to her lips. Funny how apple juice could look so much like beer. . . .

"*. . . one drink, it won't kill you. . . .*"

. . . So much like poison. Of course, Flynn had not been there *that* night. But he wasn't the type to forget anything.

"I'm a young and beautiful woman," Robin reiterated. "I'm a famous fictional character in a classic movie."

"Several classic movies," Park said.

"Don't tell me! I want to get it." Robin pondered. "If I'm the same character in several movies that must mean there were sequels. Hmm. I got it! *Star Wars*! I'm Princess Leia! And here I was sitting right next to Luke." She hugged Flynn. "I should have guessed."

"I got it!!!" Bert interrupted, leaping to his feet. "Paul Bunyan!!!" he exclaimed.

Amazing, everyone had to agree.

They hashed around the possibility of other games: Angie's Spin the Bottle, Bert's Monopoly, Sol's Russian Roulette, Park's Marco Polo in the ocean, Lena's Strip Poker. They were nowhere near a decision when Shani, out of curiosity, asked, "Robin, where did you get that eagle pendant? It's fascinating."

Robin was suddenly wary. "It's a gift. A friend who lives around here gave it to me."

"What is it?" Park asked.

Robin shrugged, her manner — for her — very peculiar. "Nothing, an eagle. It's nothing."

"An eagle," Sol repeated, exchanging a frown with Park. Shani was sure she was missing something. Sol asked,

"Does this friend of yours have long stringy hair, a tan robe tied at the waist with an orange belt, and weird eyes?"

"Is he a sorcerer?" Park asked.

"He's not a sorcerer," Robin said quickly, sharply.

"That's what I say," Lena muttered, picking at her toenails.

"You have something to say about a lot of things you know nothing about," Robin said.

Lena was not impressed. "I was only agreeing with you . . . this time. Why don't you make up *your* mind? Is this cat for real or not?"

"What are you all talking about?" Angie asked.

"What do you want, a miracle?" Robin asked her sister. "If you can't see or touch something, you assume it isn't real. There's no in-between for you, only black and white."

The tone of the evening had suddenly become chilly, as had the breeze through the dark windows overlooking the sober ocean. The foam from the waves was no longer white, or even black, but Robin's in-between — gray. Shani hugged her arms across her chest. She was not sure, but a shadow, like that of a bird, seemed to have swept by their window on its way out to sea. Far away, she heard a faint cry. It could have been a bird's, but it sounded strangely human. Robin seemed to be the only other one to hear it.

"He only spoke Spanish," Sol said. "How do you talk to him?"

"Robin's fluent in Spanish," Lena said.

"I never knew that," Park said. "That's interesting. So, tell us about this guy. I take it Lena and you disagree over his magical powers."

"I said nothing about magic," Robin whispered, withdrawing. "I'd rather not talk about it." She finished her apple juice.

The topic would have been dropped right there, except that Flynn took up the prod. He spoke carefully. "I, also, am curious about him. At the canteen Bert and I visited, the owner—an extremely old lady who spoke good English—mentioned him when we told her that we were coming here. She indicated that he visited here often."

"No, not often," Robin said.

"I've always been curious about people like that," Flynn said, letting the statement hang.

"I wouldn't call him a sorcerer," Robin answered reluctantly. "That word gives a picture of someone who has powers that he uses to his own advantage. He doesn't do that. He could, if he wanted. But he has no need to. He's a desireless man."

"If he has never demonstrated unusual abilities, how do you know he has them?" Park asked.

"Because he *knows* me," Robin said, suddenly emotional. She quieted. "I'm sorry, this is nothing I should talk about."

Flynn, however, was getting interested. "Did he give you the eagle as a protective amulet?"

"No."

"Robin." Lena said, as if accusing her sister of lying.

"Well, he didn't," Robin protested. "He gave it to me as a gift. He never said it was to protect me or to make me bet —" Robin halted, but was too late, having revealed more than she had wished. Was she staying down here to be near this peculiar man because she believed he could cure her? Perhaps that was why Lena viewed him cynically.

"What did he say about your kidneys?" Flynn asked.

Robin was defensive. "What makes you think I asked him?"

Flynn's tone was apologetic. "I was just thinking of myself. I would have asked."

"I did ask him, once," Robin admitted, sounding tired.

"I'm being nosey. I'm sorry," Flynn said. "Let's talk about something else."

Lena sighed. She was getting exasperated and bored. "This is all sounding more mysterious than it really is. Robin, just tell them the story that he told you when you asked about your health. Don't be embarrassed, wise men are always telling short parables that no one understands."

"I don't want to."

"Why not?" Lena insisted.

"Because . . . it doesn't have an ending."

"You brought up the subject and got everyone going," Lena said.

"I did not."

"If you won't tell them, I will."

"If it's private, Robin doesn't have to tell us," Shani said. Yet she, too, was curious.

"Okay, okay," Robin said. "I'm supposed to be the hostess. I guess I shouldn't be so rude. It won't matter to talk about it now, anyway. Lena, I'm feeling awfully tired. Could you get it for me? I wrote it down that day he told me. It's in a manila envelope in my desk, second drawer on the right. Thank you."

Lena returned in a minute with the envelope, plus a woolen blanket, which Robin accepted gratefully, wrapping it around her shoulders. The breeze coming in from the ocean had turned the room absurdly cold. Robin cleared her throat, saying, "This is what he told me when I asked him if I was going to get better. It doesn't really say yes or no and, like I said, it doesn't have an ending. Also, my Spanish is okay, but I'm not fluent. I can only give you the gist of what he told me. It reads like a parable.

"Once, not so long ago, there were two birds, Dove and Eagle. They were as one, very close, and would talk long and deep together. They made a vow to one another that they would always be together. But one terrible day, a storm came, and they were separated, and Dove flew alone, always searching for Eagle, but never finding him.

"Now it came to happen one day that Dove met Raven, and they became good friends. Raven was clever and strong, and helped Dove live. And Dove respected Raven, for she could do many things that Dove could not. But Dove could sing, whereas Raven could not. Often, Raven pleaded for Dove to sing to her, and Dove always would.

"After being many days together, Raven told Dove of a new and exciting place she had heard of. She wished to go to this place, for Raven was very inquisitive, and she persuaded Dove to come with her, though Dove did not really want to go. But coming to this place, they found nothing but desert and got lost—or so it seemed—and became very thirsty. Flying high, Raven spotted a pond, and said, 'Let us drink here,' and Dove followed.

"Now, this pond belonged to Snake, and Raven knew this. Long ago, Raven had promised to bring Snake tasty food in exchange for its rattle, for more than anything, Raven wished to be able to make music like Dove. But Raven did not intend for Dove to be killed, for Raven in truth liked Dove. Together, Raven thought they could kill Snake, and she would get its rattle. But Snake had no intention of giving up its rattle. And Snake really wanted to eat Raven, for it thought Dove was thin and frail, and wouldn't be tasty. Both intended to cheat the other.

"While Dove was drinking from the pond, Raven waited for Snake to appear. And all of a sudden Snake came sliding out with its teeth wide, and surprised Raven, and Raven was barely able to escape into the air, calling for Dove to do so, also. But Dove staggered and could not fly. What neither Raven nor Snake had realized was that the pond was poisoned from Snake having drunk of its waters. Now Snake curled its tail around sick Dove, trying to lure Raven closer. Alone, Raven did not feel she could kill Snake. And Raven was afraid that if she tried, Snake would bite Dove with its strongest poison, and Dove would die.

"Suddenly, Eagle appeared, landing between them. Eagle was very powerful and could easily kill Snake. But when he went to try, Snake tightened its grip on Dove and said, 'If you come closer, I will bite Dove. Kill Raven for me, and leave her body, and I will give you Dove.'

"Eagle turned to Raven, and Raven grew frightened. She said, 'Dove and I are friends. She would not wish for you to kill me.'

"But Snake said, 'If Raven was Dove's friend, why did she bring her here for me to eat?'

"Raven said, 'That is not true.' But Raven feared Dove would feel that she had been betrayed, and would allow Eagle to kill her for Snake.

"Eagle thought for a moment, and said, 'I will let Dove decide if you are a friend, Raven, and whether I should buy her freedom with your death. But I have decided this: If Dove should die, both of you will die.'"

Robin stopped, resting her papers on her lap. "I've read enough," she said wearily.

"But is that it?" Park asked. "What did Dove do?"

"I . . . I . . ." Robin put her hand to her forehead, where perspiration had sprung. "I don't feel very good."

Shani bolted upright. "What's wrong? Should we call for a doctor?" Curse that Lena for having insisted that Nurse Porter leave!

"You don't want to call doctors around here," Lena said. "There isn't one within fifty miles, anyway. Robin gets like this sometimes. There's nothing you can do."

Sol was not convinced. "I could drive you to a doctor. I don't care how far he is."

"I could carry you," Bert said.

Robin smiled weakly. "Lena's right. This is just the way it goes sometimes. Rest is all I need. Having you all here has been so exciting, I've worn myself out." She slipped her story back in the manila envelope. Flynn helped her up.

"Is that all of the story the man told you?" Angie asked.

Robin caught Lena's eye. "Yes, it is," she said slowly. "He told me I was to fill in the ending."

Lena escorted Robin to her room. When they were out of view, Shani said, "I wish the nurse was here. Her skin looks awful."

"Like she has hepatitis, yeah," Park said, worried.

"She'll probably feel better in the morning," Sol said.

Park nudged Sol's outstretched leg with his foot. "Are you thinking what I'm thinking?"

"I never think like Tweety Bird," Sol said. Then he got serious. "Maybe the old man only knows one story and wanted to tell it to us. Hell, if I'd been Eagle, I would have just wasted the two jerks."

"What about Dove?" Shani asked, realizing that Park and Sol must have met the old man. "Then she would automatically have died."

Sol went to speak, but paused, his eyes involuntarily drawn down the hall where Robin had disappeared. "Oh, yeah," he said casually. "I had forgotten about that."

Sol was being polite. He hadn't forgotten; none of them had. From the moment she had drunk the poison, Dove had already been a goner.

FLUFFING UP HER PILLOW, SHANI WONDERED IF SHE would have insomnia, as she often did when she didn't sleep in her own bed. The plan had been for their class to crash on the beach in sleeping bags, but since less than the square root of their class was present, Lena had offered them all individual rooms in the Carlton Castle. Bert had refused the offer, saying he'd take the sand and stars any day. Looking out her third-story window, Shani could see him smoothing himself a bed not far from the outstretching fingers of the remains of the largest waves.

When the tide came up, Bert would have one hell of a wet dream.

Which reminded Shani: Who, besides herself, would be sleeping alone tonight? Kerry and Bert, surely, though Park would probably try to slip in a quickie with Angie before hurrying back to his own room lest Harvard Admissions or his mother catch wind of the sin. On the other hand, he might make do with a cold shower with Robin resting a few doors down. Lena would not be worried about Kerry's proximity. Tomorrow, Sol would be lucky if he could stand up on his board.

And Flynn . . . The fantasy started in third gear as Shani turned off the light and hit the pillow, pretending he was there beside her, his left hand caressing her lower back — they already had their clothes off — her right hand stroking his silky brown curls, their free hands absorbed in unspeakable acts. He was kissing her deeply, whispering between moist mouthfuls that what they were doing was wrong but that he couldn't help himself. And she was sighing with pleasure, crooning sweetly that she was glad that it was wrong. He began to —

The phone on the stand beside her bed rang. Shani sat up and turned on the lamp, putting Flynn on hold. It rang again. She hesitated, then picked up the receiver. The instant she did so, before she had time to raise the phone all the way to her ear, she heard Lena say, "Hello?"

"Lena, this is Ellen."

"Hi, Nursey. Catch your plane?"

"Yes, I'm in Seattle now at my sister's house. And don't call me that."

"I am certainly sorry, *Ms.* Porter. What *may* I do for you this fine evening?"

"You're impossible. I wanted to . . . Is there someone else on this line?"

"No. Anyone there? No one's there. Why should there be? What's up?"

Shani did not know why she had not already replaced the receiver. Since she had not done so immediately, she was, in a sense, caught. However, perhaps half-formed fears were guiding her instincts. Lena was too meticulous to have "accidentally" placed the wrong date on the party invitations. Anything she said in private might be useful.

"How did the dialysis go?" Nurse Porter asked.

"Fine."

"How is Robin feeling?"

"The same."

"Good. I spoke with your mother. She said that she had talked with you earlier."

"Your information is correct. Checking up on us?"

"Don't get paranoid. No one's threatening your independence. It's natural that I should call and ask about Robin. But that's not the main reason we're talking." Ms. Porter paused. "That boyfriend Shani had with her, how well do you know him?"

"For one thing, he's not Shani's boyfriend. He's not even interested in her."

The words cut like an icy scalpel. Shani almost yelled, What the hell do you know, bitch? But Lena might very well know, that was the problem. Oh, God, how her heart hurt. And after he had read the lines under her yearbook picture, and everything. . . .

"Have you spoken to him alone for any length of time?"

"I haven't slept with him, if that's what you're asking. I know he's from England, moves like James Bond, and doesn't like to talk about himself. What's all this about?"

"Does he seem especially interested in Robin?"

"Yes. He waited on her hand and foot this evening."

"Keep him away from her! Don't leave them alone together."

"Why?"

"He . . . he might have . . . bad motives."

"Show me a guy that doesn't."

"That's not what I meant. Sleep with him yourself, if it helps keep him away from Robin. Listen, Lena, I would tell you more but your father has strictly forbidden me to do so. If he knew I was making this call, he would be furious. We only have suspicions, nothing concrete. He's making some checks."

Lena was shrewd. "If there was a one-in-a-million

chance of Flynn being dangerous, Daddy would already have a carload of men here with guns. Are you sure you're not suffering from severe jet lag?"

Apparently Nurse Porter was used to this kind of talk. "You *must* take me seriously. Flynn may not be who he pretends to be. That's why I asked about his passport. I wanted to see it. You saw how he evaded me. And if he has taken a false name, his motives cannot be honest."

Lena knew how to play her cards. "Tell me your suspicions, and *I* will decide how seriously to take your advice. Otherwise, my man will be here in a minute and I must get a few things in place, if you know what I mean. Be concise."

"We're worried about . . . who has sent him. That's all I can tell you. It won't kill you to keep an eye on him, and I know you will with what I've already told you. Tomorrow we'll know more, and I'll call you then."

Suddenly, Lena sounded uneasy. "Tomorrow's no good. Tell me now."

"No."

"Yes!"

"I told you, our information's incomplete."

"But there will be a ton of kids here tomorrow. You said this was private. . . . Look, I'll call you. Do not call me. Give me your sister's number."

Nurse Porter told her the number.

"Got it. Now you've got me curious, damn you. I think

I'll have a peek at his passport. He must have brought it if he was planning on reentering the States."

"Don't! God only knows what he'd do if he caught you fooling with his things."

"Okay," Lena said, but she wasn't convincing.

"You're sure Robin's fine?"

"If she wasn't, she would have told me. Oh . . . a brown, hulky babe just slid in my door. Got to go."

"Take care, dear."

After they had hung up, Shani unplugged her phone before replacing the receiver, afraid a jingle in Lena's room would betray the eavesdropping. She turned off the light, hugging the blankets to her chin. Flynn was no longer caressing her sweaty limbs, and she was no longer nibbling on his salty ears. If he had knocked on her door this instant, she wouldn't have invited him in. She would have screamed.

If she was searching for a suspect with intentions toward Robin, she would have scrutinized everyone in the house *but* Flynn, for he was the only one who hadn't been at the party when Robin had had her accident. At least, no one had seen him there.

Odd how the rest of them were all here, and no others. Odder still how none of them—after almost a year—ever referred to Robin's misfortune as anything but an accident

Of course, they all knew that it had been no accident.

"One drink, it won't kill you."

Sure.

If only she could forget, or clearly remember, it could be put to rest. This "in-between" gave her no peace.

Shani closed her eyes, listening to her heartbeat. A cool breeze stirred her curtains. Far away, over the black sea, a bird cried. Even as the darkness outside merged inside, she knew she would dream of poison.

～ CHAPTER 5 ～

LAST NOVEMBER

SHANI WONDERED IF SHE WAS DRUNK. SHE WAS PRETTY
sure she wasn't sober. To a stomach accustomed to carrot
juice and watermelon, three-and-a-half beers must be the
equivalent of downing a keg. At least she did not feel like
vomiting—not yet. But her bladder was another story.
She wished whoever was in the bathroom would hurry up.
Next time Angie threw a party, she would tell her to rent
an outhouse.

Shani glanced around for someone to help her out of her
chair. It was late, past midnight, and people—many, total
strangers—had been coming and going for the last two
hours. There weren't many left, too few to help clean up
the half-eaten pizzas and spilled chip bowls. What a mess.

"Listen here," Park was saying to Sol in reference to
"Good Vibrations" on the stereo. "This melody structure is one of the most sophisticated ever created by the
human mind." Park shook his head in dumbfounded awe.
He was plastered. "Brian Wilson was the genius of the

sixties, the king of the century! Love the colorful clothes he wears. . . ."

"Gringo trash," Sol scowled, using his half-finished beer as an ashtray. Kerry tugged at his arm, trying to get him off the floor.

"Let's go home, Sol. I've got to work tomorrow morning."

"Yeah, sure, babe, just another minute," Sol said, beginning to search through Angie's albums, littering them over the already cluttered floor. Shani wondered what Kerry was talking about. She had come in her dad's car; she didn't need a ride. Poor girl, she didn't know yet that she was spoiled goods. Thankfully, Lena had taken Angie's suggestion that she not put in an appearance. Probably because her sister had not come, Robin had also bowed out; a shame. Shani had been looking forward to seeing her. Robin didn't drink either, usually.

"Beethoven incarnate," Park swore, belching loudly. Having no respect for the melody structure, Sol shut off the music. "Hey!" Park protested.

"Surfing crap gives me a headache," Sol muttered, putting on hip hop music and twisting the volume dial.

"You surf!" Park said loudly.

"I've got to get up early," Kerry whined.

"I don't sing about it," Sol said. "Listen to this; it's got a beat." The booming bass vibrated the lamp on the glass table beside her. "It makes you want to move." He stood and started to dance. Half his gray matter was anesthetized but his style, nevertheless, was fluid. Now if only he could find a place for his beer and cigarettes, he would really be in business. He poked Kerry in the stomach. "Shake your ass, babe. What do you got to go home to?"

Kerry went from angry to pleased in a moment. She kicked off her shoes, and joined Sol. She was very clumsy, tripping over empty Coors cans. They would have to organize a repair crew, or Angie's parents would have a fit when they came home tomorrow. Damn whoever was in the bathroom! Shani closed her eyes, concentrating on her bursting bladder. Someone walked by, brushing her leg.

"Anyone want chocolate chip cookies!?" Angie shouted over the music.

"I'll take one," Park said, his slurry voice nearby. Shani was too tired to open her eyes to be sure, but he seemed to be sitting on the floor by her chair. He must have moved. Angie appeared to plop beside him.

"I baked these this afternoon," Angie said.

"Best I've ever tasted!" Park said.

Angie laughed. "Are you stoned?"

Park giggled. "I'm bouldered! What is this music that Sol's put on? It's so loud."

"Don't know. Want another cookie?"

"Yeah! Ate my first one, I did. Give me that big one. Thank you very much. You're a fantastic hostess. You ought to have a party every week, every blessed week."

"Park?"

"Huh?"

"Robin didn't come."

"Right! Where is she?"

"She didn't come. Did you invite her?"

"I did, but Kerry hates Lena and I hate Sol. He switched my music, without permission. . . . God, I'm so wasted. What time is it?"

"It's not too late. Do you want to go swimming?"

"Don't got my board."

"We can swim in the pool. It's heated; just the two of us."

"Don't like chlorine. Goes through your ears, rots your brain, pickles it, like too much beer."

"Come on, it'll be fun; just the two of us."

"Gimme another cookie."

"Take as many as you want. Shani, do you want any? Shani?"

She was still conscious, but couldn't be bothered answering. She wondered, if she did fall asleep, if she would pee in her pants. Interesting how Angie was trying to get Park alone . . .

"She's bombed out," Park said. "Too much grain in her syrup." He was proud of that one, laughing his fool face off.

"You really like her, don't you?" Angie asked.

"Love Shani. We're like twin brothers. Did I tell you

how in kindergarten she stunk up her pants? Wasted them! Are you wasted?"

"Sure am," Angie said. Shani had not seen her drink more than a can of beer all night. Angie continued: "I meant, Robin. How do you feel about her?"

"Wonderful! We're like mother and wife."

"She's more like a friend?"

"Good friend, great friend. Sol's face should lower down those drums, there. Hurt my ears."

"I thought so. Have you ever, you know, done it?"

Park giggled. "You mean, have we ever had *sex*?"

"Shhh. Yeah, have you?"

"Yeah! No . . . I don't know. Kind of, I think. Not really."

"It's none of my business. I was just wondering. So, let's go swimming."

"Sure! Wait! I don't have my trunks."

"So what? I won't wear my bikini. We can go skinny dipping."

"You mean, *naked*?"

"Sure, why not?"

"I dunno." He sounded interested. Shani was wide awake now, listening closely. Was this the real Angie, Robin's good friend? "Are you drunk, did you say?" Park asked.

"Yeah! But let's go. The others are dancing. We'll leave the pool light off. We'll have fun."

"But if you're drunk, you might say in the morning: 'I hate myself.' You might say that."

"You're not afraid of a naked girl, are you, Park?"

He giggled. He was doing a lot of that. "Noooo."

"So, let's go now. We can go out the front door like we're going for a walk, and circle around to the back."

"Will you tell Robin?"

Angie didn't like the question. "No, but what would it matter if I did? I like you, Park. Don't you like me?"

"Oh, sure. But Robin, she . . . "

"What about her?"

Park couldn't remember, it seemed. "Nothing. Let's do it, yeah."

Shani kept her eyes closed while they skipped off for their erotic aqua sports. But she had to smile when they opened the front door.

"Hi! We made it!" Robin exclaimed, her voice as sweet as an angel's. Shani opened her eyes. Sol stopped the music, quickly putting distance between him and Kerry. Wearing a short dress the exact shade of red as her hair, Lena swept into the living room and claimed her man. Arm in arm with Park, Robin followed, with a frustrated Angie bringing up the rear. Quickly, Shani closed her eyes again. "Hi, Kerry," Robin said. "You look hot. Were you dancing?"

"Sol and I were," Kerry replied thinly.

"Hi, beautiful," Sol said, kissing Robin. Sol often called Robin beautiful. "You're late."

"Lena and I went to the movies. We had the best time. Anyway, afterwards, we stuffed our faces with junk at Jo Jo's and then Lena wanted to drop by and check out the action. So here we are."

"Looks like we missed a good time," Lena said. "This place is a mess. What's Shani been smoking?"

Park giggled. "She's a lightweight. One beer and she goes into a coma." He pinched her big toe through her tennis shoes. Shani opened her eyes slowly.

"Where am I?" she asked, knowing full well; best she act like she was out cold lest Angie realize that she had been listening. The toilet flushed and the bathroom door popped open. Grabbing the arms of her chair, she pulled herself up. "Excuse me, I've passed overflow." Laughter followed her wobbly steps.

Bert was splashing cold water on his face from the bathroom sink. Between them, he and Sol had killed a quart of whiskey.

"Do you feel all right?" she asked.

"Great!" He roughed a towel over his red cheeks, shaking like a horse. "I was just taking myself a little nap in here."

"Do you know how long I've been waiting to get in here?"

"Since I fell asleep?"

"Exactly. Are you done?"

"I heard music. You want to dance?"

"I can hardly stand up."

"Throw up, you'll feel better."

"I don't have to throw up. I have to pee. Hurry up!"

"Stick a finger down your throat." Bert demonstrated, not improving her condition. "Works every time."

Shani put her hand on her stomach as it lurched three inches to the left. "Get out!"

Ten minutes later, tucked back in her chair with her bladder *and* stomach empty, Shani felt better, though still extremely sleepy. On her left, singing to himself, Bert was flipping through the music. Sitting on the floor at Robin's feet, Park was eating Angie's cookies, his girlfriend all the while running her fingers through his hair, talking about the movie. Kerry and Angie were fretting together on the couch. Lena and Sol had disappeared, probably into a bedroom to discuss Euclidean geometry.

"And at the end," Robin was saying, "he got to experience the record of the woman's death. It was so beautiful! What happened was . . . I probably shouldn't tell you. I don't want to ruin it. All of you have got to see it. They have it on the big screen at the mall."

"Where's Lena?" Park wondered aloud, floating in the ozone. "She can go swimming with —"

"I was surprised to see Lena show up," Angie cut him off.

"It wasn't planned," Robin said. "After we ate, she insisted on coming. Sorry, Kerry, if her coming upset things for you."

"Why should I care?"

"Where's Sol?" Park asked, blowing it left and right.

Robin lightly rapped the top of his head with her knuckles. "This poor little boy can't seem to hold his medicine."

"I'm bouldered," Park nodded pleasantly.

"Anyway, for myself," Robin said, "I was hoping you'd still be here, Kerry."

"Why?"

"Nothing important, just wanted to talk."

"About what?"

"A private matter. We can discuss it later."

Kerry chuckled sarcastically. "Nothing's supposed to be private with me, anymore. Say what you want. I don't give a damn."

"I had a long talk with Lena," Robin began. "I'm convinced she had nothing to do with it."

"I'm thankful for your objective opinion," Kerry said.

"I know my sister. She acts the tough cookie, but she would never intentionally try to hurt anybody."

"Her subconscious must be the culprit," Shani mumbled. The conversation was heating up, but her head was cooling down. She couldn't remember having closed her eyes, but a moment came when there were only voices to distract her dreamy thoughts.

"Come off it, Robin," Angie said. "Lena did it. She delayed Kerry; she drenched her with Coke. She set her up."

"I believe a lot of this could be explained by coincidence."

"And the paper shorts?" Angie said.

"I'm going to put on The Beach Boys!" Bert exclaimed.

"Pure, unadulterated brilliance," Park said.

Music, soft and pleasant, floated through her ears, mingled with Robin's polite defense, and Angie's and Kerry's sharp prosecution. But there were gaps, where Shani saw colored pictures as vague as her mushy thoughts, and gray voids, where she saw and heard nothing at all. Yet she continued to surface periodically. The outside voices changed, in personnel and tone. Her name was mentioned, her foot pinched again. Doors opened and closed. New music started playing, people started dancing. The party was getting a second wind. Her bladder began to call for attention again. She opened her eyes.

Park, Bert, Robin, and Angie were dancing as one big couple. Sol was stretched on his back on the couch smoking, Lena sitting on his lap drinking vodka and orange juice. There was no one in the bathroom but it was such a bother to get up. Shani assumed that Kerry had gone home until she saw her come out of the kitchen.

"My car still won't start," she said to Sol.

"Jap junk," he scowled, blowing a cloud of smoke. "I'll take you home in a minute, babe."

"When? It's one-thirty. I've got to work in the morning."

"Shani will take you home," Lena said. Shani deeply appreciated the offer of her services. She doubted she could start a car, never mind drive one.

"Shani's asleep," Sol observed, though her eyes must have been at least half open because she could see. The album came to an end. Angie broke from the dance floor, heading for the kitchen. Bert made for the bathroom—naptime again. Robin fell, winded, into her chair, sweating and laughing, the picture of youth and vigor. Park collapsed at her feet, forever giggling.

"Why don't you just walk?" Lena asked.

Kerry had been doing an admirable job of avoiding Lena. Her approach underwent a dramatic revision. "Why don't you just go to hell?" she blurted.

Lena sipped her drink, said casually, "When the time's right, I probably will."

But Sol sat up suddenly, causing Lena to fall on her ass on the floor and spill her drink in her face. He put out his cigarette. "I'll take you home now, Kerry."

"The hell you will!" Lena yelled, wiping at her dress. "You clumsy Cholo! Look what you've done."

Sol must have still been riding his Jack Daniel's buzz. In a normal state of consciousness, he would not have dared his next words. "Shut up, Lena."

Shani waited for the explosion. Lena's brown eyes widened. She sucked in a breath. "What did you say?" she asked very slowly, very softly.

Shani hoped that Sol actually did carry the switchblade Park accused him of keeping. "You heard me," he said.

"I guess I did," Lena whispered ominously. Everyone waited. Yet the bomb was suddenly diffused, or else put on hold. Lena appeared to realize she was moving into a no-win situation. And Lena hated to lose. She smiled at Kerry. "Sol's so drunk, I know you wouldn't want him to drive. Robin and I won't be here much longer. We can give you a ride home."

What could Kerry say? She had scored the most points, but Lena had still somehow come out on top. "Fine," Kerry muttered.

With the fireworks over, Shani contemplated unconsciousness again. Angie reappeared with a tray laden with freshly tapped liter mugs of beer. Park, Sol, and Kerry each took a glass. Angie set the remainder of the drinks on the corner table next to Robin. Lena went into the kitchen, probably to clean up.

"You running for sainthood?" Angie chided Robin. "Have a drink."

"I'll pass. I have to drive."

"Come on," Park said. "I've been drinking all night and I wouldn't hesitate to climb on top of the wheel."

"You mean, *behind* the wheel," Robin laughed.

"Wouldn't hesitate!" Park swore, drinking deeply.

Sol changed the music. His brain cells must have been drowning. They listened to an entire album before Bert came out of the bathroom and stumbled into the stereo, turning off the music. Kerry jumped up for a nature call, but ran into Lena at the bathroom door. They exchanged unheard words. Kerry ended up following Bert—who was wandering aimlessly—into the kitchen. Sol shook his head sadly and got to his feet. He did not go into the kitchen or the bathroom, but drifted out of sight down the hall.

"You look like you need a beer!" Park called at Shani.

She closed her eyes. "Don't bother me, I'm asleep." And she must have been for the next few minutes. When she opened her eyes next, everyone was back in the living room. This party would go on forever. Sol was sitting on a chair next to Robin, offering her his mug of beer. Lena was planted precariously on the arm of the chair. Angie was on the floor at their feet with Park, whispering in his ear. Bert was lying facedown on the carpet. Kerry was sitting on his butt, her back to Shani.

"We've got to get Robin drunk," Park announced. "It's our duty, our God-given duty."

"How are you going to lose your virginity if you won't let a guy get you drunk?" Sol asked, nudging Robin with his half-full glass. Shani wondered if they had spiked it with whiskey. It looked darker than ordinary beer.

"Yeah!" Park cheered.

Robin blushed and took the glass, weighing it in her hands. "You won't believe this, but I've never even tasted beer before."

"You haven't missed a thing," Shani muttered.

"Sleeping Beauty's awake!" Park said. "Did I ever tell you guys how she messed her pants in fifth grade?"

"In kindergarten," Shani said. It came to her then how the mood of the room had changed. They had had drunken dancing, bursting bladders, spilled food, frustrated seductions, sharp arguments, and none of that had seriously dented the upbeat feeling of the party. Yet now, even in her dull condition, she sensed a building tension, as tangible to her as if a foul stench were being pumped into the room. She studied her friends, finding no explanation.

"Finish it in a gulp," Lena advised her sister. "You'll be a new person."

"I don't know why you're badgering her," Kerry said. "If she doesn't want it, she doesn't want it."

"I better not. It will just put me to sleep."

"Wimp," Lena said.

"To the eternal virgin," Park toasted with his empty glass.

"I guess you're going to be the one to drive us home, then," Sol said, lighting another cigarette.

Angie whispered in Park's ear, his eyes widening. She said out loud, "One drink, it won't kill you."

Shani sat up with a start. Afterwards, she would be unable to clearly explain to the others why. She did not believe in precognition, and her foreboding did not necessarily require its existence, for her nose may simply have picked up the poison and triggered a subconscious warning. Yet if that were so, Robin, who was closest to the glass, should have smelled it also. In either case, to Shani the room seemed suddenly permeated with death. She was afraid and she did not know why. Robin picked up the mug, took a sip. She frowned.

"This tastes awful."

"Finish it," Lena said.

Like a hardened guzzler, Robin did so, in one continuous swallow. Perhaps she thought that would impress them. But they only laughed. Bert rolled over, spilling Kerry, taking interest. Robin put the glass down, touching her stomach, staring straight ahead.

"So, what do you think?" Park asked.

Robin coughed, hard, twice. "Tastes awful," she breathed.

"Are you okay?" Shani asked, nevertheless beginning to relax. She must study about these impending-disaster sensations when she went to college. They came and went like lightning. Robin nodded, smiled weakly.

"Was that enough to get me drunk?"

"How do you feel?" Sol asked.

"Weird."

"Then it was probably enough."

Robin wiped her forehead. She was sweating like after dancing—heavier. "I think I'll stick to Coke. Does it always leave such a bad taste in your mouth?" She leaned back in her chair.

"I've never noticed," Sol said. "Kerry, you still want a ride home?"

Lena butt in. "Robin and I are giving her a ride home."

Kerry yawned. "I'm so tired. Maybe I'll just spend the night."

"You're welcome to," Angie said, "if you'll give me a hand cleaning up."

"Okay."

"How about you, Park?" Angie asked. Lena left for the kitchen. Sol had to use the toilet. Bert rooted his face back in the carpet.

"Count me in! Are we still going to go —"

"Shh," Angie said. She leaned over, spoke in his ear. Park nodded eagerly. Shani required no ESP to know what she had said. How could they swim nude with Robin present? But then she understood. Robin had gone to sleep. That was quick. Angie and Park headed for the front door. Shani stopped him.

"Park?" she called.

He spun around. "Yes, madam?"

"Robin just passed out."

"So?"

Shani stood. "She was awake a second ago."

"She drank too much."

"As if she had a choice. She only drank one glass."

Kerry moved to Robin's side and took her limp hand. Robin's head lay bowed like a puppet's whose strings had been cut. "She's out cold," Kerry said, worried.

Park knelt by his girlfriend's side, brushed aside a soft brown curl from her face, and glanced back at Angie. "That's weird," he whispered.

Angie spoke quickly. "Carry her into my parents' bedroom. Let her sleep it off."

"Good idea," Park said, slipping his arms under Robin's body, lifting her easily. She only weighed 110.

"Maybe we should wake her," Kerry said, "have her drink coffee."

"Sleep's the best thing," Angie said.

Shani held her peace. So Robin was out. They would be fools to try anything with Lena around. She hoped they did and got caught. She was suddenly angry at Angie and Park, especially at him. What a hypocrite, the care he showed carrying his girlfriend to the bedroom.

Sol finished in the bathroom. Shani took his place, washing her face and brushing her teeth. When she returned to the living room, Sol and Lena were leaving out the front door, Kerry was fixing the bed in the guest room, and Bert was asleep on the floor. Shani turned out the nearest lamp and lay back on the couch, swearing that if the roof caved in, she wasn't getting up.

An indeterminate time went by. Behind closed eyelids,

Shani noted the rest of the lights going out. Someone with alcoholic breath covered her with a blanket. Doors opened and closed. Far away, she thought she heard splashes and laughter, but she wasn't sure.

Someone was shaking her. She opened her eyes. It was dark, and a shadow loomed over her.

"What is it?" Shani mumbled. She had a headache.

"I'm sick," Kerry said anxiously.

Shani remembered Bert's advice. "Stick your finger down your throat, throw up." She rolled over. "You'll feel better."

Kerry had the bad manners to yank her into a sitting position. A yellow glow from the porch light strained through the kitchen's curtains. It was sufficient to show Kerry's tears. "I've thrown up," she coughed. "I've got cramps. I can hardly breathe."

Shani was not alarmed. Kerry often panicked. "You're going to be fine. You've just had too much beer. A hot bath will help." She took her trembling hands. "I'll run the water for you."

Suddenly Kerry doubled up in dry heaves, gasping for air.

"No! I never get sick from beer! It was bad! There was something in it! I have a strange taste in my mouth!"

Shani reversed her diagnosis. "Try to relax. Who else is still here?"

"Park's asleep in—hall—Angie—Eeeh! I can't take this! Help me, Shani!"

"I will." She turned on the lamp. Bert was where she had last seen him, snoring peacefully. She jumped to her feet and kicked his butt. "Wake up! Get up!" He groaned, began to stretch. Running down the hall, she stumbled over Park, who was crashed outside Angie's partially cracked door.

"Huh?" he muttered, sitting up. She turned on the hall light.

"Kerry's sick! I think there was something in the beer!"

Park was barely awake, scratching his head. "There's alcohol in beer. God, my head hurts. It makes everyone sick."

"How do you feel?"

"Terrible, how else? Why did you wake me?"

"You don't have cramps?"

He grimaced, rubbed his bloodshot eyes. "Girls get cramps, Shani, not boys. What time is it?"

"Where did you put Robin?" she demanded.

His eyes focused. He was suddenly alert. He pointed to the door at the end of the hall on the left. "In the master bedroom. Why do you say there was something in the beer?"

Shani did not answer him. She raced to the door, threw it open, snapped on the light. Robin was huddled in the fetal position in the center of the king-sized bed. Shani jumped on the mattress and rolled her friend on her back.

"Robin! Robin!" she shook her. *"Robin!!!"*

Park came up at her back. "Get out of the way," he ordered. He put a finger under Robin's nose, checked her pulse. "Robin!" he shouted. She did not respond. He slapped her across the face, her head rolling like a mannequin's. He moved to her feet, pinching her Achilles tendon. Nothing.

"Is she dead?" Shani moaned, a weight beyond comprehension crushing her chest.

Park pulled the pillow from beneath Robin's head and pried open her mouth, checking for obstructions with his fingers. Taking a breath and forcing his lips against hers, he exhaled. Robin's diaphram rose sharply, once. He listened at her chest, muttered, "Clear."

"Is she dead? Answer me, damn you!"

Park stood, pale as a winter moon, but sober, in command. "No, but she's in a shock or a coma. Use the phone in the kitchen. Call the hospital. The number is taped beside the phone. Tell them we're bringing in two poison victims." He picked Robin up, cradling her in his arms. "I'll start the car."

"Shouldn't we call for an ambulance?" There was no time to feel hurt. Yet later, she knew, there would be too much time.

"This will be faster." He kissed Robin's forehead, moving for the door. "Now do as I say."

Angie and Bert wanted to come, but since they felt fine, Park told them to contact Sol and Lena, and to wait by the phone and keep the line open. He also suggested they sniff the glasses and mugs they had used during the party for suspicious smells. Unfortunately, Angie had washed them all before going to bed. Angry, Park told them to look around, anyway.

Park held Robin and they lay Kerry in the backseat. Shani drove like a fiend and ran a red light, picking up a flashing highway patrol car. After explaining the situation to the officer, they had a police escort. At the hospital, the doctors were waiting. Kerry disappeared on a stretcher through swinging doors while the officer carried Robin inside. Park called Angie. She had found a half-empty bottle of Insect Death in the refrigerator. Park copied down the insecticide's ingredients and gave the paper to a nurse, who hurried through the door where Kerry and Robin had gone. The two of them sat down to wait.

Ten minutes later — showing no adverse symptoms — Sol arrived. Ten minutes after that, Lena and her parents showed up. Lena was silent. Mrs. Carlton was heartbroken. Mr. Carlton was furious. He called the police and told them to get to Angie's house and begin a complete investigation before any of the evidence could be tampered with. Kerry's mom and dad came next. Together, the four parents comforted each other.

A nurse brought them news. Kerry's stomach had been pumped and she was feeling better. But, although Robin had been revived, her condition was critical. She was vomiting blood, and flirting with circulatory failure. Later, a young internist updated their conditions. Given her symptoms, Kerry had in all probability ingested a small amount of the insect killer. Robin, however, had definitely swallowed at least three ounces of the poison. Two ingredients in Insect Death, phosphorous and mercury, were particularly toxic to the kidneys and were therefore endangering her heart. *If* Robin made it through the night, there was a chance — looking back, the doctor must have known that it was more than likely — that she would suffer permanent damage.

Shani took a seat far away from the others. At the end of the corridor, through glass doors, she saw an orange glow in the east. But the way she felt, the night could have been just beginning.

Kerry made a swift recovery, though she would often afterwards complain of stomachaches. Robin did not leave the hospital till two months later, twenty pounds lighter and a ghastly yellow with a slightly damaged liver and two all but useless kidneys. Unless she had a successful transplant, the doctors said, she would be tied to a dialysis machine the rest of her life. And that life would not be nearly as long as average.

Two pairs of fingerprints were found on the bottle of Insect Death: Angie's and Bert's. Of course, they had both studied the bottle when Park had called from the hospital to see if they had located a source of the poison. Mr. Carlton blamed them all, even Lena. At his insistence, the police gathered them in Robin's hospital room three times and tried to reenact the sequence of events that had led to the fateful drink. The police ended up with eight different stories, not always the same one from the same individual. All of them had gone in and out of the kitchen all night long. Who could remember when and why and with whom? Everyone agreed that Sol had given her *a* beer, but who had given it to him, and was it the same person who had initiated the prodding to have Robin drink the beer, and had she actually drunk *his* beer? For a while, Sol was on the burner, but he had made himself too obvious a suspect to be a suspect. Too much alcohol had blurred their memories, not to mention the fact that almost all of them had something to hide. And Robin herself was no help. Though anxious to catch the culprit—if there was one—the trauma of her injury had created a mental block against the night. It was finally recorded in the books as an "accident," caused by "one or more intoxicated adolescents mistaking an insecticide for a common beverage and inadvertently mixing it with a glass of beer." No lawsuits were filed, no fingers were pointed. Life went on as usual. Except for Robin.

But Shani was often to ask herself, No matter how drunk you were, how could you take a bottle covered with insect sketches and labeled, in bold black letters, CAUTION POISONOUS, and pour it in a glass a person was to drink out of, unless you wanted to kill that person?

∽ Chapter 6 ∾

Sitting on his surfboard, Park stared down at his legs dangling in the blue-green bathtub-temperature water and started to worry about sharks. A couple of hours ago Bert had mentioned seeing a few sharks. But at the time, the waves had been rolling and the tubes curling and the information had not seemed important. Now the sets were well-spaced and he had too much time to think. He could imagine a baby shark, just breaking in its teeth, swimming by and biting off his big toe. The blood would spurt and he would scream and mother shark would hear and come to investigate what her youngster was up to. Then she would smell his blood and bite off his leg. He had read about such tragedies. He had also read that when you started to worry about losing a limb, it was time to get out of the water. He pulled up his legs, resting his feet near the nose of the board and holding the rails to maintain balance. One more wave and he would call it quits.

The beach and conditions were a surfer's dream. Unadulterated golden sand stretched north and south to the horizon. Except for a few white clouds far out at sea, the sky was a cerulean dish whose depth it was easy to believe was infinite. He could feel the warmth of the sun's rays in his blood. He was floating in twenty feet of salt water, but the bedrock was as clear as if it were simply the bottom of a swimming pool. And the waves had ruined him for life. An easy eight-foot or he was a dwarf, an off-shore breeze held their form to the last crucial instant. He was in heaven, but he was exhausted.

"One more and I'm going in!" he called to Bert, a hundred yards to his left. A strong riptide was pulling them south. Several times since sunrise, when they had started, they had had to go ashore and walk back to the house. Once again, the Carlton Castle was a mile up the beach.

"I'm with you! Where's Sol?"

"He went in half an hour ago!" Tired of shouting, Park lay down on his board and paddled toward Bert. The aroma of his coconut-waxed board filled his head, making him nostalgic for Hawaii. Last summer, Mr. and Mrs. Carlton had sent Robin and him—along with Nurse Porter as an escort—to the islands. The waves hadn't been nearly as good as today, but he had been happier then, a lot happier.

He pulled up alongside Bert. "Sol said he had a side-ache. Lena probably wore him out last night."

"Did I tell you about the sharks I saw?"

"Yes, and I don't want you to tell me again."

Bert's ears must have been plugged with water. He continued: "One of them was bigger than me. It couldn't have been a sand shark. It looked like that fish in that movie, that one — what was it called?"

"*Jaws.*"

"What?"

"*Jaws!*"

"Yeah, that one. Are you sure Sol went in?"

Park again pulled up his feet. "You know you're making me pretty damn paranoid. Would you please just shut your mouth?"

Bert grinned. He was impossible to offend. "You're afraid of sharks? I thought you didn't like snakes."

"I hate anything that wants to bite me — Oh!" Distracted, he hadn't noticed the approaching set. The first swell looked the killer. He pivoted his board expertly. Bert was also maneuvering into position. "You go right, I'll go left!" he yelled.

"Gotcha!"

The wave was a monster. On his knees, Park dug hard to gain the necessary speed. A powerful force began to take hold, raising him up. One last stroke and he sprang to his feet, leaning forward to compensate for what may have been a premature stand. But he was okay, sliding down the face, when Bert suddenly crossed his path, six feet below, a perfect place to be for a decapitation. Park reacted immediately, twisting to the right. The tunnel was closing in that direction. A raging foam hammer belted him off his board. Park felt a violent tug at his left ankle, saw splintered, whirling bubbles, had his spine twisted to the other side of a chiropractor's fantasies. Yet he had hold of a good breath and was able to ride out the bad weather. When the washing machine turned off, he was a hundred yards offshore in a relatively calm region between the first and second break. His board was already on the beach. The tug on his ankle had been his leash snapping.

Bert cruised by. "I thought you meant 'right,' looking out to sea," he apologized.

"That's okay. I think I just got a free neck adjustment. Give me a ride in."

During the walk back, Bert told him how he had awakened during the night and had found himself circled by a bunch of bright-eyed birds. Tonight, he said, he was sleeping indoors.

Sol was flat on his back on a red towel blowing smoke rings toward the sky. Shani and Angie were on the north side of the carport, piling wood into a concave hole they had dug. The Carlton Castle had an antenna dish and recording studio, two spas and three computers, but no barbecue. The girls were improvising. They said they were going to roast wienies for lunch. Park wasn't hungry.

"How's your sideache?" Park asked, setting down his board.

"It hasn't gone away," Sol said, rolling over, digging in the sand, and pulling out a quart of tequila. "I think I need my medicine. How about you?"

Park shook his head. "It's too early for me."

Bert beamed. "You got a bottle for me?"

"We'll split it," Sol said. "Hell, this is enough for anybody." Bert looked disappointed.

"Where're the others?" Park asked.

"Kerry's wandering all over looking for rocks for her collection. Lena's —"

"For *what*?" Park interrupted.

"Kerry collects unusual rocks," Sol explained. "She reshapes and polishes them. At her house, she has a closetful of pretty things. A lot of them make Lena's ten-grand jewelry look like plastic. Kerry has a knack for that kind of stuff." He shrugged. "It makes her happy."

"If Lena catches her, she'll charge her duty on the rocks," Park said.

"Lena's putting Robin through her usual torture. I don't know where Flynn is, haven't seen that cat all day." Sol uncapped the bottle, sniffed it, and took a slug. He held out the tequila. Park shook his head. Bert took a big swallow. Sol screwed the cap back on, adding, "Why don't you go talk to her?"

"I don't want to disturb her."

"She just sits there, reading. She gets bored. Go talk to her."

"I can't stand the sight of blood."

Sol was angry. "The sight of your own blood's a lot worse."

It was an unpleasant task that would be better over with. He owed her an explanation. Besides, Sol might kill him if he didn't. "I'll talk to her now," he said, walking toward the house. Shani waved to him, a can of lighter fluid in her hand. Angie called out something he couldn't quite catch. He waved back and went inside.

The dialysis machine was in a tiny room on the top floor. Park found it by following the mediciney smell. The door was open. He peeped inside. Robin was alone, wearing a light blue robe. Two blood-filled tubes—one leading from her left arm, the other, from beneath her robe—hooked her to the artificial kidney. The unit was largely self-contained, a shiny metallic box four feet at the edges. Two closed half-filled beakers sat atop it, connected by plastic pipes. What looked like a fire extinguisher, but probably wasn't, was bolted to the side. Robin was sitting propped up by pillows, a facedown paperback on her lap, a breeze from an adjacent window brushing her short brown hair. She used to have such beautiful hair. . . . On the windowsill was perched a black raven. Robin was talking to it, stroking its shiny mane.

". . . I don't remember, my friend. Human minds usually don't go back that far. And I could have nothing to remember. I don't know if I even got to see her. Sometimes it's done that way. And I could have been blind but for light and shadow. Still, I think about her a lot."

The bird chirped. Park thought it was alerting Robin to his presence, but she did not turn. There were many blackbirds in the neighborhood, yet he could have sworn that this was the one the Shaman had had in his hand. Robin offered a bread crumb. The raven took it hungrily. Robin continued: "I told them the story; Lena made me. I should probably have never mentioned the talks to her. To Lena, to have a master is to be a slave. But maybe I wanted to tell the others. Maybe . . ." She stopped petting the bird, touched the golden eagle at her throat. "Maybe the one . . . no, it couldn't be." She smiled to herself. "Of course, I didn't tell them the end. How could I do that?" She leaned over, kissing the bird on the top of the head. "Now, go, my friend. Do what you will do. Maybe soon we will fly together."

The raven shrieked, launching into the wind. Thinking of deals with the devil, he knocked lightly. Robin turned and smiled.

"Come in, Park. I was hoping you would visit me."

"THE STOVE WOULD HAVE BEEN EASIER," ANGIE SAID.

"Get back!" Shani called, striking the wooden match, tossing it on the lighter-fluid-drenched wood. The flames ignited in a black billow of oily smoke. "But just think of the superior taste."

"Think of the carcinogenics."

"We'll let the lighter fluid burn off before we roast the hot dogs. That won't take long. It'll be like old times."

"We've never done this before," Angie said.

"But in the future, when we do it again, we'll be able to say, Gosh, this is like old times!"

Angie fished through the cooler at her feet, pulling out a packet of Farmer John's one-footers. "You're awfully chipper today. Did Flynn visit you last night?"

"Only for sex," Shani said. In reality, she did not feel well. She had tossed until the sun had risen. The label on Insect Death had hung like a billboard in her dreams. When she had awoken, for a moment, the entire party had been clear in her memory. But only for a moment. Then the flashback had clouded, leaving her doubtful and with an upset stomach, which was getting worse as the day progressed. She would probably pass on lunch. "How about you and Park?" she asked.

"I never kiss and tell."

"Whoever says that, has nothing to tell."

"Look who's talking."

"Really," Shani agreed.

"When do you think the others will start arriving?"

Shani consulted her faithful Timex. "It's close to one. I would think that someone should have showed up by now. That Lena . . . I don't know, maybe she put down the wrong month along with the wrong day."

She wiped her hands on her shorts. "I'm going to go inside."

"*What?* You're the one who talked me into this bonfire."

"I just want to see how Robin's doing. I'll be back in a minute." And she wanted to run into Flynn. Dangerous or not, he was still cute.

"How long should I wait before sticking these wienies in the fire?" Angie impaled a hot dog on a sharp branch.

"Wait until I get back."

On the way to the house, Shani passed the carport. Open bottle in hand, Bert and Sol were climbing into the back of the van. She waved to them but they did not see her.

Climbing up the front porch steps, she stopped and laughed. Angie was cursing venomously. A blackbird had snatched her wienie stick—hot dog and all—and was racing away, trying to get back in the air with the goods. Angie was chasing the poor bird with a fiery branch and face. Shani considered going for her camera when she saw a tan-clad figure approaching along the northern beach.

The dry air rippled with rising ground heat. He flowed in the distorted landscape like a phantom in the wind. Bright orange gleamed at his midsection. Shani did not know why, but she was certain he was staring at her as she was at him. From Sol's description, she knew this was Robin's sorcerer.

The man stopped and sat down, staring out to sea. Shani

shielded her eyes from the glare and watched him for a full five minutes. But he did not move. When she spoke with Robin, she would ask if it was appropriate to simply walk up to him and say hello.

Inside, Shani discovered that she had no idea where the dialysis was done. In this big house, it was a problem. She called but no one answered. The basement was probably the most likely place to stick a lab, she decided. She started down the stairs.

Instead of an infirmary, she found an elaborate recording studio—that made sense, as music was, after all, Mr. Carlton's business, and Robin's voice had been potential platinum. The room was a perfect circle, the top half of its walls ringed with double-glazed glass, undoubtedly separated by a soundproof vacuum. An elaborate control panel stood outside a solitary entrance door. Shani went inside, stepping onto a heavily padded floor. She was reminded of the room in the ride at Magic Mountain that spun around and around and pressed you against the walls, just before the floor dropped out. That ride had made her sick.

The ventilation must have been out of whack. It was freezing inside the studio. Opposite the door, on the floor, was sprinkled sawdust from recently drilled holes. Red, green, and black wires passed through the punctured paneling to a tiny metallic box arrayed with colorless buttons. In the center of the room was a high stool, supporting, of all things, an old tape recorder. Curious about the small metal box, Shani picked it up, pressing a button. An electric motor hummed, a microphone attached to an aluminum pole descending from the ceiling toward the stool. She released the button, afraid she might break something. The microphone halted.

Inside the tape recorder was a tape labeled MAY 30 — R.C. Robin must have recently made the recording. Shani depressed PLAY. On this tune, at least, Robin's kidneys had not hurt her voice. If anything, she sounded better. It was a Beatles song.

"Blackbird singing in the dead of night,
Take these broken wings and learn to fly.
All your life, you were only waiting for this
moment to arise.

"Blackbird singing in the dead of night,
Take these sunken eyes and learn to see.
All your life, you were only waiting for this
moment to be free.

"Blackbird fly, blackbird fly,
Into the light of a dark black night. . . ."

"What are you doing in here?"

Shani jumped, and pushed STOP. It was Lena. "Is this a restricted area?" she asked. Lena had frightened her.

Like a lion approaching its prey, Lena moved into the room. She was not smiling. "My father doesn't let anyone, outside the family, down here."

"Sorry, I didn't know."

Lena strolled by, glancing around as if checking to see if anything had been stolen. "Were you looking for something?" she asked.

"Robin."

"She's upstairs."

"I didn't know."

Lena looked at her, suspicious. "You said that already."

Shani was suddenly sick of her tone. "Do you want me to say it a third time, on my knees?"

Lena smiled. "Yeah, then kiss my feet. Then get the hell out of here."

"Lay off, would ya?"

Lena smiled. "Okay, so I was abrupt. But there's a lot of expensive equipment down here. You can play anywhere else in the house." She consulted her watch, whirled, and headed for the door. "I've got to get back to Robin. Follow me."

Lena moved like a racewalker. Shani lagged behind, not enjoying the feeling of being a dog on a leash. She allowed Lena a substantial lead, and when she came to turn the corner, no one was to be seen. Lena could have gone in one of four directions. Shani didn't care. She would find Robin in a minute. First, she decided, she would call her mother. She went looking for a phone.

"This tube in my arm leads from my radial artery," Robin was saying. "This is where the process starts. My blood is pumped from the artery to one side of a semi-permeable cellophane membrane. That's inside this metal container. I'd let you open it and look, but Ellen would know and she'd throw a fit. Anyway, the other side of the membrane is continually washed with the dialyzing solution, which is in that full beaker there. The other beaker has the used solution. All blood going inside the machine is treated with an anticoagulant. Only about half a liter of my blood is inside at a time. All the stuff—including the junk—in the blood can cross back and forth through the membrane, except, of course, the protein molecules and the blood cells. The electrolyte level is controlled —"

"I'm familiar with the process," Park interrupted.

She was surprised. "Are you?"

"I once researched the subject." Two days after her accident. "Too bad they can't compress this all inside you."

"Maybe one day they will be able to." She added, "In a hundred years."

He was sitting on a chair three feet from her couch. Through the open window, the ocean was between sets, flat and peaceful. He studied the floor. "I wanted to talk."

"Really? No, you don't. Do you?"

He glanced up, noting the gray circles around her eyes. "Do *you* want to, or do you want me to leave?"

She sighed, laying her head back. There was a dark red stain on her blue robe where the blood returned via her—he even remembered the name—saphenous vein. "I don't know."

"I'll leave."

She sat up quickly, reaching for his hand. "Please don't. I want to talk, I really do." She smiled. "We used to talk all the time. Remember? Especially late at night. I would turn off the light in my room and make my parents think I was asleep, and be on the phone with you until three in the morning." She chuckled. "The next day I would call in sick to school. But you never did. I used to envy your endurance. I still can't figure out what we talked about. It must have been interesting."

"Robin, I don't —"

"I'm sorry, I'm being nostalgic. You're probably not in the mood." She squeezed his hand. "Tell me; I will listen."

He stared her straight in the eye. There, it was clear that she was dying. "God, Robin, you look terrible."

Her right cheek twitched once, her eyes moistened. "I feel terrible," she said softly. "It's like someone is tightening a clamp on my head. And my back—everything aches. And I'm so tired."

"This isn't normal for you?"

She shook her head. "It's usually not this bad."

"We should call for a doctor."

"No! I . . . I'll be okay. I'm just . . . changing the subject. I know why I feel bad."

"Is it me?"

She nodded, turning away, letting go of his hand. "You and Angie."

"I wanted to say that I'm sorry."

"For what? You're young, full of energy, full of life. You should have a girlfriend that you can have fun with. And no, I'm not playing the martyr. I'm being practical, as you have chosen to be. I can't have a boyfriend. How? I'm either hooked up to this gizmo or taking a nap."

"You can still talk on the phone."

She brightened, for a moment. "I'd have nothing to talk about. I don't do anything. I read, watch TV, listen to music. Occasionally, I try to sing, but I'm even beginning to lose my voice. My life's pretty dull." She paused, searching the sea. Her left hand clenched. She whispered, "This last couple of months, I waited for *you* to call."

"I wanted to."

"Did you lose the number?" She grimaced. "Forgive me, I didn't mean that."

The bitterness actually helped. "I deserve it. I wish you hated me."

"I did, I think, for an hour here, a day there." She had closed her eyes, wearing a dreamy expression. "But it was never for long. You want to hear something silly, a line from a soap? I think if I had known at the beginning when

I drank that poison that you would leave me, I think I would have died that night. I don't think I could have seen such a dark future, and known that there would be no outside light, and have lived." She found his hand. "That must make you feel pretty rotten, but that's not why I told you. I told you to let you know how much you meant to me, and still mean to me." She looked at him, wrinkled her nose. "Pretty silly, huh?"

"Totally irrational." He paused. "I don't love Angie."

"You should; she's a nice girl. I hate her."

"Do you really?"

"I wanted to poison her drink last night."

"Why didn't you?"

"I didn't think she would be dumb enough to swallow a glass spiked with hemlock."

"You weren't dumb. It wasn't your fault."

"Whose was it then?"

There was an edge to her question. "It was an accident."

"Lena doesn't think so."

"What do you think?"

"How could —" she began, stopping herself, shrugging. "I think beer tastes awful. But here I go again, changing the subject. I told you I would listen. What did you want to tell me?"

She asked casually, but not without hope. He wanted to give her the world. Why couldn't he give her his own self? "I stayed away because I was afraid. What happened to you scares me. I guess I worry that it could happen to me. That's irrational, too, but that's the way I feel. But seeing you again, I'm not so scared now."

She waited. He was torturing her. "And?" she asked.

"And I was wondering if we could start talking on the phone again?"

"Are you going to call collect?"

"Of course."

"What will we talk about?"

He leaned over, kissing her lips lightly. "Right now, everything isn't clear to me. But if we talk, maybe things will get clearer. Is that enough, for now?"

She smiled, clasping his neck with her free right arm, pulling him within inches. "We can plot a way to kill Angie."

"Should it be slow and painful?"

Robin nodded. "In payment for her sins."

Park chuckled, yet such talk made him uneasy. Robin was only joking, but she *had* suffered grievously. He stood and walked to the south window. A flock of blackbirds was circling the house. He pinpointed the source of his disquiet. "What were you talking to that bird about?"

"I didn't know you were listening."

"Only for a moment. He seemed to like you."

"*She.* Her name is Rita."

"Lovely Rita."

"I was telling her about my mother." She saw his

confusion. "My *real* mother. I think about her a lot, nowadays. Must be the little girl in me. I'm sick and I want my mommy." She took a deep breath and scratched her short hair, her melancholy returning. "I wish I could find her. She gave me my body to begin with, I guess I feel she could somehow help me with getting a part fixed." She wiped at her eyes. "What am I saying? For all I know, she's dead."

An idea, bright with unlooked-for hope, blazed in his mind. "Robin, is it possible that . . . ?"

He didn't finish. An explosion, powerful enough to shatter every window in the room, drowned out his voice.

SHANI PICKED UP THE PHONE. THERE WAS NO DIAL TONE. This was the third phone she had tried, all dead. She would have to tell Lena, or Robin.

But restarting her search for the dialysis room, she was troubled. They were isolated in a foreign country. No one else from their class, not one single one of them, had arrived. And now the phones were out. Was she being paranoid, or was there a pattern to all this?

The way Robin had caught Lena's eye last night suggested there was more to the shaman's story. Shani did not feel her paranoia would be soothed by knowing the parable's ending, but she was curious as to why Robin felt secrecy necessary. Suffering only minor conscience qualms, she headed for Robin's bedroom.

The door was closed, but unlocked. She pushed it open

gently. Flynn was inside, up to no good. Using a wire and metal pin, he was working on the lock of a green filing cabinet tucked in the corner beside Robin's desk. Atop the desk was the manila envelope that held the story. Robin had closed it before retiring last night. Now the envelope was open. The cabinet lock snapped. Flynn pulled out a drawer. Quickly, methodically, he began to scan the files.

Shani closed the door carefully, backed down the hall slowly, then turned and ran. She would tell Park and Sol. They would know what to do.

A second later, she changed her mind. She rationalized that his crime was insignificant; she needed more facts. But the truth was apparent to her from the start. She didn't want to get him in trouble because she liked him. His picking locks actually made him more interesting.

But she was no lovesick fool. She would continue to probe his past, starting with seeing if he was really Flynn Powers. If he could search Robin's room, she could search his.

She had been with Lena when rooms had been assigned, so she knew where his things were stowed. However, her hurried beeline was interrupted by a necessary stop at the bathroom. Ordinarily she had a nervous stomach, but this was ridiculous. She sat grimacing on the toilet, worried that she would vomit on top of her diarrhea. Fortunately, the spasm was brief. With cold water splashed in her face, she felt fine, only a bit drained. She ran for Flynn's room.

He had brought only a flight bag. However, it was packed tight and she couldn't get by jammed shirts and pants using a careful approach. Frustrated, she inverted the bag and smacked the bottom, dumping the entire contents on the bed. Sitting atop the pile was a British passport.

MICHAEL RYAN RICHARDSON. HEIGHT: 5'11", WEIGHT: 155. ADDRESS: 307 13TH STREET #B , PLYMOUTH, ENGLAND, 00642-A.

Shani liked the picture, but that was all. She memorized the information and repacked the bag as best she could. On the way out, she decided she could risk a quick inspection of his desk. It would take him a while to go through all the files in Robin's cabinet.

Despite his lock-picking and false name, she was surprised to find a gun at the back of his lower left-hand drawer. It was a small black pistol, and she couldn't help noticing that it was loaded. He was a fox and he had an enchanting voice and style running out of his beautiful hands, but guns were for killing, and that was too much for Shani. She would tell—

"Can I help you?"

It was Michael Ryan Richardson. Shani jumped, dropping the pistol. There was a delay, it couldn't have gone off. The violent explosion made no sense.

ROBIN CALLED AFTER HIM, BUT PARK DID NOT WAIT TO unhook her tubes. One look through the blown-out window at the carport and garage—what had been the carport and garage—and he was racing for the front door. An absurd idea flashed in his head: They had been hit by a meteor.

The damage was beyond comprehension. The carport and garage and everything that had been inside them were *gone*. A dark cloud sparking with red lightning mushroomed toward the sky, obscuring the sun and temporarily plunging the landscape into a grim twilight. Through ashen mists, a torn black crater emerged, littered with rubble. Charred, dusty debris rained down. He doubted there was now anything he could do that would make any difference. The convulsion had simultaneously ignited and extinguished its flames. Besides, there was nothing to burn.

As if awakening from a dream, he noticed that Shani, Flynn, Sol, and Lena had joined him. With relief, he saw Angie and Kerry approaching from the far side of the cataclysm. The smoke began to disperse. The sun blazed down. Park wiped the sweat from his upper lip.

"Where's Bert?" Shani asked. "He was with you, wasn't he, Sol?"

"I had to go to the head," Sol said evasively. Park understood in an instant. It did not seem possible.

"But he was with you," she said, not hysterical, but getting there.

Park asked Sol, "Was Bert in your van?"

Sol studied the desolation. "He was there when I went into the house."

"Maybe he had to go to the bathroom, too," Shani said quickly. "Bert! Bert!"

"Shani . . ." Park began.

"Bert! Come out, Bert! Where is he? Maybe he went surfing. Maybe went for a walk. *Bert!*"

Sol grabbed her by the shoulders. Her last "Bert" stuck in her open mouth. "He was in the van, Shani," Sol said. "He's dead."

She nodded slowly, relaxing in his hands. "I know," she whispered. "I saw him in there when I walked by." Sol hugged her. She began to cry softly.

"I'll go get Robin," Lena said, as cool as when the internist had come through the swinging green doors early one morning with the bad news about her sister.

"Wait a minute," Park said.

"I don't know how it happened," Lena said. "We don't keep nuclear warheads in our garage."

"How about dynamite? A propane tank? Drums of gasoline?"

Lena shook her head. "We have a propane tank, but it's buried on the far side of the house. There was absolutely nothing in the garage that could have made an explosion one hundredth that powerful. I'm going to get my sister. I'll be back in a minute." She squeezed Shani's arm. "I'm sorry about Bert."

Kerry and Angie joined them. Kerry started to cry when told about Bert, dropping her brightly colored rocks on the cement walkway. Angie was bleeding from her head but it was just a scratch. Of them all—except for Flynn—Angie had known Bert the least. She did not appear unduly upset.

"You were next to the carport," Park said. "How did you escape?"

"A bird was driving me nuts," Angie said. "It had already stolen one hot dog; then it came back and stole a whole packet. I was chasing it down the beach when what happened, happened."

"Did you see Bert leave, maybe?" Shani asked, having accepted the truth but unable to stop hoping. Angie shook her head.

Park wanted to question Kerry but she was in no condition to give straight answers. It would probably accomplish nothing. Shani was trying to comfort her. He spoke to the men. "Any ideas?"

"Perhaps there was a natural gas cavity beneath the garage," Flynn said, "and the barbecue fire ignited it."

Park thought the idea insightful. Robin had once told him that there was a major oil field not far southeast of their house. Indeed, Mr. Carlton owned a portion of it. However, there was a more likely possibility, at least to his own mind. Sol had picked up a lot of *something* in Tijuana, and had stored it in the back of his van. He had assumed that it was drugs Sol would sell for a profit in L.A. But perhaps it had only been an ingredient to a drug. PCP—Angel Dust—required ether for its production. Ether was explosive, highly unstable.

"What do you think, Sol?" Park asked.

He hesitated. "Flynn's idea sounds good."

"You don't have any of your own?"

"I'm no scientist."

"I don't suppose it matters," Park said, hoping to goad him. "The experts will figure out what blew."

Sol stared at the crater. It could easily have swallowed a house. "They'll have a hell of a time doing it."

Shani walked with Kerry to the front door, glancing nervously at Flynn, who seemed to want to speak with her. Park followed briskly, passing them on the porch steps. He had to make a call. Before he contacted the police, he would have to tell Bert's parents that their only son was dead.

But the phone in the front hall was broken, as was the one in the kitchen and the one in the second floor hallway. The explosion must have been somehow responsible.

Park put down the silent receiver. They were thirty miles of desert from nowhere. None of the other kids had come and he was beginning to believe they never would. Their transportation was destroyed. They couldn't even call the outside world. They were stranded.

And his friend was dead. He had been concerned about

the girls — how they would take the shock. He hadn't even given himself a chance for his own grief. Surfing would not be the same without Big Bert. Nothing would.

Sick sorrow rocked his guts. He groped for the bathroom.

∽ CHAPTER 7 ∽

THE HILL WAS TALLER THAN IT HAD APPEARED FROM A distance. Altitude couldn't be a factor. Nevertheless, the air was unsatisfying, hot and dry, burning her lungs. And the path had gone to the dogs. Tumbleweed clawed through her pants, irritating her sunburn. Sharp pebbles slipped under and inside her Nike running shoes. The sun would set in minutes but the thermometer would have had no way of knowing. Sweat salty as seawater covered her body. She should have brought water. She should never have come. A snake would bite her next. Stumbling across a boulder, Shani sat down.

Far beneath her feet, two miles in the distance, the Carlton Castle was lit up, window by square window. On the surrounding sandy canvas, the late garage and carport were spilt black ink. The ocean was dark, but the tips of the rolling swells still caught the rays of the fading sun, crashing in orange foam on the deserted beach. Overhead, like torn cotton dipped in red dye, clouds raced to blot out the first stars. Yet, where she sat, there was no wind, no noise, only a deep silence that made her internal turbulence stand out in painful relief.

"I need some air," she had told the others, meaning, *I need to get away from you all*. Park had told her to be back before dark. There was small chance of that, as the blotted sun was already touching the horizon. Kerry had wanted to read prayers for Bert from the Bible. But it was too soon for her to even mourn properly. And she still hoped, in spite of all reason, that he was alive.

Robin had fainted upon hearing the news. By the time Shani had started on her hike, she had regained consciousness, but all had agreed that she should remain in bed. If only grief had been the sole cause of her collapse. Robin's pulse was unsteady, her skin a sad color. She had every symptom of uremia, a buildup of urea and other wastes in the blood. Lena was perplexed. Kerry was dropping hints that it was Lena's fault. After all, she said, who was doing Robin's dialysis?

Shani closed her eyes, massaging her aching temples. Another reason she had gone for her walk was to have the necessary solitude to figure out who in their group was both a friend and potential murderer, an analysis she should have completed last November. For maybe *they* were preparing to kill again. Bert may simply have been the first.

Lena: Definitely the number one suspect. She had both the guts and motive to poison Robin. The Carlton fortune and a greedy heir was the stuff of prime-time serials. Was she filtering her sister's blood, or merely sending it in useless circles through the plastic tubes? The peculiar absence of the other kids could be easily explained by Lena having manipulated the invitations. Had she brought all of them who had been at the party here to exterminate them, lest a sudden memory on the part of one of them come back to incriminate her?

Angie: At the party, she had had the most immediate ulterior motive. Her frustration at Robin's "dropping by" had been obvious. Was it simply chance that Park was now her boyfriend? Angie spoke seldom, but she was no dummy. She was fully capable of *planning* for a future romance. Also, for what it was worth, she had been closest to the garage when it blew. She was right up there on the list.

Kerry: Humiliation was powerful motivation for revenge. If Lena truly loved her sister, what better way to hurt her than to kill Robin? However, even though Kerry had a sharp tongue, Shani did not feel she was capable of murder. Nevertheless, she had to be placed near the top of the list. Kerry was fully capable of hate.

Sol: He had a violent past. During the investigation following the party, the police had hammered on him the most. If he hadn't acted alone, he had at least been used, for he had given Robin a (poison?) beer. But he had absolutely no motive. He adored Robin. She put him at the bottom of the list.

Park: They had grown up together. It was impossible for her to be objective. Nevertheless, Angie's skinny-dipping offer wouldn't have been sufficient enticement for him to spike his girlfriend's beer. And, once he had realized her condition, he had taken the wisest possible course of action to save Robin. On the other hand, he had been plastered that night, and horny. . . . She would not cross him off the list.

Bert: He would have been incapable of using Insect Death for its primary purpose; he couldn't have hurt a fly. In spite of what some said, he hadn't been dumb enough to accidentally pour poison in a beer mug. But maybe he had seen something at the party no one else had. Maybe that was why he was dead. She wished that she *could* put him on a list — for wonderful, living people.

The final two, Flynn and Robin, were difficult. He had a dozen strikes against him, yet he was the only one who couldn't have poisoned Robin. Still, she didn't trust him farther than she could throw a piano. She didn't know why she hadn't told Park about the gun. She would do that first thing when she got back. Flynn followed Robin closely. He wanted something from her. He deserved a list all his own.

Obviously, Robin had not poisoned herself. But she could have arranged for their present isolation. Sweetheart was her middle name, yet poison affected every organ, even the heart. Did she want revenge? She was deathly ill. Maybe she had fallen into a confused mental state where she wouldn't mind destroying the innocent if it allowed her to get to the guilty. And she had a sorcerer for a friend. A remark Angie had made about the destroyed garage and carport came to mind: "Like they had been struck by the wrath of God." The old man had been in the area. Two days ago, she hadn't been too hip on the supernatural, but now she was game for just about anything. Supposedly, sorcerers possessed powers. Wasting the carport and garage may have been merely a minor demonstration. His story could be seen as a parallel to their situation. Eagle had granted Dove the decision of who was to live, and who was to die. Had the old man granted Robin similar authority, and had she made a deal for her life?

Interesting how, by simply thinking about the old man, she could tell he was near. It was as though he was surrounded by an invisible shell that alerted both parties of impending contact. Shani stood. It was still warm but she shivered. The sun was gone, the light failing swiftly. Thickening clouds threatened a downpour. Only moments ago she had been contemplating his evilness. Now she felt impelled to climb the remainder of the hill and—she *knew* he was there—meet him. A flickering orange glow from a hidden fire served as a beacon. She glanced back at the house. She was being given a choice, she felt, and not being controlled. But her suspicion list was long and jotted with question marks, with not a single answer. She had to return to the house with more than she had left. Whispering a prayer for protection, she started toward the light.

He was alone, dressed in white, sitting cross-legged near a small fire, facing the twilight. He did not look up as she approached. She noticed yellow flowers—dandelions—blooming in a nearby bush. Instinctively, she plucked them.

"Hello," she said, holding forth her small bouquet. He looked at her then and smiled faintly, stretching out his hand to accept her gift. His hair was long and silver, his posture straight and firm. Energy sparkled in his clear eyes. Taking the flowers, he touched her briefly, gesturing that she should sit beside him. His hand was warm, soft. She made herself comfortable.

"I don't speak Spanish, but I wanted to talk to you. Do you understand me?"

He nodded, putting the flowers in a clay vase filled with water. He smiled for her to go on. He had a nice smile. It seemed on the verge of bursting forth into laughter, a frail cap on a well of unfathomable joy. Any thought that he was evil dissolved.

"I know you know Robin . . . Robin Carlton?" She took a breath. "Is she going to die?"

What was she waiting for? He couldn't speak English, even if he could somehow sense her meaning. Yet he seemed to be considering her question. He raised his head, whistled softly. A few seconds later a blackbird landed at the edge of the camp and walked purposefully toward him, hopping onto his shoulder. He whispered to the bird. The way it nodded in response, Shani could not help but believe it understood what he was saying. The bird stared at her, cocking its head quizzically, as though wondering, What's your problem, girl? She wanted to laugh, but it suddenly left its perch on the old man's shoulder and landed on hers. For a moment she was frightened, lest it peck at her eyes. But then it began to tug lightly at her hair with its beak, creating the same sensation as when she got her hair cut, a sensation she found divinely relaxing. The old man began to hum softly. The fire crackled and sparked, the flames dancing in rhythm with the pleasing chant. She was suddenly so very sleepy that she had to close her eyes. The bird teased individual hair shafts, which she imagined were attached deep inside her brain, stimulating areas she seldom used, soothing areas she used too often. Her anxieties began to fall off. And her head began to fall. . . .

IT WAS DARK; THE MAN AND FIRE WERE GONE. FAR BELOW, *the hill was slipping quickly behind as her perspective glided effortlessly over the weed-choked miles. Up ahead was the Carlton Castle, the black ocean beyond, both approaching swiftly. A warm light shone through a window on the top story of the house. Her course focused there, and a moment later she hovered outside the closed window. Robin lay inside, asleep beneath a patched quilt. She wanted to speak to her, reassure herself that she was okay. Was that not why she was here? But when she tried to tap on the window, her arms were sluggish and lacked strength. Robin dreamed on. However, there were two others in the room, and they heard the knocking. One of them rose from Robin's desk and hurried to the window, pulling back the curtains. In amazement, she stared back, staring at herself.*

"Good-bye," Shani said, standing. "I'll have to come visit you again with Robin so we can talk together." She chuckled, embarrassed. "Next time I promise I won't fall asleep. I don't, usually."

He nodded, returning her smile. Though they had been unable to converse, she felt his calming presence had relieved many of her worries. Her doubts and questions were still there, but they seemed far away, troubling someone else. Her untimely nap had been especially refreshing. She'd had the strangest dream . . . one she couldn't quite remember. She wondered where the bird was. Vaguely, while she had been dozing, she recalled it having launched itself into the night, plucking a beakful of hair off the crown of her head in the process. The old man took one of the flowers, gave it to her.

"*Que bonita,*" he said.

Leaving the warmth and peace of the man, she clutched the memory of his smile as tightly as the dandelion.

HALFWAY BETWEEN THE HILL AND THE HOUSE, IN A DARK no-man's-land of silhouetted cacti and starless sky, she heard a sudden rattle. It appeared far in front. No problem, she would circle around. Leaving the right side of the path, she steered a wide arc through the sharp shrubs toward the beach. Before this weekend was over, her legs would be a mass of scratches. The rattle faded behind her.

But once off the path, she could not find it again. On the way to the hill, if her memory served her correctly, the trail had followed a fairly straight course. Veering to the left should have brought her automatically back to the path. Wait a minute, maybe she hadn't been on the same trail as before! Maybe the second one had simply dead-ended, and there was nothing to veer back to.

Still, Shani was not worried. All she had to do was head in the direction of the ocean and she would be okay. As soon as she could climb out of this dry ravine she had managed to stumble into, she would be able to tell which way that was.

On what she thought was the west side, the walls of the gully were steep and slippery. Chunks of gravel broke under her clawing fingers as she tried to pull herself up. Walking fifty yards farther along through a congestion of weeds and stones, she tried again. Unfortunately, on the verge of climbing free, the thumbnail on her right hand broke. Crying in pain, she lost her balance, sliding slowly back into the ditch and starting a minor avalanche. Dirt toppled down her drenched shirt, sticking to her chest. She thrust her wounded finger in her mouth, grimacing in pain, tasting blood. She wished the old man were with her now. Somewhere, she had lost her flower.

Shani was preparing for a third effort when she heard the rattle again. It was louder this time, much closer. Plowing on all fours, she tried to scamper up the disintegrating wall. But the harder she tried, the more she slipped. Rocks disappeared in the black bushes below, angering her assailant. A shadow squirmed, breath hissed. Shani kicked off her shoes, praying for better traction. But she was only digging her own grave.

"Help!!!" she wailed. Turning, she searched for a decent stone. The direction of the rattle was impossible to ascertain, but if the thing bit her, it was going to leave with one hell of a headache. Why had she gone and taken off her shoes?

"Are you stuck, Shani?"

"Flynn!!!" She couldn't see him, but the voice was from above. "Help me up! A snake's got me cornered!"

"It won't bite you unless you corner it."

"I don't think this one knows that! Where are you!?"

He crouched into view, leaned over, binoculars hanging from his neck. "Give me your hand."

She tried, and failed. "I can't reach you!" The rattle shook to a frenzy. "Shoot it!"

"I can't see it. Calm down. You're slipping because you're in a hurry. Dig your hands and feet firmly into the dirt, climb slowly."

She did as he suggested, and a moment later he was pulling her safely to her feet. The rattling stopped, but she wasn't crazy about the neighborhood. Flynn ended up chasing after her. "Are you running from me or the snake?" he called.

"Damn!" she cried, stepping on thorns. She had forgotten about her bare feet. Plopping down miserably in the dark and dirt, she pulled the stickers, one by one, out of her tender flesh, blood trailing from each puncture.

"What's wrong?" Flynn asked, coming up to her.

"I gave my shoes to the snake."

"I'll get them for you." He snapped on a flashlight, dazzling her eyes. In his other hand, he held his gun.

"Don't! It might bite you." But if he left, maybe she would make another dash for it. She had been running from both of them.

"I can't carry you back to the house. Don't worry, I have thick skin."

He left her, and she was more afraid. She would wait. A minute crept by . . . two. Suddenly the silence cracked. Shani jumped. He had used his gun. For a moment she had thought that it had been on her. A bobbing light approached. He handed her the shoes. While brushing the soles of her feet, she asked, "Am I next?"

He laughed. "Now that's no question to ask your knight in shining armor. I did, after all, just rescue you."

Her laces, her fingers, were in knots. "I could have killed the snake myself. And I wouldn't have needed a gun, *Michael*."

"I'm sure you could have. How're your feet?"

"Fine, thank you."

He smiled. "And I thought you liked me. Here I was worried about you, and volunteered to prowl the snake-infested wild to find you. What have I done to deserve that tone?"

"Are you making fun of me?"

"Probably."

She pulled on her shoes. "I don't trust someone who lies about who he is, breaks into people's filing cabinets, and is such a coward that he has to carry a gun."

"Well, at least you're afraid of me."

"A blackbird is more fearsome than you." He terrified her. He could put a bullet in her brain right now and chances were no one would be any the wiser. However, his pistol was now out of sight. He turned away, staring up at the cloud-choked sky.

"Isn't it possible that I might have reasons for doing what I am doing? Reasons that you would approve of if you knew all the details?"

"What are your reasons?"

"I can't tell you."

"Why not?"

"I can't tell you."

"Then I don't trust you."

He looked at her, his green eyes wary in the harsh shadows cast by the flashlight. "Don't tell the others who I am."

"Why shouldn't I?" She was gambling, playing the tough role, but she doubted that kissing up to him would deceive him. Her Nikes remained untied. Her stomach began to cramp. It had nothing in it. She'd thrown up on the way to the hill. He knelt by her side. His profile belonged on the big screen. He touched her arm.

"Because I'm asking you not to. Trust me, Shani. Please? Before the night's over, I think, everything will be made clear."

"I want to," she whispered, then hardened. "I'm not the only one who's onto you. Nurse Porter talked to Lena last night. She told her to watch out for you."

He frowned. "What else did she say?"

"I don't know if I should—"

"Tell me!"

She cowered. "Nothing else, just that you were probably up to no good."

"Did she use my real name?"

"No. She said they were making some checks on you, that she would talk to Lena today."

"Anything else?"

"No."

"You're sure?"

"She thought you were after Robin."

"The phones . . ." he muttered, looking back at the house. "Who was going to call who?"

"Lena said she would call Miss Porter. I don't know why I'm telling you all this."

Flynn was distracted, deep in thought. "The lines were down before the explosion. . . . Hmm." He smiled, patted her back. "Thank you for the information. But it doesn't surprise me. And I don't think it will change anything, not now."

Shani wondered what she had done, all out of weakness for a beautiful face. "You're not going to hurt Robin, are you?"

"Why would I hurt Robin?"

"You've been hanging around her, bringing all her food and drinks."

"I'm trying to protect her."

"From what?"

"From getting poisoned."

"*What?*"

"She was poisoned once. She now has the very same people around her as last time. I would say she stands an excellent chance of having it happen to her again."

"But that was an accident."

"I don't think so." He paused. "Did you do it? The first time, I mean?"

"No! How could you think such a thing?"

"I didn't really think that you did. But the others . . . There is a bad apple in there somewhere. Maybe two."

"It probably wasn't an accident," she said sadly. "And Bert . . . You didn't seem too upset over what happened to him."

He was harsh. "What do you know about *my* feelings?"

It was the first time he had dropped his guard. "I'm sorry. I . . . it's just that I don't know anything about you. Why are you so concerned about Robin? What's she to you?"

He went to speak, but stopped. Her question seemed to hurt him. But then he shrugged and smiled. "I'm concerned about you, too."

"Don't change the subject."

"I like you, Shani."

"You're playing with me again."

"No, I'm not."

"Why?" She wished her voice hadn't trembled.

"Because you're so sweet and beautiful"

He kissed her. For a moment, she didn't respond. Then her arms went around his neck and she was pulling him closer. This was madness! But she liked it! Not breaking contact, he sat down beside her, putting pressure on one leg. His hands crept beneath her shirt, touched her lower back. She began to cough, turned away.

Laughing, he said, "I didn't know I was that bad."

"It's not you!" she breathed. Boy, she was a real winner all around. At least James Bond's ladies got a little sex before he killed them. "This air . . . my throat's dry."

"Is that the only problem?"

"No. I don't even know you." She was still coughing.

His voice was suddenly grave. "Don't you?"

"No."

"But you recognize me. You and Park, you both recognize me."

"I don't know what you're talking about." Yet, she was lying. His face was as familiar to her as the one in her own mirror. He nodded, reading her mind.

"You knew once, at least. Before this night is over, you will know again." He stood. He wasn't going to kiss her again. He probably wasn't going to shoot her, either. "Tie your shoes. We have to get back."

With her Nikes tied, he helped her up, brushing off her pants. The tranquility the wise man had bestowed was straining against this assault of fear and danger, of passion and uncertainty.

"You said you wouldn't hurt Robin," she said as they began to walk toward the house. "Are you going to hurt any of the others?"

"Only if they deserve it."

She stopped. "What if I try to stop you?"

"Don't, Shani." He strode on without waiting for her. "You'd regret it."

How quick his cool could return. She had a crush on him but she honestly didn't even think she liked him. "I know who you are," she called. "You're Snake."

He turned. Without a shred of conceit in his voice, he said, "No, I'm Eagle."

On the road back, she had to stop once to be sick. Flynn — Michael — didn't even ask what was troubling her.

It began to rain.

∽ CHAPTER 8 ∾

POOR LIGHTING HAD ALWAYS IRRITATED HIS EYES. THE lone lamp on Robin's nightstand was little more than a night-light. Park thought of turning on the overhead lights, but he feared they might wake Robin. There was no reason for him to be sitting beside her bed, anyway. Nevertheless, he felt no inclination to move. When he closed his eyes and listened to the drowsy rhythm of her breathing, the pelting rain against the house, he could imagine they were elsewhere, in a world of enchantment and deathless bodies. However, this rain was no boon from the gods. His remark, when they had driven up in the car yesterday, had been prophetic. With the mud, the house was now an island.

Robin was covered to her chin with a colorful patched quilt Shani had sewn in their freshman year. Before falling asleep, she had taken a glass of grape juice and had reassured him that she was feeling better. He hadn't believed her. Only thirty minutes ago, she had showered, yet already her face was developing a crusty coat as her skin fought to do the job of her kidneys. What if she were to suddenly stop breathing? Out of fear of her death, he had stayed away from her, and now he clung to her side hoping to ward it off. He couldn't help feeling a crossroad was approaching, where every turn would lead to a dead end. But he was despairing, as she never did. When she awoke next, if he did not notice definite signs of improvement, he would take Sol up on his offer. Sol had suggested — surrounding swamp or not — that even if it took them to sunrise, they should search on foot for a phone or cell phone signal and get a doctor to Robin. They could even have a helicopter brought in.

Another thing, when she awoke, he would tell her that he wanted her back, one hundred percent, not just as a phone pal. That meant he would have to give up Harvard in September, and his egotistical image of being a suave Ivy League Intellectual. That was okay; he could get as good an education locally if he applied himself. He hoped that she would have him. And Angie . . . she deserved someone who really cared for her. Bert's death had somehow made this decision clear.

He was not feeling well. He had fever and chills, on top of cramps that made him glad he wasn't a female. It was probably a flu. The water in the house was safe and, besides, Montezuma's Revenge took several days to incubate. Angie had also mentioned feeling sick.

Too bad Robin didn't have their symptoms and they could pretend she merely had a virus.

"How is she?" Shani whispered, quietly entering the room.

Fresh from a shower, her long black hair drying in fine curls, her blue eyes bright in the poor light, his oldest and best friend was beautiful. She wore a loose purple blouse, tight white pants, and a bandage around her right thumb where she had cracked her nail while hiking. When she had not returned an hour after sunset, he'd been worried. A minute more and he would have gone looking for her himself. The walk had been uneventful, she had said.

"She's been sleeping awhile, now. She said that she was feeling a bit better."

"Good. Lena wanted me to tell you that dinner's ready."

His stomach groaned at the mention of food. "I'm not that hungry."

Shani pulled up a chair, and tucked in Robin's quilt. "Poor dear," she said softly. "I'm in no hurry to eat, myself."

"How are you feeling?"

She hesitated. "Not great. I guess I keep waiting for Bert to walk through the front door, laughing."

He felt the same way. "He won't be doing that."

"I know. I'm sorry about not being at Kerry's prayer reading. Maybe after dinner, we could read some more."

"If you want."

Shani sighed, glancing at the covered window. "It's raining hard. I usually like the rain."

"It's like a hurricane. Generally, they don't get any of those down here until late summer. Sol and I had to hustle to patch up the windows the blast kicked in. Of course, we had Lena prodding us with a whip."

Lightning flashed: one . . . two . . . three. . . . Thunder boomed. Shani shivered, holding her right hand to her chest. "My finger hurts."

"Are you going to lose the nail?"

"I already did."

"Ouch. I'm glad Flynn went out looking for you."

"I didn't need his help."

"Do I note a trace of hostility? I thought you liked him."

"I don't know him."

He wondered what she would have thought if she knew Flynn carried a gun. "You knew him less before this weekend. And you liked him then."

"You're not my shrink."

"I'm sorry, I didn't know it was a touchy subject."

"Everything's touchy to me right now." She glanced over her shoulder, seemingly coming to a decision. "Park, of all those in the house right now, who do you trust the least?"

"Myself."

"I'm serious."

"Are you referring to the party?"

"Yes."

"It was an accident."

"You don't believe that."

"I do. But then, I believe there are accidents, and there are *accidents*."

"What do you mean?"

"I'm not quite sure. But the police looked for the guilty, and the innocent. Maybe the truth of the matter wasn't so black-and-white."

"Someone either put the insecticide in the glass intentionally or accidentally. Where's the in-between?"

"I remember a program I saw on TV about Buckminster Fuller, the inventor of the geodesic dome. He drew a square on the chalkboard and asked the audience what they saw. Naturally, everyone said a square. But then he asked, 'What about the space outside the square?' His point being, of course, that we are conditioned to automatically focus on the boundaries in life. So when you say Robin was either poisoned accidentally or intentionally, don't be so sure."

"Nice lecture, Professor. What do you see outside this square?"

The rest of the chalkboard, he thought, was a dark board thick with plots and fears, where all of them stumbled unknowingly against each other. "Nothing," he said. "Let's go eat."

Shani stopped him. "Wait, I want to read the rest of Robin's story. It's in that desk."

"But she said there was no more." From having over-heard her comment to the blackbird, he knew that wasn't entirely true.

"I want to see."

"Why? It may be private to her."

"Because I saw the old man while I was out." She checked to be sure Robin was still asleep. "He's not like us. He *does* know things."

"What did he tell you?"

"Nothing. You know I don't speak Spanish."

"Then how do you know what he knows? Did he perform a miracle for you?"

"No. But I could sense his uniqueness. He's like a holy man. I don't think his story is frivolous."

He decided it couldn't hurt. "Okay, let's give it a look."

They moved to the desk. Shani found the manila envelope in the second drawer on the right. She pulled out three notebook pages, covered with Robin's neat printing. Park leaned over her shoulder as she flipped to the last page and began to read softly:

"Suddenly, Eagle appeared, landing between them. Eagle was very powerful and could easily kill Snake. But when he went to try, Snake tightened his grip on Dove and said, 'If you come closer, I will bite Dove. Kill Raven for me, and leave her body, and I will give you Dove.'

"Eagle turned to Raven, and Raven grew frightened.

She said, 'Dove and I are friends. She would not wish for you to kill me.'

"But Snake said, 'If Raven was Dove's friend, why did she bring her here for me to eat?'

"Raven said, 'That is not true.' But Raven feared Dove would feel that she had been betrayed, and would allow Eagle to kill her for Snake.

"Eagle thought for a moment, and said, 'I will let Dove decide if you are a friend, Raven, and whether I should buy her freedom with your death. But I have decided this: If Dove should die, both of you will die.'

"Raven and Snake waited, both striving for a plan of escape, both afraid, But Dove did not speak, would not choose. Hurt as she was, Dove began to sing. And Eagle smiled. . . .'"

Park plucked the papers from her hand. "Is that all?"

"That's all she wrote down here."

"Huh. You think there's more that he told her that she didn't write down?"

Shani was deep in thought. "I don't know."

"Well, for a wise man, he sure doesn't know how to end a story. Let's get to dinner."

Shani slid the papers back in the envelope, closing it carefully. "Maybe this isn't the end."

"Do you think she has another page somewhere?"

Shani's head shot up. "What was that?"

"What was what?"

She twisted her head around. "Someone's banging on the window. . . . There it is again!"

"For goodness' sakes, we're on the third floor. It's the rain."

Shani got up, hurried across the room, flung back the curtains. "Oh, no," she gasped.

"What's wrong?"

"It's not there." She was white as a sheet.

"Shh, you'll wake Robin." He stepped to her side. "What's not there?"

"I thought I would see a bird."

"A moment ago you thought it was a person. What's wrong with you?"

She put her hand to her forehead as though she were feeling faint. "I'm having this strangest sensation of déjà vu." She shook herself. "Now it's gone. That's weird. What were you asking?"

"If you think Robin has another page somewhere?"

Shani glanced at Robin sleeping, and back out at the black night. She shook her head. "No, I think the story isn't over yet."

THE DINNER TABLE COULD HAVE BEEN UNDER WATER. They all ate in slow-motion silence, without enthusiasm for the food or each other. A draft was chilling Shani's legs. A window must have been still out. The downpour continued unabated. The two drapeless windows cornering the dining room were like portals staring out onto a deep ocean bottom.

"You must have really screwed up those invitations," Sol commented, sipping ginger ale.

Without comment, Lena stood and left the room, returning a minute later and throwing a vanilla card on Sol's half-eaten plate of food. "You will note today's date on the invitation," she said, "which was the printer's fault, by the way, not mine. It should have been yesterday's date. In either case, I don't know why they're not here. Unless"—she scanned the table—"someone made a few last minute calls."

"For whatever reasons they didn't come," Park said, "it's just as well. More may have died in the blast." He yawned. "Boy, I'm sleepy."

"So am I," Angie muttered.

"Just looking at this food is making me sick," Sol said.

"Thanks," Lena said. "I screwed up the invitations *and* dinner. Is there anything that I did right?"

"Give me a few minutes," Sol said. Looks couldn't kill, but Lena's could wound; they were very sharp. Sol retracted his statement. "Nah, dinner was fine. I just feel like crap. First Bert gets wasted and now my guts are on fire. How about the rest of you?"

"I vomited an hour ago," Angie said. "I should go to bed."

"I feel like vomiting now," Park said.

"I'm running from both ends," Shani said, and by now she didn't care what the others thought. She felt oddly removed, floating.

"How . . . gross," Kerry stuttered. "At . . . the table . . . Really, Shani."

"You should talk," Lena snapped. "Who had the game-room bathroom smelling like an outhouse?"

"I never . . . never used it!" Kerry protested. Her voice sounded weak.

"A pig must have slipped in from the barn, then. One that looked just like —"

"Come on," Park interrupted. "We all feel lousy. Let's not make it any worse."

"Not me. I feel super," Lena said. But she had scarcely touched her food.

"So your walkie-talkie isn't working?" Park said.

"That's what I said," Lena said.

"I'd like to look at it."

"If I tell you it isn't working, it isn't working. My dad tried it last summer and it wasn't even working then. Satisfied?"

"Cool down," Sol said. "Preppy's a whiz at garbage like that. Maybe he can fix it."

Lena was cool. "After dinner you can have at it with a box of tools and the instruction manual for all I care." She paused, rubbing her eyes. "Hell, I feel so dizzy. What's wrong with me?"

"It's the flu," Park said, swaying slightly in his chair.

"Never had a flu like this," Sol mumbled, his head nodding.

"How's Robin?" Kerry asked.

"Ask her yourself when she wakes up," Lena said slowly, staring at an empty milk glass in her frozen hand.

"We have to get her to eat," Shani said. Her hike must have taken more out of her than she had realized. The room was receding, fogging at the edges, as if she were slipping down a translucent tunnel. It was a struggle to keep her eyes open.

"Juice is better for her if she's accumulating wastes in her blood," Park said, yawning like a hibernating bear.

Angie stood abruptly. "I'm going to bed." She was halfway to the hallway when she collapsed.

"Angie!" Lena called, stumbling out of her chair, kneeling by their fallen friend. "What's wrong?" She shook her, but Angie remained out cold. Lena turned to the rest of them for help. None was forthcoming. Shani saw everything through dream glasses. The situation was desperately wrong, but she couldn't understand why.

"This can't be," Lena said in useless denial, trembling, her hand going to her throat, her eyes rolling in their sockets. She dropped beside Angie.

Like a melting Gumby, Park staggered to his feet. But his knees buckled, and his height was halved. In dumbfounded amazement, he stared at his right hand as he tried to form it into a fist. Then he toppled forward.

Sol planted his face in his plate.

Kerry rolled out of her chair like a bag of potatoes.

And at last Shani thought she understood. She turned her head slowly toward Flynn. It was all she could move. Her arms were nailed to the table. Her legs were made of cement. The lights swirled like drunken fairies with sparklers. A wave of wrath permitted her a last moment of clarity.

"You," she breathed in loathing, wishing she could spit in his face. He hadn't spoken all night. He had been waiting.

Yet he, too, was fighting to remain erect, and his incredulous expression denied his guilt. "We've been . . . drugged," he whispered. The Carlton Castle turned into a ferris wheel.

"Who?" she managed as she slid toward the table linen. But if he answered, she wasn't awake to hear him.

CHAPTER 9

"SHANI! SHANI! I THINK SHE'S COMING AROUND. SHANI!"

Shani opened her eyes. The room was dark, quivering with candlelit shadows, hissing with the breath of serpents. It must be a nightmare. She closed her eyes. Her head throbbed with pain. She wished she could wake up.

"She's fading out again." That was Angie.

"Shake her." That was Sol.

"I can't reach her." That was Flynn. "This handcuff has me pinned."

Shani ventured another look. Their dinner-table fellowship was now equally spaced around the perimeter of the floor of the recording studio she had wandered into earlier, deep in the bowels of the Carlton Castle. The curtains outside the double-plated glass were drawn. Except for candles in red cups rimming a round Plexiglas container in the center of the room, there were no lights. Within the clear container, their long tongues flicking with hunger in the bloody glow, were snakes. A continuous rattle filled the muffled air. She was not dreaming.

"Oh, no," she whispered.

"She's awake," Angie said.

"Try to stay calm, Shani," Park said. "We're all together."

Attached to the top of the snake bin was the aluminum pole that had lowered and raised the microphone. If the pole was raised, the covering would be removed, and the rattlers would be set free. There were at least a dozen snakes, each individually isolated by partitions of glass, equally sized servings of poisonous pie. The temperature was icy. Shani's guts were burning.

"What's going on?" she mumbled. Her right arm was stuck, handcuffed at the wrist to a ring and bolt in the paneling a foot above the floor. She was not alone in this regard. "I feel sick."

"Someone who mustn't like us drugged and dragged us down here," Lena said, pinned opposite the closed entrance door, at six o'clock. Kerry slouched an hour over, head bowed, still unconscious. Shani had Park to her immediate right, Flynn to her left.

"That Robin," Angie cursed, on the far side of the snakes, next to Sol and the door. "She's out for revenge."

"Robin couldn't have picked up a gallon of milk," Park said, "Never mind have dragged us down here."

Shani shuddered from the cold, her intestinal cramps, the snakes. One, she was sure, had its eyes on her.

"She was just pretending to be sick," Angie said, bitterly.

"No one's that good an actress," Park said, shifting uncomfortably. "Man, I need to get to a toilet something awful."

"Could this be a practical joke?" Sol asked.

"Those snakes don't look like they've got much of a sense of humor," Park said. "Lena, could your dad have arranged this to get back at us for Robin's illness?"

"He doesn't have the imagination to think up this kind of scene. And even though we don't get along, he's never mentioned wanting to feed me to snakes."

Kerry began to scream. She had just woken up. She wasn't forming intelligible words, but she was making a lot of noise.

"Shut up!" Lena snapped. "This room is soundproof. Even if Robin were awake, she couldn't hear us."

"There must be someone else in the house, then," Shani said, unable to stop trembling. Deep-rooted impressions began to surface: the red light and flames, the darkness, the serpents. She knew it was not so, but she could not totally dismiss the idea that they had all died and gone to hell. She began to hyperventilate but fought for calm.

"What are those snakes for?" Kerry cried.

"For us," Lena said grimly.

"I hate snakes," Park said.

"So who are you, Harrison Ford?" Sol muttered, pulling at his handcuff, his straining muscles visible even in the poor light. "Damn, these are on tight."

"If they were all set loose," Angie wanted to know, "are we all goners?"

"If we get bit a few times and we don't receive treatment," Park said, "we will die."

"You're doing wonders for our morale," Sol grunted, using his legs now to push against the wall, getting nowhere. "Damn!"

"How many are there?" Angie asked.

Kerry began to panic again. "Help! God, please help me!" She fought with her handcuff, probably scraping the flesh off her wrist. Her screaming was exciting the snakes.

"Someone shut her up!" Lena yelled.

"Kerry," Shani said, with her best imitation of calm, "I am as frightened as you, but we can't panic. We have to find a way to get free." She turned to Flynn, who had blood running from the side of his head. He must have banged it when he blacked out. "Are you okay?"

"I'll live," he said, as cool as ever, alert and watchful.

"Do you have your gun?"

"I'm afraid not."

"They took my knife," Sol said, leaning back against the paneling, giving up on an immediate escape.

"I wonder what they want," Park said.

"I wonder who *they* are," Sol said.

As if on cue, a voice answered. It was heavy and thick, slow and laden with unnatural weariness, indistinguishable as either masculine or feminine. Shani had to wonder if it was entirely human, and not from the other side of the grave.

"We must have the truth of that night," it said.

"Whoever you are, you can go to hell!" Lena shouted.

A motor hummed. The pole rose slightly. The lid of the snake bin shook. The rattlers went nuts. They were anxious to get out. Every muscle in Shani's body tightened.

"We'll cooperate!" Park said hastily. The lid was lowered back into place. He added, "I should have guessed. They want to know who poisoned Robin."

"But who are they?" Angie asked, repeating Sol's question.

"Does it matter?" Flynn asked. "I suggest that all of you tell them what you know."

"What can we say that we didn't say to the police?" Shani said, knowing there might be plenty. But even if *they* learned the truth, would that satisfy them?

"The police didn't give us this incentive," Park said.

"That's one hell of a way of putting it," Sol said.

"With the police, we were all trying to downplay our own parts," Park said. "At least, I was. It was your party, Angie; you start."

"Start what? We've got to get free. Whoever's doing this is psycho. They'll kill us all."

"Whoever's doing this can hear everything we're saying," Park said. Shani had to admire his cool. However, he looked desperately uncomfortable, a shade of green.

Was the one behind this voice also responsible for their illness? And was it indeed Robin, and had she brought in outside help?

"Angie was the one who said, 'Just one drink, it won't kill you,' " Kerry blurted, addressing their mysterious examiner.

"I did not! Liar!"

"Actually, you did," Shani said. "But —"

"I never did!" Angie said, exasperated, frightened. "You traitorous—"

"We'll get nowhere this way," Park interrupted. "We have to piece the facts together. We should start with what we know. Sol gave her the beer."

"I gave her *a* beer. How do you know it was the poisonous one?"

"That's the same excuse you gave the police," Angie said.

"Robin took my beer, sure, but she set it down on the table in between us where there were several beers. Maybe she picked my beer back up, maybe it was another beer. Who knows? I sure don't."

Fear had sharpened her memory. Shani suddenly recalled a vital point. "The beer you gave her had the insecticide in it," she said reluctantly.

Sol stared at her, amazed. "How do you know?"

"I remember when you first gave her the beer, how it was darker. At the time, I thought one of you had put whiskey in it."

"Why didn't you tell the police this?" Park asked, regarding Sol suspiciously.

"I had forgotten." She banged her feet together. They were going numb, like her hands. She wondered what it would be like to die from snake venom. In movies, the victim always screamed horribly. Would the snakes just bite her, or would they chew on her afterwards? She had to stop thinking like this.

"What do you have to say about that?" Park asked Sol.

"Nothing. If Shani remembers that the beer was darker, I believe her. Look, none of this is new. The police jumped all over me on this same point. If I had wanted to poison somebody, I wouldn't have done it out loud in front of everybody."

Park was not convinced. "A subtle way to hide one's guilt is to make oneself so obviously guilty that no one would think that you were dumb enough to have committed the crime."

"That's a bunch of BS," Sol said angrily. "What's gotten into you, Park? You know me. I would never have hurt Robin."

"Yeah, I know you, sure," Park sneered. "I know you're no angel in a leather jacket. What about the drugs you push?"

"*What!* I get loaded—like you—but I don't deal."

"What about the junk you bought in Tijuana?"

"What about it?"

"Was it, by chance, ether for PCP?"

"What's that?"

"Yeah, you never heard of PCP," Park said sarcastically.

"I know what PCP is. What's *ether*?"

"A highly explosive chemical used to put people asleep, *and* used in the manufacture of Angel Dust." Park shook his head in disgust. "It's explosive enough to have wasted the garage and Bert. Let me hear you deny that that's what you were carrying!"

"I do!"

"Wait a minute. What's going on here?" Lena asked. "What did you have in your van, Sol?"

"Nothing! Fireworks."

"Fireworks?" Park winced.

"Like sparklers and cones and things like that?" Shani asked.

"Not exactly," Sol admitted reluctantly. "I had . . . M80's."

"What are those?" Flynn asked.

"You don't know?" Park said. "There isn't a kid who's grown up in Southern California that hasn't lit off at least one M80. They're like a firecracker, except thicker, with dynamite inside instead of gun powder. How much did you buy, Sol?"

"A lot. I could sell them to this guy in L.A. for three times what I paid for them."

"How much?"

"I bought three hundred."

"That's a lot," Shani said.

"Three hundred pounds," Sol added.

"Three hundred *pounds*," Park said, pronouncing each word distinctly. "At least we know now where the garage went. Why didn't you tell us?"

Sol shrugged. "I've been to jail. I figured I couldn't help Bert by going back. And I wasn't the one who lit —"

The snake lid shook. The voice spoke. *"Don't stray. We must have the truth of that night."*

"Give us more time!" Park called quickly. Sol's revelation had taken him back. Apparently the belief that Sol was a pusher had greatly prejudiced his point of view. "Sorry, Sol," he said. "I'm in such a hurry to get to the bathroom, I'll accuse anybody."

"You're going to make a crappy lawyer," Sol scowled.

"We're back where we started," Angie said.

"But we have established that the beer Sol gave Robin had the poison in it," Park said.

"We've got to trace that beer back. Where did you get it, Sol?"

He was shaking his head. "These are the same questions all over. I'll give you the same answer I gave the cops: I don't remember. I was so wasted that night."

"So was I," Park said.

"Why don't you try a different approach?" Flynn said. "Since you've been unable to trace the beer back, why don't you trace it *forward*. Start at a reasonable point during the party and reconstruct what happened from then on. It doesn't sound like you did that with the police. It might help jar a few memories, and maybe the beer will show up earlier."

"It couldn't hurt," Park said. "But it's probably going to get confusing. Where should we start?"

"After Lena and Robin arrived," Shani suggested. "I was phasing in and out all night, but I remember Kerry and Lena fighting."

A rattlesnake snapped at a candle. The impact of its nose against the Plexiglas spilt the red cup over onto the floor. Fortunately, the flame drowned in its wax. A portion of the room darkened. Yet, it would be worse, far worse, if the snakes came at them unseen.

"Lena started the fight!" Kerry said.

"You little snot," Lena said. "You were demanding that Sol give you a ride home when he could hardly see."

"But Sol told you to shut up," Kerry protested, as if that made any difference.

Sol nodded. "I remember the three of us arguing."

"Everyone agree that this fight took place?" Park asked, taking up the role of coordinator. "Good, that is one thing we didn't tell the police. We are making progress. What happened next?"

"I offered to give Kerry a ride home when Robin and I left," Lena said. "The fight ended."

"Then we drank more," Sol said.

"Who brought out the beers?" Park asked.

"Angie did," Kerry said.

"Of course I did," Angie said. "I was the hostess."

"Where did you get them?" Park asked.

"Hey, what is this? I'm not on trial."

"Yes, you are," Shani said. "We all are."

"We were out of cans," Angie said. "I broke into the keg."

"Who started on Robin to drink?" Park asked.

"You did," Sol said.

"I encouraged her," Park said. "But I did not start it."

"Angie started it," Lena said, thoughtful.

"I asked her if she was running for sainthood, that's all," Angie said. "But she said that she had to drive. Then Sol changed the music."

"I did?" Sol asked.

"Then Bert came out of the bathroom," Kerry said, "and I had to go."

"But I got there first," Lena said. "And *you* went into the kitchen."

"I went with Bert," Kerry said defensively.

"This is incredible; our memories are snowballing," Park said. "I can actually remember all this happening. Kerry got up and Lena chased after her. Wait! You weren't in the living room, Lena. How did you get to the bathroom before Kerry?"

Lena hesitated. "I came out of the kitchen."

"So you had been alone in the kitchen?" Park asked.

"Yes."

"What did you do in there?" Park asked.

"Nothing. Oh, I cleaned off my dress. Sol had rolled over when I was sitting on him and I had spilled a drink on myself. I never did get that stain out."

"Sol, Sol," Park muttered. "I remember him leaving during this time, too."

"I saw him go down the hall," Shani said. The pieces of the puzzle were coming together. Talking helped, it gave her less time to worry. The insistent rattling had quieted. The snakes seemed to be listening.

"Here we go again," Sol sighed. "I went down the hall looking for a head. I didn't find one."

"Because we only have one bathroom in our house," Angie said.

"Then what happened?" Park asked.

Their momentum stalled. A minute went by. Shani realized she could not feel her feet. She offered what she could. "I fell asleep, then. When I woke up, everyone was back in the living room. And you were saying, Park, that it was our God-given duty to get Robin drunk."

"I did say that," Park admitted. "But you were probably only asleep a minute or two. Everyone came right back. And then . . ." He shook his head, frustrated. "And then Sol was giving Robin the beer. This is no good. We're skipping over the most important part. The beer came from the kitchen, and that's where the insecticide was. Who went into the kitchen is crucial."

"Give me everything we've got so far," Sol said, scratching his chin. "Something's coming back to me."

"You, Kerry, and Lena fought," Park said. "Angie brought beers out of the kitchen. Bert was in the bathroom. Lena went into the kitchen. We started on Robin to drink. You changed the music. Bert came out of the bathroom and changed the music again. Kerry and Lena ran into each other at the bathroom door, Kerry coming from the living room, Lena coming from the kitchen. Lena ended up using the bathroom. Kerry went into the kitchen with Bert. About this time, you were looking for another bathroom."

"I went into the kitchen!" Sol said suddenly.

"Were Kerry and Bert still there?" Park asked.

"Bert came back into the living room and went to sleep on the floor," Angie said.

Sol was straining. "Man, I'm not sure, but I think Kerry was alone."

"And what was our sweet Kerry doing?" Lena asked slowly.

Kerry stuttered. "I was . . . getting a . . . a drink."

"Sol?" Park asked.

"Yeah, that's right. Kerry was fixing drinks."

"Did she give you a beer in a mug?" Park asked.

"Yeah, or I took one. I think I just picked one."

"Very interesting," Park said. "Where were you at this point, Lena? Were you still in the bathroom?"

"I think so."

"No," Angie said, excited. "I remember seeing you come out and go into the kitchen!"

"Are you sure it was at this exact time?" Park asked. They were closing in, but whether it was on the truth was another matter. They had Kerry, Sol, and Lena in the kitchen. Robin was waiting in the living room. The snakes were also waiting.

"Yes!"

"Oh, yeah, Lena came in," Sol said. "I had forgotten."

"That's right, I did," Lena conveniently agreed. She appeared off-balance, perhaps from surprise, probably from guilt.

"What happened next?" Park asked.

"We didn't stay in the kitchen," Sol said. "We went into the living room."

"Did you take the beer with you that Kerry had prepared?" Park asked, unable to mask the emotion in his voice.

Sol didn't hesitate. "No."

"What do you mean, no?" Park asked, irritated. "A minute ago you barely remember going into the kitchen. How come you're suddenly so positive you didn't carry out a glass of beer? You *must* have brought it into the living room."

"If he didn't," Shani said, "we're back where we started."

"I didn't carry the beer out," Sol said. "I'm positive. I remember now going into the kitchen and telling Kerry I would give her a ride home if Lena and Robin didn't take her home soon. Then Lena came in. I wanted to get the two of them apart as quickly as possible but I suddenly started having trouble with my balance. Must have been that quart of Jack Daniels Bert and I drank that night. Anyway, Lena gave me a hand back into the living room and I sat down beside Robin. Once I was off my feet, I felt okay."

"He's right," Angie nodded. "I remember them stumbling back into the living room. Lena was practically holding him up."

"Let's get back to the glass of beer that Kerry fixed," Park said, anxious to keep them on track. Sol was wrong; Park would make an excellent lawyer—if he lived. "You said you picked it up, Sol, but you were having trouble staying on your feet. Before Lena helped you into the living room, *what did you do with that beer?*"

"I gave it to Lena to hold," Sol said, matter-of-factly. Then the enormity of his remark hit home, not merely in his own face, but in Lena's.

"That's right," Lena gasped. "You gave it to me. And when you were seated, I gave it back to you. Then you gave it to Robin. And then . . ."

It was not necessary to complete the sentence. Kerry was suddenly the center of their attention. In the hellish light, her face was a mask of anxiety. "So I . . . I was alone . . . in the kitchen. So was . . . Angie. So was . . . Lena. Robin drank . . . just a little. She wanted to stop. She said, 'It tastes awful.' But Lena said, 'Finish it.' Lena made her finish it!"

"That's right!" Shani said.

"Yeah!" Angie said.

"Wait a second!" Lena snapped. "What I said or anyone else said is not important. It's where the glass came from that matters. Why would I want to poison my own sister?"

"You know very well why you might have wanted to," Park said. "For the other half of the inheritance. But I agree that—"

"That's crazy!" Lena interrupted.

"We know the liar she is," Kerry said, her voice gaining strength as the tide so swiftly turned. "She set me up in the pep rally. We all know that. But she denies it to this day."

"And I'll deny it again!"

"You spilt the Coke on me!"

"So I did! And, to tell you the truth, I did it on purpose. You were being such a jerk that day. But that's all I did! I didn't replace your dance pants with paper ones, though I wish I could take the credit."

"Liar! You didn't even care when Robin got hurt! You even tried to poison me!"

"Yeah, you were poisoned all right. The doctors pumped your stomach and didn't find a trace of insecticide. You were just prepping a martyr's alibi!"

"You made the nurse leave! Now that you're doing the dialysis, it's suddenly not working. You failed the first time, but you don't quit. You're trying to kill Robin again!"

They were like two rabid dogs. Influenced by the boiling hatred, the snakes hissed loudly, banging their heads on the trembling lid of their cage. Park and Sol tried to intervene, but they couldn't get in a word. For once, Kerry was matching Lena curse for curse, and Lena had forgotten that it was beneath her dignity to stoop to Kerry's level. Yet suddenly both choked off.

Someone was banging on the door.

"Who is that?" Park exclaimed. "Help! Yes, we are here!"

The aluminum pole began to rise, taking with it the lid. A snake's head reared above the edge of the Plexiglas container. Kerry screamed. Angie screamed. Shani did not feel the bite of her teeth into her lips or tongue, but she tasted the blood.

"Help!" they yelled.

The doorknob rattled. It was locked. They began to knock on the windows. The curtains were drawn back. A jolly face peered in.

"Bert!!!" they shouted.

"Hi ya, guys!" he called from what seemed miles away. Still inside the container, two snakes began to slash at each other over the partitions. Candles toppled and went out. A single flickering flame held off the darkness.

"Break down the door!" Sol yelled.

"Are you playing a game?" Bert wanted to know.

"Break down the door!" Park repeated, pointing and gesturing with his free hand. One snake decided to leave its cage. It was bigger than the others. It liked the way Shani looked. It slid toward her. Shani tried to back into the wall.

"Guys, oh, guys," she stammered. She wasn't wearing shoes and her pants were paper thin. *Don't hurt me.* Its tongue snaked out of a mouth set with jagged teeth opening wide. An oozing brown fluid dripped from its fangs. *Don't kill me.* Of all the possible horrors she had ever imagined in the darkest moments of her life, none was the equal of this. *Please don't.*

"Be very still," Flynn whispered. The others watched and waited in silence. The snake reached the end of her foot, began to slide up the inside of her leg.

"No," she wept. "Nooo." Above all else, she knew she couldn't move. A powerful blow hit the door. It remained firm.

"It won't bite you if you don't move," Flynn said.

Shani closed her eyes. Squirming skin was near the

bottom of her sweatshirt. *Nice Shani.* A sandpaper tongue licked her belly button. A moist snout slid around the curve of her abdomen, its contracting body encircling her like a belt. *Soft Shani.* Her heart shrieked. Her held lungs pleaded for release. *Cute Shani.*

"A second more, be still," Flynn said. "It's leaving."

A rattle shook a foot from her nose. *Go.* Its head crawled over her hand on the floor. She was a statue. She was made of stone. *Be gone.* There was no reason for it to bite her. *Far away.* Sleek muscles tightened against her side, then relaxed. Its tail scraped her lower vertebrae. She exhaled slowly. It glided back toward the cage, seeking more exciting game. *Don't come back.*

"You can relax," Flynn said.

She opened her eyes. The snakes were at war with each other. Incredibly, none of the others had left the confines of the cage. Her snake returned to the front line, hacking at its brothers.

She shook her head, went to speak, found she couldn't.

There was a deafening crack. The splintered door fell to the floor. Bert plowed in.

"Where did you guys get all these snakes?" he asked, decked in orange swimming trunks, five inches of rain, ten pounds of red mud, and the most inappropriate grin.

"Bert, quick, put the door over the top of the bin!" Park ordered, bent in a hunchback posture lest he have an encounter similar to Shani's. Kerry was screaming again.

"You want me to hurt the snakes?" Bert asked.

"They want to hurt us!" Park said. "Just do it!"

"Don't let any of them bite you," Sol added.

It was bad advice to have given Bert. As he picked up the door, he apparently began to have second thoughts about the playfulness of the snakes, for he remained close to the entrance. From there he tried to throw the door onto the container.

"No!" Park screamed, too late.

The Plexiglas cracked in a thousand pieces and the remaining candle was extinguished. In the feeble light that filtered from upstairs, they saw the snakes that were still alive—the majority of them—go wild, snapping at anything that moved. Kerry's screams tore in her throat and she began to whimper miserably.

"Got quite a few of them, I did," Bert said proudly. "What do you want me to do now?"

"Go to the garage!" Sol said. "Get bolt cutters!"

"There is no garage!" Park said.

"What happened to the garage?" Bert asked.

"Get the pokers from the fireplace," Flynn said, in a firm voice.

"Gotcha." Bert nodded and left.

They waited and worried. If the snakes had not been their own worst enemies, every member of their dinner party would have been dying by now. Yet there was still time. Several of the snakes had decided that the recording studio was no place to be and were exiting out the door in search of more peaceful territory. They would be all over the house.

Bert was back in a minute with a thick metal prong. He went to hack at Angie's handcuff, but she stopped him.

"Do Sol before me," she said.

"That's a brave girl," Sol said.

"I just don't want him to break my wrist," Angie explained.

Sol eyed Bert's upraised poker, then glanced at the rattlers, probably trying to decide which was more dangerous. "You hit my hand, buddy, and I'll kill you."

"Okay," Bert said. That sounded fair to him. Employing all of his considerable strength, he slashed down with the bar. The ring interlocking the handcuff cracked. Sol stood and took the poker from Bert, shoving him toward the door. But the way was blocked as more snakes slithered into the hall.

"Do me!" Kerry pleaded.

"Just a second." Sol dug at Angie's bolt, prying it loose.

"You're hurting me," Angie complained.

"Do me!" Kerry whined. Angie's handcuff broke off the wall. Sol leapt to Kerry's aid. A moment later she also was free. The two girls huddled together. Due to the passing snakes, they were unable to leave. There were seven reptiles left in the room. Four of them were converging on Lena.

Sol took care of Park next. But his path to Flynn, Lena,

and Shani was barred. "Throw me the poker," Flynn said. Sol did so, Flynn catching it expertly in his free hand. Using his foot as a fulcrum—which must have hurt—he transformed the poker from axe to lever, and pulled his ring out of the wall. Now he was faced with a hard choice. Lena's situation was critical, but she was next to impossible to get to.

"Do her," Shani said.

"You'll get bit," Lena told Flynn. "Get Shani loose. Any snake that bites me is going to poison himself."

Flynn wasted no time in indecision. "Pull away from the wall, Shani!" She leaned toward the shattered Plexiglas. Flynn wound up. His blow wrenched her wrist. He struck a second time, tearing into the paneling. She fell on her side, free. The last of the exiting snakes disappeared into the basement hallway. He pulled her up, hurrying to where the others had gathered, not far from the door. "Find an unoccupied room!" Flynn ordered. "Shut yourselves in."

"What about Lena?" Sol asked.

"I'll get her," Flynn said.

Sol surveyed the situation. There was a snake on Lena's right, another on her left, and two inching toward her feet. He was no coward but he was also no fool. He nodded. "You get her."

However, none of them left. Where they were was relatively safe, and to leave would be like abandoning their friend. Even Kerry was sweating over Lena's fate.

Moving swiftly, Flynn seized one end of the door Bert had knocked down and toppled it through a hundred and eighty degrees. Two crushed snakes flew off the back. Two others were pinned beneath the descending board. Like a cat, he sprang onto his self-made moat and in a single, perfectly aimed swing, broke the ring pinning Lena to the wall. Taking her outstretched hand, he helped her to her feet. But because one of her feet was asleep as a result of the cold, or simply because she was in too great a hurry, Lena stumbled. Flynn lost his hold. She fell back, directly on top of two snakes. She was wearing shorts. The serpents sank their fangs deep into her left calf.

"Lena!" they screamed, as she threw her head back in pain. A third snake, half dead beneath the door under Flynn's feet, reached forth and fastened onto her left arm. Blood spurted over her skin.

"Lena!" Sol cried, rushing forward. But Flynn purposely blocked his path, frantically hewing at the snakes with the poker. Two rolled over with fatal injuries, but the third had a hard hide and liked the taste of Lena. Dropping the bar, Flynn leaned over and grabbed the snake by its rattle, hurtling it against the opposing wall, its implanted teeth ripping a gruesome gash in her leg on the way out. Sol took her in his arms, carrying her toward the door. But Flynn remained crouched, studying the spot where Lena had fallen.

"Come on!" Shani cried. "What are you waiting for?"

"Coming," Flynn nodded, glancing over his shoulder, reluctant to leave.

The hallway and stairs were clear, but the living room droned with hidden rattlers. Veering into a nearby bedroom, they turned on the light and shut the door. Park checked under the bed. Sol laid Lena on the mattress. Blood soaked through the sheets, dark and thick. Angie brought a roll of toilet paper from the nearby bathroom and began to wrap it tightly around Lena's leg and arm. Sol stopped her.

"Let her bleed the poison out," he said. "Lena! Where do you keep a snake kit?"

"Kitchen . . . under sink," Lena whispered, her teeth and eyes clenched.

"All of you, stay here," Flynn said firmly. "I'll get Robin and the kit."

"There must be someone else in the house," Sol said. "I'll come with you."

"No, if they come here, you'll have to protect the girls." Flynn cracked the door, peered out. "I'll be back in a minute." He left.

In the madness, Shani tried to put her illness on hold. They gathered about Lena as she lay shaking on the bed. Her toughness still intact, she refused to cry. Sol squeezed the muscle surrounding her wounds, encouraging the bleeding.

"Stop that," she whispered.

"We've got to get the poison out, babe," Sol said.

"If I bleed to death, what will it matter? Stop it, I say."

A rifle in one hand, Robin in the other, Flynn reappeared. Robin hurried to her sister's side.

"What's happened?" she cried, pale and confused.

"That was smart, Flynn," Park said, "getting that gun."

Flynn shut the door, moved a chair in front of it, and sat down. He had the tape recorder Shani had noticed earlier in the recording studio. Pulling a box of shells from his pocket, he began to load the rifle.

"Did you get the kit?" Sol asked.

"No," Flynn said, methodically sliding in the bullets, his face grim.

Sol stood. "I'll get it."

"No," Flynn said.

"But we need it imme —" Sol stopped short in front of Flynn's pointed barrel.

"No," he said again, cocking the rifle.

"What's this?" Sol demanded angrily. "Lena needs —"

"Sit down," Flynn interrupted, his voice cold. Sol backed up. Kerry made a dash for the bathroom. "Stop!" Flynn shouted.

"But I'm going to be sick," she pleaded.

"Be sick on the floor."

"But I —"

"Sit down! All of you, sit down!"

They did as he wished. Lena sat up weakly, leaning

against her sister, each holding the other up. Of them all, Shani was the least surprised. In a sense, she had been expecting this. "At least let us get the antidote for the snake venom," she said. "I can get it. I promise I'll come—"

"Shut up," Flynn said.

"But she'll die!" she cried.

"So what?"

Sol could contain himself no longer. Springing to his feet, he charged, swearing, "Why, you bastard, I'm going to kill —"

Flynn raised his rifle. Shani covered her eyes. The explosion was deafening. Cold wind whipped her face. Rain sprinkled her hair. Peeking through her fingers, she saw Sol sit down again, unhurt. Flynn had blown out the window at her back.

"Understand clearly," he said. "That was my last warning."

"Has my sister been poisoned?" Robin asked softly.

"Snakes bit her," Park said.

"I see," Robin whispered. She was not strong enough for this.

Flynn smiled. "You've all been poisoned. That's why you're all sick. I slipped a very special concoction in your dinner last night. It takes twenty-four hours to take effect. After forty-eight hours the damage is irreversible. Don't start crying, Kerry. I'm getting more than a little tired of your blubbering. This poison probably won't kill you. But it does have nasty side effects: bleeding ulcers, blindness, severe kidney damage—we all know how bothersome *that* can be. I won't tell you exactly what poison it is just yet, but I will reassure you that it has an antidote." He pulled a prescription container of orange pills from his shirt pocket. "Two of these every two hours for a day and the majority of the damage can be avoided. That is, if you take them in time. Any questions?"

Shani shivered in the damp draft. "Where's your partner, Michael?"

"Michael?" Robin winced. She had found a handkerchief and was holding it over Lena's wound.

"That's my real name." Michael pointed the cassette's microphone toward them. "And as far as my partner is concerned, I don't have one. I don't operate like that voice in the room. I don't have the time; neither do any of you." His voice was savage. "You'll be given no chance to 'piece things together.' I will ask a question and you will give an immediate response. If I'm satisfied, you'll get a pill. If not, you'll get a bullet through your brain." He pressed the RECORD button on the cassette player. "You're first, Bert. Where have you been?"

Bert went to wrap a blanket around his soaked, practically nude body, but changed his mind, probably thinking Michael wouldn't let him. He did not appear frightened, more amazed. "I was surfing and then I got lost in the dark," he said. "Are you going to kill me, Flynn Michaels?"

"Start from when you were drinking in the van," Michael said.

"Gotcha. Sol had to go to the bathroom. I dropped the tequila bottle on the garage floor and it broke. I tried to clean it up but I didn't want to cut my hands. Sol was gone a long time. I decided to go surfing again. Am I doing okay?"

"Go on."

"The riptide pulled me far away, far out. When I got to shore, I couldn't see the house. Then I guess I started walking the wrong way. My arm got real tired carrying my board. It got dark. I tried walking the other way. It started raining. Finally, I saw the house. I thought it was the house, but it didn't have a garage like the other one. I walked around it a lot of times before knocking on the door. No one came to let me in, and I was cold, so I just came in and found you guys playing with the snakes. What happened to the garage?"

Any other time, Shani would have laughed in joy and relief at Bert's story. But Michael would not have allowed that. Ignoring Bert's question, he pointed the rifle at Park. "Your turn."

"What do you want to know?"

"You insisted that Robin drink the beer. You knew she hated alcohol. What was your motive?"

"I was drunk."

"That's not good enough."

Park sized up the diameter of the barrel, glanced at Angie, and put his hand on Robin's shoulder. "I'm a horny teenager. Angie offered to go swimming naked with me. Then Robin showed up. I thought the beer would put her to sleep and I could slip off with Angie. Skinny-dipping with a girl has always been a fantasy of mine."

In the middle of tying the handkerchief over her sister's cut, Robin stopped. Her hurt was painfully obvious. "Why didn't you swim naked with me?" she asked.

"I didn't think that you would have wanted to."

"I would have. We had a big pool at our house. We—"

Michael interrupted. "Any other confessions, Park?"

Park was angry now. "Yeah, I have something else to tell Robin. But it's none of your business. Shoot if you want; I don't care."

Michael was amused. "Famous last words. You're next, Sol."

Sol was bitter, but more than any of them, he respected a gun. "I've already said my piece."

"So you did. Lucky for you that Bert got out of that garage when he did or you would be up for manslaughter. Carting around that dynamite was pretty irresponsible of you. But you'll end up paying, one way or the other. How about you, Angie? Tell me your piece."

"I didn't poison Robin!"

"Didn't you?" He let the question hang, shifting his gun as Angie shifted anxiously.

"This is crazy," Shani blurted. "What's happened to you, Michael? No one will confess. You'd just kill them."

Michael ignored her. She was not sure that he had even heard her. Except for a slight sneer on his mouth and a thin glaze over his eyes, his face was blank. She was right. This was crazy, for he was.

"You wanted Robin out of the way," he said. "You wanted Park. And it was your house, your poison. You had the motive and the murder weapon. How convenient."

"I didn't do it!" Angie said.

"But you must have done something. Why, just this afternoon, when I caught Shani going through my luggage, I saw you out the window throwing a burning stick at a blackbird as it ran into the garage. That stick must have touched Bert's tequila; it started quite a fire. And what did you do? Did you try to put it out? No, you ran the other way. And then, of course, there was that awful explosion. I didn't say anything at the time because I didn't know about the M80's and I wanted to give you a chance to confess. But you never did. In fact, you lied. And to tell you the truth, Angie, I think you lie a lot." He hardened his voice. "The tape is running. I'm getting impatient."

"All right, so I wanted Park! What's wrong with that? Is that such a great sin that you're going to kill me? Why was it that only Robin was supposed to have him? She's so—" Angie stopped, horrified at her slip.

"I'm so what?" Robin asked meekly, having to take another sharp stab of pain. Angie would not look at her. She spoke to Michael instead.

"She's so *sweet*. So cutesy. So Miss Saintly. So virginal. She's worse than the worst jerk. If you said anything bad about her, everyone would jump on you. It made me sick."

"And you wanted to change that?" Michael said.

"I didn't put the poison in the beer!"

"Answer me!" He sweated over the trigger.

"What did you do?"

"I . . . I . . ." Angie bowed her head, rain—maybe tears—rolling down her cheeks. "I planted the paper dance pants in Robin's locker. I wanted to embarrass her. But it got all messed up. I only found out afterwards that Kerry was using Robin's locker because she had lost the lock to her own. When I went to sneak in the paper panties, there were two uniforms, but I thought they were both Robin's. Her family's so rich, they always buy two of everything. I swear, once the pep rally actually started, I was praying that Robin had put on her good dance pants. But Kerry had on the other ones. What can I say? I'm sorry, Robin."

"What about me?" Kerry complained.

"Shut up," Michael said. "Lena's next."

With the toilet paper and the handkerchief combined as a bandage, Lena had control of her bleeding. But her breathing was labored and sweat poured from her flushed face. Nevertheless, she remained indomitable. "I'll answer none of your questions. I don't give a damn about your antidote pills. I'm sure they're as phony as you."

"Please cooperate with him," Robin pleaded.

Lena shook her head.

"But you've been poisoned! You need the antidote!" Robin turned to Michael. "Please, I beg of you, help her. You were my friend. I liked you. Please help her."

Michael's cruel armor cracked at the edge. Swallowing thickly, he fidgeted in his chair, relaxing the grip on the rifle. But it was a brief lapse, a brief moment of sanity. Then a ruthlessness seemed to stir inside, like the memory of a bitter vow once sworn to for good or ill, and his eyes blazed.

"Phony!" he spat. "Who could deserve that title more than you, Lena? Look at you sitting there, basking in the sympathy of the others because of the poison in your veins. But why aren't you worried? We both know, don't we? You would never have released the snakes unless you knew that none of them could poison you!"

"*What?*" Park asked, for all of them. Michael jumped up, knocking over his chair and pressing the door with his back and the butt of his rifle.

"How much do nonpoisonous rattlers cost each?" he shouted. "Probably a lot less than a voice synthesizer to distort your recorded voice." He mimicked the sound: "'We must have the truth of that night.' What about the truth of tonight?"

"Go to hell," Lena said.

"Is this true?" Shani asked. Michael may have been insane, but he did have an uncanny ability to expose the facts. But Lena refused to answer.

"She had a small metal box behind where she was hand-cuffed," Michael went on. "It was covered with buttons."

"I saw that this afternoon!" Shani exclaimed.

"As we were running out," Michael continued, "I touched one of the buttons and the lid to the snake container began to lower." He aimed his rifle. The wild light in his eyes said he wasn't bluffing. "Pull off your shorts, Lena, and throw them over here. I want to see if by chance you have a handcuff key in your pocket."

Lena was wise enough to know when she was cornered. Reaching in her back pocket, she pulled out a small silver key and threw it at Michael's feet. No one spoke, until Robin asked, "Why?"

"To get the truth of that night," Lena said, touching her bloody leg, perhaps reevaluating the cost she had paid.

"Oh, Lena, Lena," Robin moaned. "What have you done to yourself?"

"I did it for you!" Lena cried, her own cold wall crack-ing at the seams. "And it was a good plan! If Bert hadn't come back when he did, it would have worked. And as far as I'm concerned, it did work."

"What did you do?" Sol asked.

"Everything," Lena said, but she would talk only to her

sister, as though Robin were the only one she was account-
able to. "You know it was I who talked you into this weekend, and that I was the one who sent out the invitations.
But there's a lot you didn't know, a lot I couldn't tell you
because you would have tried to stop me. Late Thursday
night, I called everyone and told them you weren't feeling well, and that they shouldn't come. I called everyone
except those here. I didn't expect Flynn—or whatever his
name is—to come, but you can't have everything. In case
any of the other kids in the class called to see how you
were, I cut the phones this morning. All this was just the
setup. Tonight at dinner I laced the food with barbiturates.
When everyone was unconscious, I dragged them down
to the recording studio and handcuffed them to the walls.
Last month when I was down in San Maritz, I bought a
bunch of rattlers whose venom sacks had been removed.
I was going to use these snakes to scare the truth out of
everyone. I even had prerecorded messages to steer the
interrogation. And it was working, better than that sham
the police called an investigation. Even I started to remember things I had forgotten. But then Bert showed up. I had
planned for so long, I was so pissed, so I just let the snakes
go." She winced at the sight of her injury, probably realizing her leg would be seriously scarred. She added quietly,
"I did it for you."

Michael was heartless. "So what's Robin to you?"

His words cut deeper than the fangs she had so bravely

suffered. And this same question had been whispered again and again behind her back this entire last school year. Apparently, unknown to any of them, its hurt had been accumulating, and had reached an intolerable level. Her reserve collapsed. Pretty, powerful Lena—it was soul-wrenching to watch. Bent with sobs, she tried to speak. "She's everything to me. I would do anything for her. If she were my sister, my real blood sister, I would give her both my kidneys." She fought for control.

Robin tried to comfort her, forcing a laugh. "Silly, you didn't have to do all this for me."

"How much did the snakes cost, Lena?" Bert asked.

Flynn reset his chair. But he did not sit down. He approached Kerry, who knelt on the floor, allowing the tip of his gun to touch her forehead. "Are you sick, Kerry?" he asked gently.

"Yes," she whispered, her eyes dilating with each light brush of the black barrel.

"Do you need to throw up?"

"Yes."

"Do you have cramps?"

"Yes."

"You're sick because I poisoned you, right?"

She nodded.

"Right?"

"Yes."

"Why is Robin sick?"

"Because she got poisoned."

"Right." Michael smiled. He was happy. "Now tell me, who poisoned her? Not last November, but this weekend. Tell me."

"You."

Michael was not happy. "You're wrong. I poisoned everyone *but* Robin. You must have noticed how I brought her all her food and drinks. That was to be sure she didn't swallow anything bad." He smiled again. "So how is she sick?"

"Her kidneys are bad."

"But they've been bad since November, haven't they?"

"Yes. Please don't kill—"

"Then why is she suddenly so ill?" he interrupted.

"I don't know."

"You're sure?"

"Yes."

"Be absolutely positive. If I find out later that you've lied to me on this point, I might become angry. Have you ever seen me angry, Kerry?"

"No."

"I lose my mind. I lose all control." A snake rattled outside their door. Michael was pleased. "You don't like snakes, do you, Kerry?"

"No."

"I bet you don't." He returned to his chair, sat down, crossing his legs casually. He rechecked the cassette player.

"We have plenty of tape left. You can take your time, Kerry."

"What? I don't understand!"

"Sure you do. Tell me how and why you put the insecticide in Robin's glass."

"Oh, no," she began to weep. "I didn't, no."

Michael sighed. "Kerry, I'm afraid you're beginning to anger me. Did you hear my question?"

She nodded.

"Answer me."

Even had Kerry wanted to confess, she probably couldn't. Her mouth wouldn't work. Michael raised his gun, pointed it at her head.

"Don't!" Shani cried. "I did it! It was me!"

"Nice try, Shani," Michael smiled. He pulled the trigger. The stucco wall behind Kerry's head exploded in an irregular crater, sharp chips riddling the room. A clock fell off the opposite wall and landed upright on the floor. It was exactly one o'clock. Michael reset his aim an inch to the right. "I doubt a blob of red and gray would go with this room's bright yellow, don't you, Kerry?"

She shook her head, her eyes bursting. It was a miracle, Shani thought, that none of them had fainted. A demon had possessed Michael.

"Your throat's dry, I understand," he said. "Park, would you please get Kerry a glass of water from the bathroom? That's a good man."

Kerry accepted the water gratefully, swallowing it in big gulps. Finished, she put the glass down carefully, staring at Michael, a muscle twitching in her neck. But it was Robin who asked the question.

"Did you do it, Kerry?"

Kerry nodded weakly. "I did, yes."

Tears swelled in Robin's eyes. "Do you hate me, too?"

Kerry's voice was hoarse, barely audible. "No, I love you, Robin. But I hate your sister. I hate her more than I can say." She began to cough, the spasm lasting a full minute. They waited and, finally, Kerry answered the mystery.

"My car wouldn't start. It really wouldn't. I wanted Sol to give me a ride home. He said he would. I wanted to talk to him. But Lena wouldn't let him. He even told her to shut up, but she still got her way. She always gets her way. So I just sat down. I didn't know what to do. Sometimes when I get mad like that, I can't think.

"I had to go to the bathroom, and when Bert was done, I went to go. But Lena got there when I did, and she said she would only be a minute. You see, it happened again. She was always going first.

"I followed Bert into the kitchen. We didn't really talk, and then he left, and I was alone. I was just standing there, doing nothing in particular. I was angry, sure, but I wasn't thinking of doing anything bad. Then I noticed a bottle inside the cupboard beneath the sink with the word *poison* on it. I picked it up and, it was weird, all of a sudden I didn't feel mad anymore. I felt kind of excited. The lid came off. The smell was awful. There was an empty beer mug on the counter, and I just sort of kind of poured some of the bottle in it. For a second, I guess I did think about Lena. But I wasn't hating her right at that moment. I wasn't thinking of hurting her. I wasn't really thinking at all. I set the bottle down behind the beer keg. Then Sol walked in."

Kerry closed her eyes. When she spoke next, her voice was firm, clearer than it had been in a long time. "I had the glass with the poison in it in my hand. He'd caught me. But he was drunk, and couldn't see straight. But I still had to be quick because the stuff smelled so strong. The keg was right there, so I filled the glass full of beer. I just wanted to get rid of the smell. Sol didn't notice. He picked up some chips and searched around for dip. While he was doing that, I put the insecticide bottle in the icebox. I had to put it somewhere. I wiped it off and hid it behind a milk carton. I guess I must have left the poisoned beer on the counter. When I looked back, Sol had picked it up.

"Lena came into the kitchen. Sol started stumbling all over the place. She took the beer and helped him into the living room. I didn't know what to do! I couldn't say, 'Hey, I put poison in that glass. You shouldn't drink it.' I couldn't, that would have been the end of me at school. As it was, I was barely hanging on. All I could do was follow them. I followed the glass closely. Lena had it, and when

Sol sat beside Robin, she gave it back to him. And he gave it to Robin. And . . . she drank it."

Kerry wasn't crying, but Lena and Robin were. Kerry opened her eyes, staring down at her hands, probably wondering how they could have done such a thing. "I was never sick that night," she said. "I made up the cramp routine to get Shani worried about Robin. And that's all of it. I did it, but I didn't mean to. It was . . . an accident."

Beyond the shattered window, the wind had quieted and the rain had stopped. Except for the snake outside the door, all was silent. Michael took his box of shells and reloaded his two spent bullets. From his pocket he drew a switchblade—Sol's eyes widening—and pressed a tiny button, bringing a deadly point into readiness. He turned to Robin and waited.

"You watched me drink it?" Robin asked finally, lost in waves of emotion she had never felt before, never knew existed, in herself or in her friends.

"Yes."

Robin shuddered. "But how? How could you have just sat there and watched me swallow that terrible stuff?"

"I was afraid." There was no life left in Kerry. She was foresaken, she knew. She was dead.

"But I drank all of it, every drop of it," Robin shook her head, clenching her fingers. "And you just sat there . . . and didn't stop me." She screamed at Michael. "Why did you make me know this? I didn't want to know!"

"I did," he said, setting aside his rifle, to where Sol or Park could have grabbed it if they were quick. Yet neither moved. Michael ran a finger up the switchblade, pausing at the tip. Sighing, he got up and knelt beside Kerry on the floor. He was no longer crazy. He looked completely sane, very sad. He asked, "Did you tamper with the dialysis machine?"

Kerry nodded. "I took out the cellophane membrane. It's in my closet."

"Did you want to make Lena look bad, look like she was hurting her sister?"

"Yes. I was going to put it back tonight. I really was."

"You know, I believed you when you said the poisoning was an accident. But this . . . this purposely hurting Robin, I can't understand that."

"I hate Lena," Kerry whispered.

Michael nodded. "And you can't say how much. I haven't forgotten."

"She took Sol away. He was mine and she just took him. Whatever she wants, she takes. She doesn't care."

Michael put the knife to Kerry's throat, and scratched her lightly. Kerry flinched only slightly. He looked at Robin. "Well?"

"Are you going to kill her?" Robin asked.

"If you want me to."

"Do it!" Lena said.

"It's Robin's decision," Michael said.

Robin was unrecognizable. Malice in Lena or Kerry was natural. In Robin, it was horrifying.

"No, Robin," Park said. "Tell him no."

Robin exploded. "But she deserves death! She ruined my life! What have I left? Nothing!"

"You have me, if you want me," Park pleaded. "That's what I was going to tell you."

"But what am I?" she cried. "I'm half human! I need a machine to keep me alive. Every day, for the rest of my life, I have to sit with needles and tubes in me to clean my dirty blood. And I hurt all the time. I'm in constant pain. I can't run. I can't dance. I can't swim. I can't eat what I want. I can't do anything! And I'm dying." She began to cry. "I don't want to die."

"Neither do I," Kerry whispered.

Michael had handled a knife before. His hand waited, motionless, narrowing the night to the blade's razor edge. With a word, Robin could pull them all—for a vengeful decision would leave none unscarred—into the nightmare her life had become. Michael was subtle and crafty, yet he had not known Robin long, and could not know that this was not the real Robin being given an opportunity to decide. In the confusion, in the plots within plots, he had lost her, and she'd become a frightened child who'd forgotten who she was. Shani recalled the old man, the calm, even perspective she had felt in his presence. Robin knew him well. Surely he had touched her in a similar way.

Robin bowed her head. "I don't know what to do."

All was quiet. Even the snake had gone away.

"Sing," Shani said.

Robin raised her head. "What did you say?"

Shani sat beside her on the bed. Even as Robin took her hand, she knew the nightmare was over. "I want to hear you sing."

"I wouldn't mind some music," Bert said.

Robin began to dry her eyes, her once bright green eyes, now dimmed because of her illness. Looking into them, Shani had a second sensation of déjà vu. And at last, she began to understand, seeing Michael in his true light. He lowered his knife, smiled back. His eyes were identical to Robin's.

"You read my story," Robin said.

Shani nodded. "I liked the ending. Can we have the same one?"

"Sure." Robin hugged her. The room breathed again. Park and Sol shook hands. Bert clapped. Robin laughed. "But my throat's too sore to sing," she said. "Michael, put away that knife and give me the tape recorder. You're so mean and smart, but you've recorded nothing. You forgot to remove the PAUSE button. It's just as well. I recorded a song on that tape that I wanted to play at this party."

Michael relinquished his command readily, giving the switchblade to Sol and the recorder to Robin. Park picked up the rifle but he didn't know whether he was supposed to point it at anyone or not. Michael was his old charming self. It had all been an act, and it seemed as if a great burden had been lifted from him. Vaguely, Shani could guess what it had been.

Robin played her song:

> *"Blackbird singing in the dead of night,*
> *Take these broken wings and learn to fly.*
> *All your life, you were only waiting for this*
> *moment to arise. . . ."*

When the song was over, everyone agreed that Robin had never sounded better. When the chatter died down, Shani said to Michael, "I know who you are." Eyebrows were raised around the room, but he was not surprised. "You're Luke Skywalker." She pointed at Robin. "And she's Princess Leia."

"You're right," Park gasped, turning from one to the other.

"Do I have to be Paul Bunyan again?" Bert asked.

"What's she talking about?" Robin asked, not having a clue.

Like a royal subject, Michael waited at her feet. "We were born together," he said. "I am your twin brother."

"It's true," Lena whispered, seeing the resemblance, which should have been clear from the beginning.

Robin did not shout or cry out. Her joy was beyond

flagrant emotions. "Before I got sick and had it cut, my hair was like yours," she said, running her bony fingers once through his dark curls. "I should show you a picture of myself from last year. We looked alike, then."

"I would like to see it," Michael said.

"How did you find me?" she asked.

"Our mother always knew where you were."

Robin sucked in a breath. "She's alive! And our father?"

Michael shook his head. "He died in a car accident before we were born. That's why all this has been . . . the way it has been. Above all else, Robin, you have to understand that your mother loves you. She's a wonderful woman."

"Oh, I believe you! I do."

"But you want to know why she let you go?"

"I didn't want to ask. But, yeah, I'd like to know."

Michael took a deep breath, preparing himself for a speech. "She was young. When our father died, her world collapsed. This was only days before we were born. She had no money, no family, no insurance. When we came along, a local paper wrote about her tragedy, focusing upon us in particular. A wealthy and powerful man was in England at this time. His name was Samuel Carlton. Recently, his wife had come to the decision—biologically too late in life—that she wanted children. Neither of them was used to waiting for what they wanted. A year for a typical adoption was too long. Besides, they were both too old and probably wouldn't have qualified. When we were five days old, Mr. Carlton sent a man to the hospital offering our mother a huge sum in exchange for her baby girl and her signature on some papers. Our mother had not expected twins. She wasn't yet twenty. She wasn't sure how to take care of even one baby. The money was a fortune to her. Without having read them, she signed the papers.

"That would have been the end of it but for a picture of Mrs. Carlton and her recently adopted daughter printed, without her permission or knowledge, on the back pages of *The London Times* ten days later. Our mother recognized the baby girl. As a result, she knew who had bought you.

"Years went by. When we were six, our mother married a nice, boring accountant. I call him Dad, but we don't have much in .common. Mom never had any other children. But she did subscribe to a newspaper from Santa Barbara, paying a faithful monthly sum to have it delivered to Plymouth, collecting clippings of a growing girl named Robin Carlton. Later, she told me how happy she had been when she had read that you had a sister. However, during this time I never knew *I* had a sister. Oh, this will surprise you: 'Robin' was the name you were given at birth.

"When we were twelve, our mother's guilt must have caught up with her. She wrote Mr. and Mrs. Carlton requesting permission to visit you. They were aghast that their identity had become known to her. Their reply was a venomous *no*. They threatened that if she so much as called or wrote again, they would *destroy*—that was the word used—her and her family. It was not an idle threat. Whether you know it or not, Mr. Carlton's reputation in the business world is one of extreme ruthlessness. Our mother backed off, though it hurt her grievously. For some not-so-mysterious reason, the Santa Barbara paper stopped coming. News of Robin Carlton's life came to a halt.

"Last November, while I was at school and my stepdad was at work, Mr. Carlton paid a personal visit to our mother. He told her of your accident, and your need for a compatible kidney. He offered a million dollars for one of her—or my—kidneys, given that the tissue types were consistent. He told her the specifics of the typing, which, by the way, I reaffirmed this afternoon by going through your medical records. Our mother threw him out of the house.

"When I came home, Mom was bent over the kitchen table, crying over faded newspaper clippings of a pretty, brown-haired American girl. And so I first learned of you.

"Understand, our mother did not throw Mr. Carlton out of the house because she no longer cared about you. It was his attitude. He *demanded* a kidney. He wanted it right then and there. He acted like his money gave him the right. This offended our mother deeply, for, as must be clear to you by now, she had been tormented with regret since the day she had let you go. Never again would she sell her flesh. However, she was more than willing to give it away, if her own kidneys would do.

"Yet when we went to the hospital and had the necessary tests, it became clear from the information Mr. Carlton had left that I was the one, the only one, who could give a kidney."

Michael paused, apparently trying to remember back to how he felt at the time. Lena grew impatient and started to speak. Robin silenced her with an elbow in the ribs. Finally, Michael continued. "I didn't know you. To me, you were a complete stranger. And maybe it sounds selfish, but I wasn't too keen on the idea of a surgeon cutting out a part of me that I imagined I might one day need. So what did I do? I did nothing. I postponed my decision. Mom understood. Together, we waited.

"Mr. Carlton did not give up on us completely. When your first transplant failed, he sent us a photocopy of a letter from a team of doctors at the Stanford Medical Center that stated that a blood relative willing to donate a kidney would be necessary before they would attempt a second transplant. He raised his offer to two million dollars.

"I had been wondering what you were like. I had a picture of you as a twelve-year-old from the newspaper, but it was of poor quality and I was really more curious about your personality. It got to where I was carrying on imaginary conversations with you in my head. When I saw the doctor's letter, I decided I had to meet you.

"I cashed in some bonds—which, by the way, had been

bought by our mother with the money that had bought you — and came to California. Getting enrolled in your school under false ID was no problem. What did worry me was that Mr. Carlton would see me, and recognize me. He had after all, been in our mother's house, and my picture had been on the wall. Then I would take it from there. You may have noticed, I never came over when either of your parents was at home. I was taking no chances. What did surprise me was that your nurse seemed to recognize me, or at least, was affected enough by my appearance to get funny ideas. Maybe because she met me with no preconceptions, she noticed my resemblance to you. It's possible that Mr. Carlton told her that you had a brother. She was awfully wary of me. Perhaps she was worried that I had come to steal you away. Later, we must ask her.

"Why did I feel I had to keep my identity a secret? For my very reason in coming, to get to know you, know you as you really were. Imagine if I had introduced myself as the one who could save you. Had you been a monster, you would still have been nice to me. Unfortunately, I was here several months and only got to meet you a handful of times. Certainly, I liked you, and I was leaning toward giving you one of my kidneys. Nevertheless, I was not one hundred percent decided. And a second objective had caught my fancy: I wanted to know who had poisoned you.

"Because they had been at the party, I made friends

with Sol and Park, and through them, with the others in this room, with the exception of Shani. Casually, in conversation, I would enquire about that night. I learned a lot, probably more than the police ever did. Indeed, I became convinced that Kerry had been the culprit. Yet, again, I was not positive. I heard talk of this weekend party. It appeared a perfect opportunity to get to know you better, and at the same time to flush out your attempted murderer. I made sure I was invited. I began to make plans."

Michael paused, studying them closely. "Here, I must apologize for making plans that *used* you all. Maybe with this insight into my motives, you will be able to forgive me." He chuckled. "But wasn't I surprised to wake up in the basement next to snakes and find that I also was being used? Lena never told me of her scheme—why should she have?—yet she simplified my task by allowing only the essential personnel to come here. I must congratulate you, Lena. Your plan was clever. But it was too complex. Mine was simple: Corner you and literally force the truth out. Poor Shani, I had her thinking I was the reincarnation of The Ripper. By the way, my major back home was drama."

"You mean, no matter what Robin decided, you weren't going to kill me?" Kerry asked. Basking in the relief that her throat wasn't going to be slit, she hadn't yet reflected upon her new social status. When she did, Shani had to worry that Kerry would cut her own throat.

"Of course not."

"But you already had Kerry's confession," Shani said. "Why did you continue, putting Robin in that terrible spot?"

"Before coming here this weekend, I had never heard the old man's story. But it got me thinking how I could once and for all decide whether Robin deserved my kidney. That, after all, had been my primary reason in coming to the States. It was still more important to me than separating the innocent from the guilty." He smiled, pleased at his sister, as pleased as Eagle had been with Dove.

"You wanted to hear Robin sing," Shani said.

"I always like to hear her," Bert said. "She has a great voice."

"And only you knew that, Shani," Michael said, climbing to his feet, pulling Robin with him and hugging her tightly. "You're going to be well, sister."

Not all the tears this night were sadness. "You'll give me your kidney? You would do that for me?"

Who would have thought that Michael could laugh louder than Bert? "You get the first one free. But if you want a second one, then we'll have to negotiate."

Robin clapped her hands together. "But I have to give you something for the first one. Name it. I have a ton of charge cards."

"How about if you give me Shani's phone number?"

"Hey," Lena said, insulted, "I can make you a much better offer than Shani."

"Want to bet?" Shani said.

Sol shook Michael's hand. "You should have been born in the barrio. You're a real man. Just don't go borrowing my knife again without asking."

Lena punched Sol. "And don't you go buying fireworks again." Bert slapped Michael on the back, almost knocking him over. "I like you, Flynn Michaels! Anytime you need a kidney, you just call Big Bert!"

Park kissed Robin. "I didn't know Michael was your brother," he said, "but I thought you might have one somewhere. That's what I was about to suggest when the garage blew."

"Then it was your idea," Robin laughed, "and you get all the credit." She whispered something in his ear.

"Of course I meant it!" Park said, indignant. Shani could easily guess what Robin had asked.

Angie and Kerry wished Robin all good luck with the operation and Robin accepted their sentiments graciously. Both were crushed: Angie for having lost Park, Kerry for having lost everything. Nevertheless, they were genuinely happy for Robin. Watching the celebration, Shani knew no word of what had really happened this weekend would be revealed to the outside world. Michael and Robin would not allow it. Both of them had too much class. The rest of them had too much to hide.

In the middle of pumping Michael's hand, Park suddenly grabbed his stomach. "Man, I've got to go to the bathroom again." He was on his way when he suddenly jumped as if shot. "Wait a second, Michael! You're not such a nice guy. You poisoned us! Where are those pills?"

Michael started to laugh so hard that Robin looked worried that he would burst one of his precious kidneys. He fell on the carpet, losing all control. Park was red with humiliation. He actually kicked Michael. "Damn you! This can't have been a joke! You must have poisoned us! We're all sick!"

"Yes, oh yes, all poisoned!" Michael gasped, quickly launching into a second binge. There was nothing they could do but wait. Finally, recovering, he managed to pull his orange pills out of his pocket and throw them to Park. With Sol peering over his shoulder, Park studied the prescription label.

"This is Aureomycin!" he complained. "What kind of antidote is that?"

Worn out, Michael sat up. "It's the best remedy there is for bacterial dysentery."

"Montezuma's revenge!" Bert exclaimed, showing the knowledgeable fellow he was when it came to the important things in life.

"Impossible," Park said. "Bacterial dysentery takes several days to incubate."

"This is what I meant about you all having to forgive

me. Lena's partly to blame. She pointed out the wonderful possibility to me when I first arrived."

"What did you do?" Lena asked sharply.

"I removed the filter from the water purifier. When was the last time you changed it? The thing was a mess: all slimy and green." He started to laugh again. "It had the worst smell."

Shani shook her head. "I don't want to hear this."

But Michael insisted. "I put the filter into the storage tank that feeds the kitchen faucet. The bacteria didn't have to incubate. You swallowed billions of the tiny creatures!"

Lena was disgusted. "That's absolutely the grossest thing I've ever heard in my life!"

Park was mad. "That was totally uncalled for!"

Sol agreed with them both. "Yeah!"

Michael grinned at their suddenly hostile faces. They provided him with endless amusement, it seemed. "It's your own fault," he said. "Didn't any of you read that big sign when we drove across the border? It said: *DON'T DRINK THE WATER!*"

✌ EPILOGUE ✌

THE STANFORD UNIVERSITY MEDICAL CENTER WAS not the towering thirty-story-plus structure Shani had expected. It was, rather, only a couple of stories tall, although the place covered almost an entire city block, and was surrounded by beautiful manicured lawns and a maze of cement walkways overrun with white-clad medical personnel and slow-moving patients. She was glad to see it. They had made the drive from Santa Barbara in one fell swoop. Park had borrowed Robin's Porsche, and the high numbers at the end of the speedometer had seemed to fascinate him. A speeding ticket one hundred miles ago hadn't dented his fascination. What had really started her worrying was the organ donor card he had had her fill out when she had gotten in the car.

"It's big," Shani said. The day sparkled and the sun was dazzling. A cool, salty breeze from the not-too-distant San Francisco Bay poured through the car's open windows.

"A very astute observation," Park said.

"How will we find Robin in all of this?"

"She sent me a map."

"Where is it?"

"I left it at home. But never fear, I memorized the directions." Without signaling, he made a sharp right. They rolled down a shadowed alley toward the parking lot. They had to take a ticket, and would have to pay, but who could complain when they were cruising in a car worth more than most people's yearly salaries? While searching for a vacant spot, Park asked, "Do you feel any different?"

"I feel *a lot* different."

"So do I."

She let a minute go by before asking, "What do we feel different about?"

"Graduating, of course. For three weeks now we have ceased to be immature, irresponsible adolescents."

"Doing ninety on the way up here wasn't irresponsible?"

"It showed I am a man of consequence."

Shani took away his rearview mirror and began to brush her hair for the twentieth time, worrying that she had on too much makeup. Maybe Michael preferred the natural look. She hadn't worn lipstick down in Mexico and he had liked her there. And this yellow dress she and her mother had bought yesterday was way too formal for a hospital visit.

"All I remember from graduation night was being sick," she said.

"You drank too much Insecticide Lite."

"I didn't drink a thing. And you should talk. When was the last time the valedictorian had to excuse himself three times in the middle of his speech?"

"I was being given important updates," he said. For some unfathomable reason, he passed an empty parking spot. "Are you feeling better?"

"Finally. How about you?"

"I still get occasional updates."

"That's one good thing that came out of that weekend. Never again can you bother me about having messed my pants in kindergarten."

"I will never mention it to the end of my days." Park swung in between a Cadillac and a Ferrari. He had been waiting for equal status in his adjoining parking spots. Shani got out and stretched. Butterflies were climbing out of their coccoons in her stomach. She had not seen Michael since their wild weekend at the Carlton Castle. Maybe he had found a cute nurse. Maybe he had forgotten her name. Why hadn't he gotten in touch? She popped a Rolaids.

"I told you that Sol's here?" Park said, locking the doors. They started toward the hospital.

"Yes. Did he drive up in his new van?"

"Lena sent him a plane ticket. They must really have relaxed the quarantine regulations to let him in to see Robin."

"I'm glad she can have visitors now. I talked to about

ten people who wanted to come up next weekend. The doctors say she's doing great."

Park nodded enthusiastically. "They say she'll be as good as new."

Shani hesitated before speaking next. She still had a warm feeling for the old man. "I wonder if the shaman came to visit."

"I can't see that."

"Maybe he visited in spirit."

"I can't see that, either."

Shani resented his conceit. "I still feel that everything that happened that weekend happened because of him."

They hopped onto a sidewalk, passing an elderly couple who were yelling into each other's earphones. "He was just an ordinary man, Shani. Don't be that simple. There was nothing special about him."

She was suddenly mad. "What about his story?"

"Broad-based metaphors, easy to interpret a dozen different ways. He knew that Robin had been poisoned and that she could sing. Other than that —"

"*You're* being simplistic," she interrupted. "His characters obviously mirrored the people in our group. Robin was Dove, Lena was Raven, and Michael was Eagle."

"Who was Snake — Kerry?"

"Snake was a more symbolic character. He or she represented the selfish motives in all of us."

"Oh, brother. So what does any of this prove?"

"The story explained how Eagle was Dove's brother, and how he reappeared at a critical moment to give her a life and death decision. And that's what happened in real life."

"Because Michael had heard the story! Don't you remember, that's where he got the idea from?"

"That's where he got the idea to be Robin's brother?"

"No! Look, your parallel breaks down in a dozen different places. In the story, Dove had to decide whether Raven was her friend or enemy. Robin never had to decide that about Lena."

"Who said Lena was Raven?"

"You just did."

"Oh. What I meant was that all of us were debating in our minds whether Lena was to be trusted or not. She fulfilled Raven's character, but in a broad way. Don't laugh at me!"

"You're too much, Shani. If he could see the future, why didn't he have Eagle donate a kidney to Dove at the end of the story?"

"How could an eagle give a dove a compatible kidney?" She knew the question wasn't going to help her argument. But Park didn't jump all over her. They were approaching the entrance, and apparently he had decided that their argument had better conclude before they got inside.

"Okay, maybe he was an oracle and could turn himself into a bird and all kinds of weird stuff like that. But I would be a lot more convinced of his powers if he had predicted the *rest* of that night. Remember, the real fun didn't start until after we found out who Michael was."

Shani had to agree there. After Michael's bad-taste joke about the water, while Lena started Robin's dialysis with the replaced filter, the men had gone after the snakes with Mr. Carlton's rifle collection. Though they weren't poisonous, the rattlers hadn't forgotten how to bite. Sol almost blew his toes off, and ended up with four neat holes in his calf. Yet that damage was insignificant compared to what Bert did with his gun. He murdered a perfectly harmless TV, refrigerator, toaster, and bathtub. But true to form, he compensated fully with a Big Bert Masterpiece later in the night when they were all sitting peacefully in the living room thinking that all the snakes were dead. As luck or fate would have it, there was still one alive, hiding in the chair where Kerry was sitting. At first, it must have been asleep, for it didn't stir until she kicked the chair back into the reclining position. Then the old serpent came alive with a vengeance and bit into Kerry's shoulder. And everyone had thought that Kerry couldn't dance. While she spun in a hysterical fit, the rest of them screaming for her to stand still, the entire room a blur of motion, Bert calmly picked up his rifle and, without blinking an eye, shot the snake into two equal halves. Kerry had fainted.

About an hour after that, a helicopter carrying Mr. Carlton and Nurse Porter landed on the beach. Their weary group had gone to bed, but the rotor blades woke them promptly. The instant Mr. Carlton saw Michael he turned an angry red, but Robin came up quickly and shouted the good news. Mr. Carlton was pleased, to say the least. It made explaining the missing garage so much easier. Being the hero of the hour, Michael's theory of an underground cavity of natural gas impressed Mr. Carlton. The shrewd tycoon even went so far as to say he would sink a well on the property. With his gold thumb, chances were he would strike oil. He promised Sol a new van, which Sol received inside a week. On the other hand, even Park's smooth words could not explain the shot TV, refrigerator, toaster, and bathtub. Mr. Carlton told them that he wanted no more parties at his house.

SHANI WINCED AT THE ODOR AS THEY ENTERED THE Medical Center. Hospitals always smelled like sickness to her—as she supposed they should—like a blend of blood, medicine, and high bills. Maybe she would become a psychologist instead of a psychiatrist. Getting through medical school without spending time in a hospital would be too difficult.

"So you're definitely not going to Harvard this fall?" she asked. A whiff of paint from the warm orange walls gave the relatively deserted reception area a brand-new tone. Park led them confidently past an information desk. She had to assume he knew where he was going.

"I've already written them a letter declining my acceptance."

"Are your parents mad?"

"Not at all. They haven't said a word to me about it."

"Have you told them?"

"No."

"Don't you think you'll miss being the Ivy League hotshot?"

"I look at it this way: If I stay here with Robin, then we'll probably end up getting married, and I'll have a hold of millions. Then I can *buy* Harvard."

"That's what I like about you, Park; you'll sacrifice anything for love. Hey!" She pointed. "There's Lena." Their red-haired tigress was sitting in a chair by the elevators browsing through a *Playgirl* magazine.

"I recognize the chest. Hey, lovely Lena!"

Lena closed the magazine, tossing it a couple of seats over for some innocent young girl to find and be corrupted by. She wore a white sweater, and long black pants that hid her scars. Next month, a plastic surgeon was going to fix those blemishes.

"You made good time," she said. "How did the car run?"

"Very, very fast," Shani said. "How's Robin?"

"She has her appetite back. During the past seven days, she hasn't stopped eating. You're going to have to talk to her, Park. You don't want a pig for a girlfriend."

"Where's Sol?" Park asked.

"Here I am," Sol said, strolling up slowly. He had lost considerable weight in the last month.

"Were you at the bathroom?" Park asked with undisguised pleasure.

Sol scratched his head. "I thought I was over it, but those damn bugs came back as soon as I ran out of the medicine. I tried to buy some of the pills here, but they told me I had to see a doctor. As if I had the dough to pay for one of these white coats walking around here."

"Daddy gave you insurance," Lena said. "You don't have to pay anything."

Mr. Carlton had hired Sol out of his Hollywood office as an all-purpose errand boy. He paid him peanuts and left him little time to see Lena. But one day at the Carlton residence, Shani had overheard the old capitalist remark that he saw in Sol the ruthlessness necessary to run his company. She could see it now: Five years down the road Sol and Park would be in the family and would be fighting each other for control of the Carlton empire.

"The insurance doesn't take effect until I've worked for six months," Sol said. "I'll be an amoeba by then."

Lena pulled a jar of pink pills from her purse. "Take my medicine, I'm already cured. How's the rest of the gang?"

"Bert didn't get sick at all," Shani said. "He lives a charmed life. Angie said she's practically one hundred percent. Oh! I have to tell you! I didn't even tell Park this!"

"What?" Park asked, excited.

"Nah, it's nothing. Never mind."

"What?" Park demanded.

"Bert and Angie have gotten together," she said.

Sol and Lena laughed. Park didn't. "Define 'have gotten together,'" he said.

Lena reached for her *Playgirl* magazine. "There's a picture in here that defines it perfectly."

"Come on," Park said, impatient, his ego bruised.

"I'd check out Lena's picture if you really want to—" Shani began.

"This is ridiculous!" Park interrupted. "What would Angie be doing with Bert?"

"The same things she did with you," Sol said.

"Shut up."

"I've found the picture," Lena said, spreading open a page. "See, Park, this is what Angie and Bert—"

"Shut up!"

"Who are you telling to shut up?" Lena asked.

"Yeah!" Sol said.

"Both of you!" Park pointed an angry finger at her. "You're making this up!"

"Why are you so upset?" Shani asked. "You're the one who dumped Angie, remember?"

"I didn't dump her in Bert's lap!"

"She was bound to get another boyfriend," Lena said.

"But it's only been four weeks! Whatever happened to a period of mourning?"

"You *dumped* her, you didn't *die,*" Shani explained patiently.

"You've got a point there," Park admitted. "And I've got Robin. There's no reason for me to be jealous." He sighed. "But Bert—I'm not going to surf with that jerk anymore."

"How's Kerry?" Sol asked, glancing at Lena.

"I'm not saying anything," Lena said, holding her magazine at various angles.

"Kerry's sick," Shani said seriously. "She's lost a lot of weight. None of the drugs are working on her. She may have to be hospitalized. Her parents are really worried."

"Mine know the feeling," Lena muttered.

Shani snatched away her magazine. "I want you to do something for me, Lena."

"What?"

"Call Kerry. She's sick because she can't stop worrying. Call her and promise her you'll never reveal her evil deed. Please?"

"They would just fight," Sol said.

"Kerry would just hang up," Park said.

"No," Lena said quietly. "We didn't fight, and she didn't hang up. I called her this morning."

"Did Robin make you?" Sol asked suspiciously.

"Robin doesn't *make me* do anything. It was my idea. We had a long talk, don't ask me about what. I think she'll start feeling better soon."

Shani was impressed. "I'm proud of you."

"Bert's kissing Angie and Lena's calling Kerry," Park told the ceiling. "What's this world coming to?"

"Just don't let it get around," Lena said. "I don't want to ruin my image." She stood, plucking back her magazine, folding it under her arm. "I've been waiting here to lead you to Robin. They've moved her to another room. Her mother's with her. She's an all-right lady. But I don't think Daddy and she are ever going to get along."

They followed Lena into the elevator. Park asked the question that was on all their minds. "Does this make you want to find your real mother?"

"Nope." Lena pushed button two. The door closed. They jerked upwards.

"But you must sometimes wonder about her?" Shani asked delicately.

"Nope."

"And it's none of our business," Shani added quickly.

But Lena's gaze was suddenly turned far away as she leaned against the back of the elevator and allowed them a rare glimpse into her feelings. "I think about my real father," she said softly. "I often dream about him." She chuckled, embarrassed. "It's just as well I'll never meet him. He's probably an ass, like his daughter."

They exited onto a blue-carpeted corridor that stretched forever in both directions. Leading her flock, Lena turned to the left. Shani had to work to keep up with her. Now would be as good a time as any. "Where's Michael's room?" she asked.

"The other direction." Lena didn't break stride or elaborate.

"You haven't been trying to impress him with your feminine charms, have you?" Shani asked. You could get away with a lot more with Lena these days.

"Hey," Sol said.

"Not yet."

"Hey," Sol said again.

"I heard he's being discharged today," Lena said, playing with her. A mild infection had kept Michael in longer than anticipated.

"I know." Robin had given her the news two days ago. He hadn't gone out of his way to let her know. True, he had called a couple of weeks ago, and he'd said that he was looking forward to seeing her. But he had been short on the phone, and hadn't explained whether he was returning immediately to England or what. This was her big worry. "What's his room number?" she asked.

"I thought you came to see Robin."

"Lena!"

"Two-forty-six."

Shani halted. "Tell Robin I'll be there in a few minutes."

She reversed her direction, treading through a herd of nurses and orderlies, feeling like she was climbing the wrong way up an escalator.

"Knock, knock." She rapped on his open door and peered inside. He stood with his back to her, folding a shirt in his suitcase. As he turned, she noticed an awkwardness in his once mercurial fluidity. Probably his incision was still healing. Had he any regrets? she wondered. His warm smile said that he didn't. He spread his arms. It was the best hug of her life, though rather feeble. Michael had lost weight.

"You look great," he said, holding her at arm's length, admiring her dress. "Is that a new outfit?"

She knew she was blushing. "Just something I dug out of the closet," she lied. It came back to her right away—instant karma. She had forgotten to remove the price tag from beneath her right armpit. Michael was holding it in his hand.

"Sixty-nine, ninety-five." He nodded. "I would say that it's worth every penny."

This would have to happen to her! She couldn't decide whether to laugh or weep, and ended up doing some of both. "I bought it yesterday, dammit!" she said, fighting with the tag.

He took a step back, amused at her language. "Well, now that you have my approval, you can throw out the receipt." He threw up his arms, warding off her blows. "Hey, I was only joking! Please, no kidney shots!"

She was easily pacified. She gestured at his suitcase. "I see that you're all ready to go."

"Just about." He returned to his packing. Shani wandered over to the window, from where she could see their parked Porsche, with plenty of room in the back for an extra passenger. There were questions she was afraid to ask.

"How are you feeling, Michael?"

"Great."

"Is your infection gone?"

"Completely."

"That's good." She noticed that her hands were trembling. She went to stuff them in her pockets, then realized the dress didn't have any. He was staring at her.

"What's the matter, Shani?"

"Nothing." She smiled quickly. "How does it feel to have only one kidney?"

"I feel lighter." He folded a pair of pants. "I should have all my spare parts removed."

"I bet you're anxious to get out of here."

"I sure am."

"I bet the food's been lousy."

"So-so."

"Did you get to see Robin much?"

"Every day."

"I hear she's doing great."

"She looks like a new person."

"That must make you feel good."

"It sure does. I just wish I hadn't waited so long to decide."

"Michael?"

"Yeah?"

"What are you going to do now?"

"Go home." He was collecting his books, preoccupied.

"Right away?" Her heart was breaking.

"Today."

"Is your mother going with you?"

"No, she will be staying with Robin. Could you hand me that notebook, Shani?"

She did so and went back to her window, not wanting him to see her cry. But his hands were on her shoulders, turning her slowly around in spite of her resistance. "What's the matter?" he asked.

"Nothing."

"There must be something wrong."

"No, I'm just . . . I'm just happy." She plucked a tissue from a box next to the sink and blew her nose. "It's just such a relief that Robin's okay, that's all."

He believed her, the fool. He was not interested. He did not care. He stepped back to his suitcase, snapping it shut. "Shall we be on our way? I want to say good-bye to Robin."

"I haven't even said hello."

They were in the corridor, and she was counting the steps, trying to slow down time. During these last four weeks, she had constructed a castle in the sky, only to find out now that all that was holding it up was misdirected hope. Why was he bothering to take her hand! "Can we give you a ride to the airport?" she asked, miserable.

"Can't I get a ride back with you?"

She stopped. "Huh?"

"Oh, is the Porsche too small? Maybe I can catch a cab, then."

"But . . . ah . . . but . . ." She took a breath, swallowed it. "Aren't you going back to England?"

"Eventually, but I want to attend college out here. The weather's so wretched back in Plymouth. I think I've been spoiled. I consider this my home now." He studied her face. "What's wrong?"

"Nothing." Nothing at all! "Where are you going to go to school?"

"The same one as you—if I can get in this late—U.C., Santa Barbara. I want to stay near Robin and the rest of you guys. Why do you ask? I explained this all in my email."

"What email?"

"I sent it three days ago."

"I didn't get it."

"Maybe it went to your junk mail. Was that the problem? You thought I was going to run off on you!"

"No! I mean, you're going to do what you're going to

do." She added lamely, "What have I got to do with any of it?"

Michael put down his suitcase. Though there were many in the hallway to see them, he leaned over and kissed her. She was such a mass of nerves that she could scarcely react. When he pulled away, he was frowning.

"I've got to get you a snake, Shani."

She caught his drift. The first time they had kissed, when she had let herself go, had been immediately after her escape from the rattler in the ravine. So he thought she was coldblooded! Tired of playing the role of the wimp, she curled her arms around his neck and pulled him down to her height. "Michael," she murmured, "I never told anyone this before, but I *sleep* with a snake."

For an instant—a gleeful moment—he tried to back away. But she had a firm hold of him, one that hopefully would last awhile.

ROBIN'S ROOM WAS A FLORISTS' SHOP, HER VISITORS LOST amid rainbows of petals and fragrances. Propped in a white mountain of pillows, the celebrated patient had the best view and the healthiest complexion in the entire Medical Center. Shani could hardly comprehend the transformation. Mother Time had swept Robin back to early November. She even had a tan.

"Shani!"

"Robin!"

And Lena had been right about her sister's appetite. Hugging Robin, Shani could feel none of the protruding ribs she'd felt during their embrace four weeks ago at the start of their weekend of fun and relaxation at the Carlton Castle.

"I'm glad you're here," Robin beamed, keeping hold of her hand. Michael remained in the background.

"I have to tell you," Shani said, "this is the last time I'm going to visit you in a hospital."

"This is the last time I'm going to be in one!"

"Is this the friend you told me about?" A handsome woman with Robin's features and Michael's hair asked the question in the sweetest English accent imaginable. She stood on the opposite side of the bed, her eyes sparkling when they looked at her daughter.

"Yes, this is Shani. Shani, meet my mom. Don't we look alike?"

Shani offered her hand. "Very pleased to meet you, Mrs. Richardson." She hoped that was her name.

"The pleasure's mine. I've heard a lot about you."

"Don't believe everything Robin tells you. We have a mutual secret pact to boost each other's public image."

Mrs. Richardson glanced at Michael. "I was referring to what my son has told me about you."

Shani reddened. If his mother liked her, she was already in good shape. "What did he say?"